ASCENDANT

Book Three of the
Chronicle of the Seer
Pentalogy

Florian Armas

Cover design by Cherie Fox

ISBN 13 978-0-9939772-7-5

For my mother

Table of Contents

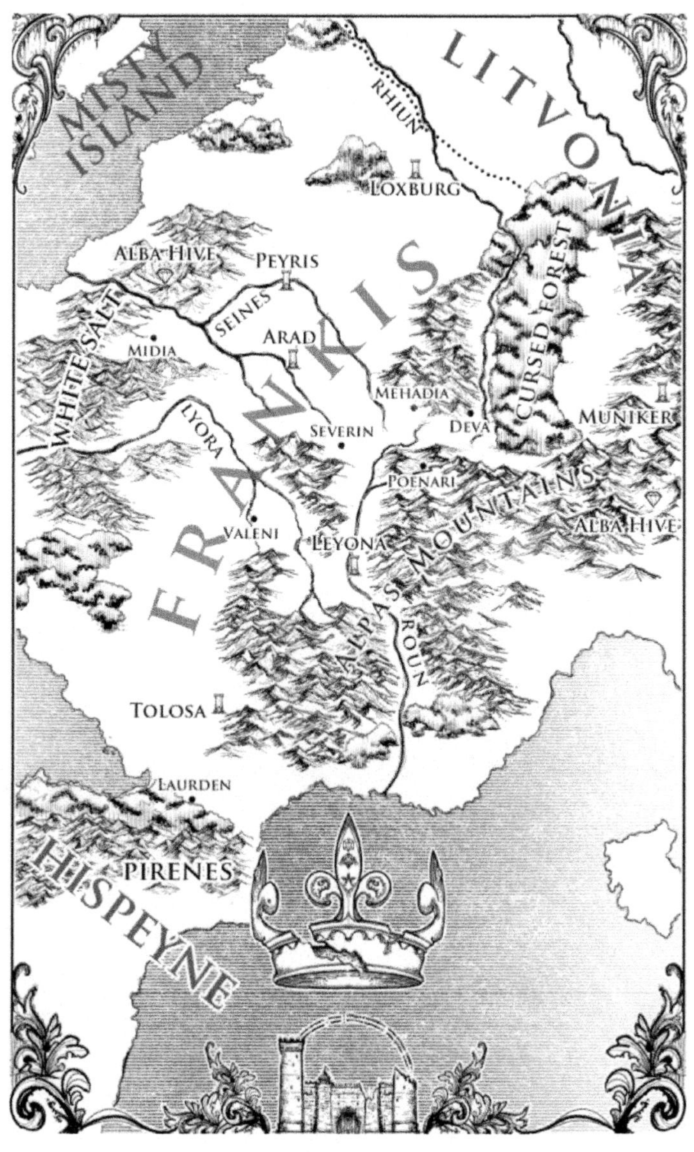

MISTY ISLAND
LITVONIA
RHIUN
LOXBURG
ALBA HIVE
PEYRIS
FRANKIS
CURSED FOREST
WHITE SALT
SEINES
ARAD
MIDIA
MEHADIA
LYORA
SEVERIN
DEVA
MUNIKER
POENARI
ALPAS MOUNTAINS
VALENI
LEYONA
ALBA HIVE
ROUN
TOLOSA
LAURDEN
PIRENES
HISPEYNE

Slippery Fate plays us, and, having played, slips further.

Chapter 1 - Codrin

Under the moonlight, the lone tent was watched by many hidden eyes. In the forest, seventy feet behind the tent, stood a hundred soldiers, half of them archers. Down in the valley, lying down behind a small ridge, two hundred fifty soldiers were waiting for the signal to attack. And on the slopes of the large meadow climbing toward the tent, another hundred were playing at being asleep. It was a waiting game.

Half of the sky was clouded and dark; in the other half, scattered clouds were dancing with the moon, so that every so often, the tent seemed to vanish from sight. Gripping their weapons, the soldiers tensed and relaxed to the rhythm of the gentle light from above. There was no lightning and no thunder to disturb the heavy silence. Just days before, a storm had raged, and not far from the tent stood a half-burned giant oak, fatally split. The old tree was broken off five feet in the air, and the end of the trunk still sat perched atop the stump. It ran at a smooth angle down to the ground where what had been its highest branches lay crushed into the earth. Archers found a good place to hide into the wall of branches and leaves. Another oak stood, unscathed, closer to the forest, and the tent was pitched next to it.

When the moon broke free from the cloud's grip, light entered the tent through the open front flap; there were two Mountes guarding it, one on each side. The back entrance of the tent flapped noiselessly, and a tall woman came into sight. Through the clouds, the moonlight became more intense, following the woman as she walked toward the lone old oak. Like a sponge, her white dress absorbed the light until it started to glow faintly. Unlit, her face remained hidden.

Leaning against the giant oak, Codrin his eyes set on her, watching with the feeling that something important was about to happen. *How did she get here?* "Vlad?" he asked in a low whisper, without moving. "Who is that woman?"

"What woman?"

"Vlad can't see me," the woman said, a banal statement, yet her voice was authoritative, the flat tone of someone versed in command. The moonlight, stronger than before, and the translucent glow coming from her clothes finally revealed her face. She walked further, at leisure, and stopped in front of the tree half-hiding Codrin. "You can't hide from me." She laughed quietly, without malice.

"I am not hiding from you." *I am hiding from many, but not from a woman who may not even exist.* Glancing right and left, Codrin stepped away from the tree, fighting the impulse to touch her. Nobody followed him, and nobody moved in the valley.

"Don't look at them. This is not what you call ... real. We are now inside your mind."

Am I dreaming? "Who are you?" Codrin asked, reluctantly, struggling to decide if he should continue, or try to break free. There was a strange power in the woman, and the foreboding sense of a temporal junction, as the Wanderers used to say. There was fear too; he could taste its bitterness. He could not say if he feared more the present or the future.

"Dochia." Her tone was flat and precise again, and Codrin frowned, saying nothing. "Do you know all the women in the world named Dochia?" she chuckled. "The one you know is now far from Frankis, and she will not return soon."

"What do you want?"

"To test the water."

"You speak like a Wanderer. Nothing concrete, only riddles."

"I am a Wanderer, Codrin of Arenia."

"Are you from Arenia?"

"I was born in Arenia. More than six hundred years ago. I founded the Order of the Wanderers."

"You are..." Involuntarily, Codrin's lips tightened. He was unable to read anything on her translucent face. His mind whirled as he struggled to find the right words. They did not come.

"Dochia." She laughed; the sound carried in the stillness of the night. Silent again, she stared at Codrin, daring him to speak. His lips stayed tight. "The last Empress, the Maiden Empress... I have many names."

"Why are you...?"

"Here? Because of you, obviously. There is interesting news in the east. Old Khad Muir from the Selem branch was killed ten months ago, and the Timurid branch has taken power in the Khadate. They have lost another Khad already, but the next one will be a Timurid too, even though nobody expects him to gain their throne. His election will be a surprise for everybody. Almost everybody. Some Assassins betrayed Fate and are now Serpentists. Meriaduk is the new High Priest of the Serpent, and he is guiding the nomads to conquer the world for his new god."

"Nothing good ever came from the steppes."

"The nomads are people too, just like you. A new Fracture is coming, and the Realm needs a Seer. Are you strong enough to be the third Seer of the Realm? Are you ready to save the Realm?"

"How should I know?" Codrin shrugged.

"Baraki told me that he is strong enough to be the one."

"Baraki!" Codrin said bitterly. He wanted to shout that his whole family had been killed by Baraki. To shout that Baraki was the Chief of the Royal Guard who killed his King and helped the Usurper take the throne of his father. To shout that Baraki even killed his fourteen-year-old sister. "That traitor," he finally hissed. "You contacted that traitor who helped the Usurper." *She contacted him first. But is this true or I am just dreaming?*

The Empress looked at him, a flicker of amusement in her eyes. "The Usurper is dead, and you still dream of taking back the Arenian throne."

"It is mine by right."

"Is it?" she asked, a trace of irony in her voice. "Your line took the throne by force from Nabal's Line."

"Nabal was a usurper."

"Maybe. Each throne is held by strength, not line."

"That's why you lost the Alban throne to your cousin, Nabal?" Codrin asked, trying in vain to control his inner voice, which sounded so real. "I apologize. I should not have asked that."

"Why not? I could tell you that Nabal was not a usurper. The Alban Empire was doomed to collapse, and I just sped up the process. Nabal was the man I trusted to help me split the Empire without much violence, and I let him rule Alba while I worked to create new kingdoms to replace the old empire. But *much* is a relative thing," she sighed. "Many people died. History was rewritten when your line took the throne, three hundred years ago."

"Then ... I am a usurper too."

"You belong to the Arenian Line, but you are not a king; you are a fugitive. And why should the Seer be a king? The last Seer was an Assassin."

"Then why me, and why Baraki?"

"Baraki is my offspring, and he is of Nabal's line too."

"Why should the Seer be your offspring?"

"It's not really necessary, it's just easier for me to know where to look. You are my offspring too. So, are you strong enough to become the third Seer?"

"How should I know?" Codrin repeated.

"That could be a good answer too. I must leave now. Do you want to ask me anything?"

"Will Baraki take the Arenian throne?"

"I am sure you can ask more intelligent questions." Abruptly, she walked toward the tent. At the back entrance, she turned and watched him intently, her eyes even brighter than before, seeming to pierce through the darkness and through him. "Three days ago, Mohor was killed, and Aron is now the Seigneur of Severin."

"Saliné?" Codrin whispered, avoiding to meet her eyes. He became aware that his hands were clenched at his sides. Slowly he forced them to relax and took a deep breath.

"She remained in Severin, as she is Bucur's *fiancée*. Jara, Vio and Cernat were sent to Arad."

"To Orban... This is the Wanderers' work," Codrin snapped, his voice echoing angrily in the stillness around. "Drusila, your First Light, is saving Frankis by killing innocent people. I no longer wonder why you chose that traitor Baraki for the Seer."

"Nothing is decided yet, and innocents always die at times like this; only the number differs from one potential ruler to another. It's difficult to count in advance, and sometimes you have to sacrifice..."

"Oh yes, Drusila made a lot of sacrifices."

"She is part of a game that may kill her too. Change is coming."

"Yes, change is coming." Codrin shrugged, to cover his nervousness. "The more we change, the more we stay the same. We fight. We kill. Sometimes, I think that only the weapons are changing. They can kill better. Some talk about sacrifices, others die. Dying is certainly a change. Drusilla tried to sacrifice me to smooth Bucur's path toward the Frankis throne. Bucur is a fraud, but I suppose he is the king with the lower body count. It all depends on the one who counts. Go, Wanderer; go to your people and to Bucur and Baraki. Leave us alone with our own sacrifices."

"Bucur is nothing but a bump on the path of history, yet history spans across time. He will stay in position for some years. Drusila did not try to kill you in Valeni, her nephew was manipulated by the Circle, and you are not alone. The Duke of Peyris will make you a proposal, and you have to decide your path. Now, be ready." She gestured down the valley and vanished before he could speak again.

I failed them, Codrin thought. *Saliné, Jara, I failed them all.* Under the moonlight the tent was still there, and Codrin shook his head. *How could the Wanderers...? If Baraki becomes both Seer and King of Arenia, my chances are lost. My future is in Frankis;* he suddenly understood. *I just need to defeat the Circle, the Wanderers, the Dukes... Only the Assassins are missing from that list. For now.*

"Did you see something?" Vlad asked, when Codrin reached the old tree again.

"They will attack soon. Let's go inside the tent." Codrin turned and walked slowly, struggling to gather his thoughts. *I need to survive this night. Then, I will see.*

In the valley, two hundred fifty soldiers prepared to crawl up the slope. The wind began to blow in short, strong bursts, kicking up old leaves and dust in small whirlpools of cold air.

The wind is helping them. "Sentries, come inside," Codrin called the two Mountes guarding the front of the tent, then took their place, and let his mind wander over the plain, trying to feel the Light and have a glimpse of the future. Nothing came, and he shook his head with anger. Far away, lightning painted the sky; it looked like an old hand with thick white veins, its white fingers piercing the ground. The ridge materialized for a few moments, void of people. Darkness came again, and finally a Vision filled Codrin's mind: soldiers crawling toward him.

There are more than we knew. Betrayal? Where did they come from? He stepped into the tent and closed the flap, watched by five pairs of anxious eyes. "Vlad, give the signal. They are coming." He said nothing about his Vision and gripped Shadow's hilt. The sword answered him with a low vibration, and he felt calmer. *This is not my first fight against a stronger enemy.*

Slowly, the moon vanished behind the clouds, and Costa, the captain from Peyris, felt engulfed by the darkness. *A terrible mission in a terrible darkness*, he thought and waited patiently for the moonlight to come again before saying, "Everything will be over soon enough. All our soldiers are in place, and you look confident, but we should not underestimate Codrin. He killed Leyonan in battle and took his Seigneury. One of the few men who have done this in a long time. He sent Devan running home."

"We need to attack tonight; we may not have a better opportunity." Leno, who was leading Aron's contingent, stared at Costa, in the feeble moonlight, trying to add more weight to his words.

"Surprise is a treacherous bitch. It works for both sides. Codrin doesn't know that I joined you after sunset with a hundred soldiers. And he doesn't know that Eagle is the Black Dervil of Peyris, not a simple mercenary leader."

"That is bothering me." Eagle rubbed his chin and stayed silent for a while. "A hundred riders could not have passed unnoticed by their scouts. I fear a trap."

"They came through the area watched by your scouts." Leno's arm gestured briefly between Costa and Eagle, his arm a dark shadow patched with moonlight; the scouts were either Duke Stefan's soldiers, from the small contingent from Peyris that had joined Severin's army, or mercenaries. Leno was slightly annoyed, but neither of the other two trusted Aron's men with important tasks. "Don't you trust your own men?" he snorted, trying to look firm and confident.

"I still don't like this night attack," Eagle muttered as if Leno did not speak. "Darkness is vicious; it may surprise us more than we can surprise them."

"There is always a risk." Costa shrugged, barely visible. Unconsciously, he gripped the hilt of his sword. "We are soldiers, risk is part of our life."

"You must do it tonight," Belugas, the new Primus Itinerant Sage of the Circle, interjected promptly, perhaps too fast, and he coughed to control his voice. "I have news from Severin. Orban helped us to take the city. Aron is now the Seigneur of Severin. When Codrin learns this, he will attack you, and even with those hundred soldiers Costa brought from Peyris, Codrin still has more men."

The last time a Seigneur was deposed, it turned out badly. Malin's death broke the equilibrium in central Frankis. Strange... His wife is now Mohor's wife. She is as beautiful as she is unlucky. Now we have two deposed Seigneurs, one of them slain in battle. Is Mohor still alive? Perhaps not, Belugas is hiding something. The Circle feeds on darkness and shadowy plots. "What happened in Severin?" Costa turned his head toward the Sage. His move was deliberately slow as he pondered how Belugas's words had changed the game in unexpected ways. Knight Costa was more than a simple captain, but he was not prepared for such a great change. He was not prepared at all. Malin's death was an accident, misfortune in a battle, the taking of Severin was not.

"Just a realignment of power. Tomorrow, I will tell you more." *And Aurelian is dead. How could they dare to kill a Sage? The Primus Itinerant.* Drown in his own rage, Belugas could no longer speak. He breathed deeply, struggling to regain his composure. Three days ago, he was outside Severin, waiting for a conclusion of their plot, ready to return and give Maud the good news. Then all crashed in a few moments, at the gate of Severin. Mohor's final revenge, coupled with Aron's stupidity, but Belugas thought Aurelian at fault too. *My place as Primus*

Itinerant is not yet approved by the Council of the Circle, he thought suddenly. *It will be after we kill Codrin... I deserve it.*

Strained, Costa fought to contain a burst of anger, and shook his head before saying, "Mohor was the rightful Seigneur of Severin." Somehow, he managed to speak in a flat voice.

"What happened there was decided at a higher level, *captain.*" Belugas's mind and voice were cold again, and his voice raised a notch, carrying into the silent darkness. "We have a problem here. Your *duty* is to solve it."

"Will you join us in the fight, Sage?" Costa asked, snubbing Belugas's title, a subtle trace of mockery filling his voice.

Belugas threw a heavy curse of silent words, and the rage inside him burned like fire. It did not bring much coolness. *Soon, I will make this captain pay for his impertinence.* "My duty is to lead you. I will leave after you capture Codrin and take him to Peyris."

"Costa, when do you want to attack?" Eagle asked, his voice calm. He was a cautious man trying to figure their next steps and give Costa enough time to recover. Inadvertently, Codrin helped with the unification of the two northern bands of mercenaries under his command, yet the way Codrin killed Sharpe in The Long Valley gave Eagle pause for thought. That and the men he lost in the mountains north of Valeni when trying to kidnap Jara on her way back to Severin.

"As soon as the conditions are favorable. Rain, wind; something to give us the least advantage. We will advance in two columns and surround the tent while Codrin is sleeping. Warn your men that I want him alive. The Duke wants to offer him a new life in Peyris." *And even his granddaughter, Cleyre, as a wife. I wonder if Codrin would enjoy marrying her. Cleyre is quite a libertine. She is nineteen now, and even the old women at court have lost track of how many men have pleased her. But she is skilled in bed,* Costa sighed; the memory of many nights, spread across half a year, with her, came back to him. *And her body is a ... marvel. She is intelligent too, so she may choose to calm down once she is married.* Once, when Cleyre was just one of the Duke's many granddaughters, and not yet a political player, Costa had aimed for more than just being a passing ghost in her bed. It took him a few months to realize that she was only interested in his manhood, or at least only slightly interested in anything else, even though he was intelligent and able to make decent conversation. Hiding his bitterness, he accepted his place as an occasional lover until she decided to drop him. Unknown to him, she liked his mind too and, while he was a capable soldier, he received his promotion to captain, a few months ago, because Cleyre had proposed it. At twenty, Costa became the youngest captain in Peyris's army. A competent one.

Finding an opportune moment, Belugas took Leno aside. "Kill Codrin, tonight or when it's the most convenient to you, but not later than tomorrow morning. Kill Costa too. He is becoming a liability. I will absolve you for his death in front of the Duke. If all goes well, you will be made governor of Corabia. It belongs to Codrin now. The papers are in my satchel. I will hand them to you tomorrow."

"It will be done. I have three archers ready to act when the torches are lit. It's better to do it now than in the morning. The night keeps its secrets better."

"You are well prepared." Belugas gripped his shoulder. "I have to leave now. In the morning, you will find me at the foot of the hill."

The wind sighed, and Costa shook his head, trying to escape the half-unwanted invasion of memories. He sniffed the dust in the air, and let the wind beat against his face, listening to its whistling. *It's strong enough.* "Give the signal to attack," he ordered and, in two minutes, his men started to crawl toward the ridge. *Is Duke Stefan thinking to give the Dukedom to Codrin? All his remaining male descendants are idiots; their only occupation is chasing young girls, even Albert, who is fifty-five years old. At least Cleyre is helping Stefan rule. In fact, she rules now, more than the old man. Cleyre and Codrin... They might raise Peyris to its old glory. Cleyre was not meant for me. I am just a Knight. I must forget her. It will not be easy.* Lost in his thoughts, Costa sighed without knowing it.

Crawling, the first batch of soldiers arrived close to the ridge and split into two wings, which moved like two huge snakes trying to surround the same prey. The left wing was the first to arrive just shy of the place from where they could be spotted if the moon showed again through the clouds. They waited patiently until the right wing arrived in a similar position too, and after another signal, which was transmitted from one man to another in hushed whispers, both wings moved forward. Playing on their side, the moon stayed hidden. Thirty paces from the tent, they stopped again, when the leading soldiers touched the stones which had been left there by scouts the previous night.

Now, Costa thought, unsheathing his sword. At his signal, silent as the night, his men ran to surround the tent. Joined by Eagle and ten old hands, he ran too, toward the front door of the tent. *I must be careful, Codrin is a devil with his swords.* The two waves of soldiers met at the back of the tent and moved fast to tighten the circle. *It was too easy.* "Surrender!" Costa shouted from the left side of the door; Eagle stood at the other side.

His shout was drowned out by the cries of the men suddenly dying around the tent. The first volley of arrows flew from the forest. Then the second one. Through the feeble light of the moon, there was no way to see the archers or the arrows. They were firing quickly and hiding again behind the trees to nock their bows. Codrin had split them into three groups and, every fifteen heartbeats, another volley of twenty arrows zipped out of the trees. At the edge of the battlefield, the hundred soldiers hidden in the grass crawled closer to the tent.

"Surround them!" Codrin shouted, when he felt sure that less than a hundred enemies were still alive around the tent.

The soldiers hidden in the grass stood up, and fifty more emerged from the forest. They all stopped at a distance which still left space for the archers to shoot. Ten torches were taken out of their buckets and thrown around the surrounded soldiers.

Costa moved toward the forest and stood alone in front of his men. “I am Costa, captain of Peyris. We have lost, and I surrender to you. Just let my soldiers live.”

“I think you are here for me.” Codrin stepped forward too. “Soldiers of Peyris, drop your weapons and go one by one toward the torches.”

“What about the mercenaries, and Aron’s men?” Costa asked.

“The mercenaries must surrender too. Aron’s men are no part of this deal.” *Aron killed Mohor and tried four times to kill me.*

“Do as he said,” Costa ordered. “Gather on the left side.”

Leno and a most of his men still alive tried to sneak away, out of the torches’ light. A new volley of arrows went through them, and soon only a few remained alive, all wounded by arrows. Pierced by more than one arrow, some of them looked like overgrown hedgehogs. The wounded survivors cried their pain in the grass. Their blood boiling to revenge Mohor’s death, Vlaicu’s guards shut their noisy mouths with cold steel. The soldiers from Peyris, and the mercenaries, dropped their swords, and one by one, they walked in front of the torches where Codrin’s men took them captive.

In the early morning, when the mist from the small river was climbing toward the hill, Costa and Codrin found themselves face to face again. “I have this for you,” Costa said, his voice level, and offered an envelope to Codrin. “A letter from the Duke of Peyris,” he added at Codrin’s mute question. “We took into account that we might fail to capture you.”

This is must be what the Empress was talking about. "Things happen." Codrin shrugged and opened the letter.

'To Codrin, Knight of Cleuny,' he read.

'If you read this, my men have failed. While I would be disappointed, there is no shame in being defeated by a more skilled enemy. This letter makes the same proposal that would have waited for you in Peyris, where you would have been my guest. I offer you the Seigneury of Crade and the position of second Spatar of my army. At the right time, marriage with one of my granddaughters will be considered.'

"Do you know the content of this letter?" Codrin asked.

"No, but the Duke asked us to capture you alive. He wants to give you a position in Peyris. And I have this letter too." Costa proffered a second scroll. It was from Dochia.

'Codrin,' the letter said.

'Things are not going well in Frankis, and I will be away longer than I thought. In our last talk, Duke Stefan's mind changed a bit. He is no longer too enthusiastic about Bucur. That doesn't mean he will cease to help Aron or Bucur. The Duke will make an overture toward you too, yet I don't know what he has in mind. It's up to you to accept or refuse it. My friend, Sybille, will contact you later.

You must learn the old language of the Talant Empire. While this may look strange to you, it's more important than you think, and I can't write you in detail about this. Sybille will bring you a dictionary and a grammar book.

Soon, you will receive Poenari. Don't refuse it. Taking the fortress will become your starting point.

PS: Jara and Saliné are in grave danger, though I don't know what will happen. Fate refused to tell me. You must protect them, even though you may need to renounce Saliné.

While Dochia could advise Codrin about the need to learn the Talant language, she had no permission to reveal Ada's Vision about the necessity of it, and the relation between the old Talant artifacts falling into the Serpentists' hands and the Fracture. She could not tell him about the High Priest Meriaduk and his devilish Maletera, which was able to carry thoughts and invade minds, and how it was almost to kill her in Silvania. Ada was the strongest Wanderer alive; none of her requests were without reason. Dochia was not even sure if Ada had revealed everything that was in the old Wanderer's Vision.

I will never renounce Saliné, Codrin shook his head. *And Dochia was wrong about Poenari. The Duke offered me Crade. I don't even know where Crade is. Her Vision was strange; Poenari is in Leyona Seigneury, and it's already in my possession. Not all the Visions come true.* "What happened in Severin?" he asked Costa.

"I heard that Aron made a mess of things. Leno may know more."

"Duke Stefan fought on Aron's side," Codrin said bitterly, "and killed the rightful Seigneur of Severin."

"You know about it..." Costa whispered. "The Duke had nothing to do with the killing. Orban helped Aron. Sage Belugas told us yesterday evening."

"Is he still here?"

"I don't think so. The Sages vanish at the smallest sign of danger," Costa said, with barely hidden contempt.

"Vlaicu, bring Leno..."

"He is dead," Vlaicu said. "And his second in command too. Five of Aron's soldiers survived, but that can wait. Our men who were embedded with them last night have some interesting news."

"I shall leave," Costa said.

"Don't," Vlaicu stopped him. "What I've learned may be of interest to you too. Belugas asked Leno to kill both you and Codrin."

"What?" Costa asked, and moved swiftly, one step closer to Vlaicu, almost to bump into him. "I am a captain of the Duke of Peyris."

"Belugas took Aurelian's place as Primus Itinerant," Codrin said. "Maybe Duke Stefan will understand more about how the Circle is playing him." *I still don't know why the Duke is helping Aron. It's not only about the Circle. I have the feeling that Dochia knows this, but she has chosen to hide it from me. Why is Aron so important?* "Tell the Duke that I thank him for his offer, but I am now the Grand Seigneur of Leyona, and I intend to remain so. Take your men and leave. The events of last night are his responsibility, but I don't want more blood between the Duke and me. And in time, we may become closer, as his words in the letter had suggested it."

"Good luck with Leyona, and thank you, Sir." Costa bowed. *Codrin is not a man to lie, but how could he conquer Leyona? Well, that's less important than being unable to deliver him to the Duke.* He shrugged, trying to overcome his worries. *My tenure as captain will be shorter than I expected.*

"Now," Vlaicu breathed after Costa left them, black anger glittering in his eyes. "Tell me about Mohor."

"I've just learned about it, but I was not sure," Codrin said, his voice heavy, and he told Vlaicu everything he had learned from the Empress. He kept the source hidden. "Aron and the Circle have joined forces with Orban, and Jara... Jara was sent to Arad with Vio and Cernat. I should have done this a long time ago, but I swear that I will kill Aron."

"Take Bucur and leave Aron to me," Vlaicu grunted.

"I will not do it without you. Will you join me now? I need good men like you in Leyona."

"Yes."

"Thank you. Talk with your men. Any one of them who wants to join me is welcome in my army."

"Most of them will join you. I am sure."

Chapter 2 - Saliné

Seen from the window, the yellow-reddish road wound left and right in large curves, following a collection of what were pompously named *hills*, mounds not much taller than a house. Close to the horizon, the road fell out of view, entering the forest. Somewhere, in the middle of the forest, it split, and the left branch headed north, toward Arad. Eyes closed, Saliné remembered the carriage which, five days ago, took Jara and Vio away, and tears ran down her face. *I am alone*, she thought for the hundredth time, wiping her face. All her days since had been the same: she played the calm game during the day, in front of Aron and Bucur, and cried during the night. *A lonely prisoner*. She shook her head. Most of the servants, and all the important ones, in the palace, were replaced with Aron's creatures, and she felt surrounded by hostile people. *I must think*. Yet all she could do was to grieve, the images of her mother and sister coming and going in her mind. And Mohor's image too. She had learned the day before about the *accident*, as Aron called it. Even her two maids were replaced, by two older women from Seged, Aron's castle, and one of them, Gria, was a shrew, repeatedly challenging Saliné in front of other people. *I have to ignore her*; Saliné shook her head again, the move seemed to calm her. *There is no way to replace Gria and receive at least Ava back*. Ava was one year younger than Saliné and, still almost a child, she always brought a breeze of cheerfulness into Saliné's life which, even before the taking of Severin by Aron, was not easy to find. She was betrothed by the Circle to Bucur, a man she despised because he had drugged and raped her, and she had to play her role with grace. *They don't just want to control what I am doing, and who I am meeting; they want to control my mind too. I must think*. Until that day, she had been confined to her small suite, consisting of only a bedroom that was small too, and an antechamber that was larger. Codrin's image came to her, and she fought hard to suppress it. Saliné had to play the role of the obedient fiancée, and twice a day, she was forced to eat with Bucur, at lunch and dinner. Codrin's lovely ghost was a risk to her game. *I hope that he escapes; the Circle will surely try to kill him*. "Codrin is strong," she said out loud, and turned her head abruptly, even knowing that she was alone in her antechamber – a prisoner is never careful enough. *They freed me today from a small cage into a larger one. I need to exploit this.*

"The market is working again," Aron said, quietly seething about how much each lost day had cost him. It was one of their dinners together where Saliné had to force the food to go down her throat.

"Things are slowly going back to normal," Bucur agreed. "Isn't that so, Saliné?"

"How should I know? I have not stepped outside the palace for a while." Her ability to understand the concealed meanings that hide behind inconspicuous words had been greatly enhanced over the last year when she had to hide herself away and learn how to interpret other people's reactions. She could clearly see a tinge of expectation in both Aron's and Bucur's postures. "I would like to see the market again."

"This not the right time to visit the market." With a swift gesture, Aron dismissed Saliné's plea. "People are stirred up by some nefarious men spreading lies about what happened when Orban took the city. There was no other way to save Severin from him. Orban forced my hand, and one day I will pay him back. Bucur will pay him. And you. Together, you will grow stronger than we are today. All this is just a temporary solution until the Circle convinces Orban to release Jara and leave Severin alone."

You and the Circle sold Mother to Orban. "One more reason to let me go into the market," Saliné insisted. "People are accustomed to see me there each week. My absence will give even more justification to those spreading the lies."

"Well." Aron rubbed his chin, seeming to consider her proposal. "Maybe you are right. You will take two guards with you."

"Ava, my maid should be enough."

"Do you want to go or not?" Aron snapped, and Saliné just nodded, trying to understand Aron's mind on that subject. "Good. For your own sake, you are not to see Ava for a while. Take one of your new maids and Karel will give you two guards." Karel was the new Spatar of Severin.

"Thank you," Saliné said and finished her meal in silence. *Aron accepted too fast. Why? The guards? They will make me look like a traitor, or make me look like a prisoner, which I am.* It puzzled her that Aron had opened the discussion about the market, in a veiled way, of course, and she knew him well enough to realize that it was more than just a slip of the tongue.

Aron took a long stare at her, but Saliné had learned from experience to lock her feelings away and try to forget them when she needed to. It was how she'd survived the last year. It was only Bucur that she could not fully play – he had more experience with all sorts of women and their feelings – and that thought always sent cold shivers down her spine. She was afraid of him, afraid that he could use his charm on her, even though they were to be married in a year's time.

Mohor's servants, those who were not thrown out of the palace, viewed Saliné with mixed feelings. Some thought her a traitor too, others saw her as a victim, but none was ready to have much faith in her. Fear stopped them. It did not help that Aron had kept her in isolation until the previous days. During the evening, she tried to imagine how her trip to the market would turn out, but she had to give up; she knew nothing about what had happened in the city after Aron took Severin over Mohor's dead body, yet the thrill of leaving her small cage kept her awake until late in the night.

Going out through the palace gate gave Saliné a sense of freedom, and the impulse to run came to her. She breathed deeply and suppressed it, walking at leisure through the plaza, followed by Gria, the oldest of her new maids, who was in her late thirties. From the time they had spent together, Saliné understood that she was as intelligent as she was mischievous. And Gria was Aron's loyal tool. Turning her head back, Saliné was happy that both Gria and the two guards were walking a few paces behind her; she was not in the mood for some forced social conversation – six days of pretending that she was pleased to have Gria as her maid were more than enough. The thought of running away passed through her mind again. She calmed herself and took the street going straight into the market; Severin was a small town. That was where she met the first persons that did not belong to the palace: a family with two children. She smiled warmly at them, only to receive back angry scowls from both adults. Once they had passed, Saliné bit her lip and walked on. A brief glance back told her that the distance between her and the guards had increased by two more paces. Her hand went to check a tiny hidden place on her dress; under the belt, she had placed one of the knives, made of flexible steel, which Codrin had given to her when they still trained together. *I must train again*, she thought, anxiety seeping into her.

"Whore," a venomous whisper woke her up, yet it was too late to see the face of the angry woman who was walking away, without turning her head.

Saliné sped up, struggling hard not to run. She was at least lucky that no one crossed her path again until she entered the market. The place was not yet full, but there were many people there, and she felt their heavy glances. At least, they were silent, making space around her, as if they feared to touch her. She slowed even more and took a deep breath. Cinnamon, cloves, perhaps and lavender wafted over the smell of many flavored pies, and over everything hung the strong aroma of apples just cooked in the stove. Abruptly, she went into the first booth on the left. It was the place she always visited first during her walks to the market.

"Good morning Velna." She smiled at the woman who sold the best silk in Severin. "Do you have new things to show me?" She waited patiently, but Velna acted as if Saliné was not there. "Velna?" she said louder this time, only to be ignored again. "Well," she said in a sad voice, "it seems that since I became a prisoner in Severin, you have forgotten how many times I visited and talked with you before."

"Don't speak, just leave," Velna whispered, and turned abruptly toward another woman who had just come in, and they started to talk in low voices. What Saliné could hear was the same word: whore. Bitterness filled her and, turning, she saw Gria approaching with a thin smile on her lips.

She went to four more booths and stalls, the ones she had visited the most in the past and forged some links with the sellers, and the same cold reception was repeated. *I have only Ferd left*, she sighed, and walked to the booth which belonged to his father, the third Mester of Severin, just that a Mester in Severin was still a small merchant. *I hope that Ferd is there.*

"Good morning, Ferd," she said, with more joy than she wanted to show. "What new sweets have arrived from Litvonia?" She locked eyes with him, her heart beating faster.

"Not many," Ferd shrugged, arranging some boxes on the counter.

"Well," she said, despondently, "it seems that there are not many things for me in the market. Being Aron's prisoner has changed me into a pariah. I wish you good luck with Aron." This time anger suppressed her bitterness, and she turned abruptly, to walk away. On weak legs, it took her more time than usual.

"Things are fluid now, but we may receive something soon, lady Saliné. Come again in three days at the same time, and we may talk more," Ferd said in a low voice; yet it was gentle, and she gestured loosely at him, walking away. The three Cerberuses followed her.

Aron told me that Saliné is a clever girl, but she seems quite stupid, Gria mused, watching her tightly. *Aron was right to send her out*; she smiled with a mischievous look in her eyes.

A few moments after Saliné left the market through the same narrow street, a woman who was leaning against the wall, moved at leisure to block her path. "Whore!" she cried, pointing at Saliné, and two men joined the woman, shouting, "Whore! Whore! You killed Mohor!" Attracted by the cries, more people came from the market to watch. Breathing deeply, Saliné ignored them and slightly changed her direction, trying to pass between the wall of the house on the left and the woman. The woman gripped her shoulder, then tried to pull Saliné by her hair. Saliné swirled and elbowed the woman in her ribs. In that fast turn, she saw her guards reluctant to interfere, and Gria smiling. Out of air, the woman gasped, releasing Saliné's shoulder, and she walked away from the three assailants, without turning back. After a few moments, the guards suddenly remembered that they were there to protect Saliné and walked to catch up with her. The cries of 'You killed Mohor,' still followed her, and she fought hard against her tears, yet her mind registered in a back corner that there were not many people shouting at her.

I know one of those two men, Saliné thought. *He is not from Severin*. She moved to walk faster, but did not try to run, even though some people had started to trail her through the plaza. Glancing back, from time to time, she saw that her guards were now just three paces behind her. She passed quickly through the gate of the palace, and silently went to her suite, followed by Gria.

Entering her suite, Saliné found her second guardian maid, Herna, waiting in the antechamber. Gria tried to follow her inside, but Saliné slammed the door in her face, almost crushing her nose, and extracting a whispered curse from the woman. Stubbornly, Gria still tried to enter, but Saliné blocked the door with her boot, two palms inside the room. It was a clever move as, feeling the free space, Gria pushed the door hard and stepped forward at the same time. This time her head banged against a door which stopped suddenly at Saliné's boot, and she mumbled another curse, but no longer tried to enter. "Leave," Saliné said to Herna who, being younger, was easier to maneuver. After the door was closed, Saliné locked it and threw herself on the small sofa.

Her mind focused again on the man shouting at her in the street. *Where have I seen him?* She recalled Gria's and the guards' reaction, but it could have been something coincidental. *I can't remember*, Saliné sighed. She stood up abruptly and went to her desk. There were papers on it and some quills and ink too. With a nervous glance behind her, she pulled out a piece of paper and started to write:

'Aron wanted me to go in the market today. He was expecting me to do it, even though he tried to *persuade* me to the contrary.'

'The guards did not interfere when the woman and the two men shouted at me. Not even when the woman became violent.'

Whore, she thought bitterly. *I am not a whore, but I am not a free woman either. Why did they shout that? Why would that help Aron?*

'They want to link Mohor's death to me,' she wrote. 'That will take some pressure off Aron and give him more space for maneuver.' She finally understood.

Remembering Mohor's death, she burst into tears, and it took her a while to calm down again and force herself to think. There were rumors in the palace that people had tried to revolt when Mohor was killed by Aron's guards. She had heard that the evening before, returning to her suite from dinner with Aron and Bucur. Two of Aron's men were talking at the junction of two corridors, but she could not stop to learn more, and had to turn the corner, as she was being followed by Gria. Seeing her, the men stopped talking at once.

'Even the sellers I knew well in the market associated me with Mohor's death.'

'They were told that. Someone is spreading rumors about me. Aron.' Her hand shaking from anger, she underlined Aron's name twice. The two sneaking parallel lines looked like a child's way of drawing water.

I need to challenge this. I started to do it today, but I need to do more. If they let me go to the market again. I must go there; she shook her head. *Let's hope that Aron will want it too.* There was no way for her to leave the palace without his approval.

The last year had been unkind to Saliné and she had grown more adept at hiding her feelings and playing the game they expected from her; but the difficulty lay in making them do what she wanted, even though all the power was on their side. She read the paper again, and then went to the fireplace. The fire from the night before was dead, but she found some small embers under the ash. The paper burned quickly.

Training now, she sighed. She liked to train, but she had always trained with Codrin, Vio and Jara, and that brought the past back into her desolate present. She undressed herself and, almost naked, started to warm her body, moving slowly and stretching; the Assassin Dance was not something to be taken lightly. When Saliné felt ready, she started a simple sequence of smooth moves, performed gradually and with muscular tension. The dance was punctuated now and then by sudden strikes in all directions, in a sequence that stretched her to the limit of her body. After several minutes, she took up her daggers. All her movements were now fluid and controlled. The dance was a deceptive exercise. It looked simple, but in the dancing steps the essence of the fighting style could be found. The Assassin Masters had gathered secrets, and tuned them during almost a millennium, hiding them within these movements.

Despite the effort, her breathing became more controlled, helping to funnel energy into her movements. Her breath and the movement of her body became one – the Assassin Trance.

In the evening, Bucur came to her suite, in what had become a ritual, to take Saliné to the living room and have dinner again, and they walked almost in silence through the maze of corridors and stairs; he always avoided the shortest route, instead parading her in front of the people walking in the palace. She forced herself to place her palm on his arm, and to accept his unwanted proximity.

"I just heard what happened," Bucur said, letting a trace of worry slip into his voice, after she was seated, and she understood that his timing was planned; Aron needed be part of the conversation too. "We will take the necessary measures, but you should reconsider leaving the palace again. The city is not yet a safe place." His hand covered hers, as he was seated next to her, and he squeezed it gently.

Saliné looked through the window, fighting the impulse to pull away, and forced herself to swipe her thumb over his fingers. She felt suddenly angry, and not only at him. At everything. "You are right about the risk. Do you think that people will attempt some more extreme acts to ... punish me?" She stared at him, and Bucur frowned – for all her acting as a docile fiancée, there was something unyielding in her that did not escape his attention.

"That woman assaulted you," Aron interjected. "Next time it may be a man with a knife. We have to consider everything carefully."

You still want me to go. "Are you advising me to stop the walks for a while?"

"That woman shouted such bad things," Bucur said, "linking you to Mohor's death, even though it was just an unwanted accident."

"They all know that I will be your wife," Saliné shrugged, "but it will take a while for some people to fully acknowledge it."

Aron frowned deeply, his eyes sparkling with anger, and no one spoke for a while; she faced the silence with strained attention.

"Yes, yes, they are aware of that." Bucur forced a thin smile to his lips, fastening upon Saliné a look which at least told her that they understood her words as she intended.

"We don't need to hide in the palace," Saliné said calmly. "Severin is our city. Unless Aron advises me differently, of course." She glanced at him, feeling the impatience in his silence.

"You may be right, and I know that you like to visit the market, but we have to think about your safety too," Aron said, avoiding to look at her.

"Then I will wait for you to tell me when security is restored in Severin."

"There are no security issues in Severin," Aron said in haste, a dark shadow filling his eyes; her wit annoyed him, and as he had no one else upon whom to vent his irritation, it was to Saliné that he displayed it.

The next evening, Felcer, the healer of Severin, came to her room. He was one of the few of Mohor's people that Aron let continue their jobs; Felcer was too skilled to kick him out, but Aron took care to provide two young apprentices to learn from him.

"You look better, today," Felcer said, and Saliné answered with a sad smile. "I went to the market yesterday," he continued, "and I talked with Ferd."

"Yes, I was in the market too," she said, neutrally.

"Do you know when I came to Severin?" Felcer asked. "Of course, you can't know. I came here three months before Mohor was born." His voice broke, but he recovered fast. "I came as an apprentice to old Miklos, and it was me who received the newborn from the midwife – Miklos's arms were too weak. From his birth, I took care of Mohor, until ... until that day. I am on your side, Lady Saliné. Before... Just before that day, Mohor told me that you only play the role of Bucur's fiancée. I thought the same – you and Bucur don't really match – even though I never voiced my thoughts, but it helped that he confirmed everything to me, and he asked me to take care of you. I am only a healer, and I am old, but I am willing to help."

"Thank you, Felcer," Saliné said, fighting hard against her own emotions.

"So, I talked to Ferd." Felcer moistened his lips. "He apologizes for the last encounter, and Velna too. There are people spreading the story that you are behind Mohor's death, that you convinced Aron and Bucur to take Severin; that you wanted to be the Signora of Severin."

"And they believed it," Saliné said, bitterly.

"Some of them, yes, but not Ferd, and not Velna, even though they acted as they acted. The woman who came to talk with Velna is known to spread bad words about you. Velna acted as she did to stop you saying things that the people who are behind that woman should not hear."

"Do you know who is behind this?"

"Not yet, but we are watching them. I understand that in two days, you will go to the market again."

"I need to talk with Ferd, if... If he is the same man I knew in the past."

"Yes, he told me that, but there is something else that we learned today. There is a rumor about some people planning to gather in the market when you arrive there. They will shout again ... those bad words, but even worse they may become violent. They want to take off your clothes and carry you naked through the city, shouting that you killed Mohor. We are not yet sure," he added, his voice trailing, "but we need to be prepared."

"What?" Saliné asked, involuntarily.

"It's an old custom, to carry whores and traitors naked through the streets."

"I understand there may be some bad feelings, but I did not think," she shook her head. "I did not think that they would go that far based only on rumors."

"You know?" Felcer smiled, "it's exactly this last rumor about being ... paraded which has convinced a lot of people that you are innocent."

"That's good," Saliné said, a thin tremor in her voice, "but the price I may have to pay seems too high. Things may get out of control, and I don't want to be paraded naked in the streets. I will pretend that I am sick and stay here. I can't bear that."

"No, no," Felcer said quickly. "We are prepared. There will be even more people shouting that you are innocent and that everything happened because of Aron. Our people will surround and defend you."

"That's not good," Saliné said firmly. "It will set me on a collision course with Aron, and I am too weak to afford that, even though more people may be on my side. Aron is the master of Severin. I have no soldiers, no authority."

"It's your decision," Felcer said gently. "Ferd asked me how we might help you, but he said that it will not be possible to sneak you out of Severin. The gate is watched closely."

Any day, I can leave Severin through the secret tunnel, yet I can't. Mother, Codrin, Vio, they will all be in danger. The only way is for Codrin to take Severin. That may turn the Circle to the right path. "However much I wish it, I can't leave. There is only one place where I would be safe, Cleuny, but that will endanger Codrin and my family. Even without me, he has enough issues with the Circle. There is no need to create another one. But we can help him." She stared with determination and a trace of hope at Felcer. "We must help him, and we must find ways to weaken Aron."

"I think I know what's in your mind, but I am an old man. Ferd has military skills..."

"I need to talk with him. The day I plan to go to the market again, Aron and Bucur will not be here, so it will be easier to talk. I will surprise everybody and ask to leave the palace two hours earlier than we planned. Those people wanting to attack me may have some spies here. A few servants think me responsible for Mohor's death. Ferd should act discreetly – no shouts against Aron – and keep most of those ... those people out of the market without a fight. Mostly the men. I can handle three or four women. Maybe..." She rubbed her chin, undecided, yet her eyes were intent and focused. "Tomorrow, I will *sprain* an ankle. That will allow you to come and see me, and me to carry a cane while walking to the market. In the right hands, a cane can be a powerful weapon. What do you think?"

"That you were born to lead," Felcer smiled. "I will meet Ferd today."

Chapter 3 – Saliné

Saliné knew how to play the game so that the other side was unable to hide its cards and waited patiently. The next evening, hearing her talking about everything else but the market, Aron reopened the issue about her visit there.

"These are difficult times, and you don't have many things to enjoy. If you really want, you may go tomorrow and see the market again." Aron spoke without looking at her, like he was preoccupied by more important things. "It seems that things have calmed down a bit."

"The market is a pleasant place indeed, full of life and colors," she said, her voice flat.

"Just please be careful." Bucur looked at her and placed his hand over hers. "At the least sign of danger, return to the castle. I wish I could join you, but we will not be here. Maybe you should take more soldiers with you."

She pondered for a while. *More soldiers would stop those people attacking me, but it may be better to let them act now, while they are less organized. I should count on the element of surprise too.* "That would only show the people that we fear something. One guard should be enough."

"But your leg," Bucur said, tentatively, and gently squeezed her hand.

"It's fine," Saliné shrugged. "It's just a small strain on my ankle. "Felcer gave me some ointment. It seems that it works, and he told me that I can walk, I just need to be careful." *An ointment always works wonders on a healthy leg*, she chuckled inside.

"When do you plan to go?" Aron asked. "I need to tell Karel, as he will take care of your safety in our absence."

"At noon. It's warmer."

"At noon, then." Aron nodded and fell silent with an expression of poorly concealed satisfaction.

In the morning, as planned with Felcer, she decided to leave two hours earlier and, unable to ask Aron and Bucur for guidance, Karel protested.

"I don't have free men now," he said.

"Do you mean to tell me you can't find one spare man in a full garrison?" Saliné asked in a mildly scolding voice, tapping with the point of her cane on his chest. "I will not go later. It's a warm day, and I can't walk fast. If you don't give me a guard now, I will stay at home."

Karel shot her a malevolent glance, but he had been ordered to let her go that day, so he yielded to her plea. But he was not Spatar without a reason; he managed to delay her for almost half an hour, and through the window of the hall, Saliné saw three of his men hurrying out through the gate of the palace.

This time, she walked as fast she could toward the market without giving the impression that she was not hurt and went directly to Velna. "Good morning, Velna. I need you to keep the shrew behind me here." She pointed toward Gria who, as in the previous visit, was walking six paces behind her, together with the guard.

"Good morning, Lady Saliné. I've received some new samples of silk. Should I show them to you? They are of good quality." Velna pointed to some samples that were already on the counter.

"Gria," Saliné said, "the samples look interesting, and I want to see how they look on me, but there is no mirror here. Velna will dress you in silk."

Gria gaped, her hand touching the silk greedily and, without a word, she abandoned herself to Velna's tender ministrations, as she started to drape her from chin to ankles.

"It's beautiful, but I am not sure..." Saliné said, after the first sample was finally wrapped around Gria. "Velna, please tie a belt around her waist, and put on two or three brooches, to keep the silk from falling from her shoulders. Make it look like a dress."

It took Velna three more minutes to arrange the silk as she was asked, and Saliné moved a few steps back, staring at Gria, who for the first time had a genuine smile on her lips. "You look wonderful, Gria, but I don't think that the color will suit me." Saliné shook her head, looking at the improvised dress. "Velna, please try with this one." She pointed with her cane to a bolt of dark green silk. Meanwhile, I will go to buy some sweeties."

Gria opened her mouth to protest and tried to move, but Velna caught her arm and kept her in place. "Don't move," Velna said, "or the brooches will pierce your skin and ruin my silk. You don't have the money to pay for it, but don't worry, each time Lady Saliné buys silk, she gives something to her maid too. Today is your lucky day."

When Saliné reached Ferd's booth, Gria was still struggling to free herself from her prison of silk.

"I've thought about what Felcer told me," he said after the greetings. "We don't have enough people to revolt against Aron, and they are merchants and servants, not soldiers."

"No, no," Saliné said quickly, "I was not thinking about that. What I had in mind was to weaken Aron in small ways, and if siege is laid against Severin, only then we should stir a revolt. Codrin may arrive soon with his army."

"That would be easier," Ferd said, "but not easy. You mentioned that killing Bucur would endanger Codrin. Now you are talking about a siege."

"I will not endanger Codrin, even if I have to remain hostage here all my life, but if he takes the decision to lay siege to Severin... It will be his decision, and he knows better what is happening in Frankis right now. If Codrin lays siege, we will start the revolt, but until then, we need to weaken Aron."

"How do you intend to weaken Aron?"

"We need to kill as many soldiers as possible we can. Let's split Severin into four areas. You and your men take responsibility for three of the walls. Someone else will take care of the northern walls of the city and palace. Perhaps we are able to kill five or six guards each week."

Out of the corner of her eye, she caught movement on a small side street; a large group of people were coming into the market, walking fast.

"We are prepared," Ferd said, seeing her reaction and, as he spoke, a cart moved slowly across the street, blocking it. For whatever reason, the horse reared, and two barrels fell, rolling down over the people on the small street. Some of them were caught, and some ran away, but a few still managed to come into the market. "Better leave now," he said, and pushed a box of cakes into her hand.

"Thank you, I will pay for it later," she said and walked toward Gria, who was now free of her silk. "I will buy the green one," she said to Velna, "and that red scarf for Gria. I will send the money later. I am not feeling well," she pointed to her leg. "Take this too." She pushed the box of cakes into Gria's arms, and Velna did the same with the silk. Gria did not complain.

Only one man and two women, the few who were able to pass the cart Ferd had used to block the street, were waiting on Saliné's return path, and she walked slowly, smiling at how hard the soldier and Gria were trying to walk even slower than a limping woman. She felt comfortable about confronting these three.

"Come here," Saliné ordered the soldier. "My foot is throbbing. Give me your arm. I hope you are strong enough to support a woman."

The guard Karel had given her was only seventeen years old, and Saliné doubted that he had ever fought a battle or used that sword he was carrying for fighting. They walked at leisure, and she chose a path that took her along the wall of the street, keeping the soldier on her right. Before she could enter the street, the man she had recognized, who had assaulted her three days ago, walked quickly past her, followed by three more women. They stopped when they reached the other three waiting for Saliné in the middle of the street.

Saliné bit her lip, yet she did not stop, just walked a bit slower, trying to find a solution. *If I turn, they will attack me from the back. I must confront them. I hope Ferd's people will come before...* She shook her head at the thought of being paraded naked on the streets.

"Whore!" the women started to shout when Saliné was only twenty feet away from them. They moved to block the street, and Saliné realized that the man who had taunted her before was leading them. When the women blocked the street, he gestured guardedly at Saliné's soldier, then less guardedly, threatening him.

"Stay calm," Saliné whispered to the soldier, gripping his arm, and turning him slightly toward her, so he could not see the other man's threatening gestures. "They are rabble. When we are ten feet from them, unsheathe your sword." Slowly, she moved half behind him, letting his arm free and, unseen, she took off the tip of her cane, revealing a thin blade, almost ten inches long. *Thank you, Felcer,* she thought. It was the old man's personal weapon.

The man in front was now staring angrily at her young guard, gesturing, trying to intimidate him.

"I..." the guard whispered. "I was told to avoid violence."

"Look at me," she said in a calm but firm tone. "That's exactly what you will do. Show them the sword, and they will back away."

"Are you sure?"

"Now!" she ordered, and the young man forgot everything Karel had told him about avoiding violence. He complied and reached for the hilt of his sword.

The five women moved toward them shouting, "Whore! You killed Mohor. Take her clothes off. Let's see what a whore looks like. Let's show the whore to the people. She spread her legs to take Severin from its rightful owner. Let's spread them again for the real men of Severin." They stopped walking abruptly when the soldier unsheathed his sword. They did not stop shouting, though.

The man Saliné thought she knew moved fast to take her timorous guard from behind with his knife. The young soldier would have been wounded, or even died, before understanding what had happened, and she stepped forward, her thin blade piercing the attacker's eye, going straight into his brain. With a half growl, he fell, his head banging hard against the stones. The women gaped, and sudden silence filled the street. Saliné moved against them, slashing their arms and legs with the blade of her cane. There were not deep wounds, but the cuts enhanced their fear, and they all started to run like chickens, crying in pain. When the street was calm again, Saliné walked away, without looking back.

In the evening, when they returned, both Aron and Bucur looked puzzled when they learned what had happened and congratulated her.

"I will find and punish those women," Aron said.

"Maybe we can out find who was behind them," Saliné said, absently. "They seemed well organized. That is not good for us. What is the Chief of the Guard doing?"

"Don't worry," Bucur placed his hand over hers, "it will not happen again. We have been warned now, and we will turn every stone to find them."

Yes, yes, you are warned. "Thank you, Bucur," she smiled.

Felcer told her later that the man she had killed was one of Aron's captains from Seged. "One scoundrel less," he said with grim satisfaction.

"Aron's man?" Saliné asked, her eyes wide with disbelief; she stayed silent for a while, trying to understand. Her hands trembled, and she clasped them at her back. "I did not think that Aron would go that far. I am supposed to be his daughter-in-law. I am just a tool." Saliné shook her head, unable yet to believe it.

❧

It was one of the last days of a long summer, but the rain felt like autumn, cold, seeming to last forever, and Saliné woke up early, when the morning was not yet fully born. Under the thick clouds, the city was still asleep. She dressed quickly in a black riding costume and went to the fireplace. Her fingers closed on a small ornament, rotating it twice, and a hidden door opened into a secret corridor. There was not even a trace of light inside, but she bent and found the things she needed, then went right, walking carefully in the darkness, her hand touching the right-hand wall. "Aron's," she whispered after a while, when her fingers stumbled over a small protuberance in the wall. Just two weeks ago, the suite still belonged to Mohor, and she bit her lip, walking further. "Bucur's," she whispered again, at the second protuberance. "Mother and little Mark slept here." Tears ran down her face, and she could no longer move. "I have to do it." Straightening her body, Saliné walked slowly to the point where the corridor ended in two sets of stairs. A spiral one going down to the small wine cellar, and a straight one going up, for about fifteen feet, leading onto a small platform. She climbed the upper one, and once she stepped onto the platform, she palmed the wall in front until she found a thick wooden plank kept in place by three, L-shaped hooks. Slowly, she took out the plank and placed it on the floor at her feet. Her fingers fumbled until she found a small iron handle. She bit her lip and pulled the handle. It did not move, and she pulled harder. With a faint noise, a stone, ten inches in width and four inches high, moved out from the wall. It was a peculiar stone, trapezoidal in section, the lower part parallel with the floor, the upper one inclined. Once it was out completely, the faint light of the morning filled a part of the platform, and a fresh breeze brushed her face, replacing the musty smell of the corridor. She breathed deeply, and placed the heavy stone on the floor, on her right. The hole in the wall formed a half arrow loop, allowing her to look down easily. Saliné already knew what to expect, as it was her third visit to the place, yet she still glanced around, fearing that maybe someone else had figured the place out too. The small platform was quiet and was seemingly undiscovered by Aron or his men – there was dust everywhere, and it seemed untouched.

It was Mohor who had disclosed the secret corridor to Saliné, when he learned that Aron would send him to Orban, in Arad, just the day he was killed. He walked with her and revealed all the secrets hidden between the walls. "Not even Aron knows about this one," he said to her, "and it may be useful to you. "But he knows about the second one, which goes out of the castle." His calm voice was still fresh in her mind.

"One day, I will avenge, you, Mohor," she whispered, looking outside, giving her eyes enough time to adjust to the faint light.

Twelve feet down, in front of her, was the northern wall of the palace, and a sentry was moving back and forth, trying to warm himself. The wall started at the corner of the palace. Invisible from outside, her small platform was part of that corner, and she was able to see the full length of the northern wall of the palace. The sentry was walking lightly, a sign that he was not wearing ring-mail. On her left, forty-five feet away and just two feet lower, was the high wall of the city, and another sentry was walking there. She had a good view there too. From time to time, the two men gestured to one another, encouraging themselves. In half an hour, the next sentry would replace the man on the wall, defending Severin. There would be no guard during the day on the wall surrounding the palace.

Saliné sighed, and watched them closely, counting their steps, and noting when the men could see each other. When she finally understood the pattern of their movements, she reached down and picked up the bow and arrow lying at her feet. She nocked and aimed. Saliné had inherited her skills from Jara, and while Vio was swift and adept with the dagger, Saliné was able to kill a running rabbit, with her bow, at more than a hundred paces. Unaware, the man was coming toward her on the palace wall, and for a few heartbeats, she hesitated. "I must do it. Men like him helped Aron to kill Mohor and to sell Mother and Vio to Orban. They are all like their master, and my only chance to be free is to weaken Aron." She aimed carefully and held her breath. Even though he was at a hundred feet from her, the man was not a running rabbit, and her arrow flew with a rasping hiss, hitting him just over his heart, a few moments later. The other sentry was going in the opposite direction, unable to see what happened. A faint growl escaped from the wounded man; his hand clutched the shaft protruding from his chest, and he half turned, falling silently onto his knees, his body leaning forward over the embrasure between two merlons. The other sentry heard nothing.

They will think that the shot came from the garden, Saliné thought, seeing the dead man's position.

The other sentry walked further, arrived at the end point and retuned. He saw the dead man, stopped for a few moments. Then he ran, sounding the alarm. The stone taken out from the wall was already in its place and, downstairs, Saliné was walking through the darkness of the corridor.

"One," she whispered, closing the secret door behind her.

In five days, Aron lost eleven soldiers, and Saliné was trying to figure out how many guards were still in Severin when Felcer came to her, in a hurry that left him short of breath. He closed his eyes, leaning against the closed door.

"Codrin," he gasped. "Codrin's army will arrive in two days. Ferd told me." He lost his breath again when Saliné embraced him, and she danced like a child, when the old man left her alone in the room.

A day later, in the evening, a column of riders approached the city. From her window, Saliné saw the colors of the Duke of

Peyris, and her hands gripped the frame of the window. Bucur came to tell her that the seventy-five soldiers would stay in Severin as long as they were needed. She played the role of the fearful woman who had received good news from him. Alone, she cried again until midnight Her night was long and without sleep.

I must continue, she thought. *That is my only chance.* She dressed fast, in the dark blue riding costume she always used in her escapades and went into the secret corridor. Despite the darkness, Saliné was able to walk fast, and she was about to go past Aron's suite when she heard voices inside, through the small spy slit in the wall. Inside the room, the other end of the slit was concealed in a wooden ornament in the corner. It offered a perfect view over three-quarters of the room. There were many splits in the old wood, masking the spy hole. Moving a few steps back, she pressed her ear to the slit. The stone was cold, but the voices were now clear, and she recognized Aron and Bucur.

"The trap is now in place," Bucur said. "With the new guards we have enough sentries to cover the garden and the attic of the palace. They are well hidden and will take up their places in the morning. The archers usually strike early in the morning. This time, we may be able to capture them, or at least understand where they are coming from."

"You still don't think that Saliné is involved in this?"

"Her suite was guarded on all the nights when sentries were killed. There was no way for her to leave. It must be the same team who killed our soldiers the day Mohor died. There were three archers then, shooting from different directions. Saliné was confined in her room that day, so she could not help them. Or maybe there are some secret corridors in the palace."

"There is only one. It links the cellar and jail with a tunnel leading out of town."

"Maybe Mohor kept some things hidden."

"He didn't even know about the tunnel. His father did not trust a boy with such secret things. It was Senal who revealed it to us. How many sentries are in the garden?"

"Two, and another one inside the palace. That small half turret at the end of the corridor which links our suites. The second one is in a sentry box at the edge of the garden. From their positions, they can see both walls. The one in the box can see the roof too. In the attic, there are three guards. From there, they can see everyone coming and going in a position to shoot at the walls."

"Gria told me that there is a bow in Saliné's room."

"I have checked it already, and it has not been used for some time. The string is not attached to the bow." Bucur remained silent for a while. "I will ask her tomorrow if she still has her bow. Just to see her reaction."

She woke up late in the morning, after a brief sleep filled with dark dreams; yet another soldier was found dead on the wall.

Chapter 4 - Cleyre

Cleyre was impatient, and maybe frightened. There were too many bad things happening now in Frankis. Some things she knew about, but she could not stop her mind asking again and again how many pieces from the larger puzzle she was still missing. *Grandfather is weaker with each passing day,* she lamented. *He was pressured to help Bucur. How could I miss that? He knew that I would oppose the move and wanted to avoid an argument. I can't deny that both Aron and Bucur are more intelligent than any other uncles and cousins I have. I don't care that Bucur is his bastard grandson, but I care that he has even less character than Orban, the other worm the Circle wanted to be our King.* She stood up and paced around her desk, trying to calm her mind.

And Dochia has left Frankis for a while. I wish I could be more open with her and she with me. Strange that she can't feel that I have the Light. I can feel hers. Maybe that's why the Wanderers missed me. Anyway, I did not want to join them. It's bad that she will be away from Frankis, more than she realizes. Dochia will not return here from Muniker; she will go to the nomads in the east. She doesn't know it yet; I saw that clearly in my Vision. Why can't we see our own future? Perhaps it would frighten us too much.

There was a knock in the door, and Nicolas, the Spatar of Peyris, entered. "Where is the Duke?" he asked, seeing her at his desk.

"The Duke is indisposed," she said. *And so am I.* "Tell me."

Nicolas frowned and half turned, then stayed like that for a few moments. "A courier just came. He almost killed the horse under him to arrive as fast as he could. Mohor is dead, and Aron has taken Severin."

"The Circle is now working with the Wanderers, and things are going from bad to worse. I know," she said. "We are helping Aron, but I don't think that killing the rightful Seigneur of Severin was in Grandfather's plans or yours. Bucur seems even worse than Orban, and now more people will learn that we have helped him. How long it will be until some may think to play the same game on us, after dear uncle Albert becomes Duke? Am I right, Nicolas? Or maybe just because I am a woman, I can never be right about these things."

"You are right. Cleyre, don't take me wrong. I take your military advice with a pinch of salt, but I will never ignore the political insight. Maybe we should agree on this."

"Politics and the military work together. I rarely contradict you in the council."

"That's true, but you piss me off every time you think yourself a military strategist. You are not."

"And from whom do you think I should learn military strategy? From uncle Albert? His best skills lie in chasing young girls to see what hides under their skirts, and even in that, he is worse than a fifteen-year-old boy. Maybe because he is so short-sighted."

Unwillingly, Nicolas burst into laughter. "So, you want to learn."

"Does it bother you?"

"No, I just did not see things from this angle. Fine, from now on, I will try to be less offended by your clever mouth."

"Thank you, Nicolas. Do we have any news from Costa?"

He shook his head and made as if to leave. "What is it?" he asked, seeing her involuntary frown.

"This thing with Severin. I am afraid that the Circle wants to push us into a war to defend and expand Aron's property. We bleed, and he prospers."

"It may happen."

"And?"

"I don't approve of it, but I don't think that we can avoid it. My impression is that the Duke has already accepted that. I supposed that the Circle pressed him into it."

"And you told me that we had nothing to fear from supporting Aron when I pissed you off about it."

"Life is like that," Nicolas shrugged. "But we can work together to ... lower the expectations regarding our help." He winked at her, a flicker of amusement in his eyes. "I have to leave now. Tell the Duke about Severin."

The Duke received the news with a good dose of indifference, his gout was becoming worse. Talking about Severin did not seem to help. Annoyed, she left him alone when the memory of her last Vision came to her, and she calculated the days. *Enough time has passed for a courier to reach Peyris and hide my unorthodox way of receiving information.* She calculated again to be sure that she could pretend her knowledge came by courier. Satisfied, she went to see Nicolas who, apart from Duke Stefan, was the only man she could trust at the court.

"I know, you are worried for Costa," he said when Cleyre entered his office. "He may be already at the border between Severin and Leyona, but I still don't see what he can do. Codrin destroyed the Leyonan army. You read the letter yesterday morning."

"There is more than you know. Codrin took Leyona."

"That can't be. He had too few soldiers to lay siege and take a city as large as Leyona. Are you sure?" Frowning, he stared at

Cleyre, who ignored his question. "I wonder how large his losses were. It may help Costa."

"Codrin had no losses."

"Leyona just fell into his lap, like a swooning lover."

"You have no idea how right you are. Sorry, for half pissing you off with military things."

"Tell me," Nicolas sighed.

"He used an interesting military stratagem to sneak into the city and take over the gate and palace."

"What stratagem? Cleyre, I've never known you so shy to speak."

"It's so heartening to hear you asking. Codrin destroyed Leyona's army and took many prisoners. Right?" She glanced at Nicolas, who just nodded. "Codrin made hostages of the sons of some Knights and important people in Leyona. Then he went in the city with their fathers. They opened the gate and asked him politely to enter the city. He obliged."

"How do you know this?"

"You know that I have my own sources."

"They are very good, I grant you that, but I wish I knew them."

I doubt that I can tell you about my Visions. "One more thing. My sources told me that Codrin may not be able to keep Leyona for long. It's hard to tame a nest of hornets, and there are several forces working against him."

"The Circle?" Nicolas asked, and she nodded. "How long is long?"

"A few months; probably his tenure of Leyona will end before the end of the year. I don't know ... yet. Of course, he may surprise us again."

"Then your letter to Codrin may have some success ... later."

"Maybe," she shrugged, and left his office. *It's just a small step,* she thought, *but it looks bigger now than a week ago. Things should be clearer come Spring.*

ঔ

At the southern gate of Peyris, a written order was waiting for Costa. He was asked to go straight to Cleyre. "Return to the barracks," he ordered his men, and rode toward the palace. At the small inner gate, there was another order waiting for him, and a page took his horse. He entered the precincts and went to the stairs, playing the paper between his fingers. *Not even a word about Codrin. They did not expect me to deliver.* The guards opened the door for him, and he walked slowly toward Cleyre's office. *I will look straight in her eyes; I want to know if she thought that I would fail.* He cut a stern figure when he was finally allowed to enter the office.

"Milady," he bowed curtly. Their eyes locked, but he was not able to read anything on her face.

He still loves me, Cleyre thought and smiled briefly; it carried a touch of sadness. "Welcome home, Costa. Take a seat." She gestured to one of the chairs in front of her desk.

"I failed you," Costa said gruffly. There was misery throbbing in his voice. Hesitantly, he threw his tired body in the chair.

"Even though you failed, I am sure you acted well. It's no shame to lose against a commander like Codrin."

"It was expected that I would lose. That's why an inexperienced captain was sent."

"Codrin is unpredictable, and we sent a captain who thinks out of the box. I am sure you learned from your encounter and, next time, you will be better prepared. Young captains are willing to take risks and to learn. That's why we sent you."

"Thank you, milady." Costa bit his lip, tried to say more, but changed his mind. *Maybe she is right.*

"Tell me what happened. I am not a military commander," she smiled, "so you must explain to me in plain words."

"We set a trap, only to find that we were already in a bigger one."

"Why are men so vague when explaining military things to a woman? Do they think us stupid?"

"I never thought..."

"I know, I know, you are a kind man."

"Codrin expected the attack, even though he did not know that I had arrived with a hundred men. He knew that Aron had taken Severin, and he was prepared for confrontation. We surrounded his tent under the cover of night. It was empty, and his men were waiting for us, hidden in the forest. He had sixty archers who made the difference. We lost before realizing what had really happened."

"How many men we did we lose?"

"Twenty-nine."

"That's a lot," she said, a rictus changing the shape on her upper lip, making it look like a broken line. "What did he say about Severin?"

"Codrin was bitter, but I took care to underline that the Duke was not involved."

"Did he believe you?"

"Hard to say," Costa frowned. "I talked with Mohor's Chief of Guard, and he told me..."

"Yes, yes, we helped Aron last year."

"Mohor was the rightful Seigneur of Severin."

"Yes, captain, I know that. How did Codrin react to our letter?"

"Despite what had happened to Mohor, he did not reject the possibility of some collaboration in the future. Yet... he mentioned being the Grand Seigneur of Leyona. From what I know, he is a man to trust, but how could he conquer Leyona?"

"Another trap inside a trap," Cleyre said.

"There was a trap for me too. Belugas, the Primus Itinerant asked Aron's men to kill both Codrin and me. He..." Costa's voice was more bitter than he intended, and he stopped abruptly.

"You can trust men like Codrin, but you can't trust the scoundrels from the Circle and their protégées." Cleyre stood up and walked around the desk, stopping close to him, her body leaning against the desk. Their eyes locked again. *Let's set another trap.* "I feel lonely tonight." She smiled, her finger tracing a line on his neck.

Costa shivered at her touch and moistened his lips a few times. She smiled, her finger moving toward the opening of his shirt. "I apologize, but a night together means very different things to us," he blurted. "There is no real place where you want to lead me, just a lovely illusion. I understand that I am not up to your expectations, and my resignation will arrive tomorrow. I will leave Peyris soon after."

Sometimes a trap has two layers. Most men fall into the first one, when a woman is involved. Costa is more mature now. "Don't be childish, Costa. I like men who have some spine," Cleyre laughed. "Forget about Codrin and go to your duties now. My feeling is that you are a better captain than you credit yourself for. Or others do." She watched him leave the room with a wry smile on her lips. *You will never know that I broke with you only because I was becoming too attached. I could not afford such weakness. Not then and not now. Not for you and not for me.* Caught in his inner thoughts, Costa did not perceive her bitterness. Cleyre knew that, with all the divergences between them, her elder brothers would have killed Costa and married her off to some nobody in the blink of an eye.

Three years ago, when she was only sixteen and almost as innocent as other girls of her age were, she had met Bucur, who was visiting Peyris. He was handsome and seductive, and she was lost when he moved to explore her body more than she was accustomed to in public, even opening her chemise. They were at a ball, in a break between two suites of dancing, hiding in the park behind the castle, together with other twenty or so young couples. Bucur pressed her too much, and she finally found some will to oppose him; there were too many eyes around them. He did not care and tried to force her even with all those people around. It was Costa who saved Cleyre, even though they did not know each other. And Costa became her love, a love that she could not afford.

At the first wrong step, my uncles and cousins would act like a pack of wolves and tear me into pieces. Even my brothers... All are brainless, but they are men of power. Only the Duke and Father were different. How I wish my parents were alive. My childhood was so short... Sometimes, I wish to be a man too; she sighed. *They think me a whore. In a way, I am, but there was no other curtain I could use to hide myself from them; yet most of the men who bragged about my legs never saw them. It's strange how not denying a lie makes it truth.*

Alone, Cleyre went to the window and watched the sunset surrender to darkness in the garden. The first stars were faintly visible on the clear sky. *It works both ways.* "Poor Dolen," she burst into laughter, remembering her first hard lesson at the court.

It was her seventeen birthday and, after drinking more than the etiquette allowed at a duke's party, some youngsters and men started to brag in front of her and many other guests about how well they had pleased her in bed. They bragged about their skills; where they kissed and touched her, and how she moaned and cried, asking for more. People were gathering around them, attracted by the spicy show, and she felt almost naked under the many eyes seeming to search for the sweet spots the others were mentioning. It was a setup, she understood that well enough, and her mind was spinning under the pressure of all those eyes fixed on her, some undressing her greedily, some filled with cruel pity. She had no clout at that time; her father, who was the only son who could take Stefan's place, had died in battle the year before. Her mother had died three years earlier, and many people whispered that she was poisoned. Cleyre was the fourth child and all others were sons who saw her more like property than sister. The only reason that she was not yet married to an unwanted man was that her brothers' interests differed, and she was able to play into that.

"Dolen," Cleyre cried and laughed as loud she could, making everybody stop talking. "You were such a poor lover that I almost fell asleep." She smiled with a charm that few could resist, and yawned ostentatiously, stretching her body, to reveal her eye-catching curves – there were only two women who could rival her beauty at the court, and they were already married.

The space around her fell into a moment of silence, and some girls and women chuckled without knowing exactly why and at whom, and then the whole hall erupted in a chain of guffaws, led by the Duke, who thought it was the right moment to help his granddaughter. Cleyre still remembered Dolen's red face, and how difficult he found it to even breathe, struggling to say something that no one could hear in the general laughter. It was a compromising moment for her, yet she had escaped less harmed than looked likely in the beginning, and that was the moment when she attracted her grandfather's attention.

"My dear, you have some wit; I grant you that, but maybe you should be more selective with your lovers," Duke Stefan told her a day later. "And more discreet. You may be too young for such games."

"I am careful, Grandfather. Most of the men bragging about being my lovers were lying, Dolen included."

"Then?" He frowned, his thick white brows drawing together.

"You may ask dear uncle Albert or that Sage from the Circle for that question. They had a brief talk with Dolen and two other men in the group which taunted me just before everything started. Those three bragged the loudest, even though they had never touched me, not even for a kiss."

"I see. Go now, my child," the Duke said, suddenly indisposed. "I will have a few words with Albert, though I think that no one will try to tease you that way again. Tomorrow morning, come into my office." There was now a thin smile on his lips, yet Cleyre thought that it was only to hide his real feelings.

Back from her old memories, she closed her eyes and began to breathe in a slow and measured way. It calmed her. *Codrin passed my test, and my letter has planted some seeds in his mind. Soon, he will learn that his position is weaker than he thinks. In the Vision I had three weeks ago, I saw him in Poenari, but I still don't understand the significance of that. Why is Fate so vague in my Visions?* She opened the window and stared out without seeing. Gently, the wind played with her long hair.

Chapter 5 - Dochia

The morning had dawned clear and cold, with a crispness that sharpened the profile of the mountains behind them. They were less than a day away from Muniker, and Dochia fought the temptation to push her horse to a gallop. The Vision came to her abruptly, like many other Visions she had experienced. She gaped, and dismounted, letting her horse free, and sat under an old oak, her back leaning on its trunk. Her guards dismounted too, and Irina caught her horse.

"Oh, no," Dochia whispered, and pulled the hood over her head. "Mohor will be killed," she said to both Mira and Irina. "Orban will capture Jara. Aron will keep Saliné prisoner in Severin for Bucur."

"Should we go to Severin?" Mira asked reluctantly, feeling the despair in Dochia's voice.

"We can't, and even if we could, everything would be over before we arrived in Severin." From the vegetation in her Vision, she was able to guess the month, but even more, she felt that Mohor would die in a few days at most. It was a three-week ride from Muniker to Severin. "Under Drusila's rule, everything is going downhill in Frankis. I hope we can return to our hive in a month. I should not have gone to Peyris but come directly to Muniker."

"It was useful to talk with Duke Stefan," Umbra, her peregrine raven, said, and flapped his wings, landing on Dochia's knee. "He agreed to reevaluate Codrin. And I think that Mohor's death was meant to be. There were some strange new paths in your Vision that we can't ignore." A Wanderer's peregrine raven was always part of the Visions. Their minds were entwined and worked together to scout the future.

"Yes, there were, but why do so many good people have to suffer, and scoundrels like Aron, Bucur and Orban gain from their suffering? Why?"

"No one can answer that question, Dochia. Maybe not even Fate herself. And there is nothing we can do except focus on the new paths."

"I grew up with Jara. How can I pass over what Orban will do to her, and that she must accept him to protect Vio and Mark, who are prisoners too? I should have killed Drusila." Tears ran down her face, and Dochia wiped them nervously.

"I never saw you crying before," Umbra said gently, "but don't let resentment take over."

"We are not made of stone, and I don't want to be just a soulless thing working for something that I have started to doubt. Feelings are good sometimes. They help you chase away the chaff." Her despair pushed Dochia back in time, to when she was thrown out of the High Council of the Seven by Drusila's machinations and Derena's weakness. *I must fight back. The sooner I return, the better.*

They passed through Muniker a day later, and Dochia was composed, though her thoughts took her back to Severin, more than into the future. It took them a day more to arrive in the Alba Hive of Litvonia, which lay in the Alpas Mountains, south of Muniker.

I always forget how tall these mountains are, she thought, seeing the snow on the highest peaks, even though autumn was still almost a month away. "Soon we will see Kostenz Lake. Just after that small mountain." She pointed in front and to the right.

"It's the Hive on the Lake?" Irina asked, with the exuberance of her nineteen years.

"No. It's higher in the mountains. The road east from the Hive passes close to the lake. We will see it better then."

Dochia was expected in the Hive; a Vision was always faster than any other communication and Ingrid, the First Light of Litvonia, saw her coming and understood the reason behind her visit.

"We know about Salvina," Ingrid said, her voice sad. They were alone, in the First Light's austere office.

"It's not her fault; any of us can be subverted by the Maletera."

"You escaped."

"It was by chance."

"Don't try to fool yourself, Dochia. It was your strength. I wish that Salvina..."

"What happened?" Dochia asked, seeing the pain in Ingrid's eyes.

"She was my pupil... Two weeks ago, she tried to escape, and..."

"Is she wounded?" Dochia asked reflexively, and Ingrid just shook her head. *Salvina is dead. Sad news, but I can return to Frankis.* "I am sorry, Ingrid. Then my mission here is finished. Tomorrow, I will return to Frankis. There are many issues there, and some of them may be related to the Fracture."

"I know from the Conclave that the Fracture will start at the edges: Frankis and Arenia, but," Ingrid glanced at her with a guilty look, "you must continue your journey. I received a letter from Ada, and this is for you," she pushed an enveloped toward her, across the desk.

Dochia frowned, knowing even before opening the letter that she had to obey the summoning; Ada, the Second Light of Arenia, was the most powerful Wanderer of their times.

'Dochia,' she read.

'You already know about Severin, I saw it in my Visions, and I saw more. I hope that it will bring some comfort to you that Jara and her children will survive Orban. There will be sorrow in their lives, but there will be joy too. You will stay far from Frankis for a while. Don't worry, Frankis will not vanish from the map. I will wait for you in Silvania, but your road will not stop here; you must go and meet Meriaduk, the High Serpentist Priest.'

Dochia closed her eyes, trying to calm her breath. The letter fell from her fingers. Her reflexes worked independently from her ravaged thoughts and she caught it before it touched the floor.

Meriaduk... Who knows if I will ever return to Frankis? Who knows if I will escape alive?

"I know some fragments of what awaits you, Dochia. Not only from Ada's letter. I saw you with Meriaduk. You were in front of a huge map where lands and oceans were depicted. It did not look like a map, not in the sense that we know them. Meriaduk played with the map in front of you. It scared me. I am sure it will scare you too, but I want you to be prepared."

At least there is a good chance that I will arrive there... A Vision is only a possibility not a certitude. "How did he manipulate the map? Like they do in theaters? A painted curtain falls, then another one..."

"It was nothing like that. He was just moving his hand, and a new map appeared on the wall, replacing the old one."

"Did I...?

"You want to know if Meriaduk will kill you. I don't know, but you know that I couldn't tell you that even if I knew it." Ingrid's voice was gentle, the tone mothers use when telling important things to their daughters.

Dochia fixed Ingrid with that feverish look people have when they see death coming for them. Ingrid's eyes were clear, and she relaxed. *She doesn't know*... Dochia sighed with relief.

"It seems that I passed your test." Ingrid placed her palm over Dochia's hand. "Ada's letter to me was long. The best way to destroy a Maletera, she wrote, is to submerge it in water."

"Meriaduk sent another one to Salvina. He revealed that to me in our last talk in Frankis. When they arrive here, you need to find and destroy it."

"How is it that he has so many Talant artifacts? We have very few, and none of them is a Maletera or anything similar."

"I can't tell. Maybe there are places where things were buried by war, or intentionally, to preserve them."

"You will need this." Ingrid pushed a silver box across the desk. "This thing keeps the Maletera contained. Don't ask me why, I have no idea what that means, just that double metallic walls with sand between them are needed. It was easier to make it from silver. Keep the Maletera inside."

"Thank you," Dochia said, without knowing what for.

Dochia allowed herself and her guards three days of rest, and they left early in the morning, under a blue sky of the kind only high mountains could produce.

At noon, to Irina's delight, they took a break on the border of Kostenz Lake, its large surface almost covering the horizon, and Dochia decided to camp there for the night. There was something that she could not grasp. It was not a Vision, just an annoying inner fever that did not leave her alone. Just before dusk, she moved the camp to a hill nearby. They had already eaten, and she did not allow another fire.

She took the silver box from its bag and moved away into the forest. "Watch me," she said to Mira and Irina, "but stay hidden. If something happens to me, take the Maletera with a piece of cloth and put it in the box. Don't touch it. If ... something bad happens, tomorrow throw the Maletera in the lake."

"Don't," Irina whispered.

"I have to," Dochia said gently. "Now hide behind some trees."

She opened the box and, breathing deeply, took the Maletera in her hand, gripping it nervously. It became warm and pleasant, until Meriaduk filled her mind.

"Dochia," he said. "Why did it take you so long to contact me?"

"I was delayed, Master."

"Did you see Salvina?"

"She is dead. They killed her, and a letter was sent to all Hives, telling them about the Maletera. I did not dare to use it in the Hive."

"That's unfortunate. You must come here, to Nerval. I need you as adviser."

"Is it necessary?"

"Don't question me again."

"What's the purpose of an adviser, if they can't question things?"

"Hmm," Meriaduk said, and she imagined him rubbing his chin. She almost smiled, but suppressed her reaction, fearing that it might be transferred to him. "Sometimes you may be right. Do it rarely and only when we are alone."

"Yes, Master."

"On your road east, you will meet three men. You will meet them tomorrow; they are not far from you. They carry the Maletera which was meant for Salvina. Join them and come here."

"How do you know...?

"I see you on the map. You are on the border of Kostenz Lake. They will reach the lake tomorrow at noon."

Despite her training, Dochia threw the Maletera away, and her first impulse was to run. Mira and Irina appeared from behind their trees. She gestured them to stay hidden. *How could he see me?* For one minute, she controlled her breath until she calmed herself enough to take the Maletera again. Her hand was still trembling.

"I am sorry, Master," she said when the link was made again. "I was just..."

"Scared, I know," Meriaduk bragged.

"How can you see me?" She waved her left hand, trying to test his vision.

"I don't really see you. It's just that your Maletera was activated and appeared on my map. Usually, I see it all the time, but yours vanished when you were still in your Hive."

"My Maletera fell during the fight. Maybe it was slightly damaged. How do I recognize the men I have to join?"

"They are different, smaller in size. Men of the steppes with a flat face and thin eyes, like slits. Their hair is half shaved, and half tied in a ponytail. All of them have moustaches and they carry round shields and bows. You will know a man of the steppes when you see one."

"Yes, Master. What should I tell them?"

"Tell them to connect with the Maletera. They will protect you on the road back."

He wants to be sure that I will not run away. "Yes, Master."

"The Serpent be with you," Meriaduk said, and closed the link.

Dochia relaxed her grip on the Maletera and placed it back in the silver box. "You may come out now," she said to her guards. "We take watches and leave early in the morning. We will meet some strangers sent by Meriaduk." She took her time describing the steppes men, and she felt uneasy. They were too strange, and her uneasiness transferred to her guards too, mostly to Irina, who was so young. "Don't worry, Irina," Dochia laughed. "Meriaduk told me that they are small. We all are big girls."

The next morning brought some clouds but no rain, and they rode fast until they reached the end of the lake. "We stop there." Dochia pointed to a place where the road coming from Silvania passed through a long defile between two ridges.

Once they arrived, Dochia sent both her guards up on the ridges, each on a different side of the road. Leaning against a tree, she stayed hidden. *Men of the steppes,* she thought. *I never saw one. Are they so different that it would strike me?*

"You are troubled," Umbra said, his black eyes fixed on her, the same understanding and worry one could find in a human stare reflected in his eyes.

"If Meriaduk learns what I want to do..."

"You think that the Maletera..."

"How should I know what that bloody tool can do? He knew that we were close to Kostenz Lake."

"Then maybe you should not try."

"I have to."

"Fine. I will go to find them." Umbra flapped his wings and flew away. He returned only fifteen minutes later. "They are coming, and they look like well-trained soldiers."

When the three men appeared at the end of the gap, Dochia saw what Meriaduk meant. The men were unlike anything she had seen before, and for a while, she just stared at them. *Later I will study them from close-up. I need to get accustomed to them*, she thought, and let her arrow fly. The first man fell from the saddle. The other two tried to turn, but it was already too late; Mira and Irina took them down.

When the three Wanderers reached them, the men were already dead, and Dochia took a moment to see how the arrows had put them down. Dochia and Mira went for the neck. Irina's arrow pierced the heart with a precision that made Dochia feel well defended.

They soon found the Maletera, and Dochia covered it with her mantle, then Mira put all the men's possessions – anything that could give them an overview of steppe men's lives – in one bag that went to Irina. It was a strange bag, with unknown decorations, but they were strange men.

Dochia went to the small river flowing toward the lake and dumped the Maletera in the water. There was a hiss, and a shock like a wave passed through the water, which started to boil, vapors rising fast around her, like a thick fog. They smelled foul, and she stepped back abruptly, out of the dangerous mist. The hiss did not last long, merely a few seconds, but it was enough to see the fish floating dead in the water through the dissipating mist. The water felt warm even at a few feet. They moved away from the small river, none daring to speak.

Before leaving, they buried the strangers. The men were enemies sent by Meriaduk to enslave the Wanderers' minds, but Dochia did not enjoy the thought of letting the wolves feed on them. *They would not do the same to me*, she shrugged.

"Let's pass through the gap," Dochia said, and they took the horses by the halter, walking slowly. *I need to contact Meriaduk*. There was a shiver and a fleeting chill down her spine. She had thought that her training, Visions and travels had led her to understand something of the world. Thinking again, she realized a new complexity, something old and terrifying, able to boil a river, something that came to her from nowhere. Dochia looked shaken, she and tightened her grip on the halter. *I must not be far from the place of their death, but I have to wait an hour or two*. When the sun was going down over the mountains, she finally found the courage to contact the High Priest of the Serpent.

"What happened, Dochia?" Meriaduk asked directly after the link was made, his voice flat. The blue shadow representing his body was slightly bent, as if he wanted to come closer, showing a badly hidden interest.

Dochia found that words did not come easily to her, and she breathed deeply before saying, "The three men you sent here are dead." Despite of a small tremolo, her voice matched the calmness of the priest's voice.

"Who killed them?"

"Men who looked like them. Ten men. Our people had no chance."

"How come you saw them?" There was a different note in Meriaduk's voice now, cold, so cold that she shivered again, wishing to throw the Maletera and run away. In his room, the High Priest was pacing back and forth, shaking the tool in his hand. His anger was too strong, so many months and a Maletera lost because of the enemy. He did not care about the dead men, they were with the Serpent now, but they were weak, and their place was low, merely servants of braver warriors. *Tonight, I will kill ten men of the Selem,* he thought. Since the Timurid branch had taken the power in the Khadate, the Selem hid in the vast eastern steppes, but they did not submit to the Serpent, and many of them filled the dungeons of Nerval. There were two more priest with Meriaduk in the room, and they moved too, trying to stay out of his path. People linked to the Maletera were blind to the real world, but he seemed to know well when to turn left or right.

"We were not that far away, but it was too late to help them. I am not sure I would have done it even if we were closer. It ended fast, and only one enemy died. The other nine survived. Then something strange happened..."

"They destroyed the Maletera."

"How did you know that?"

"It vanished from my map."

"How can the Maletera be here and on your map at the same time?"

"Don't be stupid, Dochia, the Maletera is not here with me. It's just that the map knows where the Maletera is." Meriaduk's blue hand pointed at her, as if he considered to underline the insult.

"Is the map alive?"

"In a way, the map is alive. It knows the position of all the Maleteras and other things."

"How?" *How many Maleteras do you have?*

"That's a secret."

You don't know. The Maletera is a Talant artifact. The map must be too. I think Ada wants me to learn where they found the artifacts. We should not use them. "They threw the Maletera in the river. The water started to boil, and there was mist. I found some dead fish too."

"There is great power in the Maletera. It can kill many people. Did any of them die?"

"No. If the Maletera is no longer on the map... Does that mean that it's dead?"

"Yes."

"I buried our fallen men. Should I try to find the Maletera and bury it too?"

"No. Come to Nerval," Meriaduk snapped and closed the connection.

Silent, Dochia placed her Maletera in the silver box, and rubbed her forehead. *We should not use such things*, she thought again. *We should not use them to pervert people's minds, but we can use them for communication. Some of us would not stop there, though.* Drusila's face came into her mind, and she shook her head. *I would trust Ada, but how can we trust someone like Drusila?* "Mira, Irina, let's go. We have a long road in front of us."

Chapter 6 - Codrin

The western sky was glorious gold as the sun went down behind the mountain. On top of the hill, Sava stood stiff in the saddle his lower back and legs were aching. He had no eyes for the splendor in the sky. *I slept only four hours the last two nights*, he complained mutely. *So did they;* he glanced at the thirty riders following him. In front of them lay a land of green hills, flowered plains and small rushing rivers; there was nothing spectacular in Severin County. "Dismount. We wait here. This is the shorter road to Severin." He pointed at the sinuous road winding at the foot of the hill. "We have to hope that Codrin will come this way. There may be other armies in the area, so we wait here," he repeated. "Dismount and rest. Stay on the lee side of the hill. I need two volunteers for the first watch." Despite their tiredness, more than half of the men raised their hands. "You and you," Sava chose two guards – one from Leyona and one from the Mountes – who looked less tired than the others. *It's all about perception;* he shook his head. Hard people, the Mountes were less tired than his own men, but he had to split the tasks for the cohesion of the group. Slowly, he dismounted, feeling his legs stiff and weak and, after a few hesitant steps, threw his body on the grass, his back leaning against the trunk of an old tree, and instantly fell asleep.

It was morning again when Julien, his elder son, woke Sava up after a sleep with no dreams. "A squad of scouts passed through the valley, and I think that I recognized Vlad. I already sent three riders to meet them."

"You did well." Sava stood up, stretched his bones and walked around for a while, pretending to be busy. He still felt tired but, with the skills of an old hand, his swift eyes moved from one soldier to another, both Leyonans and Mountes. They seemed to recover faster than him. Physically, at least. *They are younger,* he thought. Ending his tour, Sava sat on the grass again, his back leaning against the same old oak. Mechanically, his hand went into the leather pouch tied around his chest and took out two letters. One carried the seal of Leyona, the other one, even though it was written on the same expensive paper from Leyona's Secretariat, had only a common seal. *This may be even more important than the other one. I wish I was not the one who had to carry them.* Eyes closed, he sent his mind back to Leyona. *It will not help.* He shook his head and stood up abruptly, then began to walk around the camp again. The soldiers felt his inner struggle, and no one bothered him. When he felt calm enough, Sava went to the ridge and looked down the valley.

That's how Codrin's scouts found him; two squads arrived at the same time. One from the valley, led by Vlad, who had been warned by the riders sent by Julien, and a second one from the forest, the last three scouts being Valer's mercenaries.

"Codrin is a careful man." Sava smiled, seeing both troops arriving in front of him. *Yet, not careful enough.* "Where is Codrin?" he asked Vlad, who had the highest rank; he was now the leader of Codrin's fifteen-strong team of scouts.

"One hour's ride from here. News?" He looked at Sava, unable to read something on the composed face of the more experienced man.

"News." Sava nodded, and both walked away from all others. *Bad news.* Remembering what had happened, he felt his mouth going dry, and anger rising in him. *Stop your useless resentment, old fool. It brings nothing good.* "Go and tell him that we need to speak in private. Just the two of us. We will follow you."

"I have orders to wait at the crossroads east from here."

"There is no urgency," Sava agreed and, involuntarily, his hand touched the leather pouch.

Both men and horses were now rested, but Sava did not hurry them. There was enough time until Codrin arrived, and he still did not know how to deliver the news. He had seen many things in the past, bad or good, but this was a new experience. A bitter one. Half the way down, he saw Codrin's army, far off on the horizon. *It looks smaller.* "Vlad," he turned right, "it looks to me that there are fewer soldiers down there than I expected. Is the army split, or was the battle against Devan harder than we expected?"

"There was no battle; Devan accepted a truce and went back home, but Aron's men tried to capture Codrin, with help from Duke Stefan. They are dead now, and Eagle's mercenaries have gone back home. What was left of them."

More bad news... "Is Codrin well?"

"Yes, there was not much of a fight. We laid a trap for them, and they fell into it," Vlad laughed.

"And Duke Stefan's men?"

"They returned to Peyris. Codrin freed them, and their captain too."

Well, at least the links with the Duke are not fully broken. "Leyonan dead, Mohor dead. There are too many deaths in Frankis, and I have the feeling that it will not stop there." *Death never stops.*

"I can't answer a feeling," Vlad shrugged, "but Autumn will come soon, and we will have a respite during the Winter. Next year... Who knows?"

"I hope that Codrin has a good Secretary. He may help in preparing a ... good Spring."

"It's a she, and Codrin seems to be pleased with her work."

"Evaluating a Secretary... That's not an easy thing. You need experience."

"Codrin never speaks about his past, but Lady Jara told me once that his father was a Duke in Arenia."

"Well, a Duke's Secretariat is a place where you may learn things. My understanding is that Codrin is a good learner." *But he must learn more. A man with qualities. It will be a pity if...* He shook his head, ignoring Vlad.

"You look sour," Vlad said, his smile fading a little.

"That's my natural state of mind. I may be even more sour than usual right now. The long road and other things," Sava said, with studied careless. "It's a useful trait; people bother you less." This time he laughed quietly, even when he could not tell why, then remained silent while they walked and waited for Codrin.

"Sir Codrin, I failed you," Sava said, bitterness filling his voice. "I've lost Leyona," he added before Codrin could ask. "Garland proclaimed himself Grand Seigneur, but I doubt that it was his decision. It happened three days ago. I was allowed to leave with thirty-five soldiers. There was no chance to fight, and I thought them more useful here."

"You were right to bring them. Who took the decision? Garland's wife?" Codrin asked. "I remember that she gave up her place as a Knight's wife to become a Grand Seigneur's mistress. She carries Leyonan's bastard."

"Garland loves his wife too much to want to learn what happened between her and her lover. And she loves only power. A clever woman, yet not as clever as Maud, but they worked well together. I swore allegiance to you, and I can't work with Maud; that's why I am here with the Mountes you left behind, ten guards from Leyona and my elder son. My wife and daughter and the other son are on the road to Cleuny with five more guards."

"All of you are welcome there, and I thank you for your loyalty. This woman, Maud..." Codrin rubbed his chin, feeling strangely detached from the sudden loss. "I was expecting that she would move against me. She acted faster than I expected. I underestimated her, but the only other way was to kill her before leaving Leyona. Suspicion is not a good enough reason to kill someone. Well, what comes easy, goes easy."

"What do you want to do?" Sava asked, a touch of hope in his voice.

"What I want, and what I can do are quite different things right now. There is no way to lay siege to Leyona, and I doubt that we can sneak inside the city again. I need to know how the Knights of Leyona would react when they hear the news. I don't have much hope, and some of them may know already."

"I rode as fast as I could."

"Yes, Sava, and I thank you for that, but they may have been in touch with Maud from the point when the plot started to unravel, or even earlier, from the day we left Leyona. She seems to be a persuasive woman." *And one step ahead of me. Like Aron was too.* For some unknown reason, he remembered the letter found on Viler, the man who had tried to kill him in Valeni. *There was a link between Maud and Aron. Was she involved in Severin too? She is a Sage of the Circle,* he shrugged.

"I have these letters, maybe they will clarify things." Sava frowned and proffered the envelopes, which burned his fingers all the way from Leyona.

Codrin opened the first letter and finished reading it fast. It was the formal announcement that Garland was now the Grand Seigneur of Leyona. The writing was unknown to him, but it carried the seal of Leyona and Garland's signature. *Good that I did not announce to all Frankis my glorious conquest of Leyona.* The second envelope was thicker, seeming to contain several papers. He broke the seal, and three letters came out. The first one was written by Garland.

'They say that strong people have to rise to the occasion. I may brag that it was my decision to take Leyona, but it may be that I am only fooling myself. For you, I am a traitor, but who knows what you will think about me in a year from now? A fool? A savior? Leyona is nothing more than a nest of hornets. You will find two more papers enclosed in this envelope. I bequeathed the fortress and county of Poenari, the counties of Orhei and Saunier, and the title of Seigneur, to you. Few people know about Poenari, and most of them think that it's only an old ruin. It is more than that. In the hands of a capable commander, it may become an impregnable fortress. I know that you took twenty thousand galbeni from Leyona's Visterie. Sava will bring you five thousand more. It should be enough to make rebuild the city and hire enough mercenaries to protect you. There is one more thing you should know about Poenari. It carries a long-hidden mystery that I tried for many years to solve. I failed, or better said, I could not convince Bernart, the actual custodian, to enlighten me. He is a fine man, even though he is older now than the last time I saw him. The upper part of the wall and the city itself bear the marks of Alban architecture, but the main wall is much older. I think that it was built under the Talant Empire, and no siege catapult can even dent it. There are many signs of old sieges, and all they could do was to scratch the wall. And who knows what may be hidden between those walls?'

For a few moments, Codrin played with the letter, and then read it again. *Garland's decision is bit of a riddle, but Dochia was right; I just received Poenari, and I have no reason to refuse it. It seems to be a much stronger place than Cleuny. Did she know that I took and lost Leyona? Maybe... She wouldn't have told me.* "Do you know Poenari?" Codrin looked at Sava.

"A strange fortress, isolated in the middle of the mountains. It was a Seigneury in the past. None of the owners survived the civil war, but it's still inhabited."

"Garland gave it to me."

"He had some guts, in the end." Sava rubbed his brow, struggling to recall some old memories that fought to elude him. "Poenari is a strong place that no one can take from you. If you are not betrayed," he added with a sigh.

"Vlaicu," Codrin gestured for him to come. "We've lost Leyona. Keep it to yourself and bring me all the Knights from there." He watched Vlaicu walking away, and his mind finally started to ponder about the significance of the loss. *That was my chance to destroy Bucur's hopes of becoming a king. No, that's wrong. It was my chance to prove that he can't be the King of Frankis. His chances are still slim, but many will believe in him because the Circle wants them to believe. If the Knights of Leyona leave me, I will not have enough soldiers to lay siege to Severin. They will leave. I am sure that the Circle took care of that. Saliné...* he shook his head. *There is no way to take Severin now.*

"They are here," Vlaicu woke Codrin up, whispering into his ear.

Codrin stared at the eleven Knights aligned in front of him and felt no bonds between him and them. *They feel the same... Jara was right, it's not enough to proclaim yourself ruler; you need people to follow you. Most of them followed me because their sons or fathers are hostages in Leyona. Garland's hostages now.* "I suppose that some of you already know. Garland took Leyona and proclaimed himself Grand Seigneur. I don't intend to take the city by force; there will be too many deaths for an uncertain outcome. I will keep Poenari, Orhei and Saunier, which are linked to my lands in Mehadia and Severin. Those who want to go to Leyona and pay allegiance to Garland are free to go."

Most of the Knights chose to leave, yet all of them bowed in front of Codrin, a sign that they recognized in him a man above them. Two Knights stayed. A Half-Knight from the eastern part of Leyona, whose lands were between Poenari and the Seigneury of Deva. If he really wanted to rescind his oath for Codrin, the geography worked against him. The man did not look bothered by the situation. Sometimes, Seigneurs seems to come and go at a fast pace. The second one to stay, was Garland's brother, Laurent.

"I know about my brother's wife," Laurent said. "Some Knights told me. It will not be easy for me to stay there, knowing that she was Leyonan's mistress, and the child she carries was not fathered by my brother. Even more, I may be in danger, if she learns about my knowledge, so if you accept me..."

"I accept you," Codrin said, keeping an afterthought to himself.

An hour later, a troop of riders stormed along the road, coming from Severin, and Ban dismounted in front of Codrin, his face ashen.

"I know about Mohor," Codrin said, before Ban could speak. "We have already mourned him. You came back with fifteen riders. Will you join me?"

"Five more remained in the forests around Severin to watch Aron's movements. They will send couriers if something happens there. We already talked, and we all want to join you." He stopped briefly and glanced at Vlaicu.

"Don't think that you've escaped me," Vlaicu said.

"It was hard to think that you would kiss Aron's bloody hand. What do you want to do now?" Ban looked at Codrin, with the eagerness of a man ready to do many things, but mostly he wanted to draw blood.

"We take Seged."

Chapter 7 - Codrin

Codrin believed he had enough soldiers to take Aron's castle, which lay halfway between Cleuny and Severin. Taking Seged would weaken Bucur and give Codrin a good grip on the eastern part of Severin. From his position, on the top of a small hill, he had a good view, and Seged castle looked small and grey, yet it was three times larger than Cleuny. It had a modest barbican, four turrets that rose to different heights, and was surrounded by uneven walls. Built on a small plateau, with steep slopes on more than half of its perimeter, the castle had both strengths and weaknesses. The parts rising over the slopes were hard to assault, so he was looking at the walls around the barbican. Built on the flat part of the plateau, they were shorter than those in Severin, and Codrin was counting on the Mountes, who were as good at carving wood with their axes as they were at using them in battle, to make the tools he needed. Wandering through the forest, they had already started to look for young and tall trees that would make good assault ladders. His men were hidden in the forest lying half a mile from the castle, behind a small hill, and no one in Seged was aware of an army at their door. *I need a diversion*, he thought. From Vlaicu's memory, Seged usually had only thirty guards, and now the number could be even lower, as some had died the night Aron's men tried to capture and kill Codrin, and some could be in Severin with Aron.

He had two things in mind to lower the losses. One was to hide some soldiers in carts that were now empty of food, and sneak them toward the gate at dusk, asking for shelter for the night. Dressed as merchants, the soldiers would try to take over the gate when most of the people were sleeping. It was customary, and a source of revenue, for any owner of a fortified place: give shelter for a cost. The second idea was put forward by Laurent.

"I know the second-in-command at the gate. He is a relative of mine," Laurent said in the council. "I can enter Seged in the evening, and request shelter. Times are hard now, and I think that for a proper amount my cousin will open the gate during the night."

Codrin postponed the decision until the assault ladders were ready – if the diversion failed, he needed to attack fast, not giving the defenders enough time to organize themselves. Under the cover of night, the Mountes carried the ladders into a small ravine, three hundred paces from the section of the wall to the left of the gate, which Codrin thought would be easier to assault. The walls were slightly taller there, but the plain in front of them was smooth, allowing the soldiers to advance faster. Speed was more useful than five feet less in the height of the wall.

"Go," he finally said to Laurent when dusk was coming. "If you don't come back early in the morning, we will attack. It will give us more chance to find you alive if they catch you."

With a nod, Laurent mounted, riding out of the forest from a place that was not visible from the gate, then let his horse run at a canter toward Seged. From the top of the hill, Codrin followed him with his spyglass: the passage through the gate was without incident.

From now on, I can only wait; Codrin put away the spyglass. *Sometimes, waiting is harder than fighting.* It was late when he fell asleep, and from the slight noise around him, most of the soldiers were driven by the same inner tension. None of them had assaulted a fortress before and, where on the battlefield one could rely on his own skills to survive, climbing a wall on a ladder was a matter of luck. Luck was needed in any battle, of course, but not to such extent.

It was still dark when the night-watch woke Codrin. Under the cover of darkness, a group of twenty Mountes sneaked into the field toward the ravine, hiding the five assault ladders. Two Mountes were strong enough to run with a twenty-five-foot-long ladder on their shoulders, but Codrin wanted the reserves to be in place too. Another group of ten, half of them guards from Severin and half mercenaries, walked and stood in front of the gate, their backs pressed to the hard wood. The gate was one foot inside the wall and, at dawn, they would not be visible from above.

With ten riders, Codrin hid behind a coppice grown around a small pond lying a hundred fifty feet from the gate. It was the kind of growth that was usually cut down in spring to clear the space, but it seemed that Aron neglected that, and the young trees and bushes were now eight feet tall, enough to hide a horse. There was a reserve plan in case Laurent failed. The road to Seged was now blocked by Codrin's soldiers, and no one could go toward the town. At the opening of the gate, the soldiers hidden there would try to enter by force and block it while Codrin would ride with his men to help them hold the gate. At the same time, the Mountes would use the ladders to climb the wall.

With the dawn, nervousness grew in the main camp, and more so in the three small, scattered groups. All eyes were on the gate and the walls. With his spyglass, Codrin watched the change of sentries on the wall, and counted them again for the tenth time: there were only three guards on the front walls, one over the gate, and the other two in the middle of the walls going right and left from the barbican. There was a hundred paces distance between them. The light became stronger, and Codrin's soldiers gripped their sword hilts harder. Even though the swords were still sheathed, it was a common gesture, like a communion between the soldier and his weapon. Only the ones in front of the gate had their swords out, ready to kill.

A small postern adjacent to the main gate opened and everyone stared at it with uncommon intensity. One soldier appeared in the entryway, without going out, and he stayed there for a while, looking over the field. A minute later, he vanished inside, leaving the small gate open, and one soldier behind Codrin raised a pole with some oak branches tied to it. The men at the gate moved slowly toward the postern. Another man appeared in the entryway, and the pole with the branches went down. Codrin's soldiers at the gate froze in place. This time, the man went out and, seeing the soldiers in front of the gate, flashed a large smile at them. It was Laurent and, in a few moments, the ten men sneaked inside the city. Two minutes later, the gate opened, and Codrin stormed it with his riders.

"There are two Sages in Seged," Laurent said to Codrin. "One of them is Belugas. The other is Hadrian."

I don't know Hadrian, Codrin thought. *He is a Sage*, he shrugged with the indifference of a man knowing that nothing good could come from the Circle.

Led by Vlaicu, another group of fifty riders came out from the forest and advanced fast toward the gate. In ten more minutes, Seged fell to its new masters, and Codrin entered the large building that served as Aron's residence. Vlaicu knew the place, and he led them toward the council room, setting guards in proper places. When the first servant sounded the alarm, it was already too late.

"Don't worry," Codrin said to a servant who seemed to be less frightened than the others, "we are not here to kill you. I want Nard and the two Sages in the council room. Go with him," he ordered Vlaicu and three soldiers.

When all the people he wanted were gathered in the room, Codrin looked at his prisoners. There was one Sage more than he had been told about, a novice. *Strange*, he thought, *none of them look as if they have just woken up*.

"I demand to know why my sleep was disturbed," Belugas said.

Codrin ignored him, left the room and gestured to Vlaicu to follow him. "Were they asleep?"

"No, and they were already dressed. I found it strange, but there is nothing more to add."

"All of them were awake and dressed," Codrin said, but it was more to himself than to Vlaicu. *As if they knew that we would take the city. It can't be.* He shrugged and went back to the room, stopping in front of Nard, Aron's second son.

Nard was one year younger than Codrin and bore little resemblance to either his father or brother. He had a thin frame, almost feminine, even the face had delicate traits, partially hidden by a thick moustache and sparse short beard. *He is trying to look like a man*. Codrin almost smiled.

Nard stared at him with the same concentration; Codrin was the worst enemy of his family, but strangely, the young man did not seem to see him in a bad way.

"I am not here to kill you. You will be exchanged for Saliné," Codrin said.

Resigned, Nard closed his eyes briefly, before saying, "You should spare yourself the time and effort. Father will never accept the exchange. Saliné is more important in the political game than me, and we are not really close to each other."

"The next step is to delimit yourself from Aron's sins."

"He has some, like any of us, and I may do so, but who would believe me? You?"

Codrin said nothing and moved on to the next man in the room: Belugas the Primus Itinerant Sage. His stare was now mean, lacking the previous curiosity. The Sage was a known thing. A bad known thing.

“I am the Primus Itinerant of the Circle,” Belugas snapped with the arrogance of a man who did not accept to be denied. “I demand to be released immediately.”

“And I demand freedom for Saliné, Jara and Vio,” Codrin said, his voice cold. “And Mohor’s life back. Can you deliver that, Belugas?”

“You have no right to ask anything.”

“Sage, a prisoner should be wiser. Search Belugas for letters, then put him in jail with the other two,” Codrin said to Vlaicu, who knew his way around Aron’s castle. “In separate cells and replace all the guards there.”

“How dare you?” Belugas’s voice dripped with fury.

“The Circle must learn that there is a price to pay for the destruction it has unleashed on innocent people and for not keeping the agreement we had about Vio.” Codrin turned his back to the Sage, a trace of disgust on his face. “Laurent, take command of the gate. Come with me, Nard.”

Shaking his head like a wild animal spooked at finding itself trapped in a cage, Belugas stepped back, trying to find a way to run. His back hit the wall. “I am Primus Itinerant. Stay away from me!” he, shouted when Vlaicu grabbed his right arm, twisting it behind him while, after being searched; the other Sage and the novice went out of the room with no complaints.

“It would be my pleasure to break your arm, Belugas,” Vlaicu whispered. “Don’t give me more reasons; I have plenty already.”

“The Circle will pay you a lot to free me,” Belugas whispered, trying to overcome the pain in his arm. Codrin was already out of the room.

“Like they paid my Seigneur?” Vlaicu snapped.

“It was just an unfortunate accident.”

“And Lady Jara. She was the payment for Orban’s help in killing Mohor and making Aron the Seigneur of Severin.”

“Everything was done for the future of Frankis.”

“I warned you, Belugas,” Vlaicu growled and twisted his arm until the Sage went to his knees. “There is no future for Frankis with Sages like you and men like Bucur and Aron. Move." He pushed Belugas, who fell onto his belly, and Vlaicu searched him brusquely – he found no letters. "Move," he repeated, and the Sage rose quickly and walked away, massaging his arm. In the prison, Vlaicu waited patiently until the Severin guards he had chosen closed the door of Belugas's cell. "No favors for those scoundrels," he grunted. "But don't harm them either," he quickly added, knowing that all Mohor's soldiers were itching to kill them.

"I heard that you are the Secretary of Seged." Codrin glanced at Nard once they arrived in the Secretariat.

"Sort of," Nard shrugged.

"What is Belugas doing here?"

"He replaced Aurelian as Primus Itinerant and was on his way to Severin to talk with Father."

"I want to see the archive of the Secretariat."

"Some things are still here, but the most important letters were sent to Severin, two days ago."

"So, you think that I will find nothing of value in the archive?"

"It depends on what has value to you, but..." Nard shrugged.

"Do you know what happened in Severin?" Codrin asked, and Nard nodded. "Why was Vio sent to Orban? She was supposed to be sent into my custody."

"I don't know, but Mohor's death was an accident."

"What where the plans for Mohor?"

"They planned to send him to Arad too."

"So, the only accident was that Aron killed Mohor, when the plan was that Orban would do it."

"I had no part in this," Nard said, shaking his head.

"Maybe. Do you have anything to say about Seged?"

"No."

"Take me to Belugas's room."

Codrin stopped in the doorway of the room which had hosted Belugas and, in silence, he glanced around him. *The bed was not really used*, he observed, and stepped inside. The bed clothes did not fully cover the bed, but it looked as if someone had lain over them, across the bed. On the table, there was a large leather pouch, the type he had seen many times with other Sages; it was the container for the most important things an Itinerant Sage would carry: correspondence. He opened the pouch and found it almost empty, then threw the contents onto the table. There were only some unused papers, a small bottle of ink, feathers. Through the open window, the fresh air of the morning was filling the room, yet there was a faint scent of smoke too. After he closed the window, the scent of smoke became stronger, and he went to the fireplace.

"Was it so cold last night?" he asked Nard, and his hand went through the ash. It was still warm, but the fire had died some hours before; there were no embers.

"It's still summer, but Sages like to be spoiled."

"When did the Sages arrive in Seged?"

"Two days ago. Belugas came directly from the place where you had some problems with Father's men. The other Sage came from Leyona. He told us that you'd lost the city."

"They came a day after you sent the most important parts of the archive to Severin." Codrin stared intently at Nard, who nodded. "And they did not bring any letters for you."

"They deal with Father, not with me. You should..."

"Then why are they here?" Codrin cut in. "And where are their letters?"

"You should ask them those questions."

"Did they enjoy your hospitality?"

"I think so; this is not the first time we have hosted Sages here."

"Yes, they are family friends. You will come with us, to Severin. Now go to the council room."

Leaving the room, Codrin went to find Vlaicu. "Something is strange here, but I don't have enough time to solve the riddle. There were no letters in the Sages' rooms, only the scent of smoke."

"We took Seged so fast that there was not enough time to..." Vlaicu rubbed his chin. "Perhaps they knew that we would come here."

"I don't have enough time to solve this riddle. Tomorrow, we'll leave for Severin."

The day before they arrived at Severin, they camped on a small hill. It was a quiet night, and Codrin made his plans, for the twentieth time. All of them were bad. He did not have enough men for a direct assault. He needed a diversion, like in Seged, but Severin was a different kind of problem. They were known, and they were expected. *I need a brief attack in one place, to attract Aron's soldiers, while we carry out the main assault in a different place. How can I hide them?* Slowly, he fell asleep, and all night he dreamt of finding a solution. He woke up several times convinced that his dreams had revealed him what to do, only to find that the dream was as elusive as his plans.

Morning came with two surprises. Marcel, who was the Second Knight of Mohor, had deserted, and now Codrin had thirty fewer soldiers. Later, one of the five soldiers Ban had left behind came to tell them that a column of seventy-five riders from Peyris had come into the city.

"Well," Codrin shrugged, "there is no way to take Severin by siege. Most of the army will camp in plain view. A small part will camp in the forest, and couriers will go back and forth. They may still think that we have a larger hidden army."

Severin appeared in sight at noon, and they settled at the foot of the hill, half a mile from the walls. Codrin walked away and took Belugas with him.

"You tried to kill me," Codrin said, his voice flat.

"I never..."

"Don't lie to me, Sage. At least be brave enough to admit what you did. I don't have enough soldiers to take Severin, so we will negotiate. You, Nard and Hadrian for Saliné."

"Saliné belongs to Bucur."

"And your life belongs to me. You have half an hour to think about that."

Chapter 8 – Saliné

Aron looked with some suspicion at Hadrian. They were both Sages, but Hadrian had become one only six months ago, and Aron could not understand how such a young man had been sent for negotiations. And even worse, Hadrian was an Itinerant Sage, occupying a higher position in the Circle's hierarchy than Aron. "Why did they send you?"

"Such a young Sage, you mean? That's simple, Belugas is being kept as a hostage."

"Tell Codrin that I received a hundred soldiers from Peyris."

"Seventy-five. He knows that already."

"I have enough men to defend Severin until winter comes."

"I was asked to talk with Saliné too, and to give her a letter," Hadrian said.

"A letter from Codrin?" Aron asked, his eyes narrow. "Give it to me."

"We have a situation outside; both Belugas and your son are Codrin's prisoners, and he seems to be out of patience. Don't do something that may endanger them." Hadrian's voice became suddenly authoritative – he was an Itinerant.

"Codrin took Seged." Aron's voice was flat, but he blinked a few times like a blind man. "I will get it back. The letter," he repeated, and his hand went forward, ready to receive it. Hadrian shook his head.

"Aron, let Hadrian give her the letter," Sage Verenius said, "and I will talk with Saliné after that." He was the fourth most powerful Itinerant Sage of the Circle. Only Maud, Belugas, the Primus Itinerant and Octavian had a higher place in the Circle's hierarchy.

"What does Codrin want?" Aron asked, looking at Hadrian with badly dissimulated contempt.

"An exchange of prisoners. Belugas and Nard for Saliné."

"The Circle must take care of this." This time, Aron looked at Verenius, who ignored him, and stretched his hand toward the other Sage, to receive the letter. Aron tried to object, but clamped his mouth shut. He stepped forward, and restrained himself a moment later, then clasped his hands at his back.

When Verenius gave Saliné the letter, she moved away from him and went to the window.

"Is the light better?" Verenius asked, with unconcealed amusement, yet he was not condescending. During the last days in Severin, he came to know her better, and he liked her. He was still a man of the Circle though, ready to impose a certain policy at any cost. *You are a clever girl, but you do not trust your reactions.*

Saliné ignored him and read, then destroyed the letter.

"I have news from Arad," Verenius said in a fatherly tone. "Some of it is good." He paused and waited for her reaction. She looked back at him, her face composed. "We convinced Orban to marry Jara. It was not easy, but he yielded in the end. The wedding will be in less than a month. She now has a position in Arad; she is no longer a prisoner. That was the good news."

Orban always wanted to marry Mother. The marriage did not suit the Circle, but you failed to stop it. I don't know which is better. "Forcing her to marry the man who killed Father and Mohor... The Circle has left behind a long trail of deaths and betrayals." *It may be that he is just lying to provoke me.*

"We can stop the wedding if you think it inappropriate." Verenius let a crooked smile form on his lips. *You won't want that*. "We are working to make Frankis a kingdom again, a better place for everybody."

"You are advancing fast; Orban has made Frankis a better place indeed."

"Orban was only a transitional ruler. It's Bucur who will realize the goal. And you will play an important role too."

I am the puppet Bucur uses to have a claim on Severin, and he is your puppet. "Twenty years with Orban. Quite a long transition we had."

"It happens sometimes. We are humans after all." Verenius turned his palms up. "The bad news is that Orban is threatening to kill Vio. We are doing our best to change his mind."

"Why would he kill the daughter of the woman he wants to marry?"

"Orban was always ... unpredictable, but don't worry, we are keeping a close eye on him. Of course, it would help if we could have your cooperation too. Vio's fate is linked to you." *Now you will hate me, but trust will come later, eventually. Whatever you think of me, I am not Aron. Or Bucur.*

I thought the Sages were more subtle... They are afraid because the Primus Itinerant is in Codrin's hands. "It took you twenty years to understand that Orban is unpredictable. What do you want from me?"

"You have to refuse any negotiations with Codrin. You must let him know that. These are hard times, and you must stay beside Bucur; he needs you. There are things or people to which one is attached, but everybody has a goal in life and, with the passing of years, childhood recedes farther into the past. Like a pleasant dream. Don't let things from the past cloud your judgment or mar your future. Your place is here, and you will become our Queen. That comes with responsibility."

"Sage," Saliné said, "I am betrothed to Bucur. Everything was done with the Circle's agreement. I will not disguise myself and run from Severin for another man, but what you want is not for me to refuse or accept. That's your problem. Don't ask me to decide in your place, as I will not do it."

"Think about Vio before telling me what you will or will not do," Verenius said, sharply.

Saliné gripped the wood of the window harder, but nothing else could be seen on her face. "I am not telling you what to do, but if the Circle decides tomorrow that I have to marry a different man, would you expect me to refuse?"

"No, we wouldn't."

"As you see, I am co-operating, and my willingness will only grow knowing that my family is be safe."

"Keep that in mind. I want you to write a letter to Codrin."

"What should I write to him?"

"Tell him that your wish is to remain in Severin. Ask him to free Nard and Belugas."

"I can do that."

"Thank you, Saliné. I am glad that you understand the world around you. I need the letter today."

"You will have it, and you will deliver Vio to Codrin."

"I will." Verenius nodded, thoughtfully. *That may take a while*. He turned from her, to hide a nascent smile, and walked toward the door. *Vio is a good tool to keep the pressure on you and Codrin.*

She waited until Verenius had left her suite and went to see Felcer. "I need to send a letter to Codrin," she said. "It should leave today. Do you think if Ferd...?"

Felcer looked at her enigmatically, a trace of a smile on his lips. "This is from Codrin," he said, proffering a letter. "He is expecting an answer today."

Swiftly, she snatched the letter from his old fingers, and that only enhanced his smile.

'Saliné,' she read.

'Meet me tomorrow morning at the place where we found the little rabbit. We are in negotiations, but my feeling is that they may fail. Be ready to leave. I have a safe place for you.

I miss you.

Codrin'

The little rabbit, she thought, and the memory came back to her as if it were yesterday, in a life when they were still together and happy. It seemed like it was faraway, in another place. On one of those days when Jara went to visit Mohor, before their wedding was announced officially, together with Vio, Saliné and Codrin sneaked around the castle, and found a baby rabbit which was lost. They played with it, until the mother came to claim her baby. It was a strange occurrence, as the frightened mother came so close to them. The baby was in Saliné's arms. She moved slowly and let the baby down in the grass.

A tear escaped down her face, and she moved away from Felcer to hide her emotion. *That place was at the exit of the tunnel. Codrin knows about it and wants to free me, but the Circle have taken care to block this path.* She closed her eyes and breathed deeply. *At least I will see him. It must be at dawn when the palace is still sleeping.*

"I will give you the letter," she said finally. "But first we need to burn this one." She waited patiently until Felcer lit a candle and stared at the burning paper. "Thank you, Felcer." She bit her lip to stop the tears in her eyes and left him alone. Back in her suite, she wrote two letters and sealed them, and went to see Felcer again, then to Aron's office.

"Your letter." She handed it to Verenius.

"Give it to me," Aron ordered and, after receiving it, he broke the seal. With a wicked smile, he started to read it.

'Codrin,

We made an agreement in Valeni. I am betrothed to Bucur and you will receive Vio. I have no reason to renege on the agreement, and neither have you. Please take care of Vio. Verenius has agreed to free her. In exchange, you should free Belugas and Nard.'

"It could be better, but we can use it. Seal the letter again." Aron pushed it to her, across the desk.

"It was sealed," Saliné said flatly, and crossed her arms at her chest.

"I will seal it." Verenius took the letter to read it, then put the Circle seal on it. "Thank you, Saliné," he said and left the room. *She can be quite obedient if you know what strings to pull. Now, even when I am not particularly proud of the course of events, I am sure that we should not free Vio. Codrin would not dare to harm Belugas, and Nard is Aron's issue.* "Karel," he said when he arrived in the Spatar's office, which in the past had belonged to Aron, "send this letter to Codrin. It's urgent."

Saliné did not sleep well that night; she was afraid of waking up too late. Her sleep was fragmented, and at four o'clock in the morning she decided to leave her bed and dress herself in the dark blue riding suit. The next two hours, she walked around her room, feeling like a caged wolf. At the first sign of light, she took her dagger, opened the secret door and left her suite. Behind the door, a torch and tools to light it lay on the floor. Her hands trembled, and it took her a while to light the torch. At the end of the hidden corridor, she went downstairs and reached a bifurcation. One passage led into the wine cellar, the other one into the exit tunnel. At the end of the corridor, she took out a heavy key from her pocket and put it in the lock. *Please don't creak*, she pleaded. The door did creak but, even to a frightened Saliné, the sound seemed too weak to be heard by the guards on the next floor. When some light came into the tunnel from outside, she set her torch in one of the many empty sconces on the wall. She almost ran toward the iron gate, resembling a portcullis, closing the mouth of tunnel. It was a small one, large enough that only two people could walk abreast. Codrin was already there, and their hands clasped through the iron bars.

For a while neither of them could speak; their eyes absorbed the other's presence, both feeling the healing touch of shared love and pain. When Saliné opened the gate, he stepped forward abruptly. She rushed into his arms. Codrin embraced her, pressing her against him, feeling her body trembling in his arms, and that set him aflame. He leaned slowly down, his lips trying to reach hers. The memory of another kiss that disturbed her so much filled his mind, and he stopped just before the touch. His hand brushed a strand of hair behind her ear.

"It's not the same thing, and I am not the same girl," she whispered, waiting for him to act.

He leaned further and their lips touched. It was a fleeting thing, as if he was not completely sure about her words. She stayed still for a moment, and then pulled back enough so that he could see the spark in her eyes. Codrin needed no more encouragement, and he kissed her again. She answered him, gently at first, then passion ran through their veins. They were lost. In need of breath, they stopped, and she leaned on his shoulder. Away from the dangerous world around them, she was just Saliné. And he was just Codrin.

"Saliné," he whispered, and kissed her on the roots of her hair and neck. She said nothing. "I now have a place where I can protect you. We should go."

"I can't come with you," she said, trying to overcome the sadness in her voice and mind.

"Why are you always raising walls between us? I..." His arms retracted from her waist and he half stepped back.

Feeling the pain in his voice, Saliné kissed him with all her heart and, slowly, the stiffness in his body receded.

"The Circle threatened to kill Vio if I run away with you. I can't pay that price for my freedom." Under the shadows of Jara and Vio being taken away by Orban, her voice betrayed her, falling into a whisper.

"I won't ask," Codrin said, his voice still bitter, yet he guessed what lay behind those shadows in her eyes. They had no right to spoil the emerald of her gaze, and he wanted to take away those memories and replace them with good ones. He felt helpless. Codrin had not thought about Jara and Vio when asking her to run away. He was thinking how he could help them, but not in that chain of events. He planned to visit Arad later, taking Tudor's identity again, and enroll Cantemir to his cause. *It's the second time I've asked her to run away with me.* His mind became feverish, trying to find another solution. "Fate places stumbling blocks in our path every time we are close..."

"There is still hope, if the Circle accepts a negotiated agreement, or if you can take Severin," Saliné said gently, her hand gripping his.

"I can't take Severin; I don't have enough soldiers for an assault. Tell me about the tunnel."

"It ends in the corridor where the prison is. I have the key to that door, but there is only one way out of the corridor, through a narrow stair. The upper exit is locked from outside and, from the day of your arrival, there are always two guards there."

"I can't use it for an infiltration. Aron knows about the tunnel, but how did you...?"

"There is another one going from my suite to this one, but it's so narrow and long that it can't be used for an attack. On the right side of the fireplace in my room, there are two small stones. If you move one north and the second one south, a secret door will appear in the wall. Mohor revealed it to me, before.... Before that day."

"I wished I could have been here that day."

"You couldn't. Sage Verenius mentioned some negotiations."

"I took Seged, and Nard is in my hands. The Primus Itinerant is also my prisoner. I may have a chance to swap them for you."

Saliné stood silent for a while, rubbing her forehead. "Verenius pushed me to refuse any negotiations with you, the letter they forced me to write."

"To put pressure on me?"

"No," Saliné sighed, finally able to connect all the dots. "I think that Aron will not agree to let me go, even for Belugas or Nard, and Verenius wanted to prevent a refusal. It makes the Circle look weak. They pull the strings, but once Bucur was nominated, he can sometimes act against the Circle's will. Like

Orban did in the past. Aron wants to push the Circle to negotiate with you for his son. Later, when the bad weather comes in autumn, and no one can lay siege to Severin."

"I still don't understand why Aron is so important. It's related to Duke Stefan, but... Tell them that you think Belugas may be in danger if Aron refuses me. I mean it," Codrin looked at her grimly.

"Please don't..."

"Belugas tried to kill me. His only chance is to free you, and he knows it. I will try to use Nard and the other Sage in my custody to free Vio. What happens to Belugas should soften up the Circle. There is no other way to make them negotiate."

"Be careful," Saliné whispered, and she caressed his face. "I need to go now. One more thing... In the cellar of Grandfather's house, in the north-east corner, there are some bags of money, hidden three feet underground. Take them with you. You may need them, and I don't want them to fall in Aron's hands."

"I will take them, but I will keep them for you and Jara."

"Please use them. It would make both Mother and me happy to know that we can help you."

Codrin embraced her once more, and they stayed like that in silence until Saliné gently disengaged from him. She closed the portcullis and, with a last look back, moved through the tunnel. At the point where the light vanished, she picked up the torch she had left in a sconce. The secret door was not far, and she left the main tunnel, pulling the door after her.

"Oh, no," she whispered, staring back at the traces left by her feet in the thick dust. "I need to come back here."

"There was some movement at the foot of the northern hill," Karel said, entering Aron's office. "I recognized Codrin and Vlaicu. They were moving away from the castle, but I sent more guards to the wall just in case."

"The foot of the northern hill?" Aron touched his brow briefly, then frowned. "Bucur, take ten men and check the tunnel. Double the guards at the prison exit."

"Do you think...?" Bucur asked. He was moving before he'd finished his question. "Karel, bring the men. I will be at the door of the prison." In the corridor, he was almost running.

Bucur returned after one hour and threw himself into a chair. "You were right. Codrin talked with someone in the castle."

"I was more worried about their soldiers getting inside. We had guards at the door."

"Not during the night."

"What the hell was in Karel's mind? Any attack through the tunnel is likely to happen during the night. We need to find another Spatar. This one is useless."

"We've lost a lot of our good people. That decision can wait. I found some interesting footsteps in the tunnel. The same man passed back and forth three times. There were three pairs of footsteps, the same shoes each time, and the sole of the left shoe left a peculiar mark. It must be the man who has been killing our soldiers, and that man is in touch with Codrin. After Codrin leaves, we should set a trap for him."

"We've made a lot of obvious fuss about this. It's not good when we look so alarmed. By the end of the day, all Severin will know that something happened in the tunnel. We should wait until the memory of it fades."

Long after the last of Codrin's soldiers left the camp, Saliné was still staring through her window, her absent eyes moving without aim from one point to another. The door of her antechamber opened, and she turned her head. Bucur smiled at her and closed the door behind him. She nodded and turned back toward the window.

"I always liked the view from your suite," he said, from just behind her. "From mine, I can't see the sunset. Neither can you, but from here you can see the reflection from the Mirror Hill." The hill resembled a tall orange wall, and in the evening the stones seemed to catch fire.

"It's beautiful indeed," Saliné said, her voice flat, and she froze when his arms went around her waist. After a few moments, she tried to move away, but he kept her in place firmly, even though his grip did not hurt her.

"My betrothed," Bucur whispered in her ear, "you are as beautiful as the view in front of us. And it's even more pleasant to look at it with you in my arms."

Saliné bit her lips, realizing that he would not let her go, and she could not reject his closeness without creating a situation that would not work in her favor. She was dependent on them for now, and Bucur's behavior was normal for their official status. For a while, neither of them spoke, and she forced herself to look through the window, seeing nothing. Her body accommodated itself to his embrace, and she was finally able to ignore it, but she could not ignore the kiss on the back of her neck. She shivered, and tried again to move away from him, and again he kept her in place, pulling her closer to him, until her body leaned into his.

"How long until the sun leaves the Mirror?" he asked, as if nothing had happened.

"Half an hour."

"Then we have half an hour more for our pleasure."

"Bucur, we had an agreement on how we are to behave as betrothed," she said, alerted by both his words and the tone of his voice – it was seductive in a way that he had not used with her before, and the memory of Jara's words that Bucur was a well-known seducer came back to her. That, and the fact that he drugged her to get her pregnant.

"Of course, my dear; I promised you that we will not make that mistake again, and I will keep my word. I will ask nothing more than a man would ask from his fiancée." He turned her gently, and she realized that she had fallen into his trap. "I hope that everything will be as pleasant for you as it is for me." His finger traced a line on her face, and went down to her lips, and further down her chin, applying pressure until he parted her lips. Before she could think, she felt his lips on hers, trying to part them further. She closed her mind, and let him play, without answering him, her lips almost rigid. "You know," he whispered after a while, "your arms should move around my neck." He did not wait for a reply, and lifted her arms, and she had no choice but to lace them around him. His lips found hers again, while his arms were moving up and down her back until one found the skin on her nape and caressed it gently. The pressure from his lips grew, and despite her bad feelings, a wave of pleasure spread through her.

Codrin, she spoke his name inside her mind. *Codrin is the man I love.* That helped her, and she no longer shivered, just abandoned her body to Bucur, staying alert enough to stop him if things went too far.

Maybe Bucur felt her indifference, or maybe he was just satisfied with her abandon as a first step, but after a few minutes that were much too long for her, he stopped, and kissed her hand. "Good night, Saliné," he said and left the room.

"Good night, Bucur." She turned back to her window after he left and, remembering everything with unwanted clarity, Saliné realized that this would from now on be a normality from which she could no longer escape, and she feared that once it became normal, it might switch more and more to pressure, and unwilling acceptance. *Each day I tell myself that today will be better and it is just getting worse.*

At least she was alone for the moment. And solitude was something she needed and hated at the same time.

Chapter 9 - Codrin

"What's the meaning of any negotiation if only one part is doing it in good faith?" Codrin asked, without looking at Belugas, the Primus Itinerant of the Circle. His voice was flat, and he needed no answer. They were gathered at half distance from the gate of Severin and from the site where most of his soldiers were camped. The place was known as the Old Oak, from the huge, lonely tree overlooking the area. It was a miracle that lightning had not cut its long life. Maybe because the place was in a small valley. The sky above was a deep blue, but fringes of almost black clouds were visible in the west. "Aron rejected the exchange of Saliné for you and Nard. Orban rejected the exchange of Vio for you and Hadrian. That is to say, the Circle did not want it to happen." While Codrin had expected the negotiation with Aron to fail, he hoped at least to free Vio from Orban. It had not happened either, and he was still wondering what kind of pressure the Circle wanted to put on him.

"What did you expect? That the Circle would renege on its own policy? Saliné was given to Bucur." Belugas put on a brave face yet, with all his capacity for restraint, there was a touch of uncertainty in his voice. "In due time, you will have Vio, and our conclave will stamp your position as Spatar of Frankis."

"In due time; meanwhile she is in Orban's hands."

"Some trust is needed..."

Codrin moved away from his soldiers and nodded to Belugas to follow him. "Don't speak to me about trust, Sage. We are alone, and I will grant you an honest talk. We made that pact in Valeni and agreed that Vio would be in my custody. You've sent her to Orban instead. You killed Mohor and sent Jara to Orban too."

"We did not want to kill Mohor. We don't know what really happened there. Our Primus Itinerant was killed too."

"And Jara?"

"That was a temporary solution, which keeps her alive."

"Ah, your Black Warrant. Parents refuse to marry their children on your orders, and you kill the children."

"We need to reinforce the rules."

"By killing the children..."

"We are getting nowhere. Forget about Saliné; she will marry Bucur. When the time is ripe, perhaps in Spring, Vio will be sent to you. I will work for that." Belugas extended his lips in a tight smile. His eyes watched Codrin even tighter.

"Bucur will not marry Saliné. She has just been used so that he could take Severin. Your plan is to give him the young Duchess of Tolosa. You are playing Saliné. You are playing me. I can play too, and you still don't realize that, from now on, we are at war."

A vein on Belugas's temple bulged. Several thoughts came into his mind at once. There was panic too. The secret about Saliné and Marie of Tolosa was no longer a secret, but he recovered fast, and cleared his throat before saying, "You can't afford a war with us." A calculated touch of derision filled his voice, and he turned his palms up. *And we can't afford to let you alive.*

"I can or I cannot, but *you*, Belugas, you certainly can't afford it."

As Codrin had begun to speak, slowly, his words falling like stones into the stillness around, Belugas's bravado seemed to vanish. "You will not dare to harm me." As if seeing him for the first time, his wide eyes measured Codrin, who smiled that half wry smile, which frightened people more than his anger. Belugas blinked rapidly, and his hands trembled. He clasped them behind him. "You accuse us of killing people, but you plan to do the same, just because some negotiations did not end the way you wanted."

"You are wrong, Belugas. I will not hang you because of some failed negotiations, which you torpedoed from the shadows. I will hang you because you planned to kill me at Severin's border. Aron tried – five times now – to kill me, and I never made him pay. I was afraid of the consequences his punishment would bring on Jara's family. We are past that now, but Frankis would be a much better place now if I had dared to do things right."

"You will not dare," Belugas snarled and stepped back.

"Take him."

"Codrin! I am the Primus Itinerant. I represent the Circle. I..." His voice became strangled, and his last word ended in a cry. Recognition dawned on Belugas's face like a river running out of a broken dam. It broke him.

"Don't worry, people will know that. There will be a placard with your title on your chest. Just be aware that they may spit on it, or on you. But I think it will not matter for you anymore. Hang him." There was sudden coldness in Codrin's voice, resembling a cloudless winter's night. It did not match the fever inside his mind. Vlaicu and Boldur were ready for his order. Boldur was waiting like a soldier. Vlaicu resembled an avenger sent by Fate to punish a rotted sinner.

"You would not dare," Belugas repeated. "The Circle will hunt you to death."

"That may be," Codrin shrugged, "or it may be that they will learn accountability for their acts. You tried to kill me and failed. Even if someone else manages to kill me, people will already have learned that Sages can be killed too. Your impunity diminishes with each hanged Sage. Bring the other Sage," he said to his soldiers.

"No!" Belugas shouted, trying in vain to escape from the grip of both Vlaicu and Boldur.

"Learn to die, Sage," Vlaicu snapped. "Mohor died with dignity, fighting for his wife and child; you will die like a rat. Write *Sage* on a placard and hang it around his neck."

A soldier tied Belugas's hands, and the rope was placed around his neck. The placard was placed too, its red letters contrasting with the Sage's mostly white clothes. Belugas howled like a wounded animal, struggling and writhing until he was forced to stand on a barrel, and the rope, which was passed over a thick branch of the huge oak, tightened around his neck. Afraid of falling from the barrel, he became still, breathing heavily.

"Does anyone want to speak for or against this Sage?" Codrin asked. There were not many people around the place, three hundred paces from the gate of Severin. A few merchants and their caravans, some servants who had escaped from Aron and people from the closest village.

"I will speak." A young woman came running on the road. She stopped, bending forward, her palms resting on her knees. Recovering her breath, she spoke again. "I am Ava, and I was Lady Saliné's maid. Aron threw me out of Severin, and now he keeps her locked in the palace. She is a prisoner in her own home. This man," she pointed at Belugas, "came to Severin and agreed with Aron and Bucur to use Lady Saliné for their schemes. And they all laughed about Lady Jara being in Orban's bed. In the morning, before the Sage left Severin, they met again and decided to kill Sir Codrin. They said that a hundred soldiers from Peyris would help."

"You are not a Sage, Belugas; you are a scoundrel," Vlaicu spat. "A worm."

"Ava, how that you know this?" Codrin asked, struggling to maintain his calm, his face white with anger. He knew for some time already about the Circle's schemes, and what he did not know, he guessed. What unsettled him was that piece about Jara being thrown in Orban's bed. He recalled their first moments together, when he saved her from Orban's son, and his accommodation in her hunting house. He recalled training with Saliné and Vio. He recalled Saliné playing for him at her lyre. *I failed them. I failed everybody.* An old anger rose in him again, and the difficult pain from having failed the people he loved. Both feelings had haunted him from the day his parents and twin sister had been killed.

"They were in the living room, eating. They were careless." Before she had finished speaking, Ava bent down suddenly and grabbed a stone from the road. The motion itself seemed odd and unnaturally slow. The stone hit Belugas on the nose, making him bleed.

"Murderer!" another woman shouted, and more stones flew toward Belugas.

Recovering from his moment of weakness, Codrin gestured, and a soldier shoved the barrel away with his spear. The next flying stones hit Belugas's corpse. "Come with me." He pointed toward Hadrian when Belugas's last spasm had ended, and they walked away from the soldiers guarding the hanged Sage. "We are alone here, and I will give you one chance. Write, on this piece of paper, the name of the Master Sage and all the Sages and their social positions in Leyona, Arad, Deva and Dorna. Don't waste my time," he snapped, seeing that the Sage was reluctant to deliver. The sharp tone persuaded the man, who quickly filled the paper with a column of names; he gave the paper to Codrin, who took it and read it in silence. He did not recognize a single name, though he already knew four Sages from those cities. "Tie his hands," he ordered.

"Let me write again!" the Sage cried.

"You had your chance," Codrin said dryly. "Bring me the novice Sage," he ordered, and when the man was left alone with him, Codrin studied him in silence for more than a minute. *He is so young*. He shook his head, looking at the eighteen-year-old novice. *I hope that he will write the right names.* "I will give you the same chance that the other Sage threw away. Write down the name of the Master Sage and all the Sages and their social positions in Leyona, Arad, Deva and Dorna."

"And then you will hang me too."

"Novice, I always keep my word; the Circle knows that well enough. You have two minutes." Filled with names, the paper returned to him in under a minute, and Codrin took his time to read it. *Cantemir, Balan, Maud,* he pondered. *These names I know, and their position is right.* The other five names told him nothing; the Master Sage was unknown to him. "So, Folio is the new Master Sage." Over the paper, he looked at the novice, who nodded eagerly. "Who is he, and where is he from?"

"I've never met him," the novice said and wiped his palms, suddenly sweaty, against his fine pelerine.

He is lying, Codrin thought, *but I have no reason to kill him. One day, I will find out who the new Master Sage is*. "You are lying about the Master Sage," he said bluntly, staring at the novice, who defiantly kept his eyes locked on him. *There is strength in him. What a pity that he is fighting for the wrong side.* "But I will still free you, as some of the names here are right."

"What should we do with these men?" Vlaicu came back, followed by five soldiers pushing Belugas's guards along in front of them.

"Release them too," Codrin said, and Vlaicu wrinkled his brow, though he said nothing. "I know they are not without sins, but who is these days? And the more mouths to spread word about the hanged Primus Itinerant, the better." He patted Vlaicu's shoulder and offered a tentative smile. "Hadrian will rot in Poenari's prison until his freedom buys Vio's. We leave for Cleuny."

After an hour, the army moved away. It had started to rain, and patches of gray fog rose from the warm ground. Codrin glanced behind him from time to time, until Severin disappeared at last behind a curtain of almost white mist. Saliné resurfaced in his mind and, with her, the heavy feeling of regret. He bit his lip and pushed Zor to a gallop. The noise of the horses' hooves was muffled, and all sounds carried strangely through the humid air, so that words from one end of the long column of soldiers were sometimes heard easily through the distance. Most of them were curses against Aron and the Circle.

Chapter 10 – Maud

That afternoon, Maud was relatively happy or, at least, content – she could not remember the last time she was really happy. Maybe when her husband and two sons were still alive or when her daughter, Laure, was still a little girl, in the home that they had left a long time ago. After three weeks of struggles, she was now fully in control of Leyona. *It's a pity that I must kill that young wolf*, she sighed, *but he almost derailed my plans. Drusila will not be happy...* She poured some Porto wine into her glass. It was sweet and strong, the flavor of the southern sun in a dry land bordering the desert. Absently, she picked a slice of cozonac, a tasty cake, filled with a creamy walnut paste peppered with resins, baked slowly in the oven. If Porto came from the most western part of the continent, cozonac came from the east, from Arenia, with the colonists the Alban Empire moved into Frankis, almost a thousand years ago. Frankis and Hispeyne were the worst affected lands in the White Salt wars, and the last to recover. While Frankis was now fully healed, Hispeyne still bore the marks of that war; half of its lands were still uninhabited. There were rumors that the Misty Islands, north-west of Frankis – which some called Inglis – were even more affected, but no ship had gone west for many centuries to confirm or deny their existence.

Maud's dark intelligent eyes drifted over the large map on the wall; it was one of the few, printed by the defunct Royal

Cartography of Frankis, which still survived. At first, she looked at Leyona, then moved over Tolosa in the south and jumped north to Peyris. *I may enter the history books as the woman who pacified Frankis and gave it a new king. I may or I may not, but I have tried my best. If it happens,* she closed her eyes, leaving her mind to drift, *I will be the real Queen until Marie can take over. She is still young, but she is a clever one.*

"Dreaming?" Drusila smiled, seeing Maud, and closed the door behind her.

"I can pretend that I was thinking intensely about my next step," Maud chuckled.

Even though she was fifteen feet away from Maud's desk, Drusila sniffed and laughed quietly. "Porto. Soon, everyone in the palace will know how hard you are thinking. I might indulge in some too." She filled a glass and stared at it in the strong light of the dusk. "Dark Ruby is the best. Figs and nuts and... What's that drink made from sugar cane in Hispeyne?"

"Rumy."

"The further south you go the better everything tastes. I don't like rumy, but in Porto, the faint taste of it works well. And this..." A knock at the door interrupted her. "Are you expecting someone?" Drusila asked, raising an eyebrow; they had planned to spend their afternoon alone.

"A courier." *And you will not like the news he is carrying.*

Gren bowed deeply when he entered Maud's office. He was a simple man, and this was his first visit, not only to her office – which was larger than his whole house – but to Leyona too. It impressed him, and he was even more impressed by the two women in front of him. He already knew that Maud had more power than most people realized. His master had warned him about that. The other woman looked as if she was made from the same vein, radiating power and maybe coldness.

"Maud is a woman with a temper," his master had said. "Say only what is needed, and keep in mind that our future depends on her goodwill."

Maud looked briefly at him before asking, “You must be?”

“Gren,” he said promptly, then his mouth snapped shut, remembering quicker than his mind the instruction to remain silent. It stayed like that for a while. *Yes*, Maud nodded. “I have a letter.”

“Are you waiting for me to come and take it from you?”

“No, my lady,” he whispered and walked briskly to her desk, his eyes moving left and right from one woman to another. More slowly, he pushed the envelope across the desk.

Maud read it quickly, and kept the paper gripped between her finger for a while. *Another failure. Well, at least Drusila will not try to burn me alive.* She almost smiled and handed the letter to Drusila.

“Who tried to kill Codrin?” Drusila asked, taking her eyes from the paper. Suppressing her anger, she looked stonily up at Gren from her chair.

“Aron, my lady,” he breathed.

“Have you more to say?” It was Maud this time.

“No, my lady.”

“Tell your master to keep watching for us.” Maud looked at the man again, a hard look making him shift nervously from one foot to another, then handed him purse across the desk.

Gren grabbed the purse and felt its weight. *At least five galbeni*, he thought, struggling to hide his emotion. A drop of perspiration went down his face. Then another one. “Thank you, my lady.” He bowed several times in swift succession, and left the room, walking backward. Outside, he went through the corridor until he arrived at a quiet spot. *Five galbeni*, he counted. *This is mine, there’s no need to tell my master about this gift.* Five galbeni was his pay for a month.

“I thought we had an agreement about Codrin.” Drusila said, seeming absently, rotating the glass in her hand. A slow, calculated move.

"The assassination attempt was ... unfortunate. Aron is playing his own game, but I have to say that I did not try to stop it."

"If everybody is playing their own game..."

"I will write to him." Maud stood up abruptly, and her chair screeched in the silent room. "But I am more worried about this thing with Poenari. I did not know." She shrugged in reaction to Drusila's stare. "Garland is more spineless than I thought."

"Oh, my dear, and what about our own spines? Weren't we bending them back and forth to our own purposes? And Garland... hmm, on the contrary, my feeling is that he showed some spine. He disobeyed the Circle and, in contrast to Aron, he did not do it for his own gain."

"He just wanted to buy Codrin's forgiveness."

"Then Garland may be a visionary."

"Why are you putting so much destiny on Codrin?" Maud snapped.

"Come on, my dear sister, don't tell me that you are upset. You have to move on from what happened here. Codrin outsmarted everybody when he took Leyona, and you outsmarted him. That's life."

"What am I missing about Codrin? Even after that mess in Valeni, you still seem to put a lot of trust in him."

"Don't worry, it's not about Frankis; he was meant for a greater cause." Drusila sipped some wine, wondering how much she could tell her sister about Ada's vision of the Fracture and Codrin.

"The Fracture. Is it real or...?

"You should know me better."

"I am sorry, but it means nothing to me. There are no records about the previous Fractures."

"Some wise people considered the matter and erased everything from the history books. It's an awful thing, and if it does happen, there will be no more Frankis. Your toy will vanish."

"Fine, I will take care to ensure that Codrin remains safe. Physically. Maybe you should convince him to leave Frankis." There was a touch of exasperation in Maud's voice that made Drusila smile.

"I can't. Even if I could, until I know more about his role in healing the Fracture, he will stay here. Did you tell Marie about her ... marriage?"

"Not yet; my dear granddaughter thinks that she is in love with a handsome White Knight," Maud sighed.

"She is or she thinks that she is?"

"My granddaughter is only seventeen, and at her age, she thinks that whatever she thinks really is."

"We were all seventeen once. Is the man actually a White Knight?"

"Nineteen years old, handsome, and with some traces of a brain. I can't say that I would not have enjoyed someone like him at her age, but who cares? I've allowed her to gain some experience in handling men."

"Let her dream."

"For a while..." Maud picked carelessly at a slice of cozonac and filled her mouth before ending her phrase.

"One who is not a dreamer until he is twenty-five years old, has no heart. One who doesn't have his feet back on earth at twenty-five, has no mind." *That was a piece of useless philosophy I used to snub people with when I was as young as Marie*, Drusila thought. *Why did it come to me now?*

"In times like these, we should lower the threshold to twenty, but you are still allowed to dream, a little, later too."

"Different kind of dreams, my dear. More ... tangible. Like the one we have to bring a new king. Marie's marriage with Bucur is planned for next autumn. Are you sure that she can handle Bucur?"

"She is clever, and she has her mother, you and me behind her. And four thousand soldiers. If I count the vassal Seigneurs, we have six thousand. Next year, some of them will rally behind

Bucur, because he has almost nothing. At least in this respect, Codrin has helped us, and made Bucur even more dependent on the Circle and Tolosa. Stefan will send soldiers too, and Orban will send half of his army. Deva and Dorna should fall to Bucur, but that will be handled by our soldiers from Tolosa. Leyona will fall without a fight, and it will become part of the Tolosa Duchy. I can't wait to kick Garland out. Duke Stefan will die at some point, and then there is no one to keep Peyris from falling into civil war."

"You may even help them," Drusila laughed.

"Yes and, after a year of war, they will welcome the army from Tolosa bringing a most desired peace. This is the first time that we have managed to put such a plan in place, and it was possible only because we could work together."

"We have only one weak point," Drusila said absently, and Maud's brows drew down in thought, but she remained silent. "Bucur. He has never won a battle. How many soldiers will you give him next year?"

"Three thousand, and a good commander. I am thinking at Pierre, the Spatar of Tolosa."

"That should be enough, and Pierre is a skilled army commander. And Saliné? What are you planning for her after ... the other marriage is announced?"

"We have to block the marriage between Saliné and Codrin. My Sages report that we have a resurgence of support for Cernat, even though he is in Orban's hands. After what happened in Severin, some people have started to think that he may offer a way to bring some order. I still don't know if Aron was being stupid or playing a game again. Mohor's killing is affecting us. Some Seigneurs are discontent, as one of them was assassinated. A marriage with Saliné will only enhance Codrin's status. By Spring, she will be pregnant. Bucur will take care of that, but Codrin is too obstinate and it may be that he will still want her. He may be a good army commander. He lacks political skills."

"I am afraid that you are falling in your own trap." Drusila smiled thinly, then sipped some wine. *My dear sister, the world is getting more complex than before. Or than you know.*

The fine lines of Maud's face deepened with her frown, and she hesitated before saying with calculated coldness, "We shall see if Codrin has those skills." For a few moments she studied her hands, spread on the table. "By Spring, I want to force his hand into signing a marriage agreement with Vio."

"You are worrying about Saliné becoming Codrin's wife, but not about Vio."

"Vio is young, and a hypothetical marriage will occur in three or four years. Things should be settled by then in Frankis. In Autumn, before Saliné becomes free, I will send Vio to Poenari, or wherever Codrin is. Saliné will be kept in a hidden place for a while."

"Vio should stay in Arad. We have an interest in her. She has a powerful Light, but she may be reluctant to join us. Like her grandmother was, once. Orban will make her dream of finding refuge with the Wanderers. Promise Codrin a minor Duchess. Stefan has plenty of granddaughters ready to marry in two or three years, and Cleyre is a good prospect. Manuc has two daughters. They are a bit older than Codrin, though. I said promise," Drusila laughed at Maud's concerned stare. "As you said, in three years we will know if our plans have come to fruition."

"I think they will."

"Then why are you trying so hard to stop the marriage between Codrin and Saliné? Inheriting Cernat's influence can't be so dangerous in the short term. At a certain stage, we may use that to our advantage."

"Cernat should have been our Candidate King, but that ... *Master Sage*, wanted Orban because... Well, because Orban was his nephew. Because it enhanced his influence. Orban did not even become a Duke. And Cantemir was so weak."

"Cantemir was weak?" Drusila did nothing to hide her amusement.

"Orban did not even become a duke," Maud repeated.

"Cantemir did not consider Orban fit to be a king, not even a Duke. He *inherited* Orban – that much you know – but he prepared a Dukedom for Orban's son, who died in mysterious circumstances." *The name of that circumstance was Codrin.* Drusila recalled an old Vision in which Codrin saved Jara. It was something that had puzzled her for some years, as she did not know Codrin at that time. Neither did she know where he had vanished to. It was only in Valeni, when they negotiated a sort of collaboration between Bucur and Codrin, that she made the link.

"You want to say ... that Cantemir did not want Orban as king...?"

No, Drusila shook her head. "But you did not answer my question. Why are you trying to stop the marriage between Codrin and Saliné?"

"Because if the stars don't align well for Bucur, I will give Marie to Codrin. I still prefer Bucur because he is easier to handle."

"That makes sense." Drusila smiled and, closing her eyes, she remained silent. The Vision came to her and she shivered. "Tomorrow, I have to leave," she finally said, and Maud's eyes questioned her. "There will be trouble in Arad." *Cantemir is betraying us... I understand the reason for his move. I can't let it happen, but I have to keep this from Maud.*

"What has happened?"

"Nothing has happened yet, but we may have a problem. We, meaning the Wanderers."

"Ah, your Visions," Maud said, a touch of envy in her voice; they were sisters, but she did not have the Light.

Leaving the office, Drusila crossed paths with a young novice, who seemed reluctant to enter Maud's office. "Young man," she smiled at his fear, "there is only a woman inside, not dragons."

Yes, the young man nodded, unable to make up his mind. *She is more terrible than a dragon. And real.*

"Come," Drusila grabbed his arm and went back with him.

"Yes, Paul." Maud looked at the young novice, trying to understand his state of mind.

"I come from Severin, Master Sage, and I don't bring good news."

"Don't tell me that Severin fell into Codrin's hands," Maud snapped.

"No, but Hadrian was taken prisoner and Belugas, the Primus Itinerant was killed. Hanged."

"What?" Maud stood up abruptly and walked in front of Paul, who made himself small. "Say it again." Her eyes bored into his, and she shook him.

"I am sorry, milady, but it's true. Belugas is dead."

"Hanged. Who dared to hang a Sage?" Maud's voice became feral, yet she already guessed the answer. Her eyes became even more intent as if trying to obtain a different answer from the novice.

"Codrin, milady," Paul breathed and remained silent.

"And you wanted to..." Stifled by her sudden fury, Maud could not finish; she threw an angry glance at her sister.

"Why was Belugas hanged?" Drusila asked, her voice calm. She took the time to pick up the glass again and sip some wine, giving her sister enough time to calm down.

The novice cleared his throat. "Belugas tried to kill Codrin at Severin's border. He used Aron's men, fifty of them, and some soldiers from Peyris, but they were all killed in the fight. And because the negotiations to free Lady Saliné and Lady Vio failed."

"You may leave, Paul." Drusila pushed the young man toward the door, trying to shield him. "Well, my dear," she said when she was alone again with Maud, "you need some decent soldiers to kill someone like Codrin. But, to use your own words, losing fifty soldiers makes Bucur even more dependent on your goodwill. And, as for Codrin, I am counting on you to put some order in your house."

Caught between the need to punish Codrin and the restriction the Wanderers put on her, Maud breathed deeply. Sensing her turmoil, Drusila placed a gentle hand on her shoulder.

"I understand that doing nothing to revenge Belugas would be a hard decision for you, but you have to take it. You know why." *It was your fault.*

Maud just nodded.

Chapter 11 - Codrin

Leaving Severin, Codrin split his army into four parts. Considering the Mountes, who agreed to stay as his guards, Vlaicu and Sava's men, he now had a one hundred forty strong army. And there were ten more guards in Cleuny.

Five soldiers went north with Damian and Sara's men. After some consideration, Codrin and Valer decided that Varia's family was no longer safe in the Long Valley. She would sell everything there and move to Poenari with her three children. The soldiers would protect her and her family on their way to Poenari. Codrin wrote a long letter, explaining in detail what had happened and why they were in danger. He was keen to have them in Poenari. Good and trusted people were rare, and while Varia was a skilled administrator, her sons, Damian and Lisandru, were promising soldiers, and he liked her daughter, Livia; she reminded him of Vio, and it was little Livia, with her cheerfulness, who had made his stay over the winter, in Long Valley, more amiable.

Thirty soldiers were left behind to escort all the servants who had once worked for Jara and Mohor and had been thrown out of Severin by Aron. They were twenty-seven adults in total, including Milene, the woman who took care of Cernat's hunting house, and her family, and some children. The carts which carried food for the army, and were now empty, would take their belongings.

Laurent would stay in Seged as governor, keeping his soldiers with him. He also hired five mercenaries as guards.

At noon, the remaining soldiers went with Codrin to Cleuny, where they arrived three days later, in the afternoon. Seen from the valley, Cleuny did not impress much; from close, even less. It was not really a castle, but it looked blunt and solid, even without turrets or toothed battlements. This was more a large, fortified house, with thick stone walls and high, narrow windows. The gated entrance of the fortified house was wide enough to accommodate one large wagon and a pedestrian side by side. *I hope Poenari is better,* Codrin thought. Even with all the information he had received from Sava, he did not want to make up his mind until he saw the fortress. It might have strong walls, as the description suggested, but it all depended on their actual state.

Pintea took over his usual tasks and gathered Codrin's main people in the council room. He wanted to present Sava to Mara and Calin, but to his surprise they already knew each other.

"I was still a young soldier when Calin found refuge in Leyona," Sava laughed. "And you, Mara," he said embracing her, "you were a pretty girl who scavenged my house for books. Now, you are a wonderful woman. Calin has changed too, but I will let you guess in what way."

"I think we've both changed in the same way," Calin mused as they clasped hands.

There was laughter in the room, and only Codrin did not seem touched by it. "Mara, take care of the soldiers. They need food. We brought provisions for one week, but maybe you need to buy some more. Ask the servants to prepare rooms for Vlaicu, Ban and Sava."

"Sava will stay with Neira. His wife," she added, seeing Codrin frowning. *What's happening to him? He looks confused and sad. It's like he is not himself.*

"I'd forgotten that they are already here. Vlad, Pintea, find places for the soldiers to sleep in the barn. It will be crowded, but not for long. We are moving to Poenari," Codrin said to Mara and Calin.

"I know the place, and I've heard that it is haunted." Calin looked at him with an amused glimmer in his eyes.

"That's a good thing, people will not disturb us. I will be in my office if you need me."

For the remainder of the day, Codrin stayed in the antechamber of his bedroom, which he used as his office, leaving word to be left alone. Over and over, he recalled everything that had happened in the last month, wracking his brain to see if he could have done something different, something that could have saved Mohor, Jara, Saliné and Vio. He couldn't find anything. *I need to save Vio*; he shook his head and tried to move his mind into finding a way. He could not concentrate.

"We need to talk." Mara sneaked into his room and sent a questioning frown at him. It was late in the evening, and she was worried; he had skipped dinner, and had not talked with anyone for hours, and she was worried about what she needed to tell him. *I have to*, she encouraged herself.

Leaning on his elbows over the table, Codrin was thoughtful, his mind still lost in Severin. Mara stepped forward, and her hands moved to massage his neck.

"You are tense," she said. "Tell me."

"I failed to free Saliné," he sighed. "And I don't know when another opportunity will arise."

"Tell me," she insisted, and Codrin recalled the whole story, even though it pained him. "You must free Vio, then Saliné will follow you through the tunnel." Her hands move back and forth on his shoulders and nape until she felt him become less tense.

"It may be more difficult to use the tunnel again. Ferd wrote me that Aron learned about my visit, but he thinks that I met a man. The tunnel is now guarded."

"After a while, they will forget."

"Maybe. But she may soon be married and with child."

"Codrin, as I know you, it does not matter if she is with child. You will take them both. It's not her fault if she is forced to marry. Free her, and you will be together. That's the only thing that counts."

He nodded, biting his lip. "In three days, I will leave for Arad to look for Vio. I may be luckier there, then Saliné... You wanted to talk."

"Yes," she sighed. "I have wonderful news, but it may upset you." She leaned against the table in front of Codrin, and placed her hands on his shoulders, her large black eyes locked on his. They offered such a strong contrast against her fair skin.

"Why would something wonderful for you upset me?" His right hand covered hers, and he looked up, intrigued, trying to read her face. She looked happy, but some shadow seemed to loom behind her eyes.

"Fate blessed me, and I am with child. Somehow, my body had recovered after all those years of pain spent with my husband, and... I did not expect it, but I am happy. I feel like a normal woman again, and it's only because you freed me and helped me to have a new life. Thank you."

Eyes half closed, Codrin tried to think. Caught in his inner struggle, he did not realize the tension in Mara's body and her stare, fixed on him. Saliné's beautiful face came into his mind. *Saliné was not meant for me. Fate.* Trying to control his weakness, he calmed his breath just before releasing a sigh. *I like Mara, and she is a wonderful woman, one that I could love.* "I am glad, for both of us." When he spoke, nothing of his inner struggle transferred into his voice. He kissed her hand and, taking her waist with his free arm, he pulled her onto his lap. It was a gentle move. *She should not think that I will marry her just because of the pregnancy.*

Mara did not resist him, if only from pure instinct, and her arm went around his neck. A flash of their first and last night together came to her. Codrin's reaction when she sneaked into his bed had amused her, biting into her inner tension. *But now I am pregnant.* She leaned against him, feeling comfortable in his arms. *At that time, I was sure that I couldn't have children.*

There were a few moments of hesitation in Codrin, a part of him fighting against his will. *I am a man of honor.* He pulled her even closer, and his lips covered hers, pressing gently until she answered him. "You will make wonderful children," he said when they pulled apart, "and I am happy to be with a woman like you."

He wants to marry me. Mara's eyes strayed away from him, and her hand moved gently through his hair. *I would have liked it, but he needs a younger woman. We already agreed on that. Why did I have to marry a monster instead of having a man like Codrin? Fate... Now he needs to forget about Severin. He was not himself today. At least, I can help him to overcome this,* she thought and laced her arms around his neck, kissing him. This time, they did not stop, and passion passed through their veins while their hands searched for each other.

His fingers glided along the edge of her chemise, gently pulling it back to expose her warm skin. It didn't take long for his hand to unbutton the upper part and slip inside. Mara stood up, and he pulled her between his knees. She helped his uneasy hands to undress her further, his keen eyes searching her body, absorbing it; last time when they were so close, it was fully dark. A mellow light flickered from the candles, enhancing their feeling of intimacy.

"You seem less scared this time, but still... Don't worry, I am already pregnant," she laughed, her black eyes squinting in the low light.

"When we were in Orhei, was it so obvious that it was my first time?" he laughed too, standing up. He lifted Mara in his arms and walked toward the bedroom.

"How should I know? It was my first time too. Being raped by a monster doesn't count as making love."

He waited until she pushed the blanket away, and laid her in the bed, the trembling light of the candle playing on her body.

"You are beautiful." His hand touched her knee, then moved slowly, as if afraid of losing something important on its way up, then he leaned his head over her belly which, naked, showed some incipient signs of pregnancy. "You are so warm." He stood up to undress himself while she moved to make place for him.

"Make me feel even warmer," she whispered when he came closer.

His hands and lips went to explore her, and they got lost, lips against lips, body against body, rhythm against rhythm. At the end, they stayed entwined, her head on his shoulder, until their breaths and hearts slowed down.

"Once we arrive in Poenari, we will marry," Codrin said, his hand caressing her hair.

"We already agreed that we won't marry."

"Mara, it must be done, and I want you. You know it."

"We like each other." She raised her head and pressed a finger onto his lips, then rolled over him, her breasts pressing on his chest. "But nothing will change my mind on that. I will always stand behind you, but I will never marry you. If you are lucky, you will marry Saliné; if not, another girl who can expand your power. I am too old for someone of your age. Never make a woman repeat that. For people of your rank, marriage is mostly a political thing. You need a Seigneur's or even a Duke's daughter, but my intuition is that you will be lucky, and Saliné will be your bride."

"Mara, I take full responsibility," he said, moving his hand gently through her hair, "and we will marry..."

She pressed her lips on his, and he responded. It was a brief thing, as she had planned it.

"I am expecting that you will take responsibility for the child, but nothing else. Now that we are both agreed that we will not marry, let's talk about our relocation to Poenari," she said, disengaging from him.

"Mara..."

Her palm swiftly covered his mouth. "Please don't insist. It will only harm our relationship, and I will have to leave. I don't want to leave. My children are safe with you, but either we remain close friends or I will leave." She stared at him, her hand still over his mouth, until she felt that, at least for the moment, he would no longer claim her. "Your relocation will bring unexpected costs, and I am still your Vistier. Father told me that Poenari is a beautiful ... ruin. To make it habitable may cost much more than your revenues, so we may need to carry all the furniture from here."

"I brought twenty thousand galbeni from Leyona," Codrin said, "and another four thousand from Severin. The last amount belongs to Jara, but we will use it if needed, and I will give it back later. Sorry that I forgot to tell you about them."

"We can add your reserves – four thousand – and the other five thousand that Vava's wife brought here from Leyona. That means thirty-three thousand galbeni. We are quite rich, aren't we? My fingers are tingling at the pleasant thought that I can spend so much," she mused. "And I need new dresses; soon I will become round. You don't need to worry, that's something normal when a woman is pregnant. Do you know how much women like to buy new dresses?"

"Not really, I thought that they like jewels more."

"Well, I was thinking to take things slowly, but if you insist..."

"Insist? What did I insist on?"

"On spoiling me," she laughed, "but we must wait until we see Poenari; there are ruins and ruins, after all."

"Sava told me that it's still inhabited."

"That may bring us some issues we will need to figure out. And there are your soldiers," she sighed. "Your little army needs more than eight thousand galbeni per year. You may be a Seigneur now, and brag about having an army, but I don't know if you have a Seigneur's revenues."

"You know the south of Mehadia well. It's mine. If there are problems, those hundred fifty soldiers will solve them. How much money it will bring?"

"It's the richest part of the former Mehadia Seigneury. Five to seven thousand, depending on weather and other things, but not from the first year, not even the second. It takes time to assert authority and collect taxes."

"Orhei?"

"It's a small, mountainous place, maybe six to eight hundred galbeni a year. Saunier may bring around one thousand."

"I have no idea about Poenari, but the eastern part of Severin, which I control, should bring three to four thousand galbeni a year. As you said, not from the first year; my power is still weak. So, we need eight thousand for the army, and let's say two thousand more to run everything else in Poenari. In a good year, we may gather thirteen thousand galbeni. Let's say that we can count on six thousand galbeni this year, and ten thousand next year. If we are lucky, the third year should be normal. For two years we can use a part of our reserves and still have enough money to rebuild Poenari."

"Well, that's a good start, but we can talk about it later." She rolled over him and laced her arms around his neck while her lips touched his shoulder. "I don't think that you will sleep much this night," she whispered.

Codrin woke alone in the morning, and for a few moments, he thought that everything was a dream. "It was not a dream," he spoke to himself, as memories of pleasant moments swept through him. "My life took an unexpected course, again. Today, I must convince Mara. She carries my child. What difference would there be between me and men like Bucur if I make a woman pregnant and don't marry her? And Saliné, what I will tell Saliné? I will always love her." Head in hands, he stood at the edge of the bed, and for some long minutes, he could not think at all. "I can't stay here all day." He stood up abruptly. "There are things to be done. Poenari is waiting for me. Arad too. And Mara," Codrin repeated and walked to retrieve his clothes. He dressed quickly and left the bedroom just as Mara entered the antechamber.

"Lazy man, you must come now if you still want to eat." Mara looked briefly at him, but long enough to see how troubled Codrin was. She walked in front of him, worried and struggling to find some proper words to say. Nothing came to her. *He is still not himself, and I am part of his worries. I did not expect this child, but how I want it now.*

"I am hungry," he said, then took her in his arms, his mouth searching hers. Both stopped at the same time and burst into laughter. "I still need to manage Cleuny."

"During the day," she said, a playful glimmer filling her eyes.

"After breakfast, I will go to see the soldiers. Everybody is free today but, in the evening, I need the councilors. Sava will join the council too."

"Yes, master." She smiled, not really herself, and pulled him forward. Once they were out of the room, she relinquished his hand.

I think that today she will accept, Codrin thought.

After dinner, which was earlier than usual, all his people were gathered in the council room when he entered.

"Poenari is not far from here." Codrin tapped the map on the wall, and his finger traced a line between Cleuny and Poenari. "It's less than a day's ride, but we can't go there yet. Moving so many people into a new city requires good preparations, and I have some urgent business in Arad. Mara, we need to feed two hundred people for at least three months. Fate knows what will await us in that ghostly fortress."

"It's quite a savage place," Sava said. "Not the fortress, but the surroundings. There are not many villages around, so it makes sense to buy provisions from here. We may find that we need to buy even more from Orhei, Saunier and other places."

"Orhei and Saunier are not famous for their wealth," Calin said, "and I don't think that we can buy too much from Leyona either."

Codrin pondered for a while before saying, "We can buy from Corabia. It's a wealthy place. Mara, write a letter to Marat, the governor, and ask him to buy as much food he can and extract the money from taxes."

"I will write, but..."

"Vlaicu will deliver the letter. Take fifty soldiers with you." Codrin looked at Vlaicu. "That should convince Marat who owns the south of Mehadia.

"Sava, you will take fifty soldiers and guard Poenari, just in case Garland or the Circle try to make a move. Discreetly, and at some distance; no one inside should know that the roads are watched.

"Ban, you will guard Cleuny with the remaining soldiers. You know what to do." Wondering if he covered everything, Codrin looked round at the people gathered in the room. "In two days, I will leave for Arad. Vlad and Pintea will come with me. And five soldiers."

There was a knock at the door, and one of the guards at the gate poked his head inside. "We have a courier from Peyris," he said, and at Codrin's nod, the guard let Costa enter the room.

"Seigneur Codrin," he bowed, "I have a letter for you."

"That's good to know, Costa; I was about to raise the alarm when I saw you." Codrin smiled, and Costa smiled back, more a deliberate reaction, the result of his survival skills at the court of Peyris. "Take a seat."

Peyris is more sophisticated, Costa thought, *but full of people who can't be trusted. Codrin may be raw, but...* He almost shrugged and pushed the letter across the desk. *Cleuny is a small place.*

For a reason he could not understand, Codrin felt more eagerness to read the letter than he wanted to show and forced himself to open it with deliberate leisure.

'Codrin,' he read.

'There have been some developments in Leyona that will work against you. They are led by Maud, the Master Sage of the Circle.'

Codrin's eyes grew wide, and he read the passage again. *Maud is... Well, that explains why I lost Leyona. I should be glad that it happened while I was not there. Maud would have killed me.* The letter moved to slip from his fingers, and he gripped it stronger, almost tearing the thin paper. Caught in his thoughts, he closed his eyes, and all the eyes in the room turned to him, their move slow, almost unnatural. Unconsciously feeling their concern, Codrin started to read again.

'You may lose Leyona soon, but don't return there to fight for it, as you may be in danger. Let it fall and go to Poenari. Cleuny is not easy to defend, and the isolated fortress suits you better for whatever comes. Next year, a two thousand strong army will gather to capture or kill you. You will need provisions for at least half a year; you need to rebuild the main gate and to replace the bridge with a drawbridge.

Please burn this letter.

Cleyre Peyris'

Two thousand soldiers... Only a Duke can gather such large army. The Circle again. Duke Stefan...? Then why this letter from Peyris? This will never end. No, everything has an end. "Who is Cleyre?" Codrin looked at Costa.

"The granddaughter of Duke Stefan and a member of the Peyris Council."

That Cleyre... The brief memory of a young woman came to him. *She knows me as Tudor. Does she know the link...? Perhaps.* "Thank you, Costa. I will write an answer... When do you want to leave?" He looked through the window and saw the strong yellow red of the sunset filtering through scattered clouds. "You are welcome to stay here tonight. Pintea, take care of him." Codrin started to read the letter again, ignoring the tension in the room.

That letter seems to have burned you," Sava said, after Costa went out. "I can smell charred skin from here," he sniffed. "Bad news?"

"Interesting would be a better word. How bad or good depends on us. Mara, by the winter we need to gather provisions for nine months. Send a letter to Laurent to buy us more food from Seged. Don't mention the idea of nine months to anyone else." *Cleyre's knowledge can't be just a coincidence.* He looked at the letter again and played the paper between his fingers. *Why did she write this and not the Duke? Is Dochia behind it? This looks like a Wanderer's Vision. Visions reveal faces. Visions reveal... She knows that I am Tudor too. Well, I am still alive. But why?* "If you think that we can't get everything we need, contact the Merchant Guild in Deva. I will give you names. We are done. Mara, please stay," he said, when she stood up, and waited until everybody else left the room before speaking again. "Read it," he offered her the letter, "and memorize it. Keep everything to yourself. We will talk about it tomorrow."

"Interesting indeed," she said after reading it. "Should I burn it?" *Yes*, he nodded, and she went to a candle and let the paper burn slowly, the scent of the melting wax from the seal filling the room.

Codrin stopped in front of her and, as she was leaning against the table, took her hands and kissed them. From his pocket, he took out a ring set with a black gem and, before she could react, put it in on her finger. "The color matches your beautiful eyes," he smiled. "I apologize for not doing it properly yesterday, but men are sometimes less ... sensible than women. Will you marry me, Mara?"

"Why are you trying to make me leave?" she asked, her voice rough, touched by sadness, and tears that did not fall filled her eyes. "I thought that we had agreed on this."

Codrin bit his lip, staring at her and, for the first time, he understood her determination, even though he did not fully understand the reason behind it. His right hand went around her head, and pulled it onto his shoulder, both to soothe her and to mask his confusion, and his left encircled her waist; the tough soldier, accustomed to making decisions in a split second, felt helpless. *What should I do now? It's not fair to her.* "I don't know what to..."

"I do," she cut in, a thin smile on her lips, and she leaned her head back, until their eyes locked. "We remain close friends, and I will keep the ring. It will be the link between us and our child. Now, you have to carry me in your arms."

Codrin's eyes grew larger, but he obeyed without saying a word, and lifted her, walking toward the door going out into the corridor.

"Men are so useless in these situations," Mara chuckled. "The other door." She pointed to the one opening into his bedroom. "You've upset me, and there is a price to pay for that." *Strange this desire burning in me. It must be love, but he was not meant for me. I must overcome my weakness. I am happy enough to have a child from him and to stay with him.* It was her turn to hide the trouble in her eyes, leaning her head on his shoulder. *But until his wedding, he is mine.*

When their fever vanished and their hearts slowed down, they lay on their backs, Mara waiting for him to fell asleep. Codrin couldn't, and he was moving restlessly, small movements, a foot, a hand, his head. He thought Mara was already sleeping, as she stayed still, waiting for a sleep that did not come.

He is like a child, Mara thought, slightly amused. *Restless. Mihail acts the same when something is bothering him. He is only eight years old, but I am glad that Codrin will take care of my son.* She turned slowly and placed her palm on Codrin's chest. He stopped moving and, in a minute, fell asleep. *I should leave...* But instead of leaving, Mara leaned her head against his shoulder. *It feels so good.*

In seven years of marriage, her only good nights were the ones when her husband left her alone. She was at least lucky that he did not visit her bed often. Even so, their nights together always started with a beating, and left her bloody and aching both outside and inside. Sometimes it took her weeks to fully recover and once, he was so violent that she was bedridden for more than two months. She woke up at midnight and, with a sigh, left Codrin alone, her fingers trailing on his skin.

Before he left, Costa visited Codrin again in his office, and found him with Mara.

"Did Cleyre ever visit Leyona?" Codrin asked.

"I don't think so."

"Maybe her husband."

"She is not married. Cleyre is only nineteen years old."

"So young and she is part of the council," Codrin said, raising an eyebrow, and that brought an amused smile to Mara's lips; he was only one year older. "She must be intelligent."

"Yes," Costa said, and a hint of jealousy touched him. *I must be stupid,* he thought. *Cleyre wants him and will have him. At least Peyris will be safe with them. If Cleyre is to become a Duchess, she needs a strong man like Codrin to protect her, and us. She deserves it more than that stupid Albert, even though he is the Duke's son.*

"How did you know to come to Cleuny? I was away most of the time."

"She told me that I would find you here." There were a few moments of silence, both Mara and Codrin struggling to hide their surprise, for different reasons though. "She is well informed," Costa felt the need to add.

"I realized that from her letter. This is for Cleyre." Codrin offered an envelope to Costa. "You should know that I appreciated her help. Five of my soldiers will escort you to Cleuny's border."

Costa had three guards from Peyris with him, but he did not object to Codrin's offer.

"That's strange," Mara said after Costa left. "Peyris has probably the best Secretariat in Frankis, and I'm sure they have contacts everywhere, but there is no way they could learn about Leyona and Poenari and warn you in such a brief time. Even if they had learned it before you, from Leyona, the time still doesn't add up. And there was no way to know that you would be in Cleuny now. I don't understand."

Codrin stopped pacing around the room and picked up a glass from the table, turning it this way and that way. The fingers of his free hand rasped the old wood of the table, and he avoided looking at her.

"Tell me."

"Why do you think that I have something to tell?" he asked, a touch of amusement passing through his voice.

"Seigneur Codrin," she said, standing up, then went around the table, leaning on it, in front of him. "I may be just a poor woman working hard for your highness, but that doesn't mean that you have to trick me. Don't even try." Her hand went through his hair and shook his head gently. "Now tell me."

"Poor men, they have no chance of hiding anything from a woman."

"Men are anything but poor in this world. Feel free to trade your place with me if you don't believe what I said." She shook his head again. "I would shake it harder, but I am still waiting for an answer."

"It's complicated."

"And now you are insulting my intelligence too."

"I would not dare that. You are right, there was no way a courier could manage to ride from Leyona to Peyris and then Costa get here in such a short time. Cleyre knew when I would arrive here before I left Severin. *Before* I knew it. A Wanderer must have been involved in this charade."

"That's complicated," Mara mused, and Codrin found himself smiling. "Don't laugh at me. Are you sure that the Wanderers can...?" Her hand gestured loosely up, toward the sky.

"Yes, they can have Visions about the future, and one of them told Cleyre about Poenari and when I would arrive in Cleuny. In fact, this is the second warning I've received. The other one told me about Poenari, even before I learned about it being given to me. The letter came from Peyris too, brought by ... Costa, when he tried to capture me, but it was not sent by Cleyre."

"The same Wanderer hiding behind two ... women? That's my guess," Mara smiled. "It's quite strange how many women are involved ... one way or another, in your life."

"Maybe because I am such a nice man. The first letter was from a Wanderer, but I don't know if she was behind this letter too."

"Two Wanderers working for you."

"I would doubt that. It's more that I may be part of their plans, though one of them I like to consider as my friend."

"I need to think," Mara said, rubbing her forehead.

"Mara," Codrin took her other hand in his. "We need to agree on something."

"Please don't start again with the marriage thing," she said, her voice suddenly tense.

"No," Codrin sighed. "But it's another thing that you will not like."

"Don't you have anything pleasant for me? I am sorry, I should not have asked that. Not even as a joke. Sometimes my desire to look ... witty, goes too far. But it's your fault." She smiled guiltily, and her hand moved down his face until she touched his lips, and her thumb played there for a while.

"That's why I like you. You are my Secretary, and the woman I trust. The letter from Cleyre, and this supposition about the Wanderers, should stay between us. I know it will be hard for you, but even Calin should not learn about this." He leaned his head forward and kissed her palm.

Mara smiled wryly, and it took her a while to say, "Father is a better Secretary than me, and he may be able to help."

"You are as good as him. I don't want to put Cleyre in danger. Whatever the motivation, she tried to help me. If you tell Calin, he may tell somebody else for a good trade of information, and it may be that another Wanderer will have a Vision and... As you said, it's complicated. And dangerous."

"At least let me tell him about Maud being the Master Sage."

"Tell him, but not how you have learned about it."

"What about those two thousand soldiers? I am," she held her lower lip in her front teeth long enough to make them glisten, "afraid." Involuntarily, she placed her right hand over her belly.

"That's my worry." Codrin smiled and his hand covered hers, making Mara aware of her own gesture. "Besieged by a large army, Cleuny would fall fast. Everything depends on what we find in Poenari. Both Sava and Calin talk about a strong fortress. It may be partially damaged, but we have seven months to fix the weakest points. From the letter, it seems that there is no need for major works."

Chapter 12 - Jara

The carriage bumped over a boulder and woke Jara up. Not that she was really sleeping; her week on the road had been a strange stream of daydreams; mostly old recollections from the past. It was her way to avoid looking into the future. One week on the road, and she was still not prepared to face Orban. She stared outside, followed by Vio's inquisitive eyes. *It's afternoon*, Jara thought. *I still have a day to sort my mind out.* Something hurtful clenched in her, and she shook her head. Their journey from Severin to Arad had taken longer than she'd expected. Not that she wanted to complain. *Is Doren trying to shield me?* Her hand caressed Mark's hair; he was sleeping, his head in her lap. Still too young to fully understand what had happened, Mark was the only one finding pleasure in their journey; it was his second time out of Severin, a much longer one, and he was voicing his joy at each new thing, his cries sending cold shivers down Jara's spine. Sometimes, he rode on Cernat's horse, and that always made him sleepy.

As if reading her mind, Doren, the Spatar of Arad, lowered himself in the saddle and knocked in the window. "We will stop at that inn," he said, pointing somewhere down the valley.

"Thank you, Doren," Jara managed to say, and closed the window, returning to her daydreams. Even though she had lost Mohor only the week before, some of her dreams involved her first husband, Malin, who had died five years earlier, killed by Orban.

At the inn, she ate her dinner absently, but when she tried to leave the room, Doren gestured discreetly for her to stay.

"Take Mark and go upstairs," she told Vio, gently squeezing her hand under the table. "Yes, Doren," she said, when they were alone with Cernat.

Doren looked at her, a touch of hesitation in his eyes. He was that rare sort of mixture between soldier and philosopher, more a soldier though. Orban liked to have such men at his court. There was silence, and tree pairs of eyes flicking back and forth from one person around the table to another.

"I think that I have to thank you for this week on the road," she finally said. They should have arrived in Arad two days ago, but Doren always stopped the caravan early in the evening, and always at an inn, and started it late in the morning.

"There were issues related to your safety." The tone in Doren's voice contradicted his statement, a deliberate thing. "I wanted to tell you something." He stopped for a while, in search of proper words, this was going to be delicate. "I did not agree with what happened in Severin. Neither to Mohor, nor to you and Vio."

Jara tried to answer, but her lips refused to open, and she just nodded.

"Maybe you have not changed much from your time in Midia," Cernat said, remembering that Doren had spent almost a year in their old city, which was conquered by Orban five years earlier.

"They were good times," Doren said, evasively. "I have this letter from Cantemir." He pushed an envelope across the table.

Jara's face changed suddenly at the name, and there was an increased intensity in the line of her mouth. "Cantemir," she spat the word; his name was an awful reminder of her precarious position. "He must be happy about all this. He and Orban."

"He told me that you would react like this," Doren said, his voice calm, almost gentle. "But he was not involved. Please read it."

She sighed and, not willing to upset Doren, opened the letter.

'Jara,' she read.

'The only reason I wrote this is that I may not be in Arad at the time of your arrival. Whatever you think about me, I am not your enemy, and neither is Doren. We both knew you and Malin from the time spent in Midia. In my absence, my cousin, Herlo, will take care of you until my return. Please cooperate with them both.

PS: I was not involved in what happened in Severin, as Orban kept me out of the loop. Without Doren I would not have known at all.'

"Cantemir reminded me that both of you stayed for a while in Midia," she said, questioningly.

"It's where I met my wife, Vali." Doren smiled a touch of sadness visible on his face and, for a while, his eyes were lost in the room. Even more, young Vali was part of Jara's entourage at that time. "I lost her last year."

"I am sorry; I still remember her; she was close to my age."

"We have some things in common, mostly what we have lost. I don't know how much I can help you but, at least, I will try."

"Thank you, Doren, but I am still uncomfortable with Cantemir."

"From your voice, that was a ... mild way of saying it. Talk with him first, before deciding your next steps."

"I think that I don't have much choice about avoiding him. Good night, Doren," she said and stood up, then left the room, her limbs suddenly stiff.

"Mother?" Vio asked, when Jara entered their bedroom. She jumped from chair, and in a blink of the eye, stood in front of Jara.

"Everything is fine," she said, embracing her daughter. "All the way along the road, I had the impression that Doren was trying to give me more time."

"We traveled slower than usual."

"You noticed it too?" Jara smiled.

"Yes, we should have arrived two days ago in Arad, but I did not know if that was a good or a bad thing to tell you."

"You did not want to worry me." She embraced Vio tighter. "I think that, next time you observe something unusual, it would be better to worry me."

"Yes, Mother."

ஜ

Cantemir's assumption of absence was wrong, and he greeted Jara on her arrival. Their first exchange was both cold and short, yet the coldness came from Jara; Cantemir looked like a man trying to handle a hot potato. They followed him inside Orban's palace, up to the point where a large corridor diverged.

"Sir Cernat," Cantemir said. "Please follow Herlo to your suite. Jara and Vio will be hosted in a different place. We will meet again at lunch. We need to talk."

There was a touch of panic in Jara's eyes when she looked at her father, but she composed herself fast, and they both nodded. They walked further until they arrived in front of a double door, made of dark red wood and sculpted with floral motifs. Seeing Cantemir, the two guards opened the door to let them pass.

"There is nothing unusual about to the guards," Cantemir informed Jara. "They are here all the time."

She glanced around at the large antechamber, from which four more doors were opened. Closing her eyes, she ventured into the past, her single visit to Arad. She was still not married at that time, and it was her worse visit ever, as Orban saw her and, three months later, shortly after his first wife died, he asked for her hand. "This is Orban's suite."

"This is the S'Arad suite. That door," he pointed to the one in front, "leads to Orban's suite. The one on the left is ... yours. For a while, Vio will stay with you. All the suites have their own antechamber, bedroom and utility rooms."

Jara had the sudden impulse to ask about Orban's presence, but she stopped herself at the last moment.

"Take your time and make yourself comfortable. Two bathtubs are waiting for you. In one and a half hours, I will come here with Cernat. Lunch will be served in that room," he pointed to the last door on the right.

Lunch went on in almost silence, only some banal exchanges passing between them, even though Cantemir tried to animate it, in the beginning. He failed and resigned himself to the same almost silent behavior.

"Now, we have no choice but to talk," Cantemir said, after all the servants left the room, and Mark was already sleeping in Jara's bed, watched by a maid.

At Jara's nod, Vio stood up, ready to leave.

"Please stay," Cantemir stopped her.

"Are you trying to stop me talking about the past?" Jara asked coldly, yet she nodded to Vio, who seated herself again.

"Maybe," Cantemir smiled. It looked wryly, and perhaps a little sad, but not unpleasant. "We have important things to discuss that Vio may need to hear. She is no longer a child, and ... navigating through Orban's court is not easy. Let's start with the past; sometimes it hurts, but it may help us to arrive at some conclusions. Did you read my letter?"

"It changed nothing," Jara shrugged. "We never tried to hurt you, while you always planned to ruin us. Malin blocked your marriage, but it was a political thing, as she was betrothed for three years already, and you knew that when you arrived in Midia. That did not stop you from courting her in secret, and we did not know until two weeks before her wedding was planned. Cancelling the marriage contract would have meant a political crisis, and no one expected what happened to Lynda. Her suicide affected all of us and weakened us too. In fact, our problems started that day. We tried to come to an understanding with you, but you just left to join our enemy, to plan these two ... murders, even though Mohor had done nothing wrong to you. How much you must have hated us. Are you satisfied now? Will this stop your thirst for revenge?"

"Jara," Cernat said gently, as her voice became louder. He had chosen to stay behind, as a last line of defense. This was mostly between Jara and Cantemir, as they were friends once. His fine political sense told him that once a certain threshold was passed, a new reality could be born, one that could help Jara survive.

"It's good that she spoke her mind," Cantemir said, his voice restrained, only his fingers, playing with an inch-wide button on his jacket, betraying his inner tension. The dark red wooden button contrasted with his pale hand. Each person in the room was marked by contrasts, some visible, some hidden deep inside. Each one being able to see them just partially. "I could not remain in Midia; it was too difficult for me. I went to Arad only because I had a relative here who was the third secretary."

"Was Lydia pregnant?" Jara asked, coldly.

"No," Cantemir breathed and shook his head vehemently. "We did not... You are right that I had my share of guilt. We wanted to run, but ... I think that Malin sensed something and put more guards..."

"Lynda was his sister, and we both considered you a friend."

"I know," Cantemir said meekly, and bit his lip. "And I loved Lynda too." The room became quiet and, distantly, the lingering noises of the city could be heard. They did not listen.

"In the letter," Cernat said, feeling that it was the right moment for a turning point, "you mentioned that you want to help us. Why?"

"Let's finish with the past," Cantemir, now fully recovered, said. "The war between Orban and Malin started before my tenure as Secretary of Arad. It was an intermittent thing during the years, yet you still find me guilty because of the last battle."

"You played an important role in that battle," Jara said, struggling to control her voice.

"We were Secretaries of the courts we represented. We were on opposite sides, and we both tried to win, but Malin's death was just an unfortunate incident." Cantemir glanced briefly at Vio, thinking that he may have hurt her, but her face was composed. *I need her to be present too.* "It was not something I planned. The same could have happened to Orban or to his son. Battles are unpredictable and can't be fully controlled."

"Where is Orban?" Jara asked, abruptly.

"I advised him to give you some time to settle in. He will return in two days. It may look strange to you, but he, in his weird way, cares about you. I also advised him about ... marriage."

Jara took a deep breath and exhaled. Everything repeated three times, the Assassin Cool. With each breath, she felt as if her mind was leaving too. *I must be calm. Whatever my shock, I must think. Marriage would help me protect Vio and Mark, but it will make it harder to break the link with Orban. If I fall pregnant again... Pregnancy would not necessarily be related to marriage. Mistresses fall pregnant too.* She stared loosely around and realized that everyone was waiting for her to speak, yet she could not. *I have to speak.* She closed her eyes and separated herself from the world around her. *Marriage*, she sighed after a while. *Let it be. As if I have a choice.* "Why?" Eyes suddenly wide open, she stared at Cantemir. "Do you want to absolve Orban? Or do you want to absolve yourself?"

"I think that both of us wanted some kind of absolution. For different reasons, though," Cantemir said, cautiously. "And you tried to kill me twice."

"Not me; your friend Aron tried to kill you; he who may be a Sage from your Circle."

"Perhaps," Cantemir said, playing again with the dark-red button of his shirt. *Tudor told me the same, yet I doubt that Mohor was not involved. He can't pay anymore, but Aron can, and he will pay.* "To move to the recent past, I had nothing to do with what happened a week ago in Severin. Orban kept it hidden from me, as he knew that I would oppose it. It was between him and the Circle."

"Are you not part of the Circle, and its previous Master Sage?" Cernat asked.

"A previous Master Sage belongs to the past, not to the future, and my relationship with the actual Master is not the best. I opposed Bucur's election as Candidate King. Unfortunately, it was too late. It was quite a mischance, as my best source of information was blocked over the winter in Long Valley." Cantemir remained silent for a while, as all the other three reacted: a frown, a twitch of the lip or a tremor of the hand. *They did not react when I spoke about Bucur; they reacted when I mentioned Long Valley. Do they know Tudor?* "Aron is indeed a Hidden Sage, so it may be that some subterranean movements against me started a long time ago. It's not usual for a Sage to try to kill another one," he said almost absently. "There are some rules against... Never mind," he shook his head. *Killing a Sage, a Master Sage... Is the Circle so corrupt?* "I suggested that Orban wait a month for the marriage, but he will ask for your hand the day he returns. More than one month would be difficult to..." Cantemir looked at Jara, waiting for answer, even though he did not ask a question.

"One month," Jara agreed, her voice lost in a weak whisper.

"Until the marriage, Vio will stay with you. That doesn't mean that Orban would not want to..." Cantemir looked again at Jara; it was difficult for him to go into such intimate details, even more so knowing that each word would hurt Jara. And Vio was there too.

Yes, Jara nodded.

"Why am I in Arad?" Vio asked abruptly. "There was an agreement between the Circle and Codrin."

"I don't really know," Cantemir shrugged. "Orban did not ask for you. Maybe they want to control Codrin or Saliné through you."

"If we take into account that it's only a maybe, would it be possible to come to an amiable agreement and send Vio to Codrin?" Cernat asked.

"I don't want to leave Mother."

"I think that Jara would be relieved if you left," Cantemir said, smiling, starting to realize that he liked the girl. "But it's too early to talk about this, and it may be dangerous."

"Dangerous because of Orban or because of the Circle?" Jara asked.

"Both."

In front of the door, she breathed deeply. Eyes closed, she tried to place her hand on the knob. Her hand trembled, and she pulled it back. *I must do this. For Vio. For Mark. For Father. I must do it.* Her hand moved, gripped and turned the knob as if trying to pull it out from the door.

"Jara." Orban smiled when she entered the room, which was prepared for their dinner. His head tilted elegantly. There was aristocracy in every trait of him, albeit a deceitful and decadent form of it. "I have waited so long to have you as my guest in Arad." He stood up and walked toward her. With a hint of theatrics, he kissed her hand, and offered her a seat.

It was Jara's fourth day in Arad, and she was better prepared to meet Orban than she was on the day of her arrival. *Cantemir was right*, she thought, even though she was not sure how much she could reevaluate him, and how much she could trust him. They had talked a few times but, for a reason that she could only guess, Cantemir preferred to spend more time with Cernat. And surprisingly, he took care of Vio too, making her meet Lanya, Orban's daughter, who was only a year older.

As she seated herself, Jara had her first shock; the plates on the table had once belonged to her, when she was still Grand Signora of Midia. She bit her upper lip and clasped her hands, feeling that, behind her, Orban was observing her reactions. "It seems that Midia moved here in more detail than I thought," she said, with the calm of a woman talking about a mundane piece of porcelain.

"Isn't that interesting?" Orban smiled while going to his chair across the table. Their places were in the middle of a long table able to host twenty-four people. "A symbiosis between Midia and Arad. Past and future. What would be more important to you, what has happened or what is about to happen?"

"Both are important to me, and how can you build a future without past. Was this ... symbiosis supposed to revive my memories about what I have lost, or to make me feel your interest?"

"Both are important to me. Speaking about ... past and future. Once I lost that precious toy of being the Candidate King, things suddenly looked less ... interesting. That business ate a lot of my past, in return for a hypothetical future. When you are free of your past, the present seems to be more alive, more intense."

"And without that precious toy, what would have changed in your past?"

"How should I know? Why should I care? Wouldn't that mean letting the past drive me again?"

"It may help to live the present differently."

"It already happened. I will make an exception, just to underline my point. The other dinner we had in Midia and this one. Don't you see the difference between them?"

The only difference is that in Midia you drugged and raped me; now I have to accept you in my bed. "There may be some differences," she said, prudently. "But they may be resemblances too."

"Like the plates," Orban smiled.

"Like the glasses too." *You put the drug in my glass.*

"You have a good eye for detail. Do you think that we've settled some things now?"

"I don't think that forgetting the past is a good way to prepare for a new future. But," she added with deliberate slowness, seeing Orban frowning, "I also don't think that the past should be the only way of looking at your future."

"Symbiosis."

"Symbiosis," she shrugged, looking oddly focused inward, as if she did not fully realize the implications.

His hand went under the table and came out with a small box wrapped in black velvet. Slowly, he pushed the box toward the middle of the table until Jara was able to see the ring, and she recognized it. "You know the ring; it belonged to my wife, and before that to my mother and to her mother. Put it on your finger."

Half hidden by the plate, Jara's hands gripped the table. She blinked a few times, until Orban's intense stare brought her to her senses, but it still took her a while to take the ring and place it on her finger, next to the one she had received from Mohor.

"I don't think that those two rings work well together."

She said nothing, and took both rings off, and put back only the one from Orban; but she left the other one in sight, on the table.

Orban frowned again and tried to say something, but changed his mind, at the last moment. “Jara, will you marry me?” he finally asked.

“Yes,” she said flatly, her eyes fixing a painting on the wall behind Orban, the hand not on display gripping the edge of her chair.

He stared at her with a narrow smile on his lips. “Finally. I have waited so long for this. We will have a great party.”

“What for?” *That’s the last thing I want, to be paraded like a trophy, together with my children while I am still in mourning.*

“It’s our wedding. I want everybody to be part of it, to enjoy it.”

“A waste of resources, and they will only laugh; both of us already had two weddings.”

“I like that.” He rubbed his chin, and Jara stayed silent, not really understanding what he wanted. “You are already thinking of *our* resources.”

This is business, not marriage, and I need to negotiate my place. “I should have a look at the Visterie and Secretariat.”

“Ah, yes, you were Secretary once. It will not be the case here, but you may have a look at the Visterie if that makes you happy. Shall we?” He pointed at the first course on the table.

ஐ

From their first day in Arad, Jara decided that they needed to train again. She had been trained to fight from her childhood, but she had also learned the Assassin Dance from Codrin, though she had not practiced much in recent years, after having Mark, while Vio trained together with Saliné. To her surprise, after two weeks, Jara felt that her body was responding well, even to the most torturous exercises Vio was making her do – the advanced moves from the Assassin Dance were not easy; they required good stamina, coordination and balance. Over the last two days, they had begun to train with daggers. Because of

Cantemir, or just through Orban's neglect, their luggage had not been checked and, in Severin, Jara had hidden four weapons among her clothes.

At this stage of their training, Vio became the teacher, and they played fast, their daggers clanging when steel met steel. They were exercising in the room that was set up as Jara's office. It was large enough and, of all the rooms belonging to her, the most distant place from Orban's suite.

"Turn more to the right, Mother," Vio said, her hand moving fast, finding another hole in Jara's defense.

"I wish I could move with your speed," Jara sighed, but she turned, and Vio lowered her speed, allowing her mother to counter a new blow.

Codrin's words were still playing in Vio's mind: a trainer must be tough with the pupils, but sometimes he must allow them to feel that they have value. Codrin was speaking to Cernat one day when they were still living in their house, but Vio had been sneaking around.

"Again," Vio said and, with a grim smile, Jara complied.

She raised her left hand at an angle against her own body and kept the right hand lower. When Vio attacked, she turned swiftly, her left hand moving up for defense, and she was finally able to parry the blow with the dagger in her right hand. Vio attacked with her second dagger, but Jara was prepared and moved forward and to the left. Her sliding foot caught a small difference of level between two planks and she abruptly fell forward, just as Vio attacked. Vio reacted instantly, but she could not avoid cutting Jara's shoulder.

"Mother!" she cried and dropped her daggers.

"Don't worry, it's just a scratch."

Vio pressed her right hand on the wound. It would have been a logical reaction if she had a piece of cloth in her hand to stop the bleeding, but she did not.

"I am fine," Jara insisted, but Vio clung to her, still pressing on the wound.

Suddenly, Vio's hand started to glow white. Eyes closed, she did not realize it, but Jara saw everything, and even more, she felt the heat passing from Vio's hand into her shoulder. Then she felt well. Opening her eyes, Vio retracted her hand, and behind it, both saw that the wound was almost healed.

"We need to talk," Jara said, seeing the surprise in Vio's eyes.

"What... What was that?" Vio asked, staring at her hand, its glow decreasing slowly. Absorbed by the strange thing happening to her, she did not hear the answer to her question, and Jara left her time to adapt. Once the light vanished, Vio raised her eyes toward Jara, who embraced her gently.

"There is nothing wrong with you, Vio," Jara said again. "You have the Light."

"Do you mean that I am a Wanderer?"

"One becomes a Wanderer by choice. The Light comes to you without any strings attached. When you are eighteen, the Wanderers will ask you to join them, but the decision will be yours."

"Are you sure that it will be my choice?"

"They will pressure you for sure, but they can't force you. Mother had the Light too, but she did not agree to join the Wanderers. She wanted to make a family, to have children. With the first child, most of the Light will vanish."

"It's a hard choice."

"Yes, one must balance between family and Light, but keep in mind that the Light will not go completely from you, even after you have children. I still have some Light, even when mine was not so strong."

"I did this," Vio pointed to the almost healed wound. "What else can I do?"

"Healing a wound is unusual. There is no other Wanderer I know with this power. I'm not sure they know that such a power exists. You must keep this secret. Don't reveal it to any Wanderer, not even to Dochia."

"I trust Dochia."

"Yes, but she would have to tell them, she is bond to her order, and ... they may try to force you to join them, or even kidnap you. Remember that they tried to kill Codrin. The Wanderers are no longer what they were before. They supported Bucur. Keep this in mind."

"What other powers do I have?" Vio asked eagerly, and Jara bit her lip. "Don't worry, I will never mention my healing powers."

"You may start to have Visions of the future."

Vio frowned, and her face suddenly became serious. "In Severin," she said reluctantly, "I saw Mohor, dead. It was just the day before... I thought it only a bad dream. I am sorry, Mother."

"You did not know," Jara said, embracing her again. "And it was already too late; Orban's soldiers were already in Severin."

"But..."

"Don't," Jara said gently. "Mohor knew what he was doing, and he knew that Orban would kill him anyway." *That's strange, Mohor's death made my marriage with Orban possible. Things would have been more complicated, if Orban had killed him... Or perhaps he would have forced a divorce. I will never know.* She tightened her arms around Vio, fighting hard against her tears. She lost the fight and began to sob.

"I am sorry, Mother," Vio said and laced her arms around Jara's neck.

"I am fine," Jara said after a while. "Let's train again." *I have to keep my mind afloat. Vio and Mark need me.*

Chapter 13 - Jara

There was only one person in the palace that Vio was happy to meet. In the beginning, she frowned at Cantemir's effort to put her in contact with Lanya, Orban's daughter. It was hard for Vio to separate her from her father but, at Cantemir's and Jara's insistence, she accepted. Lanya was a kind person who resented Orban's brash personality, even though she did not know about his many sins, and she resented her brother, Alic, even more. He was eighteen and had the mind of a fourteen-year–old, coupled with the hormones of his real age. Alic was a pest for anyone in the palace, and many maids suffered because of his obsessive interest and bad temper. Sometimes, he groped Lanya, who was fifteen, tearing her shirt or raising her skirts. Since Orban ignored his son because of his weak mind, Cantemir had to take care of him and bring Alic women from time to time. That lessened the pressure on the maids but did not erase it.

A lonely presence in the palace, Lanya enjoyed meeting Vio too; they had many things in common, like reading or painting. One day, Orban found them together in front of a book, and he frowned, not knowing about their relationship. The girls froze when they saw him, even Vio, who was not so easy to astonish.

"We are reading," Lanya said.

"That's obvious," Orban said, and he smiled suddenly, eying them with a slight dose of interest. "Let me see the book." He walked toward them and Lanya raised the book so he could see the title.

"The voyage of Cherac... I read it when I was your age or even younger. It's about Arenia and Sylvania. You may know a thing or two about Arenia," he said to Vio.

"I do."

"This book is more than two hundred years old. There is another one which was written fifty years ago. It may depict Arenia better. Some things may have changed."

"Arenia is ... less strong than two centuries ago," Vio ventured.

"And that means?" Orban lowered his head to look at her.

"Decadence," Vio said flatly, not understanding Orban's sudden interest. She knew him as a bad and cruel man and for her that meant lacking culture too. She was wrong; Orban was as intelligent and sophisticated as he was evil.

"And that means?"

"Poorer people, fewer books, less skilled writers."

"Did Codrin tell you that?"

"Yes."

"It's a good thing for a man to understand his situation. Or for a woman. What about Frankis?"

"It's even worse," Vio said, starting to think that she might need to reevaluate Orban.

"What does a girl know?" Alic asked, entering the library only because he had heard about a new girl. "Who are you?" He stared at Vio, moistening his lips.

"Alic," Orban turned. "It seems that she knows some things that you do not. You may join them and read the book."

"Men don't need books," Alic said, walking behind the girls. "But I may join them. This one may provide some entertainment." He pointed at Vio, and grabbed her from behind, trying to find her breast.

"Take your hands off me," Vio growled, blocking his hand and restraining herself from hitting him.

"Or you will do what?"

"Let her alone," Orban finally said.

"We will meet again," Alic said, and left the library, winking at Vio.

"You've met my son," Orban said. "Try to avoid him."

"Why don't you teach him how to behave?" Lanya asked.

"I gave that up a long time ago." Orban shrugged and left the library too. There was nothing more he could say about his son. His failure. A failure that marked him more than losing the Candidate King status.

"Let's go to my room," Lanya said. "Alic will not bother us there."

Before leaving, Vio stopped Lanya and glanced along the corridor: there were some servants, walking left and right, but Alic was not in sight. "We can leave," she said.

They walked at a brisk pace, glancing back from time to time. Alic's suite was in the opposite direction from Lanya's. The arrangement was Cantemir's work; he had convinced Orban to keep his children far from each other. Orban did not care about them for different reasons: Alic was not fit to rule, while Lanya was a girl who could not exercise power in Arad. However, his cold distance from Lanya was only a mask. Orban had two bastard sons, but his hidden hope was that maybe Jara would give him the legitimate son he needed.

From a side door, Alic's head sneaked into the corridor, and searched for Vio: she was forty paces in front of him, and he started to follow her and Lanya. While he was stupid, there was shrewdness in him, a raw thing, basic, that belonged better in an animal's mind. He tracked them, hiding behind other people walking in the same direction. When they entered in Lanya's suite, he quickened his pace and, at the door, put his ear to the wood. His hand silently turned the knob.

"What are you doing here?" Cantemir asked.

"What I am doing is not your business."

Cantemir grabbed his shoulder and pushed him away. “Go to your room.”

Like Lanya, Alic was frail, they had both inherited that from their mother. But where for the girl it meant grace, for him was weakness. He could beat a girl of his age, but even younger boys could defeat him easily.

“One day you will pay,” he growled at Cantemir.

“You can complain to Orban. Go now.”

An hour later, Vio left Lanya’s suite. She glanced left and right and walked toward the S’Arad suite, where Jara had her own place.

“You forgot your book,” Lanya shouted after Vio, but it was too late, she was already gone.

Ten paces along the corridor, a hand covered Vio’s mouth; another one went around her waist and dragged her into an empty room. A few servants witnessed everything, but they already knew not to interfere. They thought Vio was one of the many maids in Arad palace who had the bad luck to fell into Alic’s hands.

“I told you that we would meet again,” Alic whispered to her. “Now you will entertain me. I think that you have not yet known a man. That will make my pleasure even greater.”

Lanya put Vio’s book on the table. She changed her mind, and picked it up, and left her suite. “Vio!” she shouted and turned her head around, unable to see her friend. *She must be here*, she thought, and walked briskly toward the S’Arad suite. She found Jara alone. “I don’t know where Vio is,” she said, a touch of worry in her voice.

“What do you mean?” Jara asked calmly, thinking something trivial had happened between the girls.

“She left my room to come here, and I went after her to return this,” Lanya gestured with the book in her hands. “But the corridor was empty.”

“Maybe she entered in another room. Vio likes to explore.”

"Alic," Lanya whispered. "I am sure that he followed Vio. He ... he tried to do some bad things to her."

"What?" Jara asked and stood up instantly. "Take me to your suite."

"Anyone seen a fifteen-year-old girl with auburn hair?" Jara shouted, sitting in front of Lanya's door. No one answered them apart from a young maid who, careful not to be seen by other people, pointed toward a room, then she left in a hurry.

"Why are you shouting?" Orban appeared in the corridor too.

"Vio," Jara breathed and opened the door pointed out by the maid.

They found Vio fighting two men. One was trying to immobilize her hands, the other her feet.

"Put her on the table," Alic shouted, a line of blood trickling down from his mouth and nose.

Vio's foot moved abruptly and hit one man's jaw. Three teeth fell on the floor, and Orban started to laugh. "Leave her," he ordered. "Bunch of nobodies. You can't immobilize a girl. One month in jail for attacking my guest."

"But sir," one of them protested, as he was just following Alic's orders.

"You will flog him," Orban ordered the other one, who was missing his teeth. "Ten lashes. He talks too much. Get out." He turned his head and stared now at his son.

"I want that girl," Alic said.

"Cantemir will see to your needs," Orban said, coldly.

"If you marry her mother, I want to marry her."

"That idea merits some attention," Orban said, and a large grin filled Alic's bloodied lips.

"She is too young, and your son must be punished," Jara interjected.

"But don't you see it, Jara? He will be punished; your daughter will be the man in their marriage. Alic will become a nice obedient girl."

"I won't," Alic growled. "I want to marry her the same day as you," he pointed to both Jara and Orban.

"Orban," Jara whispered. "We need to talk alone about this situation. Come with me, Vio."

Before meeting Orban, Jara turned like a restless wolf in her room, her cage, hitting an object now and then, pondering how she could influence him. After a while, she seemed to control her emotions better, and stood in front of the window, gesticulating from time to time, mumbling to herself. absorbed in her inner world, she did not see when Orban came into her room. He entered quietly, and seated himself in a chair, his eyes fixed on her.

"Something is bothering you," he said, after a while.

She started but composed herself and turned slowly. "I was thinking to invite you to sit."

"It's my castle," Orban shrugged. "So," he smiled. "My son wants to marry your daughter. I can understand why, yet after he broke his lip and nose, I don't really understand why."

"That could have ended badly," Jara said coldly.

"Yes, but it didn't. I let the soldiers know that Vio has my protection."

"You may leave for a few days, and if your son pays one of them well, he will forget about your protection. Or your son may hit her from behind and... Don't you see how wrong you are?"

"I may be."

Jara breathed a few times, seeking the peace and clarity she had learned from the Assassin Dance that would calm her. "You don't care about your son, but I care about my daughter."

"I never doubted that you care about your daughter. I agree that Vio is too young to marry now, but she may be what Alic needs. In a few years." He stood up before Jara could answer and left her alone.

ஒ௮

Vio stormed into the room, glanced right and left, and spoke in haste, her voice almost a whisper, her eyes gleaming. "Codrin is coming to Arad. It was a Vision," she added, confidently.

Eyes closed, Jara fought to overcome a burst of hope. *Even if he comes, it will not be possible to free us.* Her wedding was planned to happen in ten days – after some negotiations, Orban had agreed to postpone it by one week. "Can you work out when he will get here?" she asked, not wanting to spoil Vio's happiness.

"How can I do that?"

"People having the Light and can recall a memory in detail. Look at the weather, how people are dressed, vegetation. They may tell you something. Both Mother and Dochia told me that it's not easy to find clues, but in time..."

Vio frowned in sudden concentration and stayed like that for a while. "I don't know," she whispered, the corners of her mouth going down. "It was dark."

"Snow?"

"No. He may come soon," Vio said, a trace of hope still in her voice, but much less than when she entered the room.

"Come here." Jara opened her arms, and Vio nestled comfortably in her embrace. "Things could be better, but we are not in a desperate situation."

"Your wedding..." Vio breathed.

"My wedding is a political thing, like the other two I had in the past. When I first married, I barely knew Malin, and I was more scared than I am now." *But I was not disgusted by my future husband.* "I was seventeen years old, and it took us more than a year to fall in love. I was lucky, your father was a man who deserved to be loved. Some of my friends weren't so lucky. They had to marry men they started to hate, yet they survived, and they had children who they loved, and who enriched their lives." *Such precarious lives women have...*

"Do you think that you and Orban can fall in love...?"

"Who knows? But most probably we may find a common way of living together. A sort of ... arrangement." *Like many other women.*

"I would prefer to become a Wanderer than..."

"Don't say that. I will try to find a good husband for you." *Codrin maybe, if Saliné...* Jara bit her lip, and tightened her arms around Vio.

"Are you thinking about Saliné?" Vio asked.

"Yes. I failed her." Jara sighed and fought hard to hide her bitterness.

"It was not your fault."

"In a way, it was my fault too, but fault or no fault, she is my daughter, and I could not protect her or you. I hope that Codrin will come and steal you from here." *And marry you.*

"I am sure he is coming for us. We must train harder."

"We shall see." Jara gathered her strength and pulled her head back to look at Vio. Her hand caressed her daughter's face. "We shall see. Let's sleep now."

Chapter 14 – Jara / Codrin

It was already dark when someone knocked at Balan's door. "Helmut," Panait mumbled, "only Helmut dares to piss me off so late. That man is a pest. Like any good Litvonian merchant from Muniker."

"You need Helmut," Delia said gently. "Litvonians are sometimes hard to work with, but it is worth the pain."

"Yeah, just because they have a king, they think us inferior, but you are right, if we manage to sign this contract, my trade with Litvonia would double."

"And you may be able to stay home more."

"Yes," he sighed. "Helmut could lead one caravan; I can lead the other. The bastard has no manners; he's knocking again."

"Let me open the door. Take your time to ... calm yourself." She smiled to encourage him and left the room. "I am coming," she cried, after a third series of knocks on the door. "Helmut, you should be...," she said after opening the door, then her eyes grew wide. "Tudor," she whispered, seeing Codrin, and her arms went up to embrace him. "It's so long since your last visit. What happened?"

"Many things," he said, embracing her too. *One day I have to tell them that my real name is Codrin, not Tudor.* "Let me in, or who knows what your neighbors will think when they see a respectable woman embracing a stranger in the night? Another child is coming," he said, finally realizing why their embrace was a bit awkward.

"Yes," Delia said joyfully while Codrin closed the door. "This one came to us quicker. Fate was kind to us. Come, Panait is in a bad mood because of a Litvonian merchant."

"Helmut," Codrin laughed.

"Bring him here," Panait's irritated voice passed through the open door.

"Yes, I will bring him," Delia chuckled.

"What do you want, Helmut?" Panait asked without raising his head from the papers on his desk.

"What should I want from such a terrible Frankis merchant?" Codrin asked in Litvonian.

"You," Panait boomed and raised his head. His mouth opened again, yet no other word left it. "I always said that there is something of a Litvonian in you. Don't worry, we all have some bad parts." He stood up, and the two men embraced. "You have changed, Tudor," he said when they disengaged. "You were tall and thin, now I get the feeling I'm embracing a bear." Panait stepped back, then went to his chair. "You are still thin, relatively, only your shoulders seem to go on forever. I fail to understand how such thin arms can be so fast and strong. And deadly."

"I am no longer a child." Codrin smiled, and sat in another chair, on the other side of the desk. There was no need for an invitation; Panait's house was like his second home.

"For us, you will always be the seventeen-year-old man-child who saved our lives in the Cursed Forest," Delia said, and she ruffled Codrin's hair. "Dinner will be ready soon, but I am still waiting to know why you did not visit us for so long."

"I've settled somehow, far in the south, and I am now a Knight."

"Then we have to celebrate," Panait said, and his hand stretched involuntarily for the hat sitting on his desk.

That made Codrin smile before saying, "And you are now the First Mester of Arad." He bowed to Panait, fighting hard to restrain a burst of laughter.

"Ah, yes," Delia said, "Panait never misses the chance to scratch someone's eye with his new hat."

"I am the youngest head of the Guild of Arad in a while," he smiled coyly, rubbing the First Mester emblem on his hat. His eyes were shining in the trembling candlelight.

"And a Sage of the Circle," Codrin said, looking keenly at him.

"Who told you that?" Panait frowned. "Cantemir informed me only three days ago, even though I was introduced to the Circle in midsummer. Ah," he puffed. "I forgot that you are the Wraith of Tolosa, or else you already visited Cantemir."

"I will see him tomorrow. You know that my first visit in Arad is to Delia and you. Always. How is Cantemir? He is no longer the Master Sage."

"I can't say that he has changed because of that, but some recent ... events are taking a toll on him."

"Like the abduction of Lady Severin and her children."

"That, and the thing with the Candidate King. There are some rumors about deception..."

"They are more than just rumors."

"Orban will marry Lady Jara," Panait said abruptly, and Codrin faked a cough to hide his bitter surprise. "The wedding is in nine days from now."

"Poor woman." Codrin finally recovered. "Her husband was killed, and she was sold by the Circle to Orban."

"What really happened in Severin?" As a new Sage, Panait was not comfortable talking about the Circle's sins, but he did not want to be uninformed either.

"There was an agreement between the new Candidate King and Orban. Orban would help Bucur take Severin, and he would receive Lady Severin and her youngest children. And Bucur keeps her eldest daughter as prisoner with a false marriage proposal."

"Even the children," Delia sighed.

"How else could Orban force Lady Severin into submission? And it's only one month since her husband was killed," Codrin said, struggling to control his voice. "Bucur is even worse than Orban."

"It's hard to talk about this," Panait mused. "I took an oath to help Bucur become our King. I had to do it."

"You did not really know about Bucur last summer, but now you do," Delia said, a touch of irritation in her voice. "If I had some doubts until now, they've vanished after what Tudor said to us."

"The Sages told me that Bucur needs a base to start his ascension to the throne," Panait said meekly.

"Bucur is a fraud," Codrin said, more fervently than he meant to. "He never won a battle, and...." He stopped abruptly, thinking that he needed to calm down. *I need their help.* His silence went on longer; he could not find the words.

"What is bothering you?" Delia asked before Codrin could gather his mind.

"There is an important quest, and it may be the last action of the Wraith of Tolosa."

"Because is too dangerous or because you want to retire?"

"Both."

"Is your quest in Arad?" Panait asked, his voice prudent and almost shy.

Yes, Codrin nodded, still unable to explain what he needed. *I may put them in danger. There is no may about it. Everything I want will endanger them.*

"Tell us," Delia said, in the voice a mother uses for her children.

"The moment I tell, you will be in danger."

"We are caravan people; we have known danger. My feeling is that you are here for Lady Severin."

"That would be too complicated. I am here for her girl."

“How do you want to...?” Agitated, Panait could not end his sentence.

“I want to speak with Cantemir. He owes me a favor.” *He owes me three favors for saving his life.*

“Three days ago, I spoke with Cantemir. The day I received the title of Sage. I had a feeling that he was not happy about what happened in Severin. I was right, and I've since learned that he knew nothing when it was planned. Everything was between Orban and the Master Sage.”

“How could a woman do such a thing to another woman?” Codrin lamented. “Maud is even worse than Orban.”

“I should have guessed that you know who the new Master Sage is,” Panait sighed. “What I wanted to say is that it may be worth talking to Cantemir. I don't know that he can or will help you, but it worth trying.”

“I want to visit him this evening.”

“Since Lady Severin came, he sleeps mostly in the High Place.” That was how Panait called Orban's palace. “We shall have dinner. I will send a servant to see if Cantemir is at home. I bet that he isn't, but tomorrow, we will meet.”

He was right, and Codrin went to learn from Vlad what else he had gathered from the people at the inn.

৩৯

Cantemir was not surprised when Jara came into his office. It was early morning, and he was still not accustomed to sleeping in the palace instead of his home.

“This thing with Vio and Alic may end badly,” she said, even before seating herself.

“I did what I could.”

“Let's forget about that. Alic will attack her again.”

“I talked with Orban...”

“Orban wants to marry them.”

"I heard that," Cantemir sighed. "Three years is a long time. He may change his mind. Things may change around us."

"Alic will attack her again," Jara repeated.

"I stopped him when he tried to harass her. The guards are now warned."

"Twenty galbeni and they will forget the warning. Fifty more and they will help Alic to rape her. Are you so corrupt?"

"What do you want me to do?"

"To free Vio."

"I am thinking at that," Cantemir burst out. "But it will take a while to negotiate it with Orban and the Circle. They even refused to trade Vio for the Sage in Codrin's hands and Aron's son."

"We don't have that time. Send her away."

"I will just escort her to the gate of Arad, and she will walk away? An escape needs reliable people. I don't have them."

"And if you had them?" Jara asked, staring intently at him, Vio's Vision fresh in her mind.

"I don't have," Cantemir said, and suddenly became silent as Panait entered his office.

"If..." Jara insisted; her back was toward the door and she did not see it opening.

"Be silent," Cantemir snapped. "Yes, Panait." He stared at the Mester, both pleased and displeased by his intrusion.

"I apologize," Panait said. "Lady Severin," he bowed. "We need to talk." Panait frowned; Jara's presence was something that he did not expect, but it gave him an idea. "The Wraith of Tolosa is in Arad."

"Tudor?" Cantemir asked, forgetting that he was not alone with Panait.

Tudor, Jara thought. *That's the name Codrin is using in Arad.* "Cantemir, you were talking about trusted people. The Wraith of Tolosa is such a man."

"Do you know him?" Cantemir asked, thinking that everything was going in a direction he did not like.

"Yes."

"Tudor wants to see both of you." Panait decided that it was the right time to make all the links.

"Fate take you, Panait," Cantemir said. "I will meet him." His hand patted his chest.

"My stand is open today," Panait said to Jara, "and the market is not far from the palace. I have some boxes of mefilene."

Mefilene... Now I am sure that Tudor is Codrin. "Thank you Panait. Vio likes them."

"Cantemir?" Panait asked.

"If Mark stays in the palace, I see no reason to stop Jara and Vio from seeing the market. Please don't ask me more." Cantemir looked resigned; he had the feeling that he was being outmaneuvered by Panait. He glared at Jara, but meeting her eyes, and seeing a mother's expectation tamed him.

"Thank you. I will go to prepare Vio." Jara stood up, with the speed of a young girl, eager to leave.

"What was in your mind?" Cantemir asked, moving his irritation from Jara to Panait.

"We don't have much time. Tudor wants to take Vio away. After what happened between her and Alic... Don't look at me like that. All Arad knows that Alic and two soldiers tried to rape Vio. I am part of the Circle too, but that's not a reason to accept such things."

"I have to talk with Orban about letting Jara go to the market. Wait here."

Escorted by four soldiers, Jara and Vio went to the market trying to look like any other woman going to the market. Cantemir had convinced Orban to let them out of the palace. Vio's visit to the market would counter the rumors about her being raped by Alic.

"There was no rape," Orban protested.

"You know well how rumors work; each person spreading them adds something from their own imagination. Rape sounds more exciting than attempted rape. This is what we are," Cantemir shrugged. "If they see Vio happy in the market, people will forget."

"Mark will remain here," Orban said.

"Of course, he is too young to go to the market. People will understand that. They will also understand the need for an escort to protect the young girl from unwanted attention. She must be ... scared, now."

For half an hour, both women walked at leisure through the market, visiting stands and booths until they arrived at Panait's stand. As before, one soldier entered first to see the place, then Vio and Jara followed.

"Lady Severin," Panait bowed, "I am glad to see you here. The ladies are safe with me." He looked coldly at the soldier, who frowned, not knowing how to react. Panait was now the First Mester, and a known figure in Arad. In the end, the guard bent to the pressure in Panait's stare and chose to leave the stand. "You may come."

Following Delia, Codrin came out from the small room at the end of the stall. "Lady Jara," he bowed, a large smile on his lips. "Vio."

"Tudor!" Vio cried and jumped into his arms with amazing speed.

"We are missing a lot of things here," Delia whispered to Panait, staring at both Vio and Codrin.

"We don't have much time," Codrin said. "I am trying to take Vio away. Sorry, but I can't take you..." He looked at Jara, his lips tightened in a wry smile, Vio still in his arms.

"I understand that," Jara nodded, "and I am grateful to you for saving Vio."

"Vlad is with me in Arad, and I have five more soldiers waiting at an inn outside the city. We must act fast, while the preparations for..."

“Yes, my wedding can hide your actions,” Jara said firmly.

“My feeling is that Cantemir will cooperate. In two days from now, I plan to enter the garden just before midnight. You must get Vio there. Panait will bring Cantemir out of the palace today, so I can meet him. Does that work for you?”

“Yes.”

Chapter 15 – Jara / Codrin

Hidden by the darkness, Vlad leaned his back against the wall, and clasped his hands together. "I am ready."

Codrin placed the tip of his boot on Vlad's hands and sprang up. His fingers grabbed the edge of the wall, and in a few moments, he was lying on the embrasure. "Give me the ropes." The first one, he tied on a merlon on the street side. The second one toward the garden. "If I don't return in an hour, run."

"We'll see about that," Vlad said, knowing that he would wait longer, but there was no need to argue about that now.

After pulling on the second rope to check it, Codrin went down the wall, inside the garden. He was on foreign ground under the faint light of the moon. Obscurity was convenient and challenging at the same time. The palace garden was a square enclosure, three hundred feet wide, surrounded by walls on three sides. The fourth side was covered by the palace itself. Two walls separated the garden from other areas belonging to the palace. The last one faced the street where Vlad was waiting.

Motionless against the wall, Codrin strained his eyes into the night, then took time to listen. A bunch of crickets were saluting the moon, on the roof of the palace an owl was hooting, the wind was stirring some leaves. *Clear*, he thought, and started to walk slowly, his boot testing the ground before each step. There were some lights in the palace, giving him the general direction, but he was not sure where the door could be found. From time to time, he looked back over his shoulder; the darkness comforted him. After some long minutes, he reached the palace itself. From what he was able to guess, the door was not far away on his right. It was easier to walk on the small gravel path than through the grass. The moon had chosen to hide behind the clouds, and the stairs were concealed in the surrounding darkness; there were no lights at the windows around it. His left hand was touching the wall, his right was fumbling blindly in front of him until it touched the stairs. He decided not to climb and sat on the first step, his back leaning against the small wall bordering the stairs. Head in hands, he waited, thinking of Saliné, as he always did when he needed to calm his mind.

At some point, the horologe announced two hours before midnight. "Cantemir and Vio may come any moment," Codrin whispered, still leaning against the wall, just a few paces from the door.

It was fully dark when Drusila entered Arad. She was not alone; a five strong Wanderer Guard was with her, and Verenius, the new Primus Itinerant Sage, with his own guards. He was the third Primus in less than a month, and still pondering if such a quick advance was a good or a bad thing. He had certain powers now, but Verenius thought that the position counted on more than his own influence. Authority is better when built slowly.

In time, I may rise to the position, he thought, and what was bothering him the most was Maud's reluctant acceptance – she was attached to Aurelian, the Primus who was killed in Severin, and Verenius was one of the few who knew that Aurelian was her lover. And she thought that, at twenty-seven, Verenius was too young to be the Primus Itinerant.

"Present yourself," the guard ordered.

"Drusila, the First Light of the Wanderers and Verenius, the Primus Itinerant," one of the Circle's men announced.

There was a hush of voices behind the open window in the postern. "We will open the gate," one guard said.

"Faster!" Drusila shouted. Once her carriage entered the gate, the guards tried to stop it. "Don't stop," she ordered, and the carriage thundered on, making the guards jump aside.

"We are in a hurry," Verenius tried to calm the guards without dismounting. "Put your crossbow down, Orban is waiting for us." That was a lie, but it had the needed effect. The guards lowered their weapons, and two of them followed Verenius. They had the disadvantage of being on foot, so they arrived at the palace gate when the troubling guests had already passed through it.

Orban was awake. It was nothing unusual, he had trouble sleeping. "What the hell are you doing here?" he snapped when Drusila stormed into his suite without bothering to knock.

"What a refined man," she said, pointing at the book in his hands, derision filling her voice. "You are reading and dreaming about the woman who will join you in your bed."

"That's not your problem."

"Cantemir is right now sneaking Vio out of the palace, where Codrin is waiting for her. Would that be a problem?"

"I don't think so," Orban said, but he stood up.

"I ran like an idiot from Leyona, to arrive here in time, just to hear that you don't think there's a problem." At that moment, the horologe of the city announced one hour before midnight. *Vio must be in the garden with Cantemir and Codrin*, Drusila thought. *I arrived just in time.*

"Come with me, Drusila."

They left Orban's suite and found Verenius waiting in the main antechamber. Orban stared at him, but the Circle's man just shrugged, nodding toward Drusila. "Gold alarm," Orban said to the guards at the main door. That was the highest priority alarm in Arad. "Send couriers to both the palace and city gates:

no one is allowed to leave until I allow it. Form patrols and search the palace and the garden for the new girl. Bring Cantemir to me. Come," he said, opening the door going into Jara's suite, and let Drusila enter first.

"Oh, you suit each other." Drusila pointed at the book in front of Jara; she was reading at a small table in the corner of her antechamber.

"Is it too much hassle to expect a Wanderer to knock at the door and ask for permission before entering?" Jara asked coldly.

"Where is Vio?" Orban asked.

"She is sleeping."

"May I see her?"

"Why should I wake her?"

"We are wasting time," Drusila snapped and went toward the bedroom.

Jara jumped from her chair, and blocked Drusila before she could arrive at the door.

"Get out of my way," Drusila growled.

"Or what?" Jara moved toward her, like a giant cat, a fluid move from the Assassin Dance, and for all her fighting training, Drusila stepped back.

Despite the tension in the room, Orban frowned with amusement. "I want to see Vio."

Without a word, Jara opened the door; in the faint light of a candle, Vio was sleeping in her bed. "You will not enter," Jara whispered.

Behind Orban, Drusila craned her neck and bit her lip at the same time. *What went wrong with my Vision?* she thought. *The day? No, I saw Orban signing a document, and it was today.*

"You are getting old, Drusila," Orban said, after Jara closed the door, a malicious smile on his lips. "Your Visions are no longer what they were in the past."

"Maybe," Drusila said flatly.

"Leave now," Jara said, glaring at Drusila, fighting hard to hide her deception – the escape was compromised. She was almost to slap the Wanderer, and half stepped forward, then stopped and clasped her hands at her back. Drusila realized that but chose to ignore it.

"Sir Orban," a voice said from the hall. "We found Cantemir. He has been wounded."

"Try not to kill each other," Orban said, glancing at both Jara and Drusila, and then he walked out of the room.

"What was this circus?" Jara asked.

"You wanted to send Vio away. Something interfered with my Vision."

"Maybe Orban was right, and you are just getting old."

"Whatever happened, he will be more careful from now on. You know that."

"That pleases you. Probably it's what the Wanderers like to do now. Killing people, selling women, keeping children captive."

"The Wanderers have a goal, a new king for Frankis. It's not my fault that you are on the losing side."

"The Wanderers have nothing, not even shame or honor. Your false Vision made you act, thinking that you would stop a girl from evading her captors. A girl that barely escaped being raped a few days ago, by Orban's son. I pray to Fate to give you only false Visions. Maybe it has already started."

"I may negotiate with Orban and help Vio leave Arad."

"We agreed once in Valeni that she would remain in Codrin's custody."

"Things change."

"They change, indeed; since you became the First Light there is not much value in a Wanderer's word."

"Do you want Vio out?"

"Yes, I want her safe with Codrin."

"I will arrange that she leaves Arad in the Spring and come to stay with us in Alba."

"You are breaking another agreement and your own rules too. She must have a choice. At eighteen she can decide if she wants to be a Wanderer."

"It's too late for that. Either she becomes a Wanderer, or she stays here, with Orban."

"In the past, it was an honor to join the Wanderers, now..."

"Do you want her out of here or not?"

Yes, Jara nodded, her nails piercing her palm. "Talk with Orban." *By Spring we may have got her away, if not... It's still better with the Wanderers than close to Orban's son.*

"You may need this." Drusila took out a piece of paper from her pocket and stretched her hand toward Jara, who ignored it. With a shrug, she let the paper fell on the table. "An ancient recipe, it helps to avoid unwanted pregnancies. I don't think that you want a child from Orban."

"As if you would care about me. Now leave me alone." *I don't want to give a child to Orban, but you are playing him too.* She waited until Drusila left her suite and locked the door. She tried to control herself, but tears filled her eyes, despite her efforts to calm herself. Taking long breaths, she gradually calmed down and, walking briskly, she went to the bedroom. "Vio," Jara whispered, and embraced her daughter. "It was so close. You may undress now." It was only Vio's Vision about Drusila's arrival, one that had happened less than half an hour before, which had saved them. *How could Vio have a Vision of her own future?*

Vio jumped from her bed, took off her riding outfit and dressed herself in a night gown. "Did Cantemir go to warn Codrin?"

"Cantemir was wounded," Jara sighed. "We may learn more soon."

"I hope he was wounded after he warned Codrin."

Jara said nothing and embraced her daughter again. *I hope so too.*

"We found Cantemir, on the stairs leading into the garden," the soldier said before they entered the room. "I've already sent for a healer."

"What happened?" Orban asked, looking at Cantemir, who was lying in bed on his belly.

"Leave us alone," Cantemir said to the soldier who followed Orban inside the room. "Someone stuck a knife in my back. I think I was lucky that it hit a rib, and two servants came down the stairs before I was cut again," he said when he was alone with Orban. "The attackers ran away."

"Who were they?"

"A stranger and your son."

Orban closed his eyes for a few moments, then his face became like a stone again. "Drusila just came here, telling me that Vio was supposed to run away this night."

"And?" Cantemir asked, his voice weak.

"I found Vio sleeping."

"Sometimes, a Wanderer's Vision can be misleading, or even worse, they try to mislead people for their own purposes."

"We shall see. Are you able to talk? I want to bring Drusila and Jara here. After the healer sees you."

"Yes," Cantemir said. *I hope that I will not faint, but I want to see Drusila's face. I am sure she had a Vision. It went wrong, but how could Jara know that Drusila was coming to prevent Vio's escape? Her mother had the Light, so maybe she has it too. Or Vio has it. It can't be Vio who had the Vision about Drusila's arrival, as no one can see their own future, so it must be Jara. She kept her power well hidden, even from the Wanderers.* He closed his eyes, feeling at peace, even content, despite the growing pain in his body. After Orban came with the healer, Cantemir, having thought things through, pretended to be too weak for a talk, and everything was postponed for the next morning. He asked that Panait, the First Mester of Arad, be present too.

ର୬

Through the door, Codrin heard hurried steps coming toward him. *It doesn't sound like a walking girl*, he thought, and moved away fast, disappearing behind a bush twenty paces away from the entrance. The door opened, and nine soldiers, carrying torches, burst out. Keeping the bush between him and the soldiers, he stepped back, without losing sight of them.

"You three, take the left," the soldier who seemed to be the leader ordered.

Codrin took advantage of their distraction and moved further away, placing a second bush between him and the soldiers. *I can't run*, he pondered, *the light from the torches is strong, and movement will catch their attention.* Half-bent, he walked fast to the wall in front of him. It was not a direct path, more a zigzag passing between scattered bushes. The wall he aimed for was not the one he had climbed to enter the garden – the space was too open in that direction.

"You three, take the right. You two, come with me." The leading soldier moved toward Codrin, who was now halfway between the palace and the wall.

Arriving at the wall, Codrin measured it against the faint light of the moon. *It's too tall*, he mused, but feeling safe behind a thick tree, he jumped, trying to grip the edge of the wall between two merlons. He failed. *I need two feet more.* Walking on all fours, he moved along the wall, his hand sweeping the cold stones, trying to find a place where he could set his foot. After a while, he found a hook. It was stuck between two stones, three feet from the ground. With some hope, his fingers closed around the hook, taking its measures. *I can't climb it*, he decided after a while. *And anyway, it's too low to reach the edge from it and too late.* A team of three soldiers, carrying two torches, were now only thirty feet from him. Out of choices, he crouched behind a bush, waiting.

The soldiers were advancing slowly, searching every bush, the ones having torches walking in front. Tense and careful, they did not go far from each other, seeming to search a thirty-foot-wide band, and planning to return through another band toward the palace. It happened that Codrin was not in the center of the band, and he waited patiently. He had no other choice. On his right, a hundred feet away, another team of soldiers were advancing and, while still far from him, the light of the torches swept over him. At one point, one of those soldiers saw him, but he was unsure. From that distance, Codrin looked like a mound or a bush. Alert to both parties, Codrin saw the soldiers looking at him, but he did not try to run, just pushed his body more into the bush, lowering his head. He moved slowly, an inch at a time. Called by another soldier from his team, the man shrugged, and turned away. A bead of perspiration went down Codrin's neck, but at least now he could concentrate on the soldiers who were closer to him. Feeling covered by the bush, he straightened a bit, and his right hand went to his boot, extracting a knife. Then he unsheathed his sword and placed it at his feet, the hilt over his boot. By habit, his fingers gripped the hilt to get in touch with the spirit of the sword, but this was not Shadow, and he struggled to fight against a burst of panic. The closest soldiers finished searching another bush and moved toward him. Codrin glanced quickly from one man to another and to the wall. The moment the other two were looking in a different direction, his knife flew, piercing the neck of the man in front of him. The man gasped, and the torch fell from his hand. With feline certainty, Codrin grabbed his sword and sprang too. He trampled the torch but could not fully extinguish it. Cries filed the garden, and he attacked the two other soldiers close to him, cutting one en passant, before the surprised man could unsheathe his sword. The third one threw his torch toward Codrin. It flew, rotating and chasing the darkness with its flames. In haste, Codrin hit it with the flat of his sword, making it fly away. A clang of swords and the man died a moment later. Codrin caught him with his left arm, grabbing the sword from his hand with his right, and hurried the remaining ten feet toward the wall, pulling the dead man with him. All the other soldiers in the garden moved to surround him.

With a push of his shoulder, Codrin sent the soldier's body against the wall, and hung him by his belt on the hook. The back of the dead man was leaning on the wall. Blindly, his fingers found the right place on the nape, and he slid the captured sword between the thick shirt and the man's skin until a third of it passed down under the belt. He shook the body, but it seemed rigid enough, and he sheathed his sword. The point of his boot pressed hard against the buckle, and he sprang up, then climbed on the man's shoulders, jumping as high as he could. At the last moment, the fingers of his right hand grabbed the edge of the wall. Codrin sighed, and his second hand went up, and clutched the stone with a strong grip. Slowly, he went up, inch by inch, until his elbow passed over the wall. From that moment it was easy and, with two swift thrusts, he was now lying on the embrasure, between the merlons, ready to roll down onto the rampart. The moment his body moved, an arrow pierced his thigh. Pain came to him, shooting up and down on his spine, banging in his head. He moaned, and finally rolled down on the ashlars of the rampart. *The arrow hit the bone*. Codrin recognized the unusual pain. His hand blindly fumbled over the arrow. *A bolt... The wound may heal faster*. The shaft of the bolt was thicker than an arrow, but its point was thinner. It was made to pierce armor. *At least the point went out of my leg*. His fingers moved around the place where the iron went out of his flesh. *They will not try to climb. Not yet.* His eyes swept the garden over the embrasure and saw six men running through the garden with torches, and some more coming out from the palace. *I need to take out the shaft and stop the blood*. With one of his remaining knives, he cut a long piece from his pelerine, then another one, and laid them in front of him. Breathing deeply, he squeezed the point between his thumb and forefinger and snapped it. The shaft broke with a crack and he moaned like a dying animal. He breathed more, in and out, in bursts, until the blinding pain diminished. Below him, the first man arrived at the foot of the wall. Codrin chose to ignore him and sucked in as much air as he could. Holding his breath, he pulled the shaft from his leg. He saw black in front of his eyes, and his mind started to sink. *Don't*! he growled to himself. *Stay awake*. The blackness started to vanish, and, unsteadily, he tied the first piece of cloth around his wound, then the second one over the first. *I hope it's enough to stop the blood.*

He breathed deeply again, then threw the remainder of his pelerine over the wall, on the side opposite to the garden, and started to move on his hands and the healthy knee, trailing his wounded leg. At the corner of the wall, he turned to the right and arrived at the merlon where his rope was tied. Absorbed by his moves and pain, Codrin did not see that the first soldier had climbed the wall on a wood ladder, at the same point he went up on the corpse ladder.

A second soldier climbed, and his torch sent light over the rampart. "Blood," he said, his fingers touching the red spots on the stones. "He was wounded," the soldier shouted, and then he saw the remains of the bolt. "He took the bolt out."

"I think he went over the wall," another soldier said, advancing slowly, trying to find more spots of blood on the stones.

"Look there!" another one shouted, pointing down the wall, on the other side. "There is a pelerine on the ground."

After a brief argument, the ladder which helped them to climb the wall was brought up, and they split in two groups. One walked along the wall, the second one went down on the other side.

Codrin grabbed the rope, and let his body slip over the embrasure. Hand over hand, he slid down until his healthy foot touched the ground.

"What happened?" Vlad asked.

“Something went wrong. We must leave. See if you can take down the ropes.”

Vlad climbed up and untied the rope which had helped Codrin climb down into the garden. They were not really tied, only turned twice around the merlon. He threw the rope down on the side where Codrin was waiting, then untied the second rope, and placed its middle over the merlon. He slid down, keeping both parts of the rope in his hands, then pulled the rope down. “Let’s go,” he said after collecting the ropes. Codrin was already a few paces away, walking slowly, limping. “You are wounded.”

“I will survive, but I may need help at some point. We need to reach the fountain.”

“They are coming,” Vlad said, seeing the light of the torches approaching them, and gripped Codrin by the elbow. They lay down behind the fountain, hoping that it was not too late.

Chapter 16 – Codrin

Close to midnight, the streets were empty, the sound of running soldiers following them, closer and closer, the light from their torches growing. At least the torches allowed Codrin to know how far behind them the soldiers were. Limping badly, he tried to walk faster, his arm around Vlad's neck. He could hardly stand on his wounded leg. They turned to the right, and for a few moments, the sound of the walking boots behind them faded.

"One hundred paces left." Codrin gritted his teeth and forced himself to lean a little more on his wounded leg, to gain speed. He moaned, but they advanced a bit faster. Behind them, the sound of the walking boots grew again. *They are at the corner,* he thought without turning, *but we are close.*

The darkness was almost complete, but he knew all the stones on that street. For more than five years, Panait's house was his second home. The horologe of the city beat for midnight, covering the boot marching on the stones; the soldiers were careless. Followed by Vlad, Codrin entered the house half a minute later. Both Delia and Panait were waiting for them, and for Vio. It took Delia just a glance to understand that something had happened, and she closed the door fast behind them while Panait put out the candle. The scent of burnt wick lingered for a while. One minute later, the marching soldiers passed by the house, and then the noise of their footsteps grew fainter and fainter. The long road from Orban's castle had taken its toll, and Codrin was breathing heavily, leaning against the wall, eyes closed. Panait came with another lighted candle, and Codrin made an effort to hide his suffering and stand without leaning against the wall.

"I just need to take my stuff, and we will leave," he said.

"You are wounded," Delia gasped.

"It's not a big deal. I just need some light to tie a better bandage, and I will be gone."

"Where is Vio?"

"We were betrayed."

"Come with me." She took Codrin by the arm, and discreetly nodded at Panait, who nodded back and left the hall. "I will send one of my men to bring a healer."

Biting his lip, Codrin forced himself to walk without leaning on Vlad or Delia. He was at least lucky that the first door was only three paces in front of him. They entered the room and he seated himself on the first chair in his path, a moan escaping his mouth.

"I don't need a healer," he breathed, "Vlad is well trained to mend a wound. I don't even need stitches."

Delia went out to bring more candles, and then helped Vlad to find Codrin's Assassin healing kit. Back in the room, Vlad untied the bandage Codrin has made while he was on the wall and examined the wound. It was soaked in blood. The edges looked fine, but the arrow had passed through the middle of the muscle, doing a lot of damage, and the flow of blood, while slower, had not stopped yet. At least in this, Codrin was right, there was no need for stitches. Vlad disinfected the wound with alcohol and made a new, tighter bandage.

"You've lost a lot of blood," Vlad said, when Delia went out of the room for a few moments. Codrin's trousers were soaked down to his ankle.

"I will be fine." Codrin unclenched his mouth to answer. "Orban will hunt us, and I don't want to endanger Delia and

Panait. Give me a few minutes, and I will be ready to go." He closed his eyes, and his breath started to follow the 'pain killer' pattern of the Assassin Dance.

Vlad looked at him and began to doubt that Codrin would be able to walk his way out of the city in less than a week. Their reserve plan was that they would hide in a small room Codrin had bought two years ago. It had the disadvantage of being far from Panait's house.

"Tell me when Delia or Panait are back," Codrin said, his eyes still closed. "Where are they?"

"I don't know. Do you fear...?"

"No," Codrin said firmly. "I trust them. When I walk out, don't try to help me. I will manage it ... for a while." He said nothing more until Delia finally returned, and Vlad shook his arm. "We have to leave, Delia."

"That wound will not let you walk much. You will stay here. Our house is your house."

"I can't." Biting his lip, Codrin stood up, went out of the room and started to walk toward the main door.

"Tudor," she said gently, "please don't be stubborn; stay here."

"It's too dangerous. We were betrayed, and Orban's men are searching for me. I even don't know what happened to Vio and Cantemir."

"We will hide you."

"No. Think of your children. I don't want to put you in danger. I killed three guards, and Orban may be more than a little mad right now." Codrin was in front of the main door and, trying to open it, found that it was locked. "Delia," he turned toward her.

"I would not have had children without you saving us in the Cursed Forest."

Just then, Panait came back into the small hall.

"Panait," Codrin said, fighting hard to keep his voice even. "Please open the door. I don't want to endanger you. We need to leave; Orban is hunting us."

"It's better if you leave through the back door," Panait said. "Follow me."

Codrin nodded, and started to walk again, ignoring the fierce pain that burned through his wounded bone into his spine. He could do nothing to ignore his weakness. With each step, his breathing became shallower. They arrived at some stairs, and he bit his lip.

"Vlad, I need your help to climb down," he whispered. "Be discreet."

Delia saw Vlad's hand gripping Codrin's arm but said nothing. Finally, they arrived at what looked like a secret door. When it was not needed, the door was hidden by an armoire which had been moved away.

"Here," Panait said, opening the door, and all four entered the secret room.

"Where is the next door?" Codrin asked.

"There is no next door," Panait said. "Sorry for this ... but you will not leave my house with such a wound. You are safe here."

Codrin opened his mouth to protest, but weakness bit him, and he went pale beneath the coppery stubble of his beard. He stumbled, and whatever he wanted to say remained between his tight lips. Vlad and Panait took him by the arms and made him lie in bed.

Delia sat on the edge of the bed and gently stroked his hair. "I hope that you will not be wounded again, but if there is a next time, don't try to deceive me. I treated many wounds when we were traveling with the caravans. Did the arrow touch the bone of your leg?"

Yes, Codrin nodded, remembering the sharp pain going up his leg and spine, into his head. Her brows rose slightly, and a grimace twisted the fine-cut lips on one side.

ᔓᔕ

Considering that Cantemir had felt so weak the evening before, he looked well in the morning when everybody who counted met in his room. Considering that he had faked his weakness, he felt no better than the day before.

"We have a little charade to solve," Orban said, before everybody could be seated.

"Did you catch the assailant or assailants?" Cantemir asked.

"Why are you thinking in plurals?"

"I had a flashback. There was a second man down the stairs. He seemed to be keeping an eye on the door going into the garden."

"There was a man there," Orban agreed.

"You caught him." *I hope not. I think not. I would have known already*. Thoughts swirled in Cantemir's mind, and he closed his eyes. His reaction did not pass unobserved, but everybody put it down to his weakness. Except Jara and Panait.

"No," Orban said. His usual rage rose inside, but nothing of it was reflected in his voice or face. "He killed three soldiers, but he escaped. Not unharmed. He took a bolt. We don't know how bad his wound is. My men are combing the city after him. After them; there was a second man waiting for him outside the garden."

"And the third one?" Cantemir asked, trying not to think about Codrin's wound.

"The third one vanished without a trace."

"Did you ask your...?"

"My son hired one of them, but as usual he doesn't know much."

"It may be that the unknown man hired him," Cantemir suggested, "and I think that the second one was there in reserve."

"The second one was there to help Vio escape," Drusila said.

"What do you mean?" Cantemir asked.

"Drusila told us a nice story about you helping Codrin to sneak Vio away," Jara said, her voice cold and calculated.

"That young wolf who gives Maud the headaches?" This time, Cantemir was genuinely surprised, and Orban slightly amused, thinking of Maud's headache, even though he had one of his own, but Codrin seemed to provoke a greater one. "How would he enter Arad?" Cantemir shook his head.

"Drusila thinks that the man who attacked you is unrelated to the other one," Orban said.

"Drusila would say whatever she wants to prove her failed Vision right. If it was a Vision. Isn't this strange?" Cantemir mused. "I was attacked, exactly when she bypassed the protocol and entered the palace without the right permission."

"Are you accusing me?" Drusila asked, coldly.

"I only want to underline that we had a strange chain of events. You claim to have had a Vision about me helping Vio to run away, and I was attacked after you entered the palace with your guards."

"And?"

"If Cantemir had been dead, Drusila would have claimed that her Vision was right, and only that *accident* stopped Vio from escaping," Jara interjected. "Of course, Vio sleeping in her bed was just another accident."

"Suppositions," Drusila shrugged.

"My wound is not a supposition," Cantemir snapped. His hand moved to enhance his words, and he bent in pain. "Verenius, Panait," he said when the pain subsided, "I want to file a complaint that Drusila and Maud planned to kill me."

"Let's not go so far," Verenius said in haste, trying to gather his thoughts. "There is nothing to prove that they were involved, and Sages don't kill Sages. You know that."

"Oh, I know it very well. Panait, please give me that casket," Cantemir pointed to the one sitting on his desk. "Open it," he said when Panait came with it, "I am too weak." When the box was open, Cantemir took out the paper sitting on the top, which

Codrin had brought him two days ago. "Read it," he gave the paper to Verenius. "Read it aloud."

Verenius complied and read quickly until he arrived at the last sentence. He finished the letter in his head, and remained silent, trying to buy some time.

"Did you lose your voice, Verenius?"

"Aron offered five hundred galbeni to kill you," Verenius said quietly.

"He could not do that without Maud's permission."

"You have no proof of that."

"At least you have a proof that some Sages try to kill Sages, even a Master Sage as I was then. This was the third attempt on my life. The assassins hired in that letter failed, and yesterday we had another attempt, just when our dear Drusila stormed our palace during the night. You should remember that she is Maud's sister. Both people who attacked me were competent, and they were able to vanish without a trace."

"You are wounded and in pain," Drusila said. "You try to find guilt where there is none. Let's wait until your head is clear."

"Oh, but my head is clear, Drusila. I wonder, though, how clear your head was when you told us that story about me and Codrin sending Vio away. Me and Codrin. How could I perform such a delicate task with a man I've never met? A man who had never been to Arad. What was in your mind, Drusila?"

"He was in my Vision," she said dismissively, trying to keep her voice calm.

"He was in your invented story, nothing else. You tried to weaken Arad by killing its Secretary. Verenius, please register my complaint," Cantemir said, glaring at the Primus Itinerant.

"We are going nowhere." Drusila's knuckles went white from the strength of her grip against the hard wood of her chair. Luckily for her, her hands were hidden by the folds of her dress.

"We did not go far, but..." Orban shrugged. "Drusila, you have an hour to leave Arad. Don't try to return without my permission. Even though I will give it, next time you should come during the day. Let Cantemir rest. Jara, please come with me."

They walked in silence for a while until Orban asked, "Would you enter into a plot to make Vio run away?"

"Would you want me to lie?" Jara replied.

"No, but don't try to send Vio away."

"Would you let her go after our wedding?"

"I know how much you care about her, but I can't," he said, and moved faster, leaving Jara alone and wondering if he could not or would not.

She followed him inside his suite before saying, "The Circle and Codrin care about her too."

"Then why is she here?"

"They want to keep the pressure on Codrin. There was an understanding that he was to marry Vio."

"I may enjoy spoiling the Circle's game and stop that wedding."

"You may, but your position may become untenable."

"And who is your best hope? The new Master Sage? Or your young champion, who is good enough to win a fight, only to lose the war? Codrin took Leyona and lost it," Orban said, feeling that Jara did not understand him. "He destroyed Aron's army and took his castle and second son but could not free your other daughter. At least he hanged a Primus Itinerant, something that I never dared to do."

"What?" Jara gasped and wrung her hands. *Why did he do that? The Circle will never forgive Codrin.*

"Codrin hanged Belugas not far from Severin's gate, and even wrote Sage on a placard and hung it around the Sage's neck. I very much enjoyed that fine piece of irony. It seems that you did not enjoy it."

"No."

"You think he is in danger. You care about him." Orban frowned, massaging his chin. "Strange that I did not realize it until now. That means that your links with Codrin are deeper than I thought."

He stood up, and walked toward the window, staring away into the distance, pondering on his new knowledge. "I will take care that my son doesn't bother your daughter and forget about their wedding." *I may try to come to an understanding with Codrin. Nothing would please me more than to piss on the Circle.*

"Thank you," Jara breathed.

"I hope you can bear me for a little longer," Verenius said, when he remained alone with Cantemir.

"After surviving Drusila, I don't imagine I'll die from talking to you."

"This thing," Verenius gestured with the letter still gripped between his fingers, "should have been discussed with a more select audience."

"Why? To let Maud bury it as soon as possible?"

"Do you really think that she was involved?"

"Yes. From the day I opposed her scheming with Aron to make Bucur our Candidate King, our relation turned sour. She chose to go forward even though Bucur is a joke. Both Drusila and Maud knew this. All his so-called achievements were actually down to Codrin. All her hopes are now with the Duke of Tolosa. With his army, as that man is the stooge of his wife, who happens to be Maud's daughter."

"I know about Bucur, but it seems that we've learned everything a little too late. Even your warning about Bucur came too late."

"And Maud, do you think the same about Maud? Did she not know about Bucur when she was so close to Aron? We are in a difficult position right now."

"I don't know. It may be that she knew, but her plan is to gather both Peyris and Tolosa behind the Candidate King. It's not the right man. It's the right plan. We have a good chance to make Frankis a kingdom again."

"Do you have more questions?" Cantemir asked coldly.

"Whatever the past, we are now bound to help Bucur. You know that."

"One day, I may tell you more about that." Cantemir closed his eyes and remained silent. Verenius had no choice but to leave him alone.

Chapter 17 - Codrin

Codrin didn't begin to wake up until late in the morning. It was a gradual process, and for a few moments he could not remember anything. Not the place and not the time. Struggling to drag himself fully awake, he stirred and rolled onto his side, sending a soft groan against the walls of a room with no windows and no echo. The walls were covered with wood. A faint scent of baked bread washed over him, and a glimpse of Jara's hunting house surged into his mind: Milene cooking in the large kitchen, and Vio sneaking around to steal fresh hot cookies. *It can't be.* The sharp, bitter metallic taste in his mouth overrode his daydream and forced him to recall the day before. *I was wounded.* That awful taste always followed a wound. Opening his eyes, Codrin found Delia sitting on the edge of his bed. He blinked against the gentle light of the candles and, silent, he ran his fingers through his tangled hair. With the returned memories came the understanding of his situation and the fears about everyone else involved in Vio's escape.

"Don't worry, everything is fine," Delia said before he could speak. "Apart from the wounds."

"Wounds?"

"Cantemir was wounded too, but his life is not in danger."

"Orban must have caught him. What happened to Vio and Jara? What happened to Cantemir?" Codrin sighed and closed his eyes, trying to think what he could do. *Nothing*. He shook his head, then breathed deeply, as he recalled walking here in the middle of the night. Despite his attempt to leave the house, he was grateful that they had tricked him stay. Even now he felt exhausted, and he was lightheaded. At least he had a night to rest and heal. *I must leave, Orban will send his men here.*

"Both girls are fine, and Orban knows nothing. Even now, it's quite difficult to understand what happened yesterday. I will tell you more when you have eaten." She pointed to the table, where breakfast was waiting for him. And that fresh bread, its scent so real. "How is your wound?"

"Like any wound." Codrin shrugged and pulled the blanket away from his leg. He looked at the bandage: it was soaked in blood, and the bed sheet was filled with small red spots, but all seemed to be dry now. "It could be better," he moaned, standing up.

"Lean on me. Panait ordered a cane for you; it should arrive at noon."

He placed an arm over her shoulders, and they walked together toward the table. "Thank you." Codrin sighed and seated himself with a grimace, his jaw clenched, waiting for the pain to recede. "Now tell me," he said, taking a piece of bread from the basket.

"Drusila came late in the evening."

"The bitch," Codrin snapped, "she must have had a Vision. How low could a Wanderer go, to stop a young girl's escape?"

"A Vision, she claimed," Delia smiled. "But it seems that there was another Vision about her arrival, and Jara canceled everything, just when Vio was about to leave. She sent Cantemir to warn you. The moment Drusila arrived, she grabbed Orban and took him to Jara's room to show him that Vio was already gone. It seems that she even knew the exact time of her escape. They found Vio in bed. Dressed in her riding suit but *sleeping*. Jara did not let them wake her daughter. I wish I could see Drusila's face." Delia burst into laughter.

"Then who wounded Cantemir?"

"It seems that Orban's son hired an assassin."

"The timing is quite strange."

"Yes, and Cantemir put the attempt on his life on Drusila too. It may be true, but we don't really know," Delia said, a touch of worry in her voice. "The man vanished, even though he was a stranger, so he was good at his job. Cantemir escaped only because some servants arrived on the stairs and forced the assassin to run. Orban has banned Drusila from Arad. I don't think that anyone will miss her, not even Orban."

Thoughtfully, Codrin pushed away the plate in front of him, but Delia pushed it back. "You need to eat."

"I need to think."

"You can't leave Arad for two or three weeks, so you have all the time in the world." She remained silent, waiting for him to finish. "I remember the day when Vio visited our stand and found you there," she said, after a while. "First I thought that helping her escape was a Wraith's job, but it seems to me now that it was more than that."

"It was a Wraith's job," Codrin smiled. "And more than that. I can't hide that I know her. Can I?"

"Not after she jumped into your arms. And Jara did not ask where you would take her daughter. She trusted you completely. You are ... close to her family."

"Yes."

"There must be a story behind such ... closeness."

"Something not much different to meeting you in the Cursed Forest."

"I considered that." Delia placed her palm over his. "You are always eager to help people, but..." she bit her lip. "I am sorry if I ask too much about this. In Severin, no one seems to know Tudor, the Wraith of Tolosa."

"Maybe now is the right time to know more about me," Codrin sighed. "There are two protectors under my skin. One is the Wraith of Tolosa, the other one is..."

"Codrin," Delia said and squeezed his hand gently. "We knew about a young man from Arenia who found a new home in Jara's home the same year you came here. A protector always dressed in black and always traveling. Like you. The strangest thing was that nobody outside Severin knew about a protector named Codrin, even though he seemed to be quite successful. Merchants have their ways of learning things," she smiled, "but I could not connect the dots until Vio jumped in your arms. I wished I had known about Codrin earlier."

"I am sorry if I upset you, but it was better to have two separate identities. No one in Severin knew about Tudor, and no one here knew about Codrin. Until now. Don't think that it was easy for me to live in two different worlds."

"I am not upset. You risked your life for people you thought deserved it. My thought was that maybe we could have helped you better."

"You helped me when it counted." Codrin raised her hand and kissed it.

"I am just a merchant's daughter and wife," she said shyly, trying to pull her hand away.

He gripped it gently, not letting her escape. "You deserved it as much as some women having a title and more than some others who have and don't deserve it."

Delia's eyes glimmered with that fondness mothers reserve for their children, and she remained silent.

"Does Panait know too?" Codrin asked, tentatively.

"Not yet, and I will let a few days pass before telling him. There is too much on his plate right now. Will you tell Cantemir?"

"Not yet." Codrin closed his eyes and smiled. *It will take a while to tell him.*

ꕥ

Even after two glasses of old cognac, Verenius was not in a good mood – during the last two days, he had too many things to worry about. There was Cantemir's wound, the previous assassination attempts on Cantemir that had been ordered by Aron, the attempt at an escape that may or may not have happened, and all the events of the night before that weren't linking well. "Too many strange things," he muttered and took another sip, which slipped down his throat like fire, then wiped his mouth with the back of his hand. The delicate scent of alcohol filled his nostrils, and he breathed deeper. *The two men that entered the palace during that night had acted very differently.* The one who had wounded Cantemir escaped through a small gate going from the garden into the stable's precincts, a gate that was usually closed. The other one climbed a wall. Because a Sage was involved, Verenius did not share his worries with Orban. *They did not work together.* He shook his head and wondered if Orban was aware of that. And there was the other piece of weirdness he had heard just a few hours before: Lady Jara visited Panait's stand just two days earlier. "I have to talk with Panait." He stood up and went to the window: there was a touch of pink in the east. "It's still early."

If Panait was surprised at Verenius's sudden visit, he did not show it. He was angry that the visit was not announced; Vlad was with him and Delia, but he did not show any irritation either. "How is Cantemir?" Panait asked, even though he had left the wounded man the evening before.

"It's not a serious wound," Verenius said. "Cantemir was at least that lucky." He looked at Vlad, then his stare moved to Panait and back to Vlad. *Did I see this young man before?* He frowned briefly, then his face became immobile.

Vlad nodded before Panait could speak again, saying, "Sage Verenius." His voice was flat and missing any trace of interest.

"Have we met before?"

"People meet sometimes on the streets of Tolosa."

"Tolosa..." Verenius rubbed his chin, trying to work out if he could place Vlad there. His face was vaguely familiar, but their brief encounter had happened on a corridor in Cleuny, when the Sage visited Codrin.

"Vlad is the right hand of Tudor, the Wraith of Tolosa." Feeling trouble, Panait interjected before Verenius could finish his thought.

"Ah, the ever-elusive Wraith of Tolosa." Verenius was still rubbing his chin. "Little is known about him in the Circle. Is Tudor here too?"

"He left two days ago. And it's quite strange to think that Tudor is not known to the Circle when he saved Cantemir's life three times, and he saved us too." Panait's hand gestured between Delia and him.

"Ah, he was the one?" *I wish he had not found the letter from Aron.* "Was Tudor in your stand when Lady Jara visited it?"

"Why would that be of interest to you?" Panait asked, flatly.

"I was wondering if he knows her."

"They saluted each other."

"Could they have met again later?"

"Tudor stayed with us when the ladies left my stand, but you can ask the soldiers who escorted them. What's on your mind?" Feigning his disinterest, Panait looked at Verenius, who did not seem to be at ease.

"I suppose that you have important things to discuss, please excuse me," Vlad said and stood up.

Verenius waited patiently for Vlad to leave before saying, "The two men who were spotted in the palace did not work together. One of them had a key, the other jumped over the wall."

"Cantemir thought that they worked together. Maybe it was just an issue of timing, the intruders could not find each other at the right moment, or it was a strategy to leave by separate routes," Panait shrugged. "What has this to do with Tudor?"

"What if Drusila was right about the escape? I understand that Vio has the Light. She could have had a Vision too and stopped everything."

"Verenius, I know that you are affected by the attack on Cantemir, as much as we are. And perhaps even more so because of that letter from Aron, but," Panait looked at him with the kind of indulgent stare an adult usually throws at a child, "how could Vio have a Vision about her future? And how could she leave the palace? Orban is known for his tight security, and we both know why. The Wanderers are a manipulative lot, and Cantemir is not quite on good terms with Drusila and her sister, who happens to be our Master Sage. Again, we both know why. Think about that letter again. If you are just trying to prevent Cantemir's formal complaint against Maud and Aron, I will not help you. What will happen if we start to kill each other?"

"You are right," Verenius said absently, thinking that he would be in an unenviable position when he returned to Leyona. "I hope Orban finds the wounded man. He may clarify some things. If Tudor returns before I leave Arad, please tell him that we need to meet."

"He always stays in our house," Panait said. "It will not be a problem."

Chapter 18 - Codrin

Cleuny did not look much different when Codrin returned, carrying with him the burden of another failure. At least he was content to have seen Jara and Vio. In the inner court, carts were lined up against the wall; the provisions Mara ordered had started to arrive in the last few days. And children were playing between them; the servants from Severin had arrived a week ago. Entering the house, Codrin tried to conceal his limp, but the pain was accentuated by the ride. He didn't need help, but there was no way to hide from Mara's perceiving eyes when he entered the council room; luckily, she was alone. He could not hide neither the wound on his leg, nor the wound inside him.

She stood up and came to meet him, embracing him, arms laced around his neck, saying in a caring tone, "Welcome back." Her words, voice and gesture were a comfort to Codrin.

He pulled her closer, and neither of them spoke for a while. "It's good to be home," he finally said.

"There are many things to talk about, but they can wait until dinner. The scouts let us know you were coming, and a bathtub is waiting in your room."

He felt refreshed after the bath. Food was waiting for him in the antechamber. And Mara. He did not speak while he ate, and she did not try either.

"I can give you the latest news," she said, while he was chewing the last piece of steak. "We have gathered food for six months. Laurent and Marat were most helpful; they brought more than half of our provisions. Laurent promised to send three more carts in a week; it seems that he was able to take over the east of Severin from Aron quite quickly. Most of it, at least. We still need to cover almost three more months."

"Deva," Codrin said, still chewing, his voice muffled. He swallowed and was finally able to speak properly. "But we will send a courier from Poenari. It doesn't make sense to gather everything here, only to transport it again. Poenari is closer to Deva. What else has happened here?"

"Nothing. Things are calm. Sava sent word that no one has come to Poenari. It seems to be a place of ghosts."

"And you?" Codrin gestured at her.

"I am fine too." Mara smiled, touching her belly, "and growing. Tell me what happened."

"I failed," Codrin said with a grimace. There was pain throbbing in his voice.

Mara stood up, and came on his side of the table, in front of him, and leaned on it, her hand resting on his shoulder. "You failed in some things; you succeeded in others. Life is like that."

"Orban's son tried to rape Vio."

"Like father like son." She looked at him, pondering how much she could ask. "Tell me everything."

"That bitch, Drusila, had a Vision about me sneaking Vio out of Arad, and she came to warn Orban. I barely escaped alive." Codrin massaged his thigh.

"Vio?" Mara risked a difficult question, feeling that Codrin needed to get things off his chest.

"She is fine; Jara aborted the plan just before Drusila arrived in Arad. It was almost midnight. Drusila traveled through the darkness. She knew when and how I would take Vio out. At least, she did not know who helped me," Codrin sighed. "I had to kill three soldiers and Orban was in a rage."

"How did Jara...?

"Vio has the Light, and a Vision came to her too. This thing about Vio stays between us," Codrin said, stroking her hand. "It was strange timing, just a few minutes before Drusila arrived in the palace. And even stranger was that someone tried to kill Cantemir at the same time. It looked as if Orban's son was behind the attempt, but that young man is not the cleverest of men, and it may be that someone else manipulated him."

"Is Cantemir well?" Mara asked, and Codrin nodded. "And you?"

"It could be better, but I am already able to walk. From how the wound looks, it seems that there will be no long-term effects. I will know more in a week or two when I start training again. I must be more careful," he said, suddenly lost in thought.

"What is worrying you?"

"The new Itinerant Sage came with Drusila, and he seems to be an astute observer. He deduced that I was not linked to the assassin who tried to kill Cantemir, and he found Vlad. Orban's men interrogated him for a few hours."

"I saw Vlad," Mara said tentatively.

"Ah, yes. They don't know me in Arad as Codrin, and in the past I saved Cantemir's hide three times. He convinced Orban to release Vlad; but I put him in danger."

"Danger is everywhere."

Poenari fortress was the strangest thing Codrin had ever seen. The main wall was a semicircle, six hundred feet long and ninety feet tall. It was squeezed between two towers which were not built by men; they were natural formations, almost circular, six hundred feet in diameter and three hundred feet tall. On their tops, some defensive structure had been raised, their merlons visible from the valley. From where he stood, the basalt towers resembled a black organ, ready to be played by a giant's fingers. Seen from above, later, Poenari was even stranger than Codrin had imagined. The two towers were, in fact, the visible parts of a huge natural structure having the shape of a horseshoe. The wall simply enclosed it, creating a four-fifths natural, one-fifth man-made fortress. It was impossible to climb the three-hundred-foot-tall basalt lateral ridges, and while the back of the horseshoe shape was lower, it was still an impressive hundred fifty feet tall, and a small wall was built on top of it. There was a difference in this part of the structure too: while it was made of the same black basalt, the back of the horseshoe did not look like a monolith. It was like a giant hammer had smashed the mountain and left the pieces in place, in an agglomeration of rocks that became cemented together over time.

"What do you think?" Vlaicu asked.

"You were right, it's not easy to conquer such a fortress, and the wall seems to be in a much better shape than I expected. The merlons and the parapet look undamaged from here. I can't say yet if we have enough men to defend it. I must see what's behind this wall."

"Let's do that. I haven't been inside yet," Vlaicu agreed.

They followed the road and, after a steep curve, two things came into sight: a young girl walking alone, and the gate of Poenari. Codrin's eyes moved from one thing to another, and even though it was strange to see a lone girl in that wilderness, the gate attracted his attention more. It was not built in the middle of the wall, but on the right-hand side, at the border between the wall and the natural tower, and it was placed thirty feet from the base of the wall. There was a road, dug into the stone, curving around the tower.

Cleyre was right, with a drawbridge in place, no one can break through that gate, Codrin thought, and pushed his horse faster to reach the girl, who was scared now and trying to climb away from the road. "You have nothing to fear." He dismounted in front of her; she was already perched on a tall rock, menaced him with a dagger, her blue eyes intent on him. "We are going to Poenari. If you want, I can take you on my horse."

Her eyes moved from him to his horse, and she bit her lip, saying nothing, her fingers gripping tighter on the dagger.

"His name is Zor," Codrin pointed to his horse. "He likes little girls."

"I am fourteen," she snapped, shaking her head, her long blonde hair flying around it.

"I apologize if I offended you. Zor likes young people. Come," he extended his arm toward her. "There are many soldiers behind me. It would have been easy to capture you if I wanted to do that."

Reluctantly, she took his hand and jumped down from the rock. Codrin extended his arm again and grabbed her basket.

"Mountain berries," he took a few to taste. "They are nicely ripe. I am Codrin."

"Amelie," the girl said. "They are for my grandfather and my sister. She wants to make a pie."

"Now, let's meet Zor." He gave the basket back to her. "But we must hide the berries from him."

Amelie smiled for the first time, and without waiting for Codrin, she walked over to Zor. When she got to him, her left hand was filled with berries, and the horse found them quickly, then let her play with his mane."

"Zor, you are a traitor," Codrin laughed. "Ready?" He looked at the girl, and when she nodded, gripping the basket, he lifted her into the saddle, and mounted behind her. "Do you live in Poenari or in a village nearby?"

"The villages are far away," Amelie said. "The closest one is six miles from here. We don't have many visitors in Poe," she said after a pause. "That's what we call Poenari. It's a bit long, the full name."

"I am planning to stay for a while," Codrin said cautiously. "How many people live there?"

"More than one hundred. Do you have enough food?" She turned swiftly and glanced back at the long row of soldiers following them.

"We have some food with us, and carts will bring more in two or three days, and more people. Are there places from we can buy food?"

"The villages, but they don't have much. Except Chevres, which is larger, but it's fifteen miles from here, and even there you will not find food for... How many people you are you bringing?"

"More than two hundred."

"Why are you coming with so many people?"

"I don't like to walk alone," Codrin laughed. "I am also carrying a little secret, but I will tell it to you later."

They were now three hundred paces from the gate, and Codrin saw that there was no gate, only the old frame and the mouth of a long tunnel passing between the wall and the mountain.

"Sava, take four men and announce our arrival," Codrin ordered.

Sava was the first to enter Poenari through the decayed gate, which could not be closed. Despite decades of neglect, the old fortress was still impressive, and he took his time to look at the thick walls. Even in its broken state, the gate could at least be used to block a part of the tunnel, but it seemed that nobody had thought of it, and there was no sentry to guard it; but there were signs of habitation and, even with his great experience in handling people, he felt uneasy negotiating free passage for Codrin, who did not want to enter by force. There was something strange in the fortress, a feeling that haunted him. The tunnel went on for longer than he thought, and it looked as strange as the rest of Poenari. It was twenty feet around, with a paved floor, and while the wall was smooth and seemed to be carved out of stone, the floor was made of laid stones and mortar. It appeared to be a hundred-twenty-foot-long circular tunnel filled with stones to make passage easier.

"Hello!" Sava shouted when he had left the tunnel, and the only answer was the echo of his horse's metal shoes on the stones. The sound reverberated off the walls. He urged his horse forward and entered the first precinct. The view surprised him; from outside, there were no signs of a second, inner wall. And from here the main, outer wall looked even stranger. Inside, it rose at an angle, making it trapezoidal in section. He rode left and right for a few hundred paces, to see only empty walls and houses and then went further toward the second gate. While smaller, this was in a better shape, but it was open too, and through it, he saw people for the first time: a few soldiers – older than him, some the age of his father, if he were still alive – two women, both in their mid-thirties, and a child around ten years old. Showing no fear, they looked at him with a trace of curiosity while he dismounted. Three of his soldiers were still with him, while the fourth went back to tell Codrin and his army that they could enter, as there was no danger.

"Good evening," Sava nodded to them. "You have nothing to fear. Seigneur Codrin will enter the castle soon," he said, with a broad, friendly smile on his lips.

His words seemed to have an effect like lightning. All those eyes which had been scrutinizing him became filled with wonder. The women covered their gaping mouths; the soldiers formed a single rank, though only one of them was armed, with a dagger. The youngest soldier ran toward a large house close to the gate.

"We come in peace," Sava said, but the people seemed too agitated to even answer him. *What's wrong?* He rubbed his chin. "Go back and tell Codrin that while there is no danger, the people here are a bit ... strange," he whispered to his closest soldier. "Maybe he should come with only twenty men."

Chapter 19 - Codrin

Out of the tunnel, Codrin, looked at the strange wall. *Why this trapezoidal section*? He had enough experience in fortifications to understand that everything was a waste of materials and money. After a while, he gave up, thinking that he might learn more from the soldiers inside. Passing through the second gate, Codrin arrived in the main plaza at the same time as a man in his late sixties came out from his house, followed by the young soldier who had gone to warn him. Codrin dismounted and helped Amelie do the same. The old man seemed to be in command, and Codrin walked in front of him. They stared at each other for a while, and Codrin saw the cataracts in his old eyes. They were not solid enough to make him blind, but his vision was impaired, and he felt the need to set his hand over his eyes, even though his eyebrows sprouted profusely from a central point, sporting long grey hairs like willow branches – the light was still strong.

"Good evening," Codrin said, "I am Codrin, the new Seigneur of Poenari. Please don't fear me or my men; no one will hurt you."

"Poenari doesn't fear its true Seigneur," the man said, a strange tone of fondness in his voice, and he tried to kneel.

Codrin reacted swiftly and caught him by the arm. "There is no need to kneel," he said gently.

"My Vision was right, Seigneur Codrin. I had it six years ago when I doubted that you were still alive. It told me that you would return home, and I have waited for you ever since. Please forgive old Bernart for the state of the castle, but the past forty-one years have been hard for us. I am sure that you will rebuild everything. You were only twenty years old when you left. You are a grown man now." Tears ran down the old man's seamed face, tears of joy.

Codrin's expression became even more confused and hesitant, and it took him a while to say, "Let's go inside and talk there, Bernart, Vlad will help you. Don't say anything to him yet," he whispered to Vlad, then waited until both men had entered the large house. He glanced around and spoke to some of the people gathered in groups. They did not seem worried. There were now almost a hundred of them, many over forty years old, yet there were some children too, and Codrin saw a twenty-year-old woman staring intently at him. Some people were gathered around her, a sign that she was someone that counted in the remnants of what was once a marvelous fortress.

"That was quite a surprise." Amelie looked at him with her wide blue eyes and frowned briefly.

"I am sorry if my surprise has upset you," Codrin said.

"I can't say that, but I don't really know what to say."

"Maybe you should go inside with the berries, and we can talk later."

Reluctantly, the girl walked away to the large house, and from the door, she glanced once more at him. *He did not take my berries, so I think that I can trust him*, she thought. *And his name... But he is not who Grandfather thinks he is. This Codrin is too young to be the old Seigneur, but he looks like someone who wants to stay longer. We need more soldiers to protect us.*

"I am Codrin, the new Seigneur of Poenari, though I am not the one you expected to return," he said, loudly enough to be heard by all. "You have nothing to fear; all of you can remain in Poenari, if that is your will."

"How can we be sure of that?" the young woman asked.

"May I have your name?" Codrin smiled at her.

"Siena," she said, bluntly. "Bernart is my grandfather."

"There is plenty of space here." Codrin gestured toward the many houses on the right, which appeared to be empty. "I have only two hundred people with me. Any city has more value when it is full of life."

"And what will my people do if they remain?"

"What they have done until now. The soldiers will join my soldiers. The servants in the castle will still work there. Let's go inside and speak with Bernart too."

"Let's speak here, for all of us."

"Siena," Codrin said gently. "I did not ask you if you wanted to come. I told you to come with me inside." She was between him and Bernart's house, and he walked toward her. "Please come," he added, seeing that she was nervous and biting her lip. He stopped in front of Siena and touched her shoulder. She started but turned and walked inside with him. "Vlaicu, bring everybody else into Poenari," he shouted from the door.

"Bernart seems to be very attached to the former Seigneur," Codrin said tentatively, after closing the door behind him. "Let's stay here for a while and talk a little before we meet him."

"From what Grandfather remembers, the Seigneur was a kind man," Siena said, coldly.

"Why do you see an enemy in me? I just want you to help me to talk Bernart without hurting him."

"I don't see an enemy in you, but why would you care about an old man who is still devoted to the rightful Seigneur of Poenari?"

"I am the rightful ruler of Poenari now, but a man who was loyal for forty-one years to a missing Seigneur deserves respect. So, will you help me?"

Siena stared at him and bit her lip again. "I don't know what to do," she finally whispered. "He doesn't see well and your ...

name. Six years ago, he had a Vision that the Seigneur would return, and that kept him alive."

"Strange," Codrin mused. "You will learn all this any way. I am from Arenia, and six years ago, I lost everything, after my parents were killed. My road to Frankis started that year. I don't want to say that it was me in Bernart's Vision, but I find it a strange coincidence."

Arenia? The name struck her, but she kept her calm. "Do you want to play that card? What do you really want from us? Why do you think that you are the legitimate ruler of Poenari?"

"Because I am. There is a different political environment around you. Things have changed in the last forty years while you were cut off from the world."

"A few weeks ago, you were the Grand Seigneur of Leyona."

"Well," Codrin smiled coyly, "it seems that you were not so cut off from the world. Given the ... political environment, Leyona was more than I could hold onto. An agreement was made, and I received Poenari."

"You gave away a large city and received a ruin in return."

"A marvelous ruin. For someone who has few resources, Poenari is the right place. It can be easily defended. I don't know if I will be able to rebuild Poenari to its past splendor, but some rebuilding will be done."

"There are only one hundred seventy-five galbeni in the Visterie," Siena sighed; for a moment, Codrin's Vision of rebuilding Poenari had subdued her. She had grown up with stories about a wonderful past, with ladies and Knights swarming the city; with balls that filled the large hall of the palace. She had seen nothing of them, and the city was almost a ruin from the day she could understand what a city was, but many nights she dreamt of dancing at a ball with men of quality, dressed in marvelous clothes. Even though he was no longer a rich man, her grandfather was still a Knight, with many lands; just that there were no people to work those lands. Poenari was now an isolated place.

"There is more money in my Visterie."

"Do you have a Vistier too?"

Codrin looked at her and rubbed his chin for a while. "I have people to fill the most important positions, but I don't have that many. If I have understood it right, you are the Vistier and maybe the Secretary of Poenari too. You may help me in both these tasks, if you want to, and if you convince me of your worth, I will give you a position in the Visterie: the second Vistier."

It was her turn to stare at him, her thoughts swirling, and in that moment, a silent current of understanding passed between them, and some trust too. "Thank you," she whispered. "Let things go naturally. Grandfather is an intelligent and experienced man; he will figure out who you really are, eventually."

"I won't go into too much detail at first, but I can't tell him that I am the man who I am not."

"I understand that," she nodded. "Follow me, or some people will worry that you are not being ... kind to me." Codrin opened his mouth, then closed it, thinking that beginnings are always strange and difficult. Already walking away, she could not see his irritation.

When they entered a large room that seemed to be an office, Codrin could see that Vlad was cornered, not knowing how to handle the old man, who was living in a past that was long gone. Bernart was asking question after question about *his* Seigneur, and Vlad's only refuge was to say that he was too young to know things that had happened long before he was born, but he told a few stories about the wars Codrin had fought in the past months.

"But why did he not come home until today?" the old man asked, for the tenth time.

"I have spent many years in Arenia," Codrin said, and seated himself in the farthest chair from the old man. "Please stay seated," he said when Bernart tried to stand up.

"Arenia? Like in my dream. Were you a prisoner?" The old man stared at him with his almost blind eyes.

Codrin started and blinked a few times, then glanced briefly at Siena, who ignored him. "In a manner of speaking. It was an unstable period there, like it is here now."

"I've just heard the news!" A young man, around eighteen years old, burst into the room.

"My brother, Alain," Siena said, and patted the chair next to her. "His name is Codrin, but he is not the one we know from Grandfather's stories. Don't speak, yet," she whispered to Alain when he was seated.

"But it's like in Grandfather dream," Alain whispered back.

"We have a map of Arenia. It's a place far from here," the old man said. "In what city did you stay?"

"Alba."

"Like in my dream."

"May I speak alone with you and Siena?"

"You are the Seigneur," Bernart smiled.

"It may take a while to get accustomed to being a Seigneur again," Codrin smiled back, without realizing that the old man could not see such details on a man's face. "Now," Codrin said, mainly to calm his mind, when only the three of them remained in Bernart's office. "Are you a kind of ... Wanderer?"

"Men are not Wanderers." Amelie showed herself from behind the corner where she had been hiding; the room was L-shaped.

"Let Bernart answer that," Codrin said, thinking that it was now too late to send her away.

"I sometimes have premonitions," Bernart shrugged. "That doesn't make me a Wanderer."

Siena and Amelie are Helpers for the Wanderers, a thought came to him from the Light. *Dochia and Sybille come here from time to time;* the thought followed its course. As sudden as it came, the Light vanished, without a trace. He waited for a few moments, but nothing more happened. *I no longer trust the*

Wanderers, but I still trust Dochia, and she wrote me about Sybille. "I know a Wanderer named Dochia," he looked at Siena," but we will talk about this later. We need to lodge my men, and to feed them. We have provisions for ten days, and some more will come with the carts that are following us, but more people will come too. Amelie told me that food is scarce in the area. How do you survive here?"

"We produce some food on the inner terraces," Bernart said. "The inner part is three thousand feet long and seven hundred feet wide. And we try to collect the taxes people owe to Poenari. It's becoming more and more difficult."

"Seen from the valley, the city doesn't seem that large," Codrin said.

Bernart nodded at Siena, who went to a small library shelf containing long thin tubes made of paper, and took out one of them, followed by Codrin's questioning eyes. She opened the tube by pulling off a lid that was cylindrical too. From the tube, she extracted a roll of paper.

"Help me." Siena glanced at Amelie and unrolled the paper with great care; it looked old and frail. The paper was quite large and looked like a sort of map, quite different from the ones Codrin was accustomed with. The girls used four small objects to pin the corners of the map to the desk. "No one outside my family knows about this," she said.

"I understand the need to keep everything in a small circle," Codrin acknowledged her caution.

"This is Poenari," Bernart pointed at the map. "The map is very old; it was drawn before the Alban Empire crumbled. This is the main wall," his finger moved in a semi-circular way on the map. "These are the basalt ridges that form our eastern and western defense walls. From the valley where you came up, they look like towers."

"Can the ridges be climbed?" Codrin asked, and Bernart shook his head before saying, "No, and here, in the back, there is a large agglomeration of stones, some taller than a horse.

They make the other part of our defenses. On top of this agglomeration there is another wall. Here," the old man tapped on the map.

"How many men do you need to defend Poenari?" Codrin asked.

"It depends on the size of the army which lays siege to us, and what weapons they are using."

"From the map, the rampart of the main wall is thirty feet wide. That allows us to move soldiers quickly on it. Can fifty soldiers defend for a month against an army of three thousand?"

"It may be possible."

"Why does the wall have this trapezoidal section? It's a ... waste of resources."

"That's the first question everybody asks," Bernart smiled. "I asked it too, but there is no one who could answer my question." During the last ten years, having a deteriorating health and enough free time, Bernart spent more days in the large library which contained many old books, and he had a theory, a very strange one – the thing was made by the Talants, more than four thousand years ago, but they did not build a fortress in Poenari. He decided to avoid it for the moment.

"I saw this kind of walls built in hill vineyards." Codrin's mind drifted briefly in the past, in Cotnari, one of the best vineyards in Arenia. "They produce small flat levels that are easier to farm than steeper slopes and manage water drainage. There is pressure from soil, and that trapezoidal shape helps to counter it. Those walls are expensive, but they absorb heat and help to get good wine. Three defensive walls could be built with the resources spent on the wall of Poenari, and there is nothing behind the wall to justify such waste."

"Yes, they look like vineyards walls," the old man said. *Should I tell him? He may think me old and crazy. He is no longer leaving, so we have enough time.* "The Albans made the top of the wall and the city, but the main wall of Poenari was built by the Talants, more than four thousand years ago."

Vlaicu entered the room and stopped the old man. "All our men are inside. Where can we lodge them?"

"Siena?" Codrin asked.

"There is plenty of space, but ... it must be cleaned. That will take a while. We don't have many people to help."

"My soldiers can help too. Go with Vlaicu and see what can be done. I want to see the wall."

Amelie was the best guide Codrin could have to visit the main wall, which puzzled him from the first moment. She knew every nook and cranny of the old city, and she was more than willing to show everything to him.

Climbing the stairs to the rampart, he saw the clear difference in quality between the Talant part of the wall, and the small one which was built on top of it by the Albans. The memory of the long entry tunnel came back to him. The difference here was similar: the wall did not seem to be built from stones tied with mortar. It seemed monolithic, like a giant carving in stone. With his dagger, he knocked on the upper wall and on the lower one. The first surface produced the expected sound of steel hitting stone, but the second hit produced a crystalline sound, as if the lower wall were made of steel too. He scraped at the wall with the dagger, obtaining a fine powder. *It's not steel;* Codrin pondered, his fingers playing with the fine powder. Walking further, he could see places were water flowed down when it was raining, and the striations – now a few inches deep – did not reveal any hidden stone, only some round traces of iron. *Why put iron bars in the mortar? To make it stronger? But iron is so expensive...*

"What are you looking at?" Amelie asked.

"The differences." Codrin let his fingers feel the wall. "The older construction is different."

"Smooth, and there are no stones in it."

"Yes, it looks like made only of mortar. A very strong mortar. Do you know why?"

"No," Amelie shrugged, "No one knows how the wall was built."

From the top of the wall, Codrin could see the plateau in front of the city, and further on, the valley which they had come through. The plateau attracted his attention; it looked so flat that it gave the appearance of being an artificial structure, covered with grass. On the right-hand side, there was a channel cut through the small trapezoidal wall bordering the plateau on the west, fifteen feet tall, also covered by grass.

"What happens on the plateau during heavy rain?" Codrin asked.

"All the water on the plateau leaves through that channel," Amelie pointed to her right.

If I block the channel, the plateau will be submerged. "Do you know when the last siege occurred?"

"Almost forty years ago. Grandfather was still young," Amelie laughed. "There were ten thousand soldiers on the plateau, trying to take Poenari. They failed, but we had more soldiers at that time," she sighed. "And the palace was still..."

"I will rebuild the palace."

"And can we dance?"

"Yes, and I will gladly dance with you if you grant me the honor."

"I will," Amelie said, a large smile flowering on her lips, and took his hand. "Let me show you something." She pulled him toward the basalt towers. "We have to climb." She pointed at a small stair going up into the stones. Only one person could pass at a time. She climbed first, and when Codrin was about to arrive at the top, she spoke again: "Don't look yet."

"I can't climb without looking," he said, amused at her enthusiasm.

"Then look toward the city. Now turn," she said when he was inside a circular wall, almost as tall as the girl. "There," she pointed south-west.

"That's Orhei."

"You knew," she said, a touch of disappointment in her voice.

"I know Orhei, but I had no idea that we could see it from here. It's a wonderful view, and I would never have guessed it without you." *And we can see an invading army from far away.*

"Let's sit," Amelie said, pleased by his words. "It's still warm."

They sat on the stone, leaning on the wall which was indeed still warm. Codrin closed his eyes and remained like that for a while. Up here, the day was curiously peaceful, a sense of things working quietly in their proper courses, a sense of safety, a refuge from his usual concerns. Amelie watched him carefully, trying to find some resemblance between the man close to her, and the other Codrin she had seen from an old painting. She found none.

"We should return now. Thank you, Amelie. Will you join me again tomorrow? I want to see all the walls and towers."

"Yes," she said at once, her voice filled with delight.

They found Bernart still in his office; the old man was spending much of his day there.

"Did you see the wall?"

"I saw both walls," Codrin said, tentatively.

"We have a kind of painting representing the wall." Bernart smiled gently, understanding the confusion in Codrin's mind.

The old man nodded to Siena, who came with another tube from which she extracted another paper, which was different from anything Codrin had seen before. It was an old painting, but in some places the colors were still vivid. Involuntarily, Codrin touched it, and found that it was not paper at all. While flexible, it had a much harder consistency than paper, and in the places where the painting was gone, the thing was almost translucent. He rubbed gently at a colored patch and felt no painting at all; the thing was flat, like printed paper.

His eyes searched the painting: Poenari did not yet have the small wall on top of the old thing. Everything looked like the painter had viewed the wall from the top of a tall mountain, but there was no such mountain around Poenari. "This part, with all those hillocks; that's missing now." His finger moved from a place on the map toward the back of Poenari.

"Something destroyed the hillocks, leaving only the ridges that are now the eastern and western mountain walls of Poenari."

"What could destroy such a large ridge?" Codrin muttered.

"We don't know, but in the document I mentioned it's written that it was blown up during the White Salt invasion that destroyed the Talant Empire."

"May I see that document?"

The old man paused and considered Codrin. *He should know this already. I showed him the paper when he was still a young man, and I told him everything I knew about the walls.* "Who are you?" Bernart whispered.

"My name is Codrin, but I am not the one you were expecting to return," Codrin said in a soothing voice.

"Arenia... Alba... Did anyone tell you about my dream?"

"No, but I understand what you are thinking about this coincidence with your dream. I was born in Alba, the capital of Arenia, and moved to Frankis after my parents were killed."

"Tell me how you left Arenia."

"I escaped with my brother and our mentor."

"Tell me about your mentor."

"A tall man dressed in black, carrying two curved swords. Like this one." Codrin placed his short sword, Flame, on the table."

"Was he an Assassin?"

"A renegade Assassin, yes."

"Are the swords named?"

“This one is Flame,” Codrin pointed at the sword in the table. “The second one is Shadow. It’s on my horse now.”

“Who is Baraki?”

“Baraki,” Codrin breathed. “Baraki is the man who killed my family and my mentor. He hunted me too, on my way to Frankis.”

“Like in my dream,” the old man said, no longer able to listen, his voice barely audible, and both Siena and Amelie stared at him, eyes wide open. “You escaped alone from that fight on the hill. I told no one this part of my dream. Strange that I never saw your face... It was only the feeling that you were my Seigneur.”

“That was not a dream, Bernart; you have the Light. You saw us fighting on that hill, and how I escaped alone.”

Late in the evening, Codrin talked with Siena, and even the skeptical older sister seemed to change her opinion on Codrin. Not that she thought bad of him, but she was a reserved person, not ready to trust without a reason, and she did not easily accept that with Codrin’s arrival, her Grandfather was no longer the highest authority in Poenari, and her status was perhaps diminished too.

Chapter 20 – Codrin

"Sybille!" Siena cried with joy, embracing her cousin. "You have not come for more than half a year. I was worried."

"Sometimes you follow the problem, sometimes problems follow you," Sybille said, embracing her too. "I am glad to be home. Home is changing," she said after both women disengaged, clasping hands like two young girls. "From what I see in the buildings and walls it looks like good changes, but what lies behind that? How is Codrin?"

"There are more good things than bad to say about him. On the surface, he is a kind man, and he has treated us well, but I can't really figure out what sort of man he is. I feel hidden pain in him, but he is somehow opaque, even when I tried to use the Light on him, and I am afraid that he is hiding something evil. I have the feeling that Codrin is aiming too high and is too eager to take risks. I fear for my people. If Codrin is crushed, the common people here will suffer most of the retaliation."

"His childhood was unusual. Codrin lost everything and has fought hard to survive. He has always aimed high," Sybille said carefully, wondering if she could reveal who Codrin really was, even though Siena was a Wanderers' Helper and her cousin. "And now he has lost the girl he loved; she is a prisoner in Severin and may be forced to marry soon."

"I've heard about Saliné, but he has already found consolation with another woman."

"Are you sure?" Sybille asked in disbelief. "I did not expect that from him."

"She carries his child, and they may have two more children together, but I am not sure about that, though Codrin acts like a father to them. Her name is Mara," Siena said, feeling the next question to come. "They came here together from Cleuny, and she is now both the Secretary and Vistier of Poenari. Well, I am acting now as the Vistier, though I don't have the title, and Mara is supervising me. He hasn't bothered to marry her."

"How good a Secretary is she?"

"She is experienced and knows many people and things. I have learned a lot from her. It may be that her father worked in a stronger Secretariat in the past; he seems skilled too, but he is even less talkative about his past than Mara. His name is Calin."

"Is Mara a tall brunette?" Sybille asked, and Siena nodded. "Calin may be the former Secretary of Mehadia, and her other two children are from her marriage with Mehadin's nephew. I need to see them without being seen. He may know me. I have something of great importance to give Codrin, but I want to be sure he is a man we can trust."

Sybille opened her bag and took out a box. "There are some important documents inside that I brought for Codrin, but now I am no longer sure... I don't want to carry them any further, so I will leave the box with you. I will come again in a few months and then I will decide if we can trust him. In the evening, I have to leave. I am sorry that I can't stay overnight."

Codrin emerged from a building just as Sybille came close to the inner gate with her two guards. *Wanderers*, the Light spoke to him. "Stop them!" he shouted at the guards, and hurried over to Sybille, who sat astride her horse.

"Sybille is my cousin, and she comes here as a dearer guest. She *was born* in Poenari. There is no need to stop her." Looking past him, Siena protested more vehemently than she initially wanted, her pleasant voice suddenly strident, making Codrin feel like a stranger. When she finally looked at him, the anger in her eyes matched the one in her voice. She met his own anger, a deeper one, and she recoiled half a step back, clamping her mouth shut.

"Stay calm," Sybille whispered. "Whatever you think of him, he is the Seigneur of Poenari."

"Let's talk inside," Codrin said sharply. "Follow me," he gestured to Sybille. "Your guards will wait here."

On the way, none of them said anything, both women struggling to understand his reaction; Codrin struggling to keep his anger in check. And some curses too. From Dochia's letter, he was expecting Sybille to come. Her sneaking in and out of Poenari only enhanced his mistrust in the Wanderers. Inside his office, Codrin closed the door after the two women entered. "Take a seat," he gestured toward the empty chairs, and went to his own across the desk. His moves were slow and deliberate. Once seated, he caught a glance from Sybille, and their eyes met for a few moments, probing each other, then both pairs flicked away. Whatever they had learned, they kept from themselves. His attention moved toward Siena, before saying, "I understand that Sybille is your cousin, but from now on, I want to know when a Wanderer comes to Poenari."

"What make you think that she...?" Siena tried to ask, even more nervous than before, but Sybille stopped her. She hid her restless hands under the table. Her gesture did not escape Codrin.

"Are you afraid of the Wanderers?" Sybille looked at Codrin.

In the strong light coming from the setting sun, his face could be seen going still. It was politics now, another type of game than he had in mind, and meant for different skills. "Some of them tried to kill me at the end of the Spring, while another Wanderer is my friend. I suppose that you are that Sybille who is Dochia's friend."

"Yes. Who tried to kill you?"

"Drusila."

Sybille's eyes narrowed for a moment before asking in a flat voice, "Are you sure?"

"She kept saying that it was a misunderstanding, yet her nephew, Viler, provoked me into a duel to the death. It happened in Valeni, when the Circle and the Wanderers played a dirty game against Jara and Saliné. They even wanted to capture and kill Jara."

"I don't know much about the agreement between the Wanderers and the Circle and you that was made in Valeni, but maybe that duel was a misunderstanding; you carry a Wing Talisman."

"There is not much trust between me and the Wanderers, so I returned it to Drusila. I still consider Dochia a friend."

"How could you return a Wing Talisman? It's a powerful thing."

"Without trust, it means nothing to me. Dochia wrote me that you will bring something important."

Sybille tried to answer, and she was now ready to give the books to him, when Mara entered the office. Codrin glanced at her.

"I will come back later," Mara said and left the room.

Siena was right, Mara is pregnant, Sybille thought. *And he treated her like she was a servant.* "I don't have it with me, but I will return in a few months."

Codrin sensed the change in her but did not know what caused it and what her reaction meant. "As I understand it, the decision related to the documents belongs to Dochia," he said, tentatively.

"We all have our own decisions to make. May I leave now?"

"Yes." *She did not ask me much about the attempt on my life*. Codrin stared after her, thinking that something important was eluding him, something that will change the future.

Once Sybille left Poenari, he decided to climb on the wall and the basalt tower offering a good view toward Orhei. It was sunny, and he sat on the stone, leaning on the warm wall surrounding the western basalt tower. Far away, the small castle of Orhei was visible like a toy from a boy's game. Columns of warm air, raising from the hot stones, fluttered in the gentle breeze, appearing alive as they danced in a swaying motion, changing the shape of the city, making it look ghostly. Codrin closed his eyes and remained like that for a while. Up there, the day was calm and peaceful, as if Poenari did not belong to the turbulent Frankis, giving a sense of safety, a refuge from his usual concerns.

His inner peace dissolved into a Vision: Dochia crossing a river. *What river is that?* While not as large as Dunaris, it was a larger than anything else he had seen in his tumultuous journeys. There was a vast plain on both sides of the river. *Nepro River?* He tried to remember an old map from the wall of the Arenian Council Room. *It can be, but what is Dochia doing there? There are only nomads on both sides of the river.* Then he saw a Triangle of Assassins joining Dochia, and the Vision ended abruptly. *Is Dochia betraying me? No, I still trust her. Is she going to Nerval?* Codrin bit his lip as uncomfortable feelings surfaced, rising above the calm of the past moments. He tried to force another Vision, but instead of some uncertain future he recalled old memories: Saliné, Vio, Jara, Cernat. Most of his wanderings into the past brought back Cernat's hunting house, in a time which was calm and happy.

Two heads appeared on the stairs. Absorbed in his inner world, Codrin did not see them.

I wish they could be here, with me, Codrin sighed. His inner eye moved to Severin, during Jara's wedding, and he shook his head. The unwanted memory did not vanish, and he opened his eyes. Two pairs of eyes were staring at him with unhidden amusement. "Sit with me." Codrin patted the ground, and the girls joined him, Amelie on his right and Livia on his left, both girls bracing their arms on their knees. Since Varia had arrived in Poenari with her children, Amelie and Livia were like twin sisters.

"When can we move in the palace?" Amelie asked. "I wish to be renovated faster."

"It will take years until we can renovate it fully," Codrin laughed. "In two months, the construction of the drawbridge will end, most carpenters and masons will go to repair the palace, and we will move before the yearend party." *The main wall was in better shape than I expected. There was almost nothing to repair there. Such a strong mortar the Talants had. Is the city which bears the marks of time, but we need to repair only the palace, the barracks and the inhabited houses. Everything should be ready by the end of spring.* Codrin used his Mountes as carpenters, and asked Balan, the First Mester of Deva, to send masons to help rebuild Poenari. The only inconvenient was that the stone workers belonged to Maximen, Balan's nephew, who knew Tudor. Each time Maximen came to Poenari, both Codrin and Vlad needed to hide in a way that did not make people ask unwanted questions – few of them knew the relation between Codrin and Tudor.

"And we can dance," Amelie said, eagerly.

"Yes, we can dance. You promise to dance with me, and I hope that Livia will allow me to invite her."

"Yes," both girls said as one.

Codrin's thoughts stretched again in the past: dancing with Vio in Severin, the lights underlining her broad smile. He remained silent, and not knowing what was in his mind, the girls stayed silent too.

Chapter 21 - Dochia

The trees around them were different, reflecting brilliant colors in the crisp sunshine, and there was a freshness in the air which filled their lungs as only high mountain air could do. Dochia and her guards were now deep in the forest, at the foot of the mountain where the Alba Hive of Silvania was situated. At the crossroads with the road coming from Arenia they saw a Triangle of Assassins and instantly left the road, taking battle stations inside the forest. The Wanderers were the best archers; the Assassins were the best sword fighters. They dismounted, hid behind some trees and nocked their bows. From their position they could wait patiently for the next move.

"We come in peace," the Master Assassin who led the Triangle said, stopping his horse thirty feet from them. He did not dismount. Neither did he unsheathe his curved swords.

"Last year, I heard the same words from Dorian," Dochia said, keeping the bow tensed in her arms.

"Dorian was a Serpentist; he was no longer one of us. We are just three brothers; I doubt that such a small number could cause problems in your hive. The First Light of Silvania and Ada are expecting us. We bring news from the east."

"Ride a hundred paces in front of us."

The Assassin Master nodded and turned his horse north, toward the hive. His brothers in arms followed him. Cautiously, Dochia left the forest when they were a hundred fifty paces ahead. She urged her horse out of the forest, followed by Mira and Irina.

"Keep your bows nocked," Dochia whispered to her guards, and they shadowed the Triangle in front of them, silent. None of them spoke until they arrived at the Alba Hive. Approaching the entrance, Dochia pushed her horse to go faster, and the six riders entered almost together.

"Quite a strange sight," Ada said from the top of the stairs of the main building. "Wanderers and Assassins riding together. For a moment, I thought that I was dreaming. Come inside; you are expected. Dinner will be served soon."

Entering the room, Dochia saw that three guards were posted inside. The Assassins saw them too, but they chose to keep their thoughts hidden.

"Welcome, Scorta," the First Light of Silvania said to the Assassin Master. "You and your Triangle are welcome to our Sanctuary."

"Thank you." Scorta bowed. "We are pleased to enjoy the peace of your Sanctuary. As I explained on the road, when we met your Wanderers, I want underline that I am not Dorian. Neither am I a Serpentist."

"Well," Ada said, "I can confirm that two months ago you were not Serpentists. I am sure that you will reassure us about the intervening period."

"You may sit." The First Light of Silvania gestured at the empty chairs separated among several Wanderers. She was less worried now that the right words had been spoken by both parties. "I am thinking that you did not eat today."

"As I remember, Dorian liked pine honey. Have you the same taste for it?" Ada asked, a hint of mischief in her eyes.

"Yes," Scorta said in mock shame. "I know such a weakness doesn't fit well with the picture of a tough Assassin."

"Why not? It just makes you more human."

"I wonder what we would be without that weakness: subhuman or superhuman?" Smiling absently, he spread butter on his bread, then honey.

"Oh, dear, too much semantic pedantry just kills a conversation. If I were a young girl, I would prefer a strong man with a few little weaknesses."

"A curious memory just came to me. That day, when I met you for the first time, Ada. My first question was if you had talked the same way when you were a young girl." He bit into his bread with the gusto of a hungry man, and that hid his amusement. Some honey slid, almost invisible, onto his fingers, glowing against the darker color of his skin.

"That was kind of you, Scorta. To remind me that you were an eighteen-year-old novice, while I was already ... almost an old woman."

"Still, you did not answer my question. I know it's not good manners, but I hate to waste good honey." He licked his fingers and took time to finish the first slice of bread.

Dochia had a feeling of a déjà view; this felt like a replay of the encounter they had a year ago, the one that ended in the death of so many Wanderers and Assassins. It felt the same. It felt different too. Unconsciously, her hand gripped her dagger. She glanced at Ada, then at the First Light, but they ignored her reaction.

"I remember that I had an awful southern accent," Ada said, with an absent smile.

"I came from the south too."

"Oh, no, my dear, you came from the far south, and your accent was worse than awful. In that half year when you were wounded and you stayed in our Alba Hive in Arenia, I spent a whole winter trying to correct it. You were still a novice Assassin."

"And that leaves me as knowledgeable as I was before. I give up." Scorta raised his hands, a broad smile stretching his lips. "Honey makes me thirsty." He licked his fingers again and reached for the carafe of water. "The more you eat, the more you want. I feel like a child," he chuckled. "Baraki is now in Nerval." He fell silent, and everybody stared at him in badly feigned surprise. "He has a thousand men with him. That's not many compared with the horde, but it still means ... something. Do you still want to send a Wanderer Triangle to Nerval?"

Ada glanced briefly at Dochia, then pondered for a while. "We still need to send one, but now..." She thought for a moment. "Now we need to think more about the risks."

"Baraki is not fond of the Wanderers. I don't mean to imply that I will not join your Triangle on the road to Nerval."

Though she had managed to keep her composure when she heard about Baraki, Dochia started, hearing that Scorta would ride with her.

"Despite some awful southern traces of accent, I am not an ogre," Scorta said, looking at her, and a wry smile settled on his lips. "I suppose that you will be the one to visit beautiful Nerval."

"Dochia, you can trust Scorta," Ada said, and he nodded his acknowledgement. "In my Vision, you will leave in a week from now, but there was nothing about Baraki. He has enough men to watch every street in Nerval and every road leading there. I wonder how he convinced the nomads to accept a thousand foreign soldiers."

"He is now the main candidate for the Khadate throne."

"Baraki was a contender for the throne a year ago. I would have expected the Khadate to have a king by now," Dochia said.

"Baraki has adopted a wait and see tactic. He has worked to undermine the other main contender, Hasn, slowly," Ada said. "Not really Hasn, as he is fourteen years old, and has the mind of a ten-year-old child. And of course, the same bad temper as the previous King, Ander. A family trait, it seems. The one who really rivals Baraki is Shana, Hasn's mother."

"There are rumors that Baraki has promised to marry Shana if he takes the throne. She is only thirty-six years old," Scorta said.

"If Baraki married every woman he offered, he would need a much bigger palace to host them all. If they can tolerate each other under the same roof. All the queens I know have sharp nails." Ada laughed, and her merriment was contagious.

They stopped talking politics and danger, and dinner continued in the lighter mood created by Ada. *Strange... The Assassins can be quite gentle and amusing when they want,* Dochia mused. *Dorian acted the same way until ... until he started to kill Wanderers.*

Five days later, it was the evening before Dochia's departure, and while her opinion of Scorta in particular and the Assassins in general had changed a little, she was still uncomfortable with the thought that they would journey together. And it was not a short journey; she had learned that the trip to Nerval would take almost two months, and that the winter came one month earlier there. They might make the last leg of their journey through snow and ice.

"I have had two Visions about you," Ada said; they were alone in the old Wanderer's room. "There will be some blood spilt on the road, but you will make it to Nerval. Scorta will make it too."

"Umbra and my guards?"

"One of them may be wounded, but all of you will arrive in Nerval," Ada replied. "There is something else that stood out in my last Vision. A particular place. Umbra may have some problems there. Apart from the fact that it's situated on a large plain, I can't figure out exactly where it is and, unfortunately, from the eastern border of Arenia and Nerval you will find plain after plain and river after river. One of those rivers is quite broad and it will not be easy to cross, but Scorta knows the area well. I digress. Think of this place in my Vision as a black spot on a map. A large circle, maybe twenty miles across. I can't tell you what you will find there, but you will sense that something is wrong. Be careful." For the first time there was a touch of worry in the voice of the hardened Wanderer. "If what you find there is not particularly important, send me a letter through the Assassins. Otherwise, I will wait for you to deliver the news personally. Go and sleep now," Ada said firmly, dismissing Dochia before she could reply.

Chapter 22 - Dochia

"So, you mean that the whole road from here to Nerval will be like this." Dochia pointed at the infinite plain in front of them. They had left the last mountains one week ago, and they had just crossed the Nestro River.

"Here and there, we will see some hills, but they are not high."

"Ada told me about a wide river." Dochia pointed back with her thumb.

"She meant the Nepro. We will arrive at the ford in about a week. It's a nasty river, ten times wider than the Nestro, but it's still the dry season. The ferries should be safe."

"Have you seen a place like this?" Dochia asked and handed a piece of paper to Scorta. The drawing had been made by Ada the night before they left the Alba Hive in Silvania.

Scorta took the paper and his eyes narrowed, as if he was trying to remember something. "I am sorry, but this drawing tells me nothing. I suppose that it comes from one of Ada's Visions, I recognize her hand. What's so important about this place?"

"There may be trouble there. I have no idea what kind of trouble. Memorize the drawing. It may be that we will see the place from another perspective than in Ada's vision."

They were just fifteen miles away from the Nepro River when Umbra flew close and flapped his wings at Dochia. "We are being followed."

Dochia brought her horse to a halt, so both Wanderers and Assassins could come closer.

"There are twenty-one riders; most of them have bows and swords, some of them have spears. Some are blond men, not very tall. Some have black hair and narrow eyes."

"The blond ones are Rhusin," Scorta said. "They make up half of the Khadate. The rest of the population is Toltar."

"The Toltars look like the Serpentists we met on Kostenz Lake," Umbra said telepathically to Dochia. "One of them is a ... half Toltar," Umbra said. "He has slanted eyes, but light brown hair."

"There are many mixed families, half Rhusin and half Toltar. How far away are the riders?"

"Some six miles behind us. Two miles ahead of us, there is a small forest in a valley. I will fly ahead and check it. You should leave the main path and follow me."

"Be careful, Umbra," Dochia thought at him. *"I have the feeling that we are close to the place Ada mentioned to us."*

Once Umbra was far enough ahead to show them the direction, they left the path and moved at moderate speed.

"Ah," Dochia groaned and bent in pain. Mira came up fast and, aligning her horse, she touched Dochia's shoulder. "Umbra is in danger." Dochia managed to take a few deep breaths, trying to calm the pain in her head. *It feels like as if a Maletera entered in my brain, but this one is a hundred times stronger.* "Gallop." Ignoring the pain, she pushed her horse forward, followed by all the others. Scorta took the lead; he was the best scout.

Pain came to Umbra in a split second. He was accustomed to pain, but what was happening now was different: it was like his head was ready to explode. *It's a Maletera... Meriaduk took over me, and I am cut from Dochia's mind. That's bad, she will not be able to find me.* Slowly, he spiraled down, trying to find a safe spot for landing: a tree or a rock. It was not just the pain that drove him, there was weakness too, and his wings were moving slower and slower. *It can't be Meriaduk; this power feels different. It's blocking my mind and body, but it doesn't try to communicate or to subvert me. I must land,* he thought, though he was still flying too fast, from his own inertia, and he gave up his search for a safe place. He lost control of his wings and hit the ground. *At least there is some grass.* His last thought.

Ovan saw the bird. He was hunting with his grandfather. He was hunting birds, and he jumped from his hidden place, his net prepared. They had not eaten each much in the last two days. His father had died half a year ago when a troupe of Toltars stormed their village. They killed him and raped his mother, who was now pregnant, and the surviving people in the village were still wondering what the child would look like. Rhusin or half Toltar? A half Toltar child would be killed to pay for the woman's slain husband. Apart from his old grandfather, Ovan, now twelve years old, was the only man in their house, which was half built underground. There was not much wood in the area, and the winters were harsh. There was not much food either.

Ovan ran and caught the bird in his net. It was not difficult; the bird was not moving. *I hope that it's not dead,* he thought. It was not permitted to eat dead birds or animals; they could bring disease into the village, and after the Toltar invasion, there were only seventy-two people left. The Toltars killed six men and raped all the young women, but only his mother had fallen pregnant. Careful not to damage his thin net, the boy took out the bird. "What kind of bird is this?" he asked himself. "It resembles a crow, but it's twice as big, and there are red spots on its head. It's not dead." The bird was still breathing. "I hope we can eat it." Holding the bird in one hand and the net in the other, Ovan ran to find his grandfather, who was hunting on the other side of the small forest, more a gathering of bushes, fifteen feel tall. While Ovan had a net, his grandfather had a bow, but his eyes were not as good as they once were. At the edge of the forest, he slowed down. Twenty feet from his grandfather, he coughed.

"I see you, Ovan," the old man said, not moving.

"I caught a bird, but it's not a big one."

"I have caught nothing, so that small bird may be all we will eat today." With his younger sister, there were four people in their house, and neither his sister nor his mother could hunt or search for food.

"Look," the child said, proffering the bird, so the old man could see it. "I don't know what it is."

"A peregrine raven. We can't eat that."

"Why not?"

"The meat may be poisonous. Kill it," the old main said, and turned his head, resuming his hunt.

"Well," Ovan shrugged, "at least I tried." He moved through the forest, looking at the unconscious bird. *What attacked the bird? I see no marks on its body.* He started to fumble through the feathers, trying to find a wound.

Riding at full speed, both Wanderers and Assassins were searching the sky for Umbra.

"He must have fallen somewhere," Dochia said, still fighting the worse headache she had ever had. She was the only one not searching; her vision was half blurred. She was trying to feel Umbra's mind, but she couldn't.

"I see the forest he mentioned," Scorta said, and turned his horse slightly to the left, followed by all others. At the edge of the scrub forest, they met an old man. "We mean you no harm. Did you see a peregrine raven?"

"What business have you with a raven?" the old man asked. "It's' not good to eat."

"Did you see it or not?"

"No, I did not see it," the old man said, plainly scared. *I asked Ovan to kill the bird.*

"You are lying," Dochia said and dismounted. "Where is the bird?" She took out her knife and advanced toward the old man.

"My grandson found one a few minutes ago, but it was dead."

"Where is your grandson?"

"He went home."

"Where is home?" Dochia tried to calm both her anger and her headache.

"You can kill me, but I will not take you there. The Toltars killed six of our men. I will not allow you to harm my people."

"We are not Toltars, and I don't want to kill you. I want the bird," Dochia said.

"It was dead," the old man replied.

"Umbra is not dead. I can feel him again." *We may be at the edge of the black spot Ada mentioned.*

"Who is Umbra?"

"My peregrine raven."

"I am sorry, but I can't help you. I don't know where the boy dropped the dead bird."

"It's here," a reedy voice spoke from behind a tree.

Despite her headache, Dochia sprang into the forest. Mira ran faster and caught the boy by his arm, then took Umbra from his hands. "He is breathing."

Thank you, Fate, Dochia thought, unable to speak.

"Why is the bird so important?" Ovan asked, with childish curiosity. "We don't eat peregrine ravens. Do they taste good?"

"We don't eat them either," Dochia said, managing to smile at the child, and then she took Umbra from Mira. "I got him a long time ago. He is like a friend." She ruffled his feathers, trying to find any wound.

"He is not wounded. I looked carefully. I don't know why he fell from the sky."

"Did you see him falling?"

"Yes, he was not really falling. He was half flying. I can't explain it to you."

Satisfied that she could not find any wounds, Dochia stretched her mind, trying to connect with Umbra, but the trace of his mind that she could still feel was too feeble to establish a connection. “We need to leave the black spot.” She glanced at both Wanderers and Assassins. “There is a band of Rhusins and Toltars behind us. All armed.” She looked at the old man.

“People don’t ride without weapons out there,” the old man shrugged. “They will go into the village for food and women. It is likely Aloxe’s band. They may kill one or two of us if they are not satisfied with the women.”

“We will go with you to the village. How far is it?”

“Three miles from here, but you should not come. They will kill more people if they find you there. And they will kill you too. I will stay here with Ovan.”

“Take them on your horses. Irina, you take Ovan.” She looked at Scorta, who nodded.

“I never rode a horse,” the boy said, his eyes wide.

“You will ride now.” Irina dismounted and, smiling at him, she took Ovan in her arms. “Fera is a nice mare, she will not bite you.” Gently, she placed the boy on her saddle, then mounted behind him.

“You come with me,” one of the Assassins told the old man, who frowned, but the other man in Scorta’s triangle dismounted and raised him onto his horse.

Fifteen minutes later, they found an empty village.

“The sentry has raised the alarm, and people are hiding inside the houses,” the old man said.

“They have nothing to fear. Tell them to come out.” Scorta turned his horse several times, searching for places where they could hide the horses. There were only twenty houses in the village, and all were half underground. “Where can we hide the horses?”

“We have a stable for cows. It’s half empty now. The Toltars killed half of them; they’d have killed them all, only the others were not here. The place is a little tight for your horses, but they will manage."

"Call the people out."

"I will call them, but they may not come."

"Call them," Scorta snapped.

Aloxe's band found an empty village, but that was expected. They visited the village twice a year. "Boros, call the rats out," he said to the man on his left. "Tell them to feed us and to give us ten young women. Dismount. You," he pointed at two men, "guard the horses."

His deputy went to the house belonging to the chief of the village. "Come out, you old rat." He kicked the door of the house, knocking it down.

A head of thick white hair appeared, and Boros pulled on a long beard. He kicked the man, throwing him into the dust. "We need women and food."

"What do you want first?"

"Women. Give us ten women. Make sure they are young. Don't forget your granddaughter. Aloxe and I have a weakness for her."

"She is not here."

Boros placed his boot on the man's chest. "Don't play games with me."

"She is not here, but my nieces..."

"You have nieces. Bring them out." He waited for a few moments. "Faster!" he shouted. "My blood is boiling for a good woman. Hope that I like your nieces, if not I will kill your wife. That old hag lived too long." Two frightened women came out from the house, and Boros's eyes widened. "Tell your wife that she is safe. These two look good." He grabbed the first one and squeezed her breast. "Don't worry, beauty, we will please you today and tonight." He pushed them until they stood in front of Aloxe. "We have fresh meat. The Chief's nieces. We should visit their village too. Which of them do you prefer?

"This one," Aloxe said, and discarded the belt with his sword, then pulled the youngest one to him and kissed her roughly. Boros did the same with the second one. Eager, both men laid them down, watched by the rest of the band, who kept their distance. Aloxe did not like close onlookers. Both men and women rolled on the ground. Aloxe and Boros liked to play games first. Sometimes the women were on top, sometimes the men.

The first three ruffians from Aloxe's band died without knowing what happened to them. They were the ones at the back, craning their necks for a better view. The next three were more observant; half turned, they learned that a sword would kill them. One of them grunted, alerting the band. It did not help them much. The Triangle of Assassins passed through them as if they were overgrown turkeys.

The two guards with the horses jumped to take their bows. An arrow from the house in front killed one of them before he could touch his bow. The second one was luckier; he died with a bow in his hand.

At the front of the fighting band, Boros rattled when Dochia cut his throat. His glassy eyes stared at the large slit in Aloxe's neck without seeing it. A third arrow from Irina took down another man, and Dochia threw her knife in another's chest. Mira's knife was ready too, but there were no more targets.

"All done," Scorta said, cleaning his sword with the tunic of a dead ruffian. "They were rabble. I can't even say that this was a fight."

"The village will be safer from now on," Dochia said and walked quickly toward the main house, where she opened her backpack. A pair of small, round eyes stared out at her. "You are awake," she sighed, and took Umbra in her hands. "You scared me."

"I am a tough raven," Umbra said jokingly, "but the black spot was dangerous. It messed with my mind. I couldn't fly any longer. At first, I thought about Meriaduk and his Maletera, but this was much stronger. It didn't try to communicate with me. We must learn more about it when we return."

"There must be some Talant ruins in the area, but it will not be easy to search the place. It messed with my mind too. I've never had such a bad headache. Shh," Dochia said. People were coming, and she did not want them to know that Umbra could talk.

Next day, they left the village, and the remaining part of their journey toward Nerval was eventless.

ꕥ

In Nerval, Dochia followed Meriaduk through a maze of tunnels until they arrived in a hall larger than anything she had ever seen. Even the Grand Hall of the Arenian Palace was smaller. In the middle of the round hall, she saw the map both Ingrid and Ada warned her about. She had arrived in the city just an hour ago, but the High Priest was as eager as a child to impress his new acolyte – Dochia was one of the most powerful Wanderers. There was nothing painted on the map, and for a moment, she thought they were wrong, but the size of the map and the place were right, just as the Wanderers had seen in their Visions. Sixty feet by twenty, the map occupied a semicircular pedestal. Meriaduk stopped in front of a strange desk, filled with light coming from underground. He gestured with his right hand, and the map came to life, depicting their whole world. Dochia did not recognize the six continents, set in a projection vaguely resembling a flower.

"Watch me," Meriaduk said, his face glowing with satisfaction.

He gestured again with his thumb and forefinger. The map changed until only their continent remained visible, but Dochia still did not recognize it – there were no remaining maps fully depicting the continent in the libraries – but at the next flick of Meriaduk's fingers only Frankis remained on the map, and that she could recognize. She gaped, her eyes wide, and she breathed hard. The map zoomed in further until her Alba Hive became visible: not just houses, but even the horses and people moving now and then.

Meriaduk was watching her, a smile on his lips. *They are all so predictable*, he thought.

It took more than ten minutes for Dochia to gather her thoughts. "How is this possible?"

"This is the great magic of the Serpent God," Meriaduk boasted, "and only his priests are able to use it. In time, if you serve me well, you will become a priestess of the Great Serpent."

Well, he may be right about the next God replacing Fate; Dochia thought, bitterly.

"There is no magic," a voice spoke in her mind, in the same way as the Maletera worked. It was a woman's voice. *"Welcome to the Sanctuary, Dochia."*

Chapter 23 - Saliné

At the Winter Solstice party, Saliné felt alive for the first time in almost four months. In keeping with his new rank, Aron had invited a lot of people, and she recognized many of them from years before, when they honored Mohor's invitation. It was not easy for her to pass over that, but for four months she had only been able to speak with Aron, Bucur and the servants, and from time to time with her people in the market. She bought a lot of sweet things from Ferd, and many servants enjoyed her gifts, yet she could not trust them. Each time someone important visited Severin, Saliné was packed off and sent to her suite. And even worse, in the two weeks before the party, she was confined to her room, talking only with Bucur and Gria. She was now like a caged animal finding itself suddenly free. To some guests, she looked like a strange curiosity, a relic from the past, and they chose to ignore her, but others, mostly women, were glad to meet her again.

Saliné could even dance. Most of the dances were with Bucur, but from time to time, he allowed others to invite her. She tried to guess if there was a tacit understanding between the young men who invited her and Bucur, but she could not discern it. Bucur reserved the third series of dances only for him, and the last two of the five in the series had a rhythm that made her feel like she was running a mile. At the end, she burst into laughter as both breathed like two tired horses.

"Let's go on the terrace," he laughed too. "I feel like I've been in a sauna."

Without waiting for her answer, he pulled her by the hand, and they went out. It was not yet fully dark, but the sky was starry, and under the full moon, the land, covered by the snow, reflected the light, making the palace look dreamlike. It was not as cold as she expected in a winter's evening.

"I don't remember the last time I danced like this," he said, leaning his hands against the railing. "It seems that you are better trained than me." He glanced at Saliné in the light coming from both torch and moon.

"As if I am not tired," she said, cautiously, and leaned against the railing too.

"Even the moon is laughing at me," Bucur mused.

The cold sneaked into them, and after a while Saliné shivered. He passed his arm around her waist and pulled her against him. She stiffened, but the warmth of his body moved into hers. A memory of Codrin came to her from another life, and Saliné let her mind drift back in time. She almost physically felt Codrin behind her and shivered again when Bucur kissed her neck. Eyes closed, she did as she had done many other times in the past months, let Bucur take what he wanted, trying to think of something else, and Bucur turned her slowly, searching for her lips while her arms laced mechanically around his neck. All her movements were nothing more than calculated reactions. She knew now exactly how much to give in her position as fiancée. Yet this time was different, even though she did not realize it. She felt so soft and so right in his arms, and her fingers were stroking the back of his neck. After the almost total isolation of the last two weeks, the fever of the party was going through her and, for the first time, she fully opened her mouth for him, and it did not take long to answer him, matching his passion with her own. Bucur felt it, and he used all his experience to make her body feel even more pleasant. His hands went all over her back, lower than he ever went before, then his left hand passed over her breast. It was a brief touch that ended before she could acknowledge it, yet a trace of pleasure lingered. Bucur embraced her tighter, and then released her slightly, and his hand went over her breast again, and this time his hand fully embraced and fondled it gently, his thumb sweeping like a metronome over the thin silk. There was warmth in the wake of every touch, and her mind acknowledged it long after her body both felt it and enjoyed it.

"It's getting cold," he said when he felt her uneasiness. "Let's go inside."

He pulled her abruptly after him, and Saliné followed, a small part of her still lost in the memory of his warm embrace, feeling a faint dose of regret that it had ended. When they arrived close to a large column, he pulled Saliné behind it, and pressed her against the stone, his fingers playing on the back of her neck. He took her head between his palms, and his lips touched hers briefly, then he leaned back, staring at her. Breathing unevenly, she remained silent, her mouth half open. Their eyes still locked, his left hand caressed her face. He touched her lips for a while, before moving down her neck and chest, sneaking inside her cleavage. He cupped her breast and fondled it gently. Slowly, he leaned forward, taking over her mouth while her hands went around his neck.

The party continued, keeping her in a feverish state and, as usual, at sunset, when the party ended, Bucur escorted Saliné to her suite.

"I don't remember ever dancing so much," she said. "I barely can walk."

"I can help with that." Bucur lifted her in his arms and walked further. "Let's hope that I don't stumble," he laughed.

"Please don't," she laughed too.

In her suite, the trembling light from two small lamps played in the corners, while the fire danced in the fireplace. Gently, Bucur set her on the fur in front of the fireplace and kissed her neck.

"Let's continue the party," he said, and took a bottle of wine and two glasses from the table. Checking the temperature of the bottle to check if Gria had carried out his orders, he nodded, satisfied. "This is a special wine," he gave one glass to Saliné. "It's a bit sweet. It works well after dancing. Cheers, my betrothed," he smiled warmly, and they tapped glasses. A delicate crystalline sound filled the room. "It resembles your laughter," he said and tapped the glasses again. "It was a nice party and, out of all the women there, you shone the most. All the men envied me for having such a beautiful fiancée."

"Maybe," Saliné said, neutrally.

"There is no maybe," Bucur touched her chin, raising her head, and kissed her. "You were the most beautiful woman there."

"I liked the two last dances from the third series, but I've never heard them before."

"They are from Tolosa. I was there once. Five years ago," he said after a short pause. "Or six. The orchestra came from Leyona, and there they know some southern dances." He moved closer and took Saliné in his arms. "We should go to the south sometime. Maybe after the wedding. While you still can," he smiled, his hand caressing her belly with soft circular moves that grew larger until his fingers stroked her breasts gently. "I am sure that we will have a lot of children. What do you want to have first?"

"A girl," she said, feeling torpid; it was much warmer than in the hall, and both the wine and warmth from the fire and his body were working on her.

"I was sure you would say that. A girl if you want, but the next one should be a son. We need sons too." He turned her head and kissed her, and her lips went soft under his. His hands moved to caress her, and soon he found a way under her chemise, fondling her naked breast.

"Bucur, don't," she whispered but, feeling her weakness, but he went further, with practiced ease, and opened her chemise even more.

"Don't worry, Saliné, I will keep my word to make love with you only after the wedding." That weakened her even more, and her body became subdued under the pleasant pressure from his hands and lips. They spent the evening like two lovers, kissing and touching. Speaking and drinking wine. Only once, when Bucur's hand tried to go under her skirts, did she react firmly, and he did not try again.

It was only later, in her bed when, still feeling that pleasure, Saliné fully realized that her reactions to Bucur's advances were different than before. She curled tightly around the pillow in her arms, thinking that the more she stayed alone in Severin, the more vulnerable she would become. Logically, Saliné was accustomed to the reality that in the next autumn she would have to marry Bucur, but in a corner of her mind, she still hoped that Codrin would be able to save her. Yet the worse danger for her was before the wedding.

Bucur may close the door and rape me anytime. I can't do anything, but he is trying to seduce me, so he can brag about it. Is my body so weak? He wants to make me pregnant. I can't do anything, she repeated. *Only try to kill him. I will do it if there is no other choice left for me. I will die too, but at least Bucur's death will help Codrin.*

Remembering again both the party and the weeks before, she realized that her isolation was just a ploy, not the result of a security issue, as Aron had sold it to her. They were softening her for the party and for the evening after it. *The wine bottle and the glasses were already here...* Her last thought before falling asleep.

The week after the party she was again confined to her suite and, at the end of it, Bucur came to spend an evening with her. She managed to be colder this time, yet she still gave more than she wanted. Once Bucur had made a step forward, he would not go back again. With his experience, he found all her weak spots, and he played them for his own pleasure and hers.

To break her isolation, Saliné pretended to be sick, and Felcer came to her room. Once inside, he closed the door quickly, and stared at her with an enigmatic smile on his face. She glanced at him and turned her head away. She could not understand his smile and was not able to answer. It was like she has forgotten to smile.

“I have this for you.” Felcer placed a box wrapped in paper on her table, but she looked at it absently. “It came two weeks ago, but I could not give it to you.”

“Thank you, Felcer,” she finally said. She wanted to talk with him, but now that he was here, she could find nothing to say.

“There is not much to tell you about Ferd and his men. It’s winter and they have slowed down with the hunting. If the need arrives, I will find a way to talk with you. Enjoy the gift; I think you already know who sent it to you.”

That was when Saliné raised her head, feeling that the box was more important than she had initially thought. She wanted to ask Felcer, but he was already gone. She jumped from her bed and opened the box quickly. The familiar smell of mefilene came to her, and she saw a letter too. She slid down to the floor and waited, her knees to her chest, her arms tightened around the box. “Oh, Codrin.” It was all she could say, tears filling her eyes. Almost blind, she tried to read the letter. She failed.

Her tears ran dry, yet she did not move, leaning against the bed, her thoughts back in a past that seemed more like a dream. After a while, she remembered the letter and opened it again.

‘In the garden, our cherry tree will always be there, waiting for us,’ she read.

There was no signature, but it was not needed; there was only one person with whom she shared a cherry tree in the garden of a hunting house. Her mind slipped into the past again, and it was long after midnight when she finally could sleep.

Bucur felt that her will was faltering under his pressure and kept Saliné in isolation for more than one month, and his visits became her only escape from talking to the walls of the room, and her only pleasure. She started to wait for him to come and take her in his arms in front of the fireplace but did not yield completely to him.

"Next time, I will have her, gently or not," he growled in his room, after failing to fully seduce her in the fifth week, and his fist hit the hard wood of the table. "No, I want Saliné to give herself to me. I want her to love me, like every other woman I've had before. I want her to cry for me. I want her to beg me. My pleasure will be greater."

Soon afterward, Bucur had to leave Severin, and said nothing to her, planning his next step.

"What happened?" Saliné asked Gria, when Bucur did not come to her room at the end of the usual week. Gria shrugged and left her alone with her breakfast.

Saliné tried to find refuge in the book she had started the day before, but once it was finished, she was not allowed to go to the library again. Gria came three times a day with food and refused to talk with her. At the end of each week, she usually had a bath in her suite, but this time Aron refused even this small pleasure to her.

After the second week alone, she thought of walking out through the secret corridor and visiting the market, just to escape the appalling loneliness. Several times she opened the hidden door, only to close it. After a while, afraid that she could no longer restrain her mind, Saliné forced herself not to open that door again. She struggled, but kept her will, and she no longer went to hunt Aron's soldiers on the walls.

She hated herself, but waited each day for Bucur to return, walking around the room. Even though she knew that Gria would not answer her, she continued to ask about him. She was like a caged animal feeling its cage becoming smaller and smaller. At the end of the third week, Bucur returned to Severin, but everything was hidden from her. Then he left again.

It was her twenty-fifth day of loneliness when Aron finally allowed her to have a bath again. The servants filled it with warm water and left four more buckets of hot water for her. When she remained alone with Gria, Saliné took off her clothes, almost ripping them, and threw everything at Gria's feet. "Wash them," she said coldly. *I stink.*

Gria picked them up without a word and left the room. Saliné checked the water in the bathtub and emptied another bucket into it. She spent the next hour just sitting in the bathtub, immersed up to her chin, until her body relaxed completely. From time to time, she added more hot water from the buckets. *It feels so good.* Finishing, she called Gria to have the room cleaned and asked for her dinner. For the first time in weeks, she enjoyed her evening.

When the horologe beat two hours before midnight, someone knocked at the door of her suite. Feeling lazy, and almost sleeping, it took her a while to answer. The knocking continued unabated.

"Who is there?" she asked.

"Bucur. I've just returned and wanted to wish you goodnight. Please open the door."

Behind the door, she bit her lip. "Just a moment, I need to dress myself; she was wearing a nightgown, leaving her shoulders naked and barely covering her knees." She moved away from the door, her eyes searching for something to cover herself.

"Saliné, I am tired, and I will not stay long. We are both tired. Don't leave me waiting here." He knocked again on the hard wood.

Her fingers grabbed a dressing gown lying on a chair, and she returned to open the door. Before she could say anything, Bucur took her in his arms and embraced her. He did nothing more, just held her tightly, saying nothing.

“I missed you, Saliné,” Bucur said after a while, and his head moved back until their eyes locked. His fingers moved to caress her face.

“What happened?” she whispered, breathing heavily. “I missed you too. No one told me why you ...” She stopped herself from saying ‘you left me alone’.

“Something unexpected kept me far from you. I was almost killed on the way back. Ah, how I wished to be here with you, to hold you in my arms in front of the fireplace.” He embraced Saliné again and kissed her with all the passion he could muster. She answered him warmly, and Bucur moved gently to undress her. She voiced a small protest, but he pressed his lips over hers, and she abandoned herself to his touch. “How beautiful you are,” he whispered when she wore only the nightgown, then kissed her again, before she could speak. “There is no other woman like you. You are so special. I love you, Saliné,” he whispered in her ear. His lips went down her neck and shoulder, edging the strap of her chemise down her arm, and stopped on her breast, while her arms tightened around his neck. His hand moved up on her thigh, and she gasped when his fingers played her.

“Bucur, don’t,” she whispered, then said nothing more.

Eye closed, Saliné leaned her head back against the wall and abandoned herself to the pleasant tension mounting in her body. When he felt that she was fully subdued, Bucur lifted her and walked toward the bedroom.

“No,” she said, seeing her bed through the open door. “Please, Bucur, we had an agreement.” Her hands caught his face between them, trying to enhance her plea.

“I love you, Saliné. I hope that you love me too,” he said, still walking.

“Please, Bucur.” She held his head to kiss him and that gave her a minute. *I need to gain some time*, she desperately thought, understanding that she had no chance to escape, if not today then tomorrow or the day after, and it would happen whether by force or her acquiescence. Her mind was working feverishly to find the less damaging path.

He disengaged from her mouth and started to walk again. They were close to the door of the bedroom now.

"Bucur, don't." She twisted abruptly, slipping from his hands and tried to run away from him. He caught her in the door and, from behind, he encircled her waist, trying to push her inside with his body. She pressed her hands against the frame of the door to stop him, but that only freed him to tear down her nightgown. "Bucur!" she cried, but he ignored her, raising the pressure on her body. Her hands left the door, and they stepped abruptly inside the bedroom. He found the right moment to turn her, and they were now face to face in the low light of a small lamp.

"I want you, Saliné," he breathed. "I can't wait any longer. I love you so much."

"Bucur, don't," she whispered, stepping back until she realized that he was pushing her toward the bed.

"You are mine, Saliné. You will always be mine."

Her knee went into his groin, and the shock paralyzed him for a few moments, even though she took care to hit him relatively softly. It was more her unexpected resistance which froze Bucur. For years, no other woman had refused him until Saliné came into his life, and two years ago, he had to drug her, to overcome her resistance. She pushed him out of the bedroom and closed the door.

"Saliné," he said coldly. "You are mine. I will give you a few days to come to terms with this. Open the door; I want to talk with you about something else. It's a weak door and has no lock. Don't make me break it."

She grabbed a bedsheet and covered her body, then opened the door. "I thought that we had an agreement," she said.

"We had; we will have others. I want you, and I don't feel the need to wait until the wedding."

"Then we should have the wedding now."

“For whatever reason, the Circle wants our wedding to be in the beginning of autumn. I have no control over that, but it’s something else we need to talk about. This evening, we caught the man who has been stirring up the people in Severin and kills our soldiers. He is now in the Gate Tower. Tomorrow, he will be moved into the main jail.”

“Who is he?” she asked, and it took Saliné all her inner strength to make her voice sound bland.

“Ferd.”

“The merchant who sell sweeties?” *Yes*, Bucur nodded. “Strange, he doesn’t look like a killer. Maybe he is only the one who pays the killer. Or killers.”

“Maybe. Tomorrow, in the afternoon, we will interrogate him. A Sage will be there, and I need you to be present too.”

“Bucur, I can’t do that.”

“You will be there. We need to show people that we are family.”

“At least not... not when they torture him. Please don’t torture him.”

“We will give him a chance to tell us what we want before we employ harsher methods.”

“Please.”

“Fine, you will leave before that.”

“Thank you, Bucur.”

“Let me wish you good night.” Gently, he pulled her against him again. “Embrace me, Saliné,” Bucur said, his voice seductive and demanding. She stood still for a while, then laced her arms around his neck, feeling the bedsheet falling along her naked body, and answered his lips. He lifted Saliné in his arms and sat in a chair, seating her in his lap. “You are so beautiful,” he said, staring at her naked body. “I am sorry for being so rude. Please forgive me. It was... I just lost my head, seeing you again after so long. I missed you. It’s more and more difficult for me. I never felt for another woman what I feel for you, Saliné. I want you. I would marry you today if the Circle would allow it. I don’t know why they are delaying us. I owe a lot to them, and I can't say anything." He kissed her briefly while his arms tightened around her. "It's so good to feel you like this. Tell me that you forgive me." Bucur leaned his head back, until they were eye to eye. Unable to speak without betraying her turmoil, Saliné nodded, and placed an arm around his neck. "I want you, Saliné."

I am alone here. There is no one to help me. Either he rapes me, or I accept him. If I accept, I may be able to control things. "It's a difficult choice for a woman to act like this before her wedding. Please give me some more time."

"In three days, when all this issue with Ferd is solved, I will invite you for dinner in my suite. Would you move in with me after that? Every evening and night we spend together would be a joy."

She bit her lip and leaned her head on his shoulder to hide her face. *I have only gained three days. We will see what may happen in three days.* "Bucur we have a certain position, we should not..."

"Please," he cut in, his voice flat, and leaned his forehead against hers.

"At least we should keep up the appearances and stay in separate rooms." *I need my room and liberty to use its secret door.*

"You will love me," he said, his voice filled with delight. "You will love me."

"Yes."

"Thank you." Bucur hugged her again, acting like a child, then stood up and went to collect her dressing gown from the floor, and came behind her. There, he kissed her shoulder, then helped her dress, and turned her toward him. "Good night, Saliné," he said, leaning his forehead against her. His hand went gently down her face and neck, then back to her nape. After a while, he kissed her hand and left the room.

"You are mine," Bucur whispered to himself. "Finally."

She locked the door of the suite, picked up her dressing gown, and put another log in the fireplace, then sat in front of the fire, her head leaning on her knees. *Now it's clear that he will not marry me. At least this is a relief. He just needed me to take Severin. Mother and Codrin were right; once Severin was taken, Bucur needed a wife who brings him soldiers. In autumn, I will be free, but he wants me for his own pleasure until then, and my pregnancy will block any marriage I could have later. I can't let it happen. Later... Ferd... Who betrayed him? I may be in danger too, but I need to help him. What if they already know...? Is Bucur playing me? I must think.*

Chapter 24 – Saliné

Ferd's interrogation started later than planned as Grigio, the Itinerant Sage, arrived in Severin with the falling of the night. There were only three people waiting for him in Aron's office.

"Some unexpected issues," Grigio shrugged at Aron's mute question. "Saliné, Bucur," he nodded. "Let's see the prisoner. Saliné, my dear, you look more beautiful with each passing day. You shone at the Winter Solstice Party, and both of you stole the show," he gestured between her and Bucur. "Will you come with us? Maybe your beautiful face will soften Ferd." He had a crooked smile on his lips, and that made his face look even more hideous. Grigio was an ugly man, with a face that seemed borrowed from a donkey.

"I wouldn't count on that," Saliné shrugged. "But the fear you impose may help us," she smiled back at him.

"Let's go then," Aron said, and even he could not stop a hint of a smile spreading on his lips, in contrast to Grigio, whose eyes could not hide his irritation.

When all four entered in the interrogation room, Ferd was already there, sitting on a chair, his hands tied at his back.

"So, this is the one," Grigio said thoughtfully. "He doesn't look like a killer."

"Saliné said the same to me," Bucur interjected. "Ferd is a merchant, and he sold her cakes and other things. She thinks that he may be the one with the purse."

"Well," Aron rubbed his chin. "Saliné, did you not tend his wounds after the second battle with Mehadin?"

"I helped many people," she said, vaguely. "Some say that I am a good healer."

"Yes, yes," Aron mused. "You are a good healer. So, Ferd? What are you really?"

"A man," Ferd shrugged.

"My fault for not being specific enough," Aron said. "How comes it that a peaceful merchant fought in a Seigneur's war?"

"I was one of Valer's mercenaries."

"See, my dear?" Aron glanced at Saliné. "That answered your doubts. This gentle merchant knows how to kill. Are you still a mercenary, Ferd?"

"After I was wounded, I decided that a mercenary's life was not for me. And thank you for healing me, Lady Saliné," he bowed as far as his restraints allowed him.

"You fought for us," she said. "It was my duty to tend your wounds."

"Saliné is always dutiful, but let's move on." Aron took a paper from his pocket. "This is an interesting paper. Do you know this paper, Fred?"

"How could I know that without seeing it?

"It's reporting to an unnamed someone, that seven guards of Severin were killed last month."

"My letter," Ferd acknowledged.

"We are making progress," Aron said, his voice confident. "To whom was the paper addressed? There is no name on it."

"The Merchant Guild of Leyona. There was an inquiry about the safety of the roads in Severin. Another letter was sent to Arad."

"Bring the other one," Aron ordered a guard standing outside, behind the door, and in less than a minute a new man entered the room. Ferd's eyes sparked for a moment, but that was all. His reaction escaped anyone else in the room, except Grigio. "You know each other," Aron's hand gestured between

Ferd and the new man. "I know, I know," Aron smiled at Ferd. "I told you that Herby was dead. "Herby," Aron addressed the new man. "To whom you were supposed to deliver the letter?"

"To the third Mester of the Guild in Leyona, and to Valer, the Dervil of Tolosa. The letter has that small sign in the lower left corner, a triangle inside a circle, to certify the sender, and it was supposed to be shown to the Mester and given to Valer."

"What do you say, Ferd?" Aron glanced at him.

"The letter was supposed to go the third Mester of the Guild in Leyona. If Herby has his own dealings with Valer, that's not my issue, it's yours."

"Are you suggesting that Herby is in league with Valer?"

"He mentioned Valer, so you will have to ask him. Many people know that I was Valer's man," Ferd said, avoiding to look at Herby. "It would not be hard to use that for one's own interest."

"Bring the other one," Aron ordered, and a woman was brought into the room. This time, Ferd's upper lip twitched. It did not escape Grigio, and Saliné saw it too.

In the few moments which followed, when all were still looking at the woman, Saliné signaled with her forefinger to Ferd, then rubbed her hands, and her lips spoke mutely: I need one day. Ferd glanced at her briefly and blinked. In an instant, Grigio turned. He found Saliné looking at the woman too; nobody was expecting her to be there. The woman looked like she had not slept for some time, and her clothes were disheveled. Even though she tried to keep them wrapped around her body, she was half naked. Her face was bruised, and both eyes swollen.

"I hope you had a pleasant evening, my dear," Aron said, "I personally selected the five men to take care of you. They are known for their politeness and skills. Is this the woman who gave you the letter, Herby?"

"Yes," Herby said, "and she is Ferd's right hand and his girl. They will marry in spring."

"I didn't know that," Aron said. "Ferd, you should talk with the men who took care of ... Alma. They may know now what she likes most. In time, you will learn that it's important to know a woman's most hidden desires, and they are usually shy about telling them to their husbands. Take it as a goodwill gesture, and I will enjoy being invited at your wedding. So, Ferd, what more can you tell me about that letter?"

"Nothing more."

"You are disappointing me, Ferd." Aron nodded at the man behind Alma, and he pulled her hands down, to fondle her naked breasts. She did not react.

"Watch him, Ferd, and learn how to do it. It's important to know how to please a woman."

"Aron," Saliné interjected, and tried to reach Alma, but Bucur grabbed her arm and pulled her back against his body.

"Don't interfere," he whispered in her ear.

"So, Ferd," Aron said. "Have you more to say about that letter?"

"About the letter, no." Ferd tried to speak normally, but the tremor in his voice betrayed his inner tension.

"Maybe about something else."

"Leave her alone." Ferd's head gestured toward Alma, and at Aron's sign, the soldier behind her stopped groping.

"I am listening, Ferd. Who is coordinating the killing of my soldiers?"

"Me and Herby."

"That's a lie," Herby growled.

"Interesting," Aron rubbed his chin. "And who is killing them?"

"We hired two assassins. I paid the money, and Herby brought them to Severin."

"Why?" Aron snapped, before Herby could protest again.

"For Mark, the real Seigneur of Severin."

"I understand you, Ferd. I also like that little man. He used to play a lot on my knees. And you should understand that my taking over Severin is only a temporary solution to keep it out of Orban's dirty hands. At the right time, Mark will return here with his mother. Saliné can confirm that. Isn't it so, my dear?" Aron looked at her.

"Yes, you told me that," she said, with studied approval.

Before Aron could speak again, Grigio whispered something to him, making him frown. After a moment of consideration, Aron nodded, reluctantly.

"He's all yours," he said to Grigio. "All others should leave the room. Put Herby and Alma in jail; we will talk with them tomorrow."

"I told you everything," Herby said, desperately.

"Yes, yes, Herby, and I thank you for that, but there are still some small things to clarify tomorrow. Sleep well; I want you to be in good form."

"We shall have a council," Aron said as they were walking along the corridor. "In my office. You will come too," he pointed toward Saliné. In the office, he sat, and gestured at Saliné and Bucur to do the same. He remained silent until Grigio joined them. "Saliné," Aron said, almost absently, "what do you think about Ferd? Other than he seems to be a gentle man who is not able to kill people."

"He was perhaps involved, but I still don't think that he did it."

"What do you mean?"

"Ferd is just a merchant who sells candies, and not a wealthy one. He is too weak to be the leader of this plot. There must be someone with real power behind him."

"Interesting. And?"

"You have to interrogate him tomorrow."

"We all have to," Aron snapped.

"We," Saliné shrugged.

"Did Ferd agree with you?" Aron asked Grigio.

"Partially. He is now half convinced that we did all this only to keep Orban's hands away from Severin, and that Mohor's death was just an accident."

"If we fully convince him, Ferd may tell us about the real leader, and there will be no need to torture him," Saliné said.

"Such a kind girl," Aron mused.

"Under torture, Ferd may say whatever you want to hear. That may lead us to a false path, and any chance to learn the truth would be lost."

"She has you," Grigio laughed. "And I agree with her. Would you then," he stared at Saliné, "convince Ferd that everything I told him was true?"

"Maybe not everything, but the most important parts, yes."

"Good. Did you learn something from the third prisoner?" Grigio asked Aron.

"We caught her only two hours ago, and my men are softening her up right now."

"That will not help us," Saliné said, more fervently than she wanted. "Send her to jail, and we will talk with her tomorrow. Who is she?"

"A woman," Aron said dismissively. "You may go now."

"As you wish." Saliné stood up, trying to keep her calm; she had already seen how well Alma had been *softened up*.

"She is right, Aron. Send the woman to jail, today," Grigio said, before Saliné could leave.

"Fine, I will send her to jail," Aron snapped and stared at Grigio after Saliné left the office. "You seem softer than before."

"Don't be stupid, Aron. I don't care how many men are taking their pleasure with her right now, but you want Saliné on your side tomorrow. Don't you? She is the only one who can convince Ferd. Nobody trusts you."

"Saliné is a clever girl, and in the last months we have become closer than I expected. I am good at that." Bucur smiled and felt sudden heat in his groin, thinking that two days would pass quickly, and Saliné will finally become his lover.

"You should have solved that issue by now," Grigio said, his hand gesturing over his belly.

"When this thing with Ferd ends, our problem will be solved. Yesterday she moaned and became wet when my fingers went inside her. She wanted me but had to play that *please give me some more time* game. Every woman does this just to hide the fact that she wants you in her bed. She is ready, and that's it."

"She should have been pregnant already. It doesn't matter how you do it, just spread her legs," Aron snapped. "The embassy from Tolosa will arrive in a week. We should be able to secure the Duke's daughter for you. And his army. The marriage will be in autumn. Saliné must be broken by then."

"I know; she must lose any chance of marriage with Codrin, so he can't claim Severin."

"You still don't understand. That idiot may marry her even with your child. She must not only be pregnant, but she must also be broken, so she doesn't have a political future anymore. If that doesn't happen, I have to kill her. I would prefer the other solution. Another death may endanger us. Or maybe..." Aron moistened his lips. "I can spread her legs."

"We can share her," Bucur laughed. "But let me have her first. I want some sweet romance, and she is ready."

"That may break her." Aron followed his thought. "After you seduce Saliné, I will take her from you, and make her my mistress. Then I will give her back to you, and so on."

"Fine by me," Bucur shrugged. "Now," he went on. "I think that Saliné wants to prove herself useful, and we have to exploit that."

"I agree with you. Aron," Grigio said thoughtfully, "you should leave Saliné alone until we no longer need her. From my understanding, that would be in midsummer. Then you can share her how much you want."

"Grigio," Bucur laughed. "I suspect that you have some feelings toward her too. We can help you."

"Well," Grigio shrugged, "I am a man, but there are some rules in the Circle regarding..."

"It will stay between us. You enter her room during the night..."

"I will think about it." *These bastards are trying to set a trap for me*. "What if you marry her?" He looked at Aron.

"It would be awkward to marry the woman who was made pregnant by my son."

"Give the baby away and keep the woman. She is young and desirable."

"Maybe," Aron shrugged, his mind undressing Saliné.

"Tomorrow will be an interesting day, but I am tired," Grigio yawned.

Chapter 25 - Saliné

One hour after midnight, Saliné left her suite through the hidden door behind the fireplace. Faint sounds of moaning and a thin ray of light emanated from Bucur's room, and she placed her eye on the small spy slit in the wall: Bucur was not alone. He stood in front of a naked woman, lying on her back over the table, her legs encircling him. Saliné blushed and moved away. *Keep him busy*, she thought. Instead of going up toward the wall, as she had so many times in the last few months, she went down, toward the small cellar which in the past kept Mohor's finest bottles of wine, trying to remember the place from a visit long ago, when she was still a child. She was playing with Vio that day, and the memory of her sister made Saliné bite her lip. *I can't afford to be weak now.* She opened the secret door that went into the cellar and the smell of countless vintages struck her. She walked slowly through the darkness, placed the rope she carried with her on a small barrel close to the door, and left the cellar, which was only thirty feet long. She peered out into the wide underground corridor. Deserted. No noises, either. She breathed out. After fifty paces, she stopped in front of a massive door and stared inside, through the small window with iron bars: there were two men in the large room, which looked raw and cold, its walls made of rough stones.

One of them was sleeping with his feet on the table, snoring loudly; the other was indulging himself with a carafe of wine, staring absently at the desolate walls. From time to time, his hand caressed the carafe, before he sipped another mouthful of wine.

Aron's men lack discipline. Vlaicu wouldn't have allowed this. Saliné sighed and knocked on the door. The sound reverberated through the corridor and she started, her ear trying to catch the faintest sound behind her.

The drinking guard cursed her and came toward the door.

Please stay asleep, she prayed to the second one.

"What?" the guard growled, opening the door. His eyes found Saliné, and he involuntarily wiped his mouth to hide the wine on his lips.

"Where is Bucur?" she asked in a cold voice, staring at the carafe the man was trying to hide behind him. "He told me to come here. We are to interrogate the prisoners."

"Now?" the guard asked, incredulous.

"Now," she said and pushed the door wide open. "We have learned that there may be an uprising tomorrow. Aron caught another man, and he was interrogated upstairs, and it seems that Herby lied to us." Unwillingly, the man made space for her to enter the room. "Where are Ferd and Herby?"

"Numbers four and seven," the guard said, eyeing her suspiciously.

"Hide that carafe," she snapped. "You should not drink while on duty. What will happen when Aron sees you? He will be here in minutes."

"Yes, Lady," he managed to say, and turned while she locked the door. "Thank you, Lady. Please don't tell him." He walked toward a small wooden door in the wall, opened it and hid the carafe inside with the care of a mother putting her child to bed. He closed the door and turned at the same time as Saliné's dagger pierced his heart.

With a faint whimper, he sagged in her arms, and she struggled to lay him on the floor in silence. The second man died in his sleep. She went to the pegs in the wall and picked the fourth key from the left. *I hope this is the right one.* There were no numbers on the cells either, and she used the same logic, inserting the key in the lock of the fourth cell from the left. It worked, and she opened the door slowly, gripping the dagger in her hand. Ferd was sleeping, and she sighed.

"Wake up," she whispered, shaking his shoulder.

Ferd opened his eyes, blinked, then blinked again, and for all his sorrow, a faint smile appeared on his lips.

"Can you walk?"

"I've taken a beating, but the real party was supposed to be tomorrow," he said, and stood up. He stretched his body, and the sound of creaking bones filled the silence. "What's the plan, Lady Saliné?"

"This is the plan." She pushed one of her daggers into his hand and walked away.

"You're as sharp as this blade." He weighed the dagger in his hand, following her. "You didn't lose any time," he said, glancing at the two bodies. "Where is Alma?"

"Arrange them at the table as if they are asleep and search each cell. Herby is in number seven. I will keep an eye on the corridor." She went to the door, checked again that it was locked, and looked out from a corner of the small window: the corridor was still empty. "There must be another prisoner linked to you, but I don't know her name."

Ferd took the keys from the wall and opened the cells one by one. Alma was in the first, and he took her in his arms. "I am sorry, Alma," he whispered, and led her out, then seated her on an empty chair. She nodded at him, her eyes fixed on Saliné. Walking briskly, he went to cell seven, where Herby was already awake.

"Kill me if you want, but first listen to me," Herby said.

"Speak."

"They captured me when I was leaving Severin and found the letter on me. That was already an issue, but Aron knew also about my last visit in Poenari to contact Codrin, and even more, he knew why I went there."

"Why should I believe you?" Ferd played with the dagger, hitting his palm in a slow rhythm.

"I have nothing to lose. It was not me who delivered Alma to them. They were watching me and found out that Alma had met me the day before, when she gave me the letter. And I think that they arrested Velna too."

"Why Velna?"

"I told Codrin that Velna was helping you to organize the merchants. If you remember, there were two more names in the letter you send with me to Codrin. He did not mention them in the meeting, and only Velna was arrested today. Aron or the Circle has a spy in Poenari."

"Who was at that meeting?"

"Vlad, Mara, Calin, Vlaicu, Sava, Laurent, Bernart and Siena. And Varia."

"I will give you a chance," Ferd said after a while, his voice cold. "I will leave your cell open, but you must wait five minutes after we leave."

"Better than nothing," Herby shrugged.

"Stay in your bed."

"Herby is ... alive," Ferd said when he returned, then checked all other cells. "He told me that Aron caught Velna, but she is not here. I don't know any of the other prisoners." He glanced at Saliné, gesturing toward the cells. "They are all men and seem to have been here for some time already, but none of them worked for Mohor. What should I do with them?"

"If we have enough time, we free them too, but they should not see me," Saliné said after a few moments' thought. "No," she whispered, still looking through the small window in the door. "Alma, go into the cell, quickly. Ferd, quench two torches and hide behind the dead guards. There is a carafe with wine behind that small door. Put it on the table. Three men are coming, with Velna. She doesn't look well. When they knock, tell them that the door is open. Speak as if you are drunk." Swiftly, she unlocked the door.

"Open the door, old rat," one man said, knocking on the hard wood. "We have fresh meat for you. Good meat. We tested it all evening. The bastards are sleeping. Hey!" he banged his fist against the door.

"It's... It's open." Ferd spoke in a muffled tone, slurring the words, and he shook the arm of the dead guard who was closer to him. "This wine is so good." He tried to take the carafe, only to push it off the table. It crashed on the floor, spilling the wine.

"Idiot," the man who was the first to enter the room, and seemed to be the leader, snapped. Velna followed him, pushed from behind by another man. "Light more torches," he growled at the man behind. "And put these two in jail." He gestured at the dead guards.

Hidden behind the open door, Saliné waited until the last man entered and sneaked behind him. The man in command hit one of the dead men with his boot, and the body fell slowly onto the floor. Taking advantage of the noise, Saliné plunged her dagger into the ribs of the man in front. It was a skilled strike, and it pierced his heart, but the man still groaned, and the other two turned swiftly. Ferd jumped on the lead man and slit his throat from behind while Saliné found herself in front of a man with a sword in his hand.

"Drop your sword," she ordered coldly and, recognizing her, the man hesitated for a few moments before falling on her with his sword. It was enough time for Ferd to plunge his dagger into the man's neck. Eyes closed, Saliné breathed deeply. "Ferd, hide all of them in a cell and lock it. Take the key with you. Then arrange the two guards we found here at the table again." She went to Velna, who was sobbing quietly. "I am sorry, Velna," she whispered and took the woman in her arms. They stayed like this until Ferd had finished hiding the bodies and came back with Alma.

"Alma, throw the keys in the cells with the other jailed men and take torches," Saliné ordered. "The position of the key on the wall matches the row of the cells."

"We are leaving, Herby," Ferd went to the man's cell, and locked the door, then threw him the key. "Wait five minutes, and when you leave, lock the main door and take the key with you."

"Are you sure?" Saliné whispered.

"He gave me something that may exculpate him partially, and we need to verify it later. It's important." He thought about telling her about the possible spy at Codrin's court but changed his mind. "Please give him a chance."

"Tell him to leave through the small wine cellar."

Ferd threw a surprised stare at her but executed her order. "Let me go out first," he said, gesturing at the door. "More soldiers may come, and from the window, we can't see the whole corridor." Without waiting for an answer, he took the sword from the fallen guard and opened the door slowly, sneaking his head out. "There is no one outside." He moved into the corridor, followed by Alma and Velna.

"Go left, the last door on the left," Saliné whispered behind them, and locked the door, then let the key fall inside through the small window. Once she had finished, all four ran toward the cellar.

"This is the small wine cellar," Ferd said when they entered the vault. "There is no other door to leave by."

"There is a window."

"There are bars too."

"Ferd," Saliné snapped. "You will go out through the window. That one," she pointed up to her left. "It leads into the inner garden. Shake the two bars on the right, push them up, and they will move."

Ferd glanced at her, then shook the first bar, and it moved. In the low light of the torch, he threw a shamed smile at Saliné and took out the second bar too. It looked strangely wry.

"Out there," Saliné said, "go to the northern wall of the palace, through the garden. It's important to escape by that route. Climb the stairs on the left and walk the length of the wall. There are no sentries on it. Then climb down at the end of the wall into the city. Alma, there is a rope in front of the door. Give it to Ferd. You must leave the rope on the wall. Here are twenty galbeni," she pushed a small purse to Ferd. "It should help you leave Severin. Take your families and go to Codrin, in Poenari. He will help you."

"Thank you, Lady Saliné, but it will not be possible to leave Severin for a while. They will wait for us at the gate. We already have a hiding place prepared for such an emergency. Herby doesn't know about it. And you?" Ferd asked.

"I will manage. Go now."

"From now on, you should contact only Felcer and Herat, the chandler."

Yes, she nodded. "Thank you for everything." Saliné embraced Alma and Velna, and she stayed until they had all left the cellar. She barely had time to hide behind a barrel when Herby entered. One of the torches was still alight, and he found the open window. He quickly climbed onto the sill and vanished into the darkness. Slowly, Saliné went to the window and put the bars back in place.

Early in the morning, it took Bucur five minutes of punching at the door to wake up Saliné up. "Saliné," he growled, "open the door."

She waited for a few moments then, shrugging, she went to open the door in her nightgown. "Sorry," Saliné said, "I struggled to sleep last night. Those women," she shook her head. "Please help them." She stared at Bucur, who nodded. "Let me dress, and I will come for breakfast."

Bucur pulled her toward him and kissed her, his hands slipping under her gown.

"Let's eat now," she said, stopping him. "I am hungry."

“Ferd has escaped,” he said.

“You are joking. How could he escape from that jail?”

“I am not joking.”

“Someone must have helped him,” Saliné frowned. “Let’s eat; I can’t think on an empty stomach.”

Breakfast was brief and morose; neither Aron nor Bucur wanted to speak. Grigio tried a bad joke on Saliné, who ignored him.

“They escaped through the small wine cellar!” A guard burst into the room.

“Let’s go and check,” Aron said and stood up.

Ferd left traces in the snow by the wall... Saliné pushed her nails into her palm to stop a smile. “I don’t think that you need me there. I am tired. It was a hard day yesterday. It may be even harder today.” She waited until the last out of them left, and she left too, through the smaller door going straight into the corridor leading to her suite. She walked at leisure and, once inside her room, she locked the door.

She waited for a few minutes to make her mind up, and then opened the secret door behind the fireplace. Her hand trembled a little. Her heart beat faster, and she pressed her hand on her chest. With a sigh, she stepped into the hidden corridor, and waited there for a while. *I must do it.* At the end of the upper stair, she took out one of the two stones, and her eyes searched the northern wall. Aron was climbing the stairs by which Ferd had escaped during the night. His face was tense, and he was frowning. That brought a brief smile to Saliné’s lips. Grigio and Bucur followed him, the same tension filling their bodies. The last man to mount the rampart was a guard, the only one who seemed not to care much about what had happened. They walked briskly toward the end of the wall, where they found the rope. Aron bent over it and looked over the wall. From her hiding place, Saliné lowered her body a bit to get a better view.

“Go down and check,” Aron ordered to the soldier, who cursed him silently.

The soldier tested the rope for safety, then climbed over the embrasure. His head vanished behind the merlon. Bucur and Grigio gathered behind Aron, their bodies touching, all of them slightly bent to follow the soldier's descent.

"There are footprints in the snow," the soldier shouted.

"Don't touch them," Aron ordered. "Go and tell Karel to come with more soldiers and follow the footprints."

Saliné's stare moved from one man on the wall to another, and she took a deep breath. "I wish I could kill him," she whispered, "but I can't. The Circle may take revenge on Codrin. But my hands are not fully tied." She grinned and released her arrow, which flew and pierced Bucur's buttock, its point smashing into his femur. He fell against the wall with a wail of shock and pain. The second one hit Grigio, and the third one too. Deliberately, she aimed at his stomach. She fixed the stone back in its place again, and walked quickly to her room, and got there just as Gria knocked at the door. "Who is there?" Saliné asked.

"Gria."

"Come later, I am tired." She went to change her dress and washed out the small stains it had suffered in the hidden corridor. Then she placed it close to the fireplace. She checked her riding costume, which she had washed after her night escapade to the jail, and it was already dry. She grabbed it and placed it into her wardrobe. Leaning against it, she sighed.

The arrow she used on Bucur was a special one; it had a dented point, and that shredded Bucur's flesh. Because of the pain and shock, Bucur fell on his back and broke the shaft of the arrow, and he needed help to return to his room. Felcer and Saliné were called to take care of his wound.

"We need to extract the point," Felcer said in a worried voice. "It won't be easy; the shaft broke inside him," he stared at Aron. "We need to make him sleep."

"Give me the potion," Bucur moaned, lying on his belly.

Felcer went out and returned with a jar and a bag filled with several small boxes and bottles. He rifled through them and took some powder from one or another and dropped it into the jar. Then he poured liquid from two bottles. Patiently, he mixed them for more than five minutes.

"Faster," Bucur growled.

"It must be done properly," Felcer said, unmoved, continuing to blend everything in the jar. "Leave the room," he said to Aron, when Bucur finally fell asleep. "Saliné and I can take care of him."

Aron frowned, and tried to object but, in the end, he obeyed; it was not good to disturb a healer when working on a serious wound.

"How long will Bucur be bedridden?" Saliné whispered when she was alone with Felcer.

I want to kill him, but even though he deserves it, I can't, Felcer thought. *I am a healer, not a killer.* "It depends on how I extract the point. Would two months be enough?" he asked.

Yes, Saliné nodded. "He tried to rape me," she said, her voice filled with anger.

"He will not bother you for a while." Felcer gently squeezed her hand and nodded at her. He turned back to Bucur, enlarged the wound with his knife and took out the arrow. "Quite a strange point." He raised the remains of the arrow to see it better.

"I chose it with care," Saliné whispered.

Felcer fought hard not to burst into laughter; it could be that Aron or somebody else was listening through the door. "This thing seriously damages the tissue, and the wound may not heal properly inside, close to the bone, and in time, he may limp. He deserves it."

There was nothing Felcer could do for Grigio, who had died during the night.

Next morning, Aron called Saliné to Bucur's room. "Grigio died," he said, his voice bland. "Why Bucur and Grigio?" His voice was edgy, and he stared at her. *I don't like to ask this bitch, but I have no one else...*

"It was not a skilled archer," she said, after a few moments of thought. "All the arrows were aimed at a large target, the belly. How far was Bucur from Grigio?"

"It was a tight place on the wall. Their shoulders were touching."

"I think that he wanted to kill Grigio. The first shot was a miss. It hit Bucur in error. There was enough time to kill both you and Bucur if the archer wanted to. One or more arrows... He did not even try."

"Why?"

"The many soldiers who were killed, now Grigio..." Saliné said, after a brief silence. "Someone wants to make you look weak. I suppose that the Circle will not be happy after losing another Sage in Severin."

"No, it won't be," Aron growled. "It must be Codrin's work."

"Codrin doesn't play like that." She looked straight into Aron's eyes. "It's the work of someone from here; someone who knows the castle well. It may be related to Mohor, as Ferd said, but it may be somebody else who wants to take your place. Like one of your Knights. Whatever the reason, they don't want to kill you yet."

"Ah, your noble Codrin," Aron snapped.

"He is not mine, but you are right about the noble part. Focus on your men here, one of them is sabotaging you. I will come at noon, to read you a book," she said, caressing Bucur's hand, and she kissed him briefly on the temple. "I just...," she said, hesitantly, from the door. "I just thought of something. It looks more like someone from the Circle is behind this. There may be no connection between this assassin and the ones killing our soldiers. Perhaps someone who opposes the Master Sage and wants to create a conflict between him and you. That could be the reason the archer killed a Sage but did not try to kill you and Bucur. To be sure things are under your control, send some of your Knights and their soldiers away from Severin. We are not in danger now."

"What do you think?" Aron asked when Saliné closed the door behind her, leaving them alone.

"Saliné is a clever girl, and in the last months we have become closer than I expected. She thinks of us as family. I am good at that," Bucur smiled despite all the pain on his back. "She may be right about a dissident in the Circle trying to harm us, but we have no proof."

"She doesn't know that Maud is the new Master Sage, and it's bad if we have an enemy in the Circle," Aron frowned. "I can't find a better explanation."

"Neither can I; we need to keep our eyes open. Promote Saliné into the council, and we will watch her closely. My wound will make her protective, and she is able to work hard."

"I will send some Knights home. It's still winter, and nobody will lay siege to Severin right now."

Felcer was right, and the wound kept Bucur in bed for almost two months, and it took him three more weeks to recover enough for riding or fighting. He still limped slightly.

Chapter 26 - Cleyre

Through the open window of the office, came the pleasant fragrances of the early spring, but Cleyre could not enjoy them. Dark clouds were gathering over Frankis. War was coming, and Peyris would become soon involved in a fight that she tried to avoid.

Fate take the Circle and their Candidate King. "Grandfather, we will gain nothing from sending half of our army to help Bucur," Cleyre said.

"I gave my word." Duke Stefan was morose, but he did not scold her. For years, he had depended on Reymont, his secretary, and his own judgment. As he aged, his judgment became less stable, and he was prone to unexpected influences. Cleyre had started to challenge the Secretary more than the Duke would have liked, but she was not without merit; he had to give her that. *I wish Albert could be like her*, he thought.

"You gave your word to help Bucur, and you kept it. You already helped him, and you will help more, but it was never assumed that we will send half of the army. Do you think that your friend, Manuc of Loxburg, will not seize the opportunity?"

"Don't talk to me about that savage," Stefan growled.

"Better to talk now, than when his army comes to Peyris."

"Reymont assured me that will not be the case."

"Your Secretary is a Sage of the Circle. Don't tell me that you don't know that. To whom is he loyal first?"

"Of course, I know that he is a Sage," the Duke snapped, "but you should consider that he worked for me from before you were even born."

"Wasn't Reymont who pushed you to have that five years of useless war with Loxburg?"

"There were reasons for that war. Well, not all of them were well founded. What do you really want?"

Cleyre walked behind Stefan and embraced him, leaning her head on his. "Send only five hundred soldiers. The Duke of Tolosa will send soldiers. Orban will send soldiers. That should be enough for any decent commander to take Deva and Dorna."

"What if it's not enough, and Bucur loses? Wouldn't that fall on my head? He is a bastard, but he is my grandson, and better than our dear Albert. We need someone to keep Peyris safe."

I hope that he will lose. The scoundrel. From her Visions, Cleyre knew much more than her grandfather about Bucur, including how he had drugged Saliné to make her pregnant. "Bucur will never help Albert, apart from taking the Dukedom from him. The Circle should ask Loxburg to send soldiers too. That will keep us ... safe." *For a while.*

"That's indeed strange," Stefan said, ruefully. "The Circle did not ask Loxburg to send soldiers."

"See, Grandfather?" Cleyre said, her hand gripping his. "Reymont avoided any talk about Loxburg. Ask him in the council today."

"Fine," Stefan sighed. "Gather the council."

There were eleven people in the Peyris Council, and ten of them were men. That made Cleyre feel lonely and insecure. And even worse, one of them was Albert, Stefan's heir, with his stupid insistence that she must be thrown off the council. For him, the value of a woman was related to what he could find under her skirts. Cleyre knew that, in fact, Reymont was the one who really wanted her out. After Cleyre moved to postpone the departure of the army for two weeks, she and the Secretary were almost at war. As Reymont wrote the agenda for the council, it was no surprise that the contingent for Bucur was the first point to discuss.

"We are delaying too much," Reymont said. "We assumed some obligations and we need to fulfill them on time."

"Yes, yes," Stefan said absently. "You know what I'm wondering, Reymont? Why Loxburg will not send any soldiers."

"He will gain little when Bucur becomes King. The King will be gracious enough to solve our borders problems in our favor. We all know this."

"It may take a while for Bucur to become King. Both Orban and I waited twenty years, and it did not happen. What if Loxburg attacks us while half of our army is away?"

"We have already touched on this subject." Reymont spoke to Duke Stefan, but his eyes were directed at Cleyre, who smiled innocently at him.

"Not entirely. Not entirely, my dear Reymont. What do you think, Nicolas?" The Duke turned toward the Spatar. "Would Loxburg...?"

"He may think of that," Nicolas said, "but I don't know if he will dare. That doesn't mean that we should not be prepared."

"What do you mean by prepared?"

"Maybe we should keep some more soldiers here."

"We will still have almost two thousand soldiers in Peyris," Reymont said, "and the Circle will watch Loxburg."

"I feel almost naked with only one thousand soldiers to protect us. The other almost one thousand is made of new men and auxiliaries. They are only good for watching the roads. Reymont, you've never seen a battlefield. You've never drawn blood. You've never shed blood. Stop advising me in military matters." The Duke looked thoughtful; Reymont's insistence was starting to bother him.

"Father," Albert interjected. "If the Circle gives us guarantees, I don't think that we have to worry about Loxburg."

Stefan glanced briefly at Albert and chose to ignore him. "I think that five hundred soldiers would be enough. They can leave in a week."

"We won't impress the future King of Frankis with five hundred soldiers," Albert said.

"I am sure that he will be impressed if you lead the army," Stefan said, with a glimmer in his eyes; Albert was afraid even to ride. "You look so much a soldier."

"My Duke," Reymont said hastily, his voice pitching, "maybe you should reconsider. Let's make a compromise and send one thousand soldiers. It will help us keep Peyris stable in the long run."

"I am not yet dead, Reymont," Stefan snapped. "I am not yet dead, and I intend to stay here for a while. I will send one thousand soldiers if Loxburg sends five hundred. It should not be hard for the Circle to convince him. What's next?" he asked before Reymont could answer.

Verenius, the Primus Itinerant, was waiting for Reymont to return, sitting in his office. A page brought him a wine bottle and filled his glass. "Leave me alone," Verenius said, and raised the glass against the window. *Good color*, he thought, but he did not start to drink. *Why does Maud need three thousand soldiers for Bucur?* Still young and new as Primus Itinerant, he did not have the clout Aurelian once had, but a Primus was named for life, and he had enough time to overcome Maud. Verenius was even younger than her daughter. *What does she know that I don't? They want to conquer Deva and Dorna for Bucur. Even though we are no longer counting on Codrin to lead the army, that can be done with less than two thousand men. After what happened in Leyona... Do they want to attack Codrin later? That would be a pity; Codrin is more of a man than Bucur, and he can help us to pacify Frankis. Why is Maud not considering him? That was a stupid question. Codrin dared to take Leyona from under her very nose. That's something hard to forget, and that bloody woman has a good memory. Perhaps too good.* He took a break in his thoughts and sipped some wine. *Codrin has no more than two hundred soldiers. He was expecting more, but we thwarted him. So?* He sipped some more wine. *Why three thousand? And why is Maud keeping me in the dark?*

Reymont entered the office and slammed the door behind him.

"You are too old for such tantrums," Verenius said. without turning his head.

"The Duke is getting old."

"As if we are getting younger. Tell me."

"He wants to send only five hundred soldiers now, and five hundred more if Loxburg send a contingent of the same size."

"After the war we pushed him into, it is no wonder that he is cautious."

"Are you sure you are on the Circle's side?"

"Sage," Verenius said absently, as if he was talking to his glass, "There are two people who represent the Circle: Maud and I." *But Maud doesn't think the same as I do.*

"I apologize. It's only that I was outmaneuvered today by that young bitch. She put those things in Stefan's head. I am sure of that."

"She would not have been able to, if Stefan didn't have had his own worries. You should have taken care of his worries; but the army will leave in two weeks. You still have time."

"Do you think that I should silence her?"

"Convincing her would be preferable."

"I don't understand that bitch. She loves men, yet it seems that she hates Bucur."

"Maybe he was not good enough in her bed." *Reymont is blind; most of Cleyre's so-called lovers never went near her bed. I still don't know who spread those lies and why. I think that Reymont hates her too much to look, but... Strange that she doesn't care about her reputation; she is an intelligent woman.*

"As far as I know, Cleyre is fond of her grandfather, and she is worried about what will happen after Albert becomes Duke."

"Albert will marry her off quickly and send her away from the court."

"An intelligent man never sends away a good councilor, but intelligence and Albert don't work together."

"Isn't that what we want? To weaken Peyris so it will fall into Bucur's hands? We need her out."

"That was a general remark. Fate gave Albert to us. It was a blessing. The marriage contract between Bucur and the little Duchess of Tolosa was signed two weeks ago. She is the only daughter of the Duke, who doesn't count anyway; it's his wife, Maud's daughter, who leads Tolosa. If Bucur takes both Tolosa and Peyris, then Frankis will have a new King. Loxburg is too weak to stand alone against two Duchies and the Circle. I will stay for three more days. Tell me tomorrow how you intend to solve our issue. You have good taste." He placed the empty wineglass on the table and stood up. *I wonder if Bucur understands that he will be the king, but he will never rule. Why should he?*

"They've changed my schedule," Costa said, his voice mildly annoyed. "Today, I will be the captain of the Western Gate. I apologize, but I can't come with you."

"Strange." Cleyre made a concerned face and remained silent for a while. "I asked for you and, yesterday, everything was arranged with Nicolas."

"Why ask for me?" There was touch of bitterness in Costa's voice, and he avoided to look at her.

"Don't be a child Costa, I always prefer to go with you. Who will lead my escort?"

"Captain Ferez, I think. That tall man there." He pointed to the left side of the gate, where a captain and five soldiers were waiting, their faces blasé.

"Ferez, then," Cleyre said and went to talk with the leader of her escort. She found that her mare was already saddled, and in ten minutes they were out of Peyris.

The place she wanted to see was in the small mountains west of the city, a long ridge that look like a man-made wall, fifteen to twenty feet tall and three hundred feet wide. The middle of the ridge was neatly dented, creating a sixty-foot gap that was easy to reach on horseback from the foot of the hill. From there, the whole Seines Valley was in view, a vista that Cleyre had enjoyed from when she was a ten-year-old girl; it was her father who has shown her the place, carrying her on his horse.

"Wait here," she said to Ferez when they were about to enter the gap after her and, from there, she went alone to a stone, rising in the middle and close to the precipice, vaguely resembling a chair. It was warm in that mid-Spring, and she seated herself comfortably. *This thing with the army for Bucur may sink me, but I must protect Peyris and make sure that we will not have such a bastard as king. Reymont is a traitor, and a Sage of the Circle too. You can't be Sage and Secretary; your main loyalty will be always to the Circle.* Absently, she picked some stones and threw them into the deep precipice in front of her. *In two weeks, we will send five hundred soldiers to Bucur. The Circle wanted a thousand more. They still claim that they want to take Deva and Dorna. Liars! I know that they want to take Poenari, but I can't tell that to Grandfather – he will ask about my sources. We will lose many men in a siege against such a fortress. Do they want to weaken us?* She threw another stone; somehow, the physical activity was helping her gain control over her bad thoughts. *Who knows what will happen when Albert becomes Duke? I must be married by then, if not... With Albert in charge, there is little hope that Peyris will survive as a Duchy.* The wind soughed between the rocks and she shivered. *I shall walk.*

Standing up, Cleyre caught movement in the corner of her eye. Turning, she found her escort leaving in an orderly way, walking at leisure, and unknown soldiers advancing toward her. *Mercenaries*, she thought. *More than ten. They send so many to kill one undefended girl. Nicolas has betrayed me.* The mercenaries were already in the middle of the gap when they stopped. Two of them pointed crossbows at her while another two walked further toward her, unhurried. *They want to make it look like an accident.* She glanced at the precipice behind her. Involuntarily, her hand touched the dagger at her waist. *I may be able to hurt one of them, but ... I have no chance of escaping.* She moved in front of the rock that was her chair before – on this side, it was taller, almost reaching her shoulders. *If I die by the sword, Grandfather will understand that it was not an accident, and that we were betrayed. That's the most I can do.* Eyes almost closed, she leaned against the stone, the dagger tight in her hand, hidden behind her. Cleyre quivered and felt nauseous from the fear gnawing at her. She stamped her foot on the stone to control her weakness. *I am so young... Fate.*

"There is nothing personal in this," one mercenary said, twelve feet away from her. "Let's not make it painful."

Cleyre could not answer, just gripped her dagger as tightly as she pursed her lips. Tensed and waiting, she heard the soft hiss of flying arrows, and saw the mercenaries with the crossbows falling into the grass. She had the feeling that her mind was no longer sound. One of them cried out, and so did some of the men behind him, to alert the other two, who were now just three feet from her, ready to kill. In an instant, Cleyre's eyes widened, and she became alert. The men in front of her half turned, and she sprang, her dagger slicing the throat of the one on her right. She stepped aside, to keep the body between her and the second mercenary. It did not matter much; coming from above, an arrow pierced his neck. Trembling, she leaned again on the stone behind her and saw three men dressed in black sliding into the gap from the ridge's edge. They were using ropes that had not been there only moments before. Each of them had two curved swords, and they formed a wedge, attacking the mercenaries with skills that she would not have thought possible. The man at the front was like a storm, and he killed with elegant efficiency, left and right, no more than three sword strokes for each falling mercenary. Arrows were still flying from the ridge and in five minutes only one mercenary remained alive. The tall man in black, who seemed to be the leader, disarmed him and pressed a sword to his neck.

"Bear is your Black Dervil, and you were hired by Reymont. Tell them that Cleyre Peyris is under the protection of the Assassins."

"What Assassins?" the mercenary asked, his voice wobbling.

"Bear will know what I mean; if not, he will ask. If he does not ask, he will die. Go now." He released the mercenary and watched him running away toward his horse. Two more men appeared on the ridge, and one of them raised his hands, six fingers up, signaling that the soldiers from Peyris, who had betrayed Cleyre, were dead too. The tall man waved his hand and walked in front of her. "Cleyre," he bowed slightly. "We've finally met."

"Thank you, Codrin," she said. "How did you know...?"

"Perhaps the same way you knew about Poenari."

"It's true, I feel the Light in you."

"Are you...?" He arched one brow, staring at her like an owl.

"You thought that I was working with the Wanderers." She smiled. "I prefer to work alone. Drusila is not my preferred Wanderer. But this is strange; I did not know that men could have the Light too."

"Things change." *Vio can heal people and has Visions about her own future, Cleyre is not a Wanderer, Bernart is a man, and Fate knows what kind of Light I really am. It must be a divergence.* "We don't know how they are changing. We may learn. You are not safe yet. Reymont, the Secretary, hired the mercenaries."

"Was Nicolas involved too?"

"I don't know. We will take you to an inn down in the valley, and you will stay there while I go to Peyris. Don't worry; I have five more men at the inn to guard you."

"It's not that. Let me go. They will kill you in Peyris if..."

"In Peyris, they know me as Tudor."

"Are you the Wraith of Tolosa? I hired him once..."

"Yes, I carried one of your letters to Tolosa. You were trying to find a ... husband. I did not read your letter," he added quickly, "but my informant there told me about your search."

"It did not happen," she shrugged. "Costa and some men from his company know *Codrin*."

"I need you to write a letter to Costa to tell him to keep his mouth shut. I may need him."

"Don't use the Western Gate; Costa is its captain today."

"Come, we will talk more at the inn." Codrin looked at the two fallen mercenaries and saw the deadly slit in one's neck. He looked Cleyre over. "Are you wounded?"

"No."

Before Cleyre could mount, Pintea gave her a pelerine and a helmet. Then he tried to tie a belt with a sword at her waist. It fell, and he caught it between his palms, together with her leg.

"It happens." Cleyre smiled gently, seeing him blushing. "How old are you?"

"Sixteen."

"You are a good archer."

"I was born in the mountains."

"Thank you for your help."

"You are welcome." Pintea looked relieved, but he looked long after her until he saw the smile on Codrin's lips. What flustered Pintea was the resemblance between Cleyre and Vio when she smiled. Strangely, Codrin did not realize it. The other thing he did not know was how close Pintea and Vio had been during his absence from Severin. Pintea was her *guardian,* before she was sent to Arad.

“Let’s go,” Codrin said. “Damian, Pintea, you stay at the rear. Vlad, Lisandru, you go in front.”

Chapter 27 - Cleyre

Built at the cross between the roads going north-south and east-west, the Lily of the Valley Inn was large. Codrin led Cleyre to her room, which had been rented for two men. "If someone asks, you are my young cousin," he whispered to her while they were walking through the hall.

In the room, she pulled off her helmet. "I hate this," she mumbled.

"Damaging your hair?" Codrin asked.

"What's more important on a woman's head than her hair? Do you know why Reymont wants to kill me?"

"Something about soldiers. My Vision was brief. I was lucky that he was signing a document in my Vision, so I learned the date. Isn't strange how Fate notifies us?"

Cleyre shrugged before saying, "I did not think that Reymont would go so far." She shook her head and threw the helmet away. It crashed on the floor with a loud bang, and Cleyre felt a little better. She imagined it hitting Reymont's head. "It's about the army Bucur is building to take Poenari. Officially it is to take Deva and Dorna. I convinced Grandfather to send only five hundred soldiers. The Circle wanted one thousand more. Sorry that I could not do more."

"In military jargon, when an enemy having a thousand soldiers is convinced to stay away from a large battle, we say that a thousand soldiers were killed by lightning. You just did that. Thank you, Cleyre. I think that you want to be alone now."

"The last thing I want now is to be alone. Stay with me."

"You may find that I am not the most entertaining man."

"Young men should know how to entertain a girl. Did you ever court a woman?" Cleyre asked with a trace of a smile on her lips.

"I lost everything at fourteen, and became a fugitive," Codrin shrugged. "You find that learning to survive has priority over learning how to court a girl."

"You may start your education with me." Cleyre looked at him, amused, but it was a friendly thing; she valued Codrin. "Your survival skills may help you survive courting too."

"Do you think that we should learn courting together?" Codrin asked, just for the sake of the conversation.

"Oh, my dear," she burst into laughter. "You are the Wraith of Tolosa, and nobody told you. And nobody taught you how to gather information from the gossip at a court. The young and noble soldier! In a way, is better to learn it from me. I started courting at fifteen, and I won most of the men I wanted as lovers. Many people would tell you that I am a whore. If they dared. Now you know," she said, staring at him. Her blue eyes glittered, and her quick, intelligent face expressed a touch of amusement.

"And are you?" Codrin asked, his voice affable because of the intuition that she was exaggerating.

"Of course not. I never asked for payment," she laughed. "Most of the things said about me are not true. Some of them are. My parents died when I was still young, and there was no other way to avoid an unwanted marriage. I made people think that I was a whore. Because of that, my potential husbands asked for a dowry that my sweet brothers could not pay. Now, you know the gossip. What do you want to do?"

"I want to know if Nicolas was involved, then it's your choice. If you feel threatened, I can take you with me."

"Thank you, Codrin. I would prefer to stay. Grandfather needs me. As yet, I don't know what will happen when he dies."

"You are always welcome to Poenari."

"Are you proposing marriage too?"

"For a while at least, I don't have a mind to marry."

"It would give you a way to claim Peyris." Cleyre went silent, staring at him. "I must look quite strange to you," she added quickly, feeling embarrassed for the first time that she had to use such ways to find her freedom.

"Why? For people like us, most marriages are political and start with this kind of informal talk. This year, I need to survive. You may need the same. Please write me the letter for Costa." Codrin pointed to a table with papers and writing instruments.

She seated herself and took her time to think. Then she wrote:

'Costa,

I have full confidence in Codrin. He saved my life. Please do what he is asking you. He is trying to help me and Grandfather.

Cleyre, the whirlpool girl.'

"The last phrase is my secret signature that only Costa knows," she said, giving the letter to Codrin. "And you. Who knows, I may need to send you secret letters."

"If Nicolas is innocent, I will send him here, and we will not meet again. Do you know about the Assassins Order?" he asked, and Cleyre nodded. "The mercenary who survived belongs to Bear. I told him that from now on, you are under the protection of the Assassins. He will spread the word to Reymont and into the mercenary world. It may take years until the truth surfaces, so you must tell the same story in Peyris. It will stop another assassination attempt."

"And if I am asked why?"

"You don't know." Codrin smiled.

Codrin and Vlad entered Peyris through the Eastern Gate, and rode toward the Seine Inn, which they knew well. From there,

Codrin adopted his other identity, Tudor, and went alone to see Gilles, the Second Secretary.

"You can't come in now," the bearded man sitting at the desk in the antechamber said. "The Second Secretary left word he was not to be disturbed."

"Tell him that we have an emergency related to the Duke. I am Tudor."

"I know who you are."

Codrin looked at him for a few moments, then at the door. He stepped forward and opened the door before the man get stand up from his chair.

Gilles glared angrily at him and snapped, "Wait outside." Codrin ignored his order. "I am sorry," the bearded man cried from behind him.

Codrin closed the door, before the man could follow him in. "Gilles, Cleyre has been kidnapped. Tell your man not to call the soldiers." He opened the door again.

"Everything is fine," Gilles said, when the bearded man appeared in the doorway again. "You may go now. Take a seat," he gestured to Codrin. "What happened?"

"She was attacked by twenty mercenaries. I was too far away to help her in time, but three men came from nowhere."

"What chance could they have?"

"Three men dressed in black, each carrying two curved swords. What chance did the mercenaries have?"

"I don't understand."

"They were Assassins. A Triangle of Assassins."

"Where is Cleyre?"

"They took her away. Ask Nicolas to come here. We need to act fast."

"And Reymont."

"Nicolas first."

Gilles pulled a cord hanging on the wall, and the bearded man reappeared. "Where is the Secretary?"

"Meeting the embassy from Muniker."

"Go and ask Nicolas to come here. Tell him that we have an emergency. Then leave a message in Reymont's office."

"We have a situation," Gilles said, when Nicolas was seated next to Codrin. "Cleyre has been kidnapped."

"Who is this man?" Nicolas asked, pointing at Codrin.

"Tudor, the Wraith of Tolosa. He saw three ... Assassins taking Cleyre," Gilles said.

"Assassins from the order or just...?" Nicolas asked, and Codrin nodded. "Then she is in danger."

"They saved her. She was attacked by Bear's mercenaries."

"Do you know where Cleyre is now?"

"With the Assassins. They went south."

"You will come with us," Nicolas ordered. "I will take fifty soldiers with me."

Codrin took his time answering. "I am going south anyway, and I can come with you up to the point where I saw the Assassins. Then I need to go in another direction."

"You will go where I need you. Now," Nicolas said and stood up. "Follow me," he added when they were in the corridor, and they went to his office, where he gestured toward a chair. Once they were seated, he looked at Codrin. "We are both men of arms. Let's go into more detail. Take it from the moment you realized what was happening."

"Before Bear's men surrounded Cleyre, her guards went away. They did not run. They looked calm."

"How close were you?"

"Three hundred paces. You don't need to see a man face to understand..."

"Even Captain Ferez?"

"How should I know Captain Ferez? Six men walked away, maybe that tells you something."

"Even Ferez... I selected him today to guard Cleyre." Nicolas was clearly taken aback, but Codrin sensed no obvious guilt in him. "Yesterday, I selected Costa, but we had a strange situation. The captain of Western Gate got sick, and I asked Costa to take his place."

"Why Costa?" Codrin asked.

"You should ask questions that give you answers. Don't go above your station. I told you about Ferez, and that should be enough for you to understand that I have been deceived."

Or that you are trying to deceive me. "So, what do you think it happened?"

"I bet that the sick captain is not sick at all, but I'm trying to recall why I chose Ferez. There were more captains in the room."

"Why don't you start with Costa's selection for gate duty?"

"Do you think Cleyre in danger?" Nicolas ignored his question.

"The Assassins saved her. Someone from Peyris wanted her dead."

"And you think it's me."

"From what I know, it is more likely that Reymont wants her dead."

Nicolas looked at him, thoughtfully. "You are not a Wraith for nothing. Bear's place is a long way from here. This was set in motion some time ago."

"Perhaps, or maybe they were hired for a different purpose and just happened to be here after the meeting about your army."

"What do you know about that?"

"Wraiths are ghostly things." Codrin shrugged. "Do you know anything about the Assassins' rules?"

"I believe they have some strange rules. As strange as their names."

"Rules are important to them, and they are sometimes strange for us. It's not a given thing that they have saved Cleyre. If they have a Black Warrant in her name, they will save her only to fulfill the warrant themselves. Rules..." Codrin shrugged.

"Why are you telling me this?"

"Because if they have a contract to protect her, some people may be in danger. They *will* protect her. Are you sure that you still want to find out where she is now?"

"I will have a hundred soldiers with me."

"They will not give a damn for your soldiers. They will not attack them; they will kill you. This business of you choosing Ferez may be already known to them. After all, they knew about the attack."

Nicolas rubbed his forehead and, eyes closed, tried to remember, Codrin's eyes fixed on him, following his every reaction. A twitching finger, a bead of perspiration. The flow of breath. He was trained like an Assassin and knew how to read a body's reactions.

"I know," Nicolas said, and sighed, relieved. "When I was told that the captain of the Western Gate was sick, Ferez was the closest captain to me and Costa. That's why I chose him to replace Costa who was to replace the sick man. I will make sure that he is sick for a while."

"Do you understand what that means?"

"Yes," Nicolas said, "there are some traitors among my closest people; but that won't be solved today, and not by you. Let's find Cleyre."

Chapter 28 – Cleyre

Cleyre gasped; it was not a Vision, just the feeling that something bad was happening. Her grandfather had been sick for some days already. The last two weeks she had been haunted by the attempt on her life, and she still did not fully trust Nicolas, even though he had brought her safely home. Nicolas had come to the inn alone, a sign that Codrin trusted him, but the mercenaries had not tried to kill Codrin; they'd tried to kill her. She stood up abruptly and hurried out of the room. It was almost midnight, and the corridor was empty, so she kept running. Close to the Duke's suite she slowed down, not wanting to alarm the guards at the door. "Is Grandfather alone?"

"Meunier, the healer, is with him," one soldier said.

With a cursory nod to the guard, she opened the door and entered the antechamber. From there, she hurried to the Duke's bedroom. As the guard had told her, Meunier was there, an empty spoon in his hand. Seeing Cleyre, he moved to hide, with his body, something on the table close to the Duke's bed.

Cleyre pushed the frail healer away and found a small open bottle on the table. She sniffed the bottle, but the scent told her nothing. She had no knowledge about medicine, but she had knowledge about people – the healer was frightened by her reactions. "You've poisoned him," Cleyre whispered and grabbed a bronze statue, ready to smash his head in.

“I am sorry, Cleyre,” Meunier cried out in terror, and fell into his knees in front of her. “Kill me. I deserve it.”

“Why have you done this?”

“They took my daughter and her children and threatened to kill them if I don’t...”

“Who are ‘they’?”

“Reymont. I used small doses of poison on the Duke until today, trying to make it slow. Reymont pushed me to hurry... It’s something to do with the army for Bucur. I am sorry.” He burst into tears, as distraught as he was terrified. Meunier had been the Duke’s healer for more than forty years. “Kill me. I won’t blame you.”

“Grandfather trusted you, and you... You...” There was a lump in her throat and Cleyre could no longer talk. She went toward the bed, but Duke Stefan was no longer breathing. His face looked rigid and serene at the same time. “Goodbye, Grandfather,” she whispered, closing his eyes, and tears coursed down her face. It took her a while to gather herself. “Stay here,” she snapped at Meunier and, wiping her face with her sleeve, she left the room.

She knocked at Nicolas’s door, and his page came to open it. “Wake Nicolas,” she said, and seated herself in a chair in front of his desk.

The page frowned, tried to say something. In the end, he obeyed the order, and a sleepy Nicolas emerged from his bedroom. Cleyre glanced at him, and then nodded toward the page. “Leave us,” Nicolas said. “This is most unusual,” he said, sleepily.

“Grandfather is dead,” she said and then she could hold back her sobs no longer.

“I am sorry.” Nicolas went to her and placed his hand on her shoulder. “The Duke was an old man, Cleyre.”

“He was poisoned.”

“Who told you that?”

"Meunier. He poisoned Grandfather on Reymont's order because of the issue with the army for Bucur. Reymont kidnapped his daughter and her children. Meunier confessed everything to me."

"That's a ... strange tale."

"Arrest Reymont."

"He would deny it all; and who will believe Meunier? Let's talk to him first." Nicolas went to his bedroom and returned in a few minutes fully dressed and carrying a dagger at his waist.

They found both Reymont and Meunier in the Duke's bedroom.

"The Duke died in his sleep," Reymont said.

Cleyre closed her eyes and took a deep breath. *It will solve nothing if I yell* assassin *at Reymont*. "Is this true?" She looked at Meunier, murder in her eyes.

"Yes, milady," Meunier whispered, avoiding her eyes. "There was nothing I could do. The Duke was an old man."

She clenched her hands into fists to stop herself from crying; and to stop herself from attacking Meunier.

"You are troubled, Cleyre," Reymont said. Go to your room, I will take care of everything."

She was on the point of accusing him of her grandfather's murder when Nicolas's hand gripped her shoulder. "I will accompany you." Holding her tightly, he escorted her out and they walked in silence into her suite.

"You don't believe me," she said, despondently.

"What I believe is that even if what you have told me is true, and it may be, Reymont acted faster than we did, and it will now be very difficult to convince anyone of his guilt. Meunier contradicted your story in front of two witnesses."

"Leave me."

"Cleyre," he said gently. "We are in a new situation now. You must forget what has happened and think about your future."

"Reymont killed his Duke. What future do I have with Albert and Reymont working against me?"

"It may not be the future you want, but you still have one."

"Reymont tried to kill me, too."

"Someone hired mercenaries to kill you, but there is no proof that it was Reymont who tried to kill you. Don't get me wrong, I believe that Reymont did it, but we have no real proof."

"You just don't want to be involved. The new ... situation," she said, her voice thin.

"New situations require new approaches."

"You are the Spatar of Peyris. Your Duke has just been poisoned. I was abandoned by a captain you chose to a band of mercenaries..."

"Careful Cleyre, I may be the only friend you have at the court."

"Yes, that's good advice. I was not careful enough to prevent Grandfather being assassinated, but at least I tried to do something. I can't say that about you. Leave me, Nicolas; in the next few days I will see how much of a friend you really are."

"Try to sleep, Cleyre."

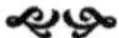

As was customary, Peyris Council gathered again three days after the Duke's funeral. Before the assembled councilors, Albert accepted the Duke's scepter and raised it above his head.

"From now on, Peyris stands on my shoulders," Albert spoke the ancient words, and from that moment, he became the new Duke of Peyris. "We mourned Father, but now we have to work. Cleyre, you are no longer part of this council. My sister, Cecile, will take your place. I shall soon find you a good husband. In fact, I already have someone in mind. You need to settle down. There have been many complaints about your behavior at the court and in the council." Albert had no living children, and only two granddaughters. By the succession rules, Cleyre's elder brother was the next in line to the dukedom and a member of the council but, thinking that Cleyre might still have some influence, Reymont had convinced Albert to appoint Cecile.

"Cleyre has disgraced our court with her shameless behavior," Cecile said. "So many men in her bed..."

"At least I am not married." She looked at Cecile who, even at fifty, had a lot of lovers that she paid generously. No one could say if her three children belonged to her husband, who lived more or less separated from her.

"And you wanted to be gentle with this viper," Cecile growled at Albert. "Don't be weak, Albert; do your duty."

"I don't think that Albert needs your advice to perform his duties," Cleyre said, her voice calm and almost gentle. "He is our Duke now, and it's not good to call him weak in front of so many people. You should apologize, Cecile."

"I will never apologize to a bitch like you, and I meant every word I said about you."

"You should apologize to Albert." Cleyre fought hard to kill the smile on her lips; Cecile was even more stupid than her brother.

The councilors silently watched the exchange, and while most of them were neutral regarding Cleyre, they felt that they were on her side this time, though they did not dare to help her. Nicolas shook his head subtly, trying to make Cleyre step back.

"Cleyre is right," Albert said, feeling the drunkenness of power seeping into him. "Cecile, you should not call your Duke weak."

"This is a private matter, and should be resolved later," Reymont interjected. "My dear," he said to Cleyre in a fatherly voice, "you should go now, and let us work on the more important problems we have now."

"What was done in public has to be undone in public," Cleyre said, "and the Secretary should be the first one to realize this. We can't let something like this stain the reputation of the Duke of Peyris."

"Cleyre is right," Albert said, raising his voice a notch. "Sister?"

"I apologize," Cecile hissed, looking daggers at Cleyre.

"I shall leave now," Cleyre said. "Let's hope that Reymont handles Peyris better than he handled the Duke's honor."

"With your approval, Duke, let's start the council." Reymont bowed peremptorily to Albert, who nodded. "We have a pressing issue regarding the army we sent to help the Candidate King. The Circle asked for one thousand five hundred soldiers. Last week, we sent only five hundred."

"I received a courier, today," Nicolas said. "It seems that Bucur's army is going to Poenari and not to Deva."

"Why should that matter?" Reymont asked.

"I don't know what you expect from your ambassadors, Reymont, but I wouldn't expect that if you send one to Leyona, he will go to Muniker. Why were we not informed?"

"Perhaps there was not enough time, and they will inform us later."

"Is the Duchy of Peyris so unimportant?" Nicolas looked at Albert as he asked the question.

"Of course, we are important, but the army we've sent doesn't match our importance," Reymont said, his hand gripping the edge of the table. His voice remained calm, but his irritation was beginning to get the better of him.

"You mean that they snubbed us?" Nicolas asked, his voice gentle.

"Of course not. We should..."

"We have a new Duke," Nicolas cut in, "and if we accept being treated like this, he will look weak. And if he looks weak now, at the beginning of his reign, they will never take us seriously. My Duke," he said to Albert, "we should clarify their miscommunication before committing more soldiers. Let's send an embassy to ask for answers."

"That would take time," Reymont said coldly. "My Duke," he said, mockingly copying Nicolas, "let's do both, send an embassy and the army."

"They will just laugh at our weakness," Nicolas said, with a calculated dose of amusement, leaning his head back as if he was about to laugh. Through his lowered lids he stared intently at Albert.

"Nicolas is right. I can't afford to look weak. Send an embassy to Bucur," Albert said, avoiding Reymont's eyes.

His lips pursed in a tight line, the Secretary swallowed hard and nodded.

From the council, Nicolas went directly to Cleyre's suite, and found her sitting with Jerome, a fifty-year-old friend of Albert.

"It seems that Jerome is my new fiancé," Cleyre said in answer Nicolas's mute question.

"Albert agreed that we should marry in a week, so you are more than my fiancée," Jerome said, "and from now on, you should no longer receive other men when you are alone."

"You are quite a cautious man, Jerome. Intelligent men are always cautious, but I hope that you will not think so low of me, the Spatar of Peyris. Cleyre has just lost her grandfather to whom she was very attached. She is also like a daughter to me."

"Of course not. Please excuse me."

"I will not stay long." Nicolas stared at him and, frowning, Jerome turned and left the room against his will.

"Reymont did not lose any time," Cleyre sighed.

"You've made powerful enemies. I don't see the need for that show with Cecile in the council."

"I did not make any new enemy, and Albert took the bait."

"Two words from Reymont, and he will forget everything. If it's of any interest to you, I was able to postpone the departure of the second troop for Poenari. We are waiting for Bucur or the Circle to inform us why they took the decision to attack Poenari instead of Deva, as we had agreed. I have to say that your stunt about Albert's perceived weakness helped me, but it did not help you."

"It will buy Albert some more time, but he is too stupid to realize that Reymont will sell Peyris to Bucur, in fact to the Circle."

"You told me that before, but how can I believe it without proof?"

"Then don't believe it." Cleyre turned away from him and leaned her head against the window. "Why do you think they murdered Grandfather and sent those mercenaries to kill me?"

"It's not me who will ask for proof. I have to leave now."

"Help me leave Peyris."

"Your place is here. Jerome is not the ideal husband, but you will manage," Nicolas said, softly and deliberately.

"I will manage it until Reymont..."

"He will not dare to kill you. The Assassins can be very persuasive, even if they don't speak directly."

"Nicolas, I need to leave."

❧

Waiting in her room, Cleyre felt alone in a way that she did not feel before. Ignoble men, her brothers were lost to her for some years already, and the only one she considered family was the Duke. That was her grandfather, for her, Albert could not be the Duke of Peyris. *I still want to call Peyris my home*, she thought, and bitterness swelled inside. The day has been long for her, and the evening even longer. She knew that she had to wait, but it did not count, she was ready from the early morning, dressed in her dark riding suite. With the first stars filling the sky, Nicolas would wait for her at the stable and help her run away from home. He promised three guards to protect her until reaching Cleuny. Alone in her room for most of the day, she waited for the sun to go down behind the hills. Leaning against the window, she watched every move in the plaza in front of the ducal palace. Other than calming her mind, it had no importance to her. The horologe of the city beat three hours before midnight. *It's time.* For the first time in days she smiled, then left the window, walking like a young girl eager to meet her first lover. She opened the door and found Albert looking amused at her, that stupid smile spread large on his lips.

"Going somewhere, niece?" he asked.

"Into the garden." As she spoke, she felt the presence of a Wanderer. *This is how they learned about my escape.*

"Would you mind if I join you?"

"Why should I mind? It's your garden, after all."

"Before that," he said, as if just remembering it, and a woman that Cleyre had never seen before came into sight. "Someone wants to talk with you. Talk with her, and then we have to talk too." Albert moved out of the doorway, and let the woman take his place. With a malicious look, he closed the door, leaving her alone with Cleyre.

"Do you have the Light?" the Wanderer asked without any introduction.

"You would feel it," Cleyre said, knowing from Dochia that a Wanderer could feel the Light only when it was used.

"Maybe you are a special type of Wanderer, and I can't feel your Light."

"I am not a Wanderer. I am just a young woman trying to escape a forced marriage to an old man. You just gave me back to him. I pity myself for that, but I pity you even more for going so low. Your order is as bad as the Circle."

"I can help you."

If they find that I can hide my Light from them, and that I can feel it in them, even when it is not used, they will keep me prisoner, or kill me. "No, you don't. You would have had contacted me, instead of selling me to the old man. And you are a woman too. Leave me."

Chapter 29 – War

The first half of Spring had come and gone, but Spring had not yet fully arrived in Poenari or in the surrounding mountains. A memory of his previous winter in the Long Valley came to Codrin. *There was much more snow there*, he thought, then returned to the papers in front of him. During the winter, Mara had given birth to his son, Radu, and Codrin felt more responsible now. Radu was named after his grandfather and uncle, who were killed together with the rest of the family and Tudor, by Baraki's men. The name brought to Codrin good old memories from Arenia. It brought pain too, but he felt the need to pay homage to both his father and brother. Until the day when he held the little body in his arms, he had not thought much about responsibilities. If he died in a fight, then he died. Little Radu made him see the future in a different way; it no longer belonged only to him; it was intertwined with the future of his son. There were consequences for Saliné, Jara and Vio, of course, but they did not feel the same. And there was another consequence; the pile of papers in front of him. Calin and Siena had taken over the Secretariat and Varia was now leading the Visterie, but they did not know his ways as well as Mara.

How is Cleyre? Codrin recalled his last journey through the northern Duchy. *I did not receive any letter from her.* They had agreed that she will inform Codrin about the last moves of the Circle in Peyris. *I hope she is well.*

Absently, he took a piece of paper and, searching for numbers in the many letters in front of him, started to write:

- The Mountes will bring two hundred soldiers.

Boldur was strong enough to convince them, he thought. In his last letter, Boldur wrote that the Circle had sent Verenius to stop the Mountes soldiers going to Poenari.

- Valer will bring a hundred mercenaries.

They are the best ones in Frankis. I hope that Valer is able to hide his actions from the Duke of Tolosa.

- Laurent and Marat will bring fifty soldiers. Other knights *should* bring a hundred more.

Laurent took faster than I thought over the eastern part of Severin. He was even able to collect more than half of the taxes and provided a lot of food for the siege.

- Orhei and Saunier will bring fifty soldiers.

- I have a hundred and fifty soldiers in Poenari, and ten in Cleuny.

"Six hundred and fifty soldiers," Codrin said, and underlined the number on the paper. "It should be enough." He burst into laughter. "I am trying to fool myself. Bucur will have more than three thousand soldiers."

Celeste was silent, but under her studied calm, Pierre guessed at her turmoil. "Wife," he said gently, "it's not the first time I have led an army to war." He took her hand and kissed it, then looked at her. That sweet, simple gesture brought tears to her eyes.

I am afraid, Celeste thought, *I am afraid in a way that did not happen before. Is this a bad sign?* "I wish you to come back whole and well." Her voice had the same studied calm as her face. Unconsciously, her hand gripped Pierre's. Her eyes widened. She wanted to protest, to beg that he simply let someone else lead the army, but she would not. Pierre was a commander; the best in Tolosa, the best in Frankis, and fighting had been his vocation since he was a twelve-year-old squire.

She hated the thought of him fighting for some dishonest scheme of the Circle, and wished he were a simple man so she wouldn't have to worry about him but, deep inside, she loved his strength and his power. He was the Spatar of Tolosa, and she loved him as much as she loved their children. As afraid as she was for him, she would never ask Pierre to be less than he was.

"I promise you that this is my last fight. I am getting old, and I have enough wars on my plate. Some youth hungry for fame should take over from me." Pierre was fifty-two years old, and for almost twenty years, he had ruled Tolosa beside the old and the new Duke. Things had changed with Baldovin's sickness and the ascent of Maud as Master Sage of the Circle. Helped by Masson, the Secretary of Tolosa and Hidden Sage of the Circle, his wife, Laure had taken the reins of the dukedom in her hands, and Pierre had once again to march to war. Laure was both the Duchess of Tolosa and Maud's daughter.

"Your children want to see you before you leave." Celeste felt her eyes sting with tears and leaned her head on his shoulder.

"I shall see them. But only after..." Pierre took her in his arms and kissed her with the vigor and desire of a young man. He did not let her go, even when their lips parted, holding her tightly in his arms. His hand reached into a pocket and picked out a small box. "In a week, it is our anniversary. Twenty-five years of marriage. I feel like it was yesterday. For our past and future happiness, wife." He opened the box, revealing a gold brooch.

"You have carved our years in gold." The brooch was sophisticated in its simplicity, something only the jewelers in Tomis could make: two figures, representing the time they had spent together, used as support for two black gems.

"The best years of my life, wife, and the most beautiful black eyes in the world."

Silently, she attached the brooch to her chemise and, unwillingly, tears escaped from her eyes. She hid her head on his shoulder again, and he pretended to be unaware of her emotion.

Early in the morning, the massive outer courtyard of the barracks was full of soldiers, and many torches lit the area brightly. Fully armed, Pierre sat astride his large destrier, solemnly watching what was going on. His orders were brief and sharp and, when needed, he moved like an efficient war machine, competent in what he was doing as he arranged fifteen hundred soldiers in order. From the window, Celeste watched everything in anguished silence, wringing her hands.

"Mother," Helene said gently, and took Celeste's hands in hers. "Father is a strong man, and he has the best army in Frankis."

"That young man in Poenari..." Celeste shook her head.

"As you said, he is young."

"Still, he has achieved so much. Some people say that his father was a Duke, others say that he was the King of Arenia."

"Why would that matter?"

"There is an aura around him. That kind of charisma that brings out the best in any soldier. This is what I am afraid of."

The end of spring sun was now half in sight over the large plain, and the army was properly in order and ready to leave Tolosa as the knights, their duties complete, began to mount their horses. "March!" Pierre ordered, his voice sharp and loud in the morning silence. The army moved like a giant snake, company after company leaving the city through the large northern gate, the Red Gate. The four gates of Tolosa were each constructed from a different color stone. They descended toward the valley of Garon River under the summer sunrise, looking like an army of ants in the distance. Like a dark blue tide of men and horses, they flowed away in a steady rhythm, watched by the guards atop the massive wall of the city.

The letter was brief, containing only one sentence, the order for him to come to Tolosa. *What could have happened to make the Duke summon me so urgently?* Valer wondered. "I need five men with me," he said to his second-in-command. "I must go to Tolosa. I may stay there overnight." It was just a three-hour ride from the fortified house in the mountains that played the role of quarters for Valer's mercenaries.

At the gate of the palace, Valer was taken in charge by the guards, and his men were preventing from joining him inside. *I don't like this*; he thought and briefly touched the hilt of his sword. This was the first time that his guards had not been allowed inside the precincts. The Duke's soldiers led him to the antechamber of the council room. One of them mutely pointed to one of the chairs aligned against the wall on the left. Valer was not alone waiting for an audience; there were six more people, and he felt a kind of amusement in their stares: he would have to wait longer than them. *Now I am sure that I have to sleep in Tolosa.*

After half an hour, one man and a woman went inside the council room, while two more men joined them in the antechamber. The reaction of the people around Valer toward the newcomers revealed the same amusement they had treated him to. Eyes almost closed, Valer ignored them, and he also had to ignore – or at least to pretend that he ignored – the fact that all the people in the antechamber were invited inside before him, even the newcomers. *The Duke wants me to stew.*

When Valer was finally allowed to enter, he found Baldovin, the Duke, and his wife, Laure. That was expected; Laure was more Duke than Baldovin. What he had not expected was Maud's presence, and her cold eyes staring at him. He bowed and waited patiently. It took a while for the Duke to gesture loosely toward an empty chair.

"How busy are your mercenaries?" Baldovin asked.

"All of them are hired for periods from a few months to half a year. More than half are already gone to their assignments." That was untrue; in three days, his main force of a hundred would be ready to leave and join Codrin in Poenari.

"How many will join Codrin? It seems that you are his preferred Black Dervil," Maud said.

"Fifty."

"Why only fifty?"

"I can't answer that question." He looked at Maud, then he chose to move his eyes to a painting hanging on the opposite wall. "I deliver as many soldiers as a contract stipulates."

"You are fighting against me," Baldovin snapped.

"I would never do such a thing, my lord. My mercenaries never fight in Tolosa. That's one of our strictest rules. Maybe someone has deceived you. If there are indeed mercenaries ready to fight here, they don't belong to me; they are from another Dervil."

"You pretend you do not know about the Duke's army going north, to Deva," Maud said, her voice even.

"How should I know?" Valer replied. "I am not part of the Duke's entourage."

"People say that you are well informed. You can't be a Dervil without being well informed. Can you?" Maud stared at him, her black eyes a contrast to Baldovin's blue stare.

"Information often flows in strange ways, Lady Maud. This year, I have no interests in Deva. None of my mercenaries will fight there. Maybe that's why I did not learn about the ducal army going to Deva."

"How many men do you still have at home?"

"Fifty."

"Keep them there. You may leave now." Baldovin's voice was cold, and he gestured dismissively toward the door.

❧

The rain was pouring when Bucur left Severin. The small river, meandering only ten miles from the city, became suddenly swollen and split his army in two. Some considered this a bad omen; some did not care much about such things. Bucur did not care either; he was more worried that only five hundred soldiers, from the promised fifteen hundred, were coming from Peyris. And all their other allies had sent fewer soldiers than they had agreed. That little series of shortfalls meant another five hundred soldiers fewer for his army. When they were all gathered, his army would have only two thousand seven hundred soldiers, and most of them would come from Tolosa.

He had expected four thousand and, even worse, he had not been able to learn much about Poenari. Few people knew about it, and most of the things they told him were not helpful. *Ghost city*, he thought. *What can I do with such superstitious people? None of our scouts has returned from Poenari. Now, half the idiots in our army think we are fighting ghosts.*

From her window, Saliné was watching the army which became smaller and smaller toward the horizon. *Fate, please help Codrin*, she pleaded. Both Aron and Bucur took care to let her know how many soldiers will come to take Poenari, and none of them tried to hide their satisfaction and how will they hang Codrin after capturing his fortress. She listened to their morbid bragging with a forced calm, and that make them repeat the same thing for several times. Only late in the evening, alone in her room, she could let her worries take over and, standing on the floor, her back leaning against the wall, she cried, sometimes long after midnight had passed. When the last soldier vanished from sight, she pressed her forefront against the cold window, trying to calm her turmoil, and tears ran down her face.

When his army arrived in the forest, Bucur signaled the riders behind him to stop under the trees. There was at least some shelter under the dense foliage, and they had to wait for the other half of the army that was hindered by the swollen river. For a moment, he considered riding ahead, and arriving earlier in Poenari. *I may fall into a trap;* he shook his head. *The best of my soldiers will come from Tolosa, and we will meet close to Poenari*. He had only seven hundred soldiers with him, five hundred of them from Orban, a man he could not fully trust. The troop from Peyris would join him close to Faget, the traditional castle of his family, now in Codrin's hands. He ached to take the castle back, but the Circle had forbidden him. Poenari first, and then he could do what he wanted. Two Itinerant Sages, Verenius, the Primus Itinerant, and Octavian, accompanied him. Which was to say, they were there to keep an eye on him. The Circle had gambled a lot on this war which, officially, was started to bring Deva under Bucur's authority. They wanted to crush Codrin.

How I will enjoy seeing him hanged, Bucur thought with morbid satisfaction. *I will force that bitch to watch him die. How pleasant will be to have Saliné in my bed while she still mourns him.*

Despite Maud's formal interdiction, a part of the Circle led by Octavian had decided to avenge Belugas and kill Codrin the same way. Octavian was Maud's closest confidant, and she knew about his plot, and each time he tried to convince her, she protested, though she did nothing to stop it. It was just a show, as she was afraid of Drusila's Visions. She would welcome Codrin's death, crying that she didn't know anything.

The only one who was not planning to kill Codrin was Verenius. Despite that great army, which Bucur was formally leading, the Primus Itinerant had come to understand that the reality was more complex, and the young man, who the most powerful forces in Frankis wanted dead, might not be so easy to kill, and any assassination attempt would only complicate the Circle's task. There was something else in Verenius' mind too; of all the Circle's people working for Bucur, he was the only one who actually knew Poenari, and knew its value as a fortress. That place was so isolated and forgotten, that most maps were not even mentioning it. Maud did not ask him, and Verenius did not tell her. *Codrin will make a better King, but we have to wait ten more years until Bucur expires. Or Fate takes him.*

Chapter 30 - Codrin

The Mountes should have arrived five days ago in Poenari, but none of the scouts could locate them. Worried, Codrin searched over the local map on the wall of the council room and compared it with the one he had brought from Cleuny. This was indeed a council room, ten times larger than his previous one, with a vast, heavy table able to seat thirty people. It resembled the one he used in Leyona for two days. The thought did not comfort him. Codrin's council of seven people was small compared to the immensity of the table, and they gathered at one end of it, so they didn't feel too lost.

"The army from Tolosa is coming by this road." Codrin tapped the map and looked at Vlad at the same time; he was the leader of the scouts.

"We can confirm now that it is led by Pierre, the Spatar of Tolosa. The army is three to four days away from Poenari, and they are marching slowly. From the correspondence we've intercepted they want to meet Bucur, at the Burned Forest crossroads, ten miles from here, before they get here.

"Thanks to Cleyre, Bucur was delayed by the late arrival of the Peyris army. Pierre is not aware of this, as we've intercepted Bucur's couriers. Bucur will reach the crossroads in six days, but if Pierre takes control of it before the Mountes get here, their way will be blocked. Well, not completely blocked, but the Mountes won't be able to use the road anymore. Vlad, place a scout team ten miles from the crossroads, on the road to Orhei.

They should help the Mountes reach Poenari through the mountains."

"I will ask Bernart for a soldier who knows the high paths through the mountains," Vlad said.

"What about our soldiers from Severin and southern Mehadia? Only seventy have arrived, and I was waiting for eighty more." Codrin looked at Vlaicu this time, but he already knew the answer to his question.

"I don't think that they will come." Vlaicu turned his palms up. "Laurent is the only one who fully answered your call. Marat and three more Knights sent some men too, but they have a foot in both camps."

"Eighty soldiers fewer," Codrin mused. "We still have five and a half hundred. At least, we will have if... Valer might have been delayed too. He is supposed to arrive tomorrow with a hundred mercenaries, but Tolosa's army could have given him troubles, and forced him take another road. Valer is an experienced commander; we should not worry. He will avoid a fight with Tolosa on the road. I can't say the same about the Mountes."

The door opened, and Pintea burst into the room, breathing heavily. He waited a few moments to gather his breath before saying, "The Mountes are coming." There was a broad smile on his lips and sudden relaxation in the council room. "Yesterday, they were in Relermont village."

"They will be here in less than two days," Codrin said.

"I don't think so, there is something strange about them," Pintea said, still breathing hard, and all eyes in the room were on him. "They have come with their families. Boldur's clan, I mean; children, women, elders and their belonging. Sixty carts. That's why they were delayed."

Codrin closed his eyes for a few moments. *Have the Mountes expelled Boldur?* "How many soldiers are coming?"

"Seventy-five, if we don't count the too young or the too old. Boldur's words."

I was expecting two hundred. "Did he tell you what happened?"

"No, but he was not in a good mood. There was a look in his eyes, like he was itching to crush a skull or two. He wants to talk with you first."

"It looks like migration to me," Sava said, "and the Mountes are not eager to leave their land. They fought hard to keep it free from Arad and Peyris."

"Did Boldur mention more soldiers coming later?" Codrin asked, and Pintea shook his head. "Boldur's clan was expelled, and we may be the cause of that."

"The mountains around Poenari are empty." Sava gestured toward the window, one of the basalt towers was visible in the strong late morning light. "Give one mountain to them and they will be happy."

"Happy may be too strong a word, but I will consider that, after Boldur tells me what happened and what they intend." Codrin thought for a while. "This means fewer soldiers for us, but we can cry later; right now, we need to help the Mountes. Pierre will arrive at the Burned Forest crossroads before them, and with the carts, diverting the Mountes through the mountains is no longer an option. We have two hundred and sixty soldiers. Vlaicu, take thirty and join the Mountes. I will take two hundred and try to delay Pierre for a while. Sava, you will guard Poenari."

"Pierre has fifteen hundred soldiers," Vlad said.

"I will not take him on in open battle, but he will not know this. All I need to do is to delay him for two days. That will give the Mountes enough time to reach the crossroads before the Tolosa army gets there." Codrin stood up and went to the map again. "Vlad, we leave in one hour," he said without turning, his eyes still searching the map. "Bernart, you will lead the council in my absence."

Leaving Poenari, Codrin met another squad of scouts bringing news about a hundred strong army coming from Deva. They had no colors, and he had to change course and intercept them.

It can't be Valer, Codrin thought, *he will come from the south not from the north*. He stopped his army in a good ambush point, and he waited. *They are acting strange*. The incoming army was falling straight in his trap. They had no scouts, and they rode fast. *Devan's son*; he recognized Filippo. *Four years ago, he was supposed to become Saliné's husband. Why is he coming here?* While Codrin still felt a grudge against the other young man; Filippo was not aware of that. For him, the marriage with Saliné was just a piece of paper, an expired contract. He never met the girl, and he did not know the storm that his marriage contract had caused in Severin. "Don't shoot yet," Codrin said to his archers. *They are not here to attack us*. "Devan, what brings you here?" Codrin pushed his horse at the edge of the forest.

"My father has a debt to you. I came here with a hundred soldiers to honor his word."

"What about your missing colors?"

"The bastards from the Circle have many eyes in Deva."

Both men dismounted and stared at each other with different feelings. Codrin's mind was still haunted by Saliné; Filippo was eager to know the famous young man.

"You are welcome," Codrin said and stretched his hand, the painful past almost forgotten. "We have a war to win."

Fate was kind to Codrin, and he arrived at the place he wanted to be just three hours before the Tolosa army. Below, on the left, the road was flanked by a ridge, thirty feet high and six hundred feet long. On the right, the ridge was only nine feet tall, but it was covered with dense forest. It was not an ideal place for an ambush, but it was all that Codrin had. As they had arrived in a hurry, there was not enough time for his scouts to take over the ridges, and some scouts from Tolosa were able to escape, stopping on a hill from where they could survey the area. It was already known by many in Frankis that Codrin had the best scouts. He used the Assassins' training methods for his scouts, and that was not known, even to the Wanderers, yet sometimes Fate tricks even the best.

"Prepare the army for battle," Codrin said to his officers, looking at the road from Poenari toward the narrow gap in front of them: it sloped downward for two hundred paces, through a large meadow. Most of his small army was still hidden in the forest behind him. "Ban, take thirty archers and set up on the left-hand ridge." He looked up toward the sky, and his eyes followed the sun, going west. When he turned, Codrin saw the worry in the eyes of his officers. "We *will* not give battle, but don't tell that to Pierre. It's an hour past noon. He will not want to start a fight today, so he will camp somewhere down in the valley. Tomorrow, we will take up position for battle again, most of our soldiers hidden in the forest behind us. Only our front line will be visible from the valley. They need to prepare for battle too, and they will know that we have archers on the ridge but, if we keep their scouts away, Pierre will not know how many soldiers we have. I'm sure he will think that we have more than three hundred. No one is crazy enough to attack more than a thousand with three hundred. Right? They have to prepare, so half of the morning will be gone when they arrive where the road enters between the ridges. They will advance with care. If they are able to climb the ridge from the valley," he looked at Ban, "mount up and vanish into the forest. If not, rain arrows on them until they are able to get to this side through the gap. You run before they can turn and climb the ridge from this side."

"Codrin sent his army to fight us," the scout said even before dismounting in front of Pierre, the Spatar of Tolosa. Unhurried, his army was ready to move again after lunch. "It is arranged in a battle line on the top of a hill overseeing the road, waiting for us. One hour's ride from here."

"What advantage does that place hold?" Pierre asked the scout. The Spatar of Tolosa was a tall man, towering over most people in his army, and he liked people who were as tall as he was. With his dark brown mane and massive frame, he resembled a lion, and the Lion of Tolosa was he called. There was even a joke, that no one was promoted to captain if he was not able to take his insignia from the Lion's raised claw. But his smile was his most outstanding feature; it was bright and distinctive and a rare sight; Pierre was now fifty-two and thinking that this was his last battle. The scouts were not usually tall men; they needed to be able to sneak everywhere, unobserved.

"The road passes through a gap between two ridges. Their archers have already taken over the ridges. Some thirty men." The scout still tried to look up at Pierre, but the Spatar was so tall he had to tip his head right back.

"How many soldiers does he have?" Pierre controlled both his impulse to smile at the short man's effort and his urge to rip off his armor, which felt like an oven in the heat.

"Difficult to say. We could see only the vanguard, around two hundred soldiers. The rest of the army remained hidden in the forest.

"You hide an army when you don't have many soldiers. Two hundred in the vanguard, and perhaps the same amount in the forest. Why are they here?" Pierre pondered. "It makes no sense, and it make even less sense to arrange themselves for battle and wait for us in a tight formation. I will not start a battle without resting my soldiers. Their soldiers can stay at battle stations until tomorrow if that's what Codrin wants."

"Maybe there are more soldiers hidden in the forest..." one captain said tentatively.

"The Circle guaranteed to me that Codrin has less than four hundred soldiers. War is a terrible thing, but this one started some months ago, with the battle between our embassies. As things stand, the Circle has won everywhere except Peyris, but Duke Stefan sent five hundred soldiers, so it is still to our advantage. Valer was coerced into keeping his mercenaries at home, and the Mountes rejected Codrin's plea for help. I still don't know how the Sages were able to buy the Mountes; they have the most rigid spines in Frankis. Even some of Codrin's knights did not answer the call. It suits us, but I despise these traitors; if you are a Knight, then you answer the call for war. How long until we are able to see the ridge?"

"In half an hour."

"Then we will talk again in half an hour. Stay close to me." Pierre looked at the scout for a few more moments, then mounted his destrier. *Is Codrin trying to attack us before we can join Bucur? He has no chance... Has he set a trap, maybe? He defeated Orban's much larger army by concealing a crevasse. But he had no time to set such a trap here. Perhaps.*

"That's the ridge." The scout pointed forward, the moment they rounded a large curve in the road. "Their army is not yet in sight. It will be in fifteen more minutes."

Pierre stopped his horse and rose in the saddle, his palm protecting his eyes from the strong afternoon sun. "Send a team of scouts to see if two hundred strong men can pass behind that small hill and get behind the ridge where Codrin's archers are hidden. Let's go." He pushed his horse to a fast trot, then stopped again when the enemy army came in sight. "We will camp here!" he shouted before dismounting.

The council started when the first squad of scouts returned with the news that a small force would be able to pass through a ravine and observe the archers hidden on the ridge. The sun was now only a thin line above the hills in the west.

"Reno, in the morning, gather two hundred soldiers and take up position behind their archers. You will not attack until our forces arrive at the ridge. We should let them think that we were caught by surprise by the archers. Don't attack them directly, just cut off their escape. It should be easy to capture thirty soldiers." Pierre shifted his weight on his long legs, from one to the other, sweating underneath his chain mail armor. "We will continue the council when the other two squads of scouts return."

To Pierre's chagrin, the scouts never returned; ten good soldiers had been lost.

It was early morning when Pierre woke again. "Still no news of our missing scouts?" He looked up at the hills, and shielded his eyes from the early morning sun, which bathed the hillside in a dazzling white light.

"Nothing," the captain said. "They must have been captured."

Killed, most probably. Pierre agreed with a nod; he had guessed as much the day before. "Is Reno ready to go?"

"Yes, Sir."

The riders were ready and waiting for the order to go, but the order did not come. Eyes closed, Pierre let his thoughts wander. It was his way of approaching the same issue from a different angle. *Why is Codrin here? He doesn't have enough men to attack me. Maybe he wants only to delay me. Why?* "Joffroy, take three hundred men and go to the Burned Forest Cross. There is a parallel road going to Orhei. You need to go fifteen miles back south, then turn north. After you pass the crossroads, leave the road and ride through the forest. Hide your men on top of a hill overlooking the cross and wait there. Watch the roads."

"What should I look for?" Joffroy asked; he was his son and the second captain of the army.

"I don't know. Maybe nothing. You have full liberty to engage if something happens. Go now and assemble your men." Pierre turned toward Reno, who was still waiting, and gave him the signal to go. "Let your men rest," he said to his other three captains. "We will attack at noon." *Or maybe even later...*

"I can't wait to fight," Dulain, Pierre's nephew said, his eyes bright, full of confidence. He was only eighteen years old, and under Joffroy's command. This was his first battle. "We have enough men to defeat whatever army we find at the cross."

"What if you find two thousand soldiers there?" Pierre asked, half-amused. *I wish I could have left him at home*. But his sister had insisted, and he thought he would be able to protect the untrained man. *I can't protect Dulain from himself.* "I admire your spirit, young Dulain, but beware of overconfidence. It will not get you far."

Dulain turned slightly red at a speed which only young people possess. "Of course, uncle, I apologize for my over-eagerness.'"

Pierre slapped him on the back. "Eagerness for battle is a virtue, but so is wisdom. Let the old wise heads decide when to start the fight." Pierre laughed. "Don't worry, you'll see action soon enough."

Reno did not hurry his men. They rode back south for five miles until the ridge vanished from sight. After a tight curve leading through the forest, he felt confident enough to leave the road, following a small creek on the left. In the camp, the scouts had told him that the creek allowed passage around a long chain of hills rising parallel with the ridge where Codrin's archers were hidden. After half a mile, they left the creek and moved north again. Now and then, Reno matched the landscape with the mental map the scouts had given him: You turn left and leave the creek in front of a yellow rock with a small yew tree on top. You go north around the foot of the hills for five miles. You turn left through a gap between two large rocks the size of a house. They are strange rocks with parallel layers of stones, some of them yellow, some of them white. There are several gaps there, so we scratched three parallel lines at the bottom of the rock on the left.

He found everything as they said, even the scratches, and a sense of pride swelled in him; they were his scouts. In two hours, they arrived at a place situated in a gap between two hilltops. The road toward Poenari and Codrin main army were no longer in sight; but he could see the ridge where he knew Codrin's archers were positioned.

Followed by fifty riders, Valer rode north, toward Poenari. He had left home the other fifty men promised to Codrin, but he had to obey the Duke of Tolosa, yet he had tricked the Duke who did not know about the fifty men behind him. They traveled through small roads that only the locals used. They were in a hurry, but they did not rush. Each road was traveled with caution, the scouts going first, then the rest of his men. Sometimes, they rode through the forest. That slowed them even more. Even with all that caution, at one point, his scouts almost bumped into Pierre's scouts. Only the swifter reactions of the mercenaries saved the day; they slid silently into the forest and hid behind some bushes. In a regular war, they would have killed the scouts from Tolosa, but Valer did not want Pierre to react because of the missing scouts. The stealthiest journey is the one that is not guessed at by the enemy, and Valer did not want to be seen; Duke Baldovin would have had him hanged.

"Army ahead," Ferio, his best scout said, stopping his horse abruptly on front of Valer. "Tolosa, but it's not Pierre. A splinter group, three hundred soldiers."

"Where are they heading?" Valer asked.

"That's a kind of a riddle. They came back south and, at the crossroads that lies three miles from here, they took the left fork toward Orhei. I left two men to watch the place; it was too risky to follow them." Valer's teams were small by necessity.

"A hard riddle," Valer rubbed his brow. "Ride again and see if Pierre's main army is camped somewhere ahead. We will wait for you at the crossroads, hidden in the forest on the eastern side."

The morning was already old when Codrin arranged his army for battle again, at the edge of the forest, trying to hide how small it was. There was no sign yet that Pierre was going to attack anytime soon, but scouts from Tolosa were swarming the area south of the ridge. He ordered his own scouts to avoid riding at the border of the ridge. *The later Pierre attacks, the better*, he thought. Early in the morning, a courier had arrived from Poenari with the message that the Mountes had increased their pace, and they would arrive at the Burned Forest crossroads half a day earlier than they had expected. He needed to delay Pierre's army for just a day and a half, and half a day's delay had already been achieved.

"Pierre's main army is less than fifteen miles away from here," Ferio reported to Valer when he returned to the crossroads with his two men. "They are preparing for battle. Codrin is waiting for them."

"How many men does Codrin have?" Valer asked, convinced that his army was much smaller than the one from Tolosa.

"Difficult to say; some parts of it are hidden in the forest. Maybe three hundred strong."

Why did Codrin chose to confront Tolosa here? Pierre is an old fox, and it's not easy to trick him. "The splinter troop from Pierre's army is trying to surround Codrin. We must warn him."

Abruptly, Valer pushed his horse on the road leading to Orhei, parallel to the one where Pierre and Codrin had assembled their armies. They dispensed with caution and rode at a full gallop until the rearguard of the enemy came into sight. At that moment, they left the road and went on, at a lower speed, through the forest on the west side.

"Strange," Valer murmured to himself. "They are not in a hurry." He thought for a while, then turned toward Ferio, who was on his left. "How far are we from the place where Codrin's army is waiting?"

"I can't tell from here. The hill between Codrin's place and this road has a peculiar bunch of rocks on the top. They vaguely resemble a bust of an old man. It may look the same from this side. I need to..." He gestured toward the road that was just visible through the trees.

Go, Valer nodded.

Ferio stopped his horse at the edge of the forest and searched the road left and right. It seemed peaceful. He prompted his horse and passed onto the other side, and entered the forest again, where he turned. He felt a moment's apprehension as they first rode among the tall pine trees. From his saddle, he looked at the hills ahead. He could not see their tops and decided to go further up, to reach an open place inside the forest that was a hundred feet higher than the road. Close to the gap in the forest, the path became too steep, and he had to dismount, and lead the horse by the halter. Arriving at the highest place in the meadow, he looked again at the hills to the east. "The old man," he said to himself, as the stones were now visible north-east, three miles from him. At the road, he glanced left and right again, then crossed the road.

Three hundred paces from him, a troop of four men watched him vanishing between the trees and rode north. They wore the colors of Tolosa.

"The *old man* is only three miles from here," Ferio told Valer. "I can't say if there is a gap between this side and the eastern edge, but these hills are small, it should not be an issue to pass to the other side."

"Captain Reno's men are now in place in a gap close to the top of the hill. They are waiting for the main army to attack." A soldier from the captain's companies had returned and reported to Pierre, who nodded. The sun was now high in the sky. "They are half a mile from the ridge where Codrin's archers are hiding."

"Did you see the archers?" Pierre asked.

"We have a direct line of view to the ridge, but the archers are hidden. They were probably expecting that our scouts would reach the top of the hill."

One hour into the afternoon, the army of Tolosa was ready to march north. Pierre sat up straight in his saddle. "Hear my command." He looked round at his army and gave the signal move to move forward.

Company after company moved in their usual marching order. The four elite companies marched in front, prepared to counter any surprise attack. During long marches, after three hours, the companies would rotate, the first one falling back to fourth place. Pierre had planned things down to the smallest detail. This time, they rode more slowly than usual, leaving their horses to choose their own speed.

"The pressure is on the enemy," Pierre said to his captains. "Let them boil." He was still pondering about the reason for the unequal battle in front of him but kept the thought to himself. His guess was that Codrin was trying to delay him, but he wasn't sure. *Joffroy may be able to find the reason; Codrin knows what he's doing. Soon, I will meet him*. Half a mile before the ridge, he halted the march, waiting for the latest reports from his scouts. This time they were able to return, and Pierre listened to their report with a calm that transferred to his men. "I want to see their army." He mounted his horse and twenty men of his guards mounted too. They advanced at leisure, up to the point where the scouts stopped them, as Codrin's archers, who were still invisible, could send a volley. The ridge on the right had the disadvantage of being too steep on this side, and Pierre's scouts could not climb it.

"We need to dismount and climb to that rock on the left. From there, Codrin's army is visible," the scout said.

Pierre climbed the rock, but he was disappointed by the view. *There is an army there, any fool can see it, but there is nothing useful to be learn from here*, he thought. *Am I a fool?* He liked to see the enemy from proximity, try to understand their emplacement and to guess their tactics. It was not possible from their position. They hurried down at the sound of riders coming from the left, through the forest. Half of his guard moved to intercept the incomers, half surrounded Pierre, who mounted his horse.

"Our men," the scout who was still on the rock said.

Joffroy's men, Pierre thought, seeing the riders, who were now at the edge of the forest. "Report."

"There is another force coming over the hill to join Codrin."

"How large is it?"

"We saw it in the forest. Something between fifty and a hundred soldiers. They will be there in half an hour." The scout pointed toward the place where Codrin's army was waiting, prepared for battle.

"One hundred men will not change the balance of things too much. Tell the rest of the army to come here."

"Will we attack now?" one captain who had arrived with the troupe asked.

"Not yet," Pierre smiled.

"Codrin's army has left the battle line." The scout was panting hard, as he went in his mission without a horse and, at first, no one believed him. It sounded like a joke.

"Explain," Pierre ordered.

"Fifty men joined their army up the hill, and in fifteen minutes they were all gone. They went north, probably toward Poenari."

"We can set the camp again," one captain said.

Joffroy... "Mount your horses. We ride now!" Pierre shouted.

ஜ

Three armed groups arrived at the Burned Forest Cross at a two-hour interval between them. Codrin was the first to arrive, then Pierre, and then Joffroy. By coincidence, the first Mountes arrived at the same time as Pierre, who rose into his saddle to understand what was happening.

That may be the reason of Codrin's actions, Pierre thought, seeing the long caravan. *I don't see Codrin's army.* Cautious, the Spatar of Tolosa stopped his army two miles away from the cross. He shielded his eyes from sun, trying to see the caravan better. "Send two more squads of scouts to verify the hills around the cross and the caravan. We stop here and wait for Joffroy." They knew already that the second group from Tolosa will arrive in two hours.

"An embassy from the Circle will come in half an hour," one of the scouts from the first squad reported.

"Who is leading it?" Pierre asked.

"Octavian."

Ah, the scoundrel. I would have preferred Verenius. "Bring him to me. Alone."

Led by Codrin, ten riders left the forest hiding his army, climbing down the hill. They stopped in the middle of the plain south of the Burned Forest Cross. Taking ten men with him, Pierre rode to meet his enemies. When he was three hundred paces away, one man came toward them. Pierre did the same, and they met in the middle.

"Tudor," Pierre said, surprised. "I was expecting Codrin, but I am glad to meet an old friend."

"Sir Pierre." Codrin bowed slightly.

"Both men dismounted, and they clasped hands. "Why are you here?"

"That's a bit difficult to explain. This time, it is not Tudor you meet. This time, I am Codrin." He looked at Pierre with a tentative smile on his lips. "I hoped that they would not send you or Joffroy, but you are the best Spatar in Frankis."

"So, you..." Pierre pointed three times at Codrin, "are ... both Codrin and the Wraith of Tolosa?"

"Yes, I am sorry for hiding it from you, but I had no choice."

"I see... Things are more complicated than they looked in the beginning. We are... No, we are not enemies. We will fight each other, but we are not enemies."

"Thank you, Sir Pierre, I was hoping for that. How is Joffroy?"

"Two years older since you saved his life, and he is becoming a good soldier. Do you want to see him? You ... vanished from Tolosa for some time. Now I understand the reason."

"Tolosa has a horrible jail. Very damp. I did not like the place. I was lucky that you freed me after two days."

"It was just a misunderstanding, but..." Pierre burst into laughter. "If Lady Laure had known who we had arrested, I would not have been able to free you. Do you want to see Joffroy? He is here, too."

"I would like to see him, but I would like even more to keep my real identity hidden. There are very few people who know that Codrin and Tudor are the same person."

"I see..." Pierre thought a moment. "So, Codrin, what brought you here?"

"The people on the road. There are soldiers among them, but most of them are women, children and old people."

"How many armed Mountes are there? And how many are unable to fight?"

"There are fifty armed men at the moment, and more than six hundred who are not fighters."

"And you are willing to fight an army which is four times as big to help those people." Pierre spoke to himself, and Codrin knew it. "There is a snake in my camp who wants me to attack the convoy."

"Octavian, the Sage of the Circle."

"Why did you let him pass?"

"I wanted you to know that Bucur's army will arrive here in two days."

"Next time, hang him. That man is worse than any other Sage Itinerant. We are lucky that he was sick when their new Primus was elected. Verenius may be a tricky man, but at least he has some honor. Tell the Mountes that they are safe. I don't attack women and children."

"Thank you, Sir Pierre."

"How is Poenari? Just an old man's curiosity."

"It's the best fortress I've ever seen. I hope that one day you will come and visit it. There is something strange there, and you are the best architect of fortifications in Frankis."

"I will remind you about the invitation." The Spatar of Tolosa stretched his hand toward Codrin's, and they clasped again. Both men turned and left the field without a word.

Chapter 31 - Codrin

Bucur's merged armies came to a halt about seven hundred paces from the fortress and set up siege lines. Sava could see the careful battle lines from where he stood, behind an arrow loop above the gate. Codrin could see them too, from the top of the hill where his army was camped. It was a classic Tolosa tactic. They raised Bucur's new flag having three stylized white flowers on light blue background. The flowers resembled more a halberd than a known flower. It was an old chimera and the standard flag used in battle by the Frankis Kings, but there was no wind, and so the banner hung limp and its boldness was lost.

"That weakling raised the Frankis flag," Sava laughed on the walls. "Even the wind mocks him."

Once the flag was raised, ten riders broke off from the main body and thundered towards the gate.

"Bucur, the Candidate King requests entry in Poenari," one of the riders shouted.

"It is denied," Sava said flatly. "Scoundrels are not welcomed here."

"Then we shall take Poenari."

"I pity you."

"We don't need your pity," the rider growled.

"Don't worry, son, in the grave you will need nothing."

By late afternoon, the army moved to make camp for the siege. Tolosa auxiliaries had already done much of the preparation work, marking out flags where lightweight wattle was to be constructed, and clearing the area of obstacles. The companies went to their assigned positions – for the Tolosa army, they had the same positions that they held in the permanent camp. The other three armies were less organized. Some of them erected tents from the baggage train, then setting about digging the perimeter ditch and constructing the wattle to protect the army from night attacks. There were not many tents.

The siege of Poenari had begun.

Late in the morning, Pierre gathered the war council in front of his tent. He needed to see the fortress, and he stayed silent, setting his mind free to absorb the environment. Once the most important details settled in his mind, he recalled the most significant sieges of a long life, filled with many wars. *Codrin was right. This is a strong fortress; the wall is some ninety feet tall; there is a twenty feet large moat, and no one from the Circle knew about it.* "We don't have enough men; we don't have assault towers, and we have only ten catapults to take those walls by force. For half a year, we prepared ourselves to take Deva not Poenari, and it seems that those who changed the target did not feel the need to check what is here. There is no way to make a successful assault with our forces. We must find solutions."

"Let's be more optimistic," Octavian interjected.

"Octavian," Pierre said absently, his eyes still searching the walls for some hidden weakness. "Interrupt me again, and I will boot you out of the camp. Codrin is there," his thumb pointed back, "and you know well how fond he is of Itinerant Sages. We will try first to burn the gate. Sandro, Doren," he looked at the second Spatar of Peyris and the Spatar of Arad, "you have assault shields and oil too. We need to form a shell. Fifty men should be enough. I have thirty, each of you should provide another ten."

The shell took the sinuous road, dug into the stone, curving around the tower. From his place on the wall, above the gate, Sava was watching them with a mischievous smile on his lips.

"Should we shoot?" one guard asked when the shell came into the range of their ballistae.

"Let them sweat."

"Do you want to keep them..." The guard could not finish, and laughter filled the wall above the gate.

"Why not?" Sava smiled; he was the only one not laughing.

The road toward the gate was not steep, but carrying heavy shield, able to resist ballistae heavy bolts was not easy, and there were five barrels with oil too. Even when they stopped each five minutes, the men were panting and cursing.

"A hundred paces to the target," the leader of the shell announced, and the men forced themselves to advance faster. *The defenders did not shoot*; he wondered.

When they arrived at forty paces from the gate, the road in front of them broke and, pulled by strong chains, the mobile bridge started to raise. Behind their heavy shields, a hundred angry eyes followed the moving bridge, which was invisible from the valley.

"Bloody bastards," the shell leader cursed. "Turn now. Do it orderly."

The soldiers tried to turn orderly, but the road was narrow, the shields were heavy, and they were angry and tired.

"Team one, fire," Sava ordered, and ten ballistae shoot heavy bolts. Some of them were deflected by the shields, some of them found a way between them, and four shields fell. "Team two, fire."

The shell lost its cohesion; the men threw their shields away and started to run for their life.

"Fire at will, the chickens are running."

"It didn't work," Pierre said, keeping an apparent calm, his cheerless eyes following the running soldiers. *I will eat some more humiliation, but we are not prepared to seize Poenari. We don't have enough men to take a ninety feet tall wall, and I don't want to lose them for nothing, yet I can't leave.* "We start positional siege. Poenari has only one gate. They are cut from the world and have no way to receive new provisions."

Bucur and Octavian looked at him, but the Spatar of Tolosa ignored them.

"Do you know who the Chief of the Guard in Poenari is?" Pierre asked no one in particular.

"Sava," Verenius said.

"From Leyona?" Pierre looked at the Sage, who nodded. *Another friend, and the best Chief of Guard I know. I know him from the time when we chased young girls in Tolosa. We ended by chasing Neira and Celeste. The girls are cousins, and they are our wives now. Vlad and Pintea are some of the best scouts in Frankis. I know both. Last year, Calin wrote to me that Mara was Codrin's Secretary in Cleuny. I met her in Sava's house, when she was just a girl. She is intelligent, and the second Secretary of Tolosa speaks well of her. How could Codrin find so many good people in such a short time? People of honor, not scoundrels like Octavian and Bucur. I am on the wrong side in this war. Only because Baldovin is ill and, and Laure leads Tolosa.* "Send men to retrieve our dead."

"We will just lose more soldiers," Bucur said.

"We won't." *Sava is a real man.*

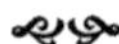

The night was overseen by a pale moon, as large as a chariot wheel, and it only took a few moments for Codrin's vision to adjust to the meager light, when he came out of the forest. He swayed in the saddle, feeling his nerves tingle with excitement. Everything had been planned down to the smallest detail. For two weeks, he had not bothered Pierre's army; none of his soldiers came close to the enemy camp, but no enemy scout, from those who ventured too far from the plain, returned to the camp either. Codrin carried his helmet in the crook of his arm because he did not want anything to obstruct his hearing. The feeble wind played in his long mane. The last two days came with a strong wind which uprooted some old trees. The evening before, the hale stopped as suddenly as it came from the ocean. It was replaced by fog and a cold frizzle of rain too. The wild outburst of the nature suited his plans, as the enemy scouts were blind, and anyway they did not know the area well. His mind flew back to Severin, to Cernat's hunting house. That evening, for the first time, he heard Saliné singing. She pulled a lyre from a large chest made of polished acajou wood, a dark red color like her hair. Gently, like a mother caressing her child, she plucked a string with delicate fingers, and the note filled the room, warm and vibrant. Sometimes she would catch him looking at her, and she would smile, making Codrin lose himself even more. An owl called out three times from the plain in front, then two times more, and Codrin jerked his head in response to the sudden warning.

"The scouts have done their job," Vlad whispered on Codrin's left. He, Vlaicu, Damian and Julien, who was Sava's elder son, would form a wedge behind Codrin to lead the riders. The second wedge was led by Laurent.

The scouts had gone ahead to take down the enemy sentries on the left side of the plain. A team of strong Mountes was prepared to level the wooden palisade Pierre had ordered to be raised. The excitement of the fight already burned through his veins; for the first time, Codrin knew that he had to fight a seasoned army commander. Pierre was a mighty Spatar, the best in Frankis; no wonder he was called the Lion of Tolosa. Despite the difference in age and the war which was impose on them, they were still friends, and each commander respected the value of his opponent.

On paper, Codrin's plan was simple. His main force consisted of two hundred men, his best riders, of which thirty were Ban's archers, and was split in two, one being led by Codrin, the second one by his main Knight, Laurent. The archers were to send volleys of arrows into the enemy camp first to cause confusion and panic. The third volley would be made of fire arrows that would burn the tents and light up the camp, making the advance of the cavalry easier.

A few dark silhouettes moved in front of Codrin; the scouts were returning. "All done," Pintea reported.

"Thank you, scouts. You have made our task easier. How long until dawn, Vlad?" Codrin asked, gazing up at the stars. He was good at reading the path of the constellations, but Vlad was a mountain man, and better than him at guessing the passing of time. During his childhood, Vlad's life was ordained by the flow of the stars and moon. Or perhaps Codrin just wanted to flush out his inner tension.

Vlad sniffed the wind, gazing up. "Two more hours. Most of them are asleep in the camp, except the sentries, who are dead."

"We march now." Codrin's words were carried by mouth, and after a minute, the riders went down toward the plain, like a black wall. They did not hurry.

Two hundred paces from the camp, the archers prepared their arrows. One volley flew, and its sound was the sound of death. Screams filled the night inside the camp and, here and there, sleepy soldiers stood up. A second volley followed. Two men, carrying buckets of pitch, dismounted, and ran from one archer to another. The next volley left behind long trails of fire. They hit the tents, which were of light colors and visible under the moonlight. Some of them burst into flames, lighting up the plain.

"Ride!" Codrin shouted.

It was like unleashing a dam of dark horses. The roar from the men drowned out the twang of bows as the dark of the night sky was pierced by invisible arrows. The archers dismounted and dropped onto their backs, tensing the bows with their feet, almost leaping into the air as their arrows went skyward. Another volley flew before the first had even landed. The camp in the plain came to life while death spread, taking her toll. Men were rising, grabbing weapons and armor, but it was too late for organized resistance. The arrows showered into the camp like rain, and the night was filled with shrieks of agony.

Codrin knew he had won the battle before the first sword fell. He also knew that he was far from winning the war. The morning came silent and serene, and with it, the full account of the night battle, which had ended in less than twenty minutes.

"We've lost four hundred and seven soldiers," the first captain of Tolosa informed Pierre.

"What about them?" Pierre asked, pointing at the horses having no riders.

"Codrin lost twenty-seven men."

"Commanders!" Pierre shouted, standing tall in the middle of the camp. "We've met a man who knows how to fight. There was a wattle to protect us, and there were sentries watching the night. It was not enough. We need to double everything, and we need men who knows how to make a watch. Warn them that they will be the first ones to die."

"Do you think that Codrin will repeat the attack?" Joffroy asked when he remained alone with Pierre.

"He may, but not soon, and not in the same fashion." *The Wraith of Tolosa is a resourceful man. Soon, I have to tell Joffroy that Codrin is Tudor. He saved my son's life.* "Learn from his attack, son. One day you may confront him, or you may befriend him." *It should be the latter. Joffroy might become one of Codrin's best commanders. In time he might even be his Spatar. Those fools from the Circle think that they can defeat Codrin. It will not happen. After this war, I will challenge that witch who pushed Baldovin into this fight.* "The commanders will gather in my tent. Go and receive them; I still have some things to check."

"It will not be a pleasant talk," Joffroy said and left his father. He found Bucur, Verenius and Octavian inside the tent. Silent, he took his place at the long table. He always sat on Pierre's right.

"Why didn't the scouts warn us of this night attack? How could they take us so unaware? Somebody must be held responsible for this disaster!" Bucur shook his head vigorously. He was red-faced and angry. Codrin led his main attack on Bucur's area, killing almost half of his men.

Joffroy stared at him, for a few moments, but ignored his question.

"I asked you a question."

"You don't have much experience in battle," Joffroy said, his words coming slowly, as if he was forcing them through his teeth. His eyes were looking attentive at a small dark spot on the ceiling. "There will be a council soon. You can voice your worries when it starts."

One by one, more commanders entered the tent, and most of them frowned, sensing the bad mood.

"You won't answer because your scouts failed us."

"It's no good blaming the scouts for this night. In this fog and rain, a full army could slip through our lines," Verenius said.

"Bad weather is not an excuse," Octavian took Bucur's part. He was not giving much credit to Bucur but settling scores with Verenius was another thing. *This weakling took my place as Primus Itinerant.* He looked at Verenius, a cold smile on his lips, but Verenius did not take the bait. *Weakling.*

"A war council is not to find excuses or to settle scores," Pierre said, entering the tent. He took his place at one head of the table, while Bucur seated himself at the other head. "Bickering is getting us nowhere. We need to understand what happened and to decide what we are to do now. A blaming game will not help."

"Let's start with the scouts," Bucur said. "A full army attacked us in the morning. Why were they not able to spot it?"

"In the past two weeks, all our scouts who went away more than five miles from the camp vanished. In the council, we took the decision to keep them closer to the camp. There was no way to find an army which was hidden in the forest, in a familiar place."

"It was a wrong decision."

"Our decision kept our scouts alive, and none of you opposed that decision. Why complain now? We still need them to check the area around the camp."

"We need better scouts," Octavian said.

"Where to find them? If you volunteer to scout the forests around, I will accept your offer." *They say that the Circle has capable Itinerants,* Pierre thought. *Octavian is not stupid, so it must be a game.* He stared at Circle's man, daring him to answer. It did not happen. *Who was his target?* Pierre glanced around and saw Verenius smiling thinly. *So, this is an internal fight.* "If there are no more questions related to the scouts..." Pierre glanced around, but no one tried to interfere. "Our next weak link in the chain were the sentries. In the area where the attack occurred, we had ten sentries last night, and most of them were behind the wattle palisade. None of them raised the alarm and when the attack occurred the palisade was down."

This time, Pierre looked at Bucur; it was his area on which Codrin entered the camp.

Bucur blasted in frustration, "That's ridiculous!" and turned his back on Pierre struggling to control his temper.

"We will split your area of responsibility in three. One goes to Tolosa, the other two to Peyris and Arad. Sandro, Doren," Pierre looked at the second Spatar of Peyris and the Spatar of Arad, "talk with Joffroy after the meeting for who will take what. This campaign wasn't quite what we expected, and it's not yet finished. Anything else?" He looked at the people around the table and found only silence. Bucur opened his mouth to protest, then shut it in a grim line. "You are free to go."

"I thought that we had the best scouts in Frankis," Joffroy said, his voice bitter, when he remained alone with his father. Before being promoted to commander, he was the leader of the scouts.

Pierre placed a hand on his shoulders, and they went out together. "We have very good scouts, but the ones out there," Pierre gestured toward the forest covering the foot of the southern mountain, "were trained by the Wraith of Tolosa."

"Tudor?" Joffroy asked in disbelief. "He is from Tolosa. Why is he working against us?"

"He is not working against us. He works for himself."

"But he is from Tolosa, and he is a man of honor."

"Son," Pierre squeezed his shoulder, "it's time for you to know this. Codrin and Tudor are the same person."

"It can't be." Joffroy stared at his father for a denial that did not came. "Since when do you know this?"

"Since I met him at the Burned Forest Cross. I suppose that Vlad is the leader of his scouts. You know Vlad." Pierre turned his palms up.

"During the night attack, we've lost just seven men who were in Arad camp. Codrin attacked only Bucur and Orban' soldiers. Peyris lost sixty something men, because they went to help the soldiers from Arad. We were on the other side of the camp, far from the battle."

"We are here to lay siege on Poenari, because Baldovin was stupid enough to listen to the Circle, but Tudor is still our friend."

"Yes, but why did he spare Peyris? They were not attacked either."

"It may be that he has a friend there too, most probably Cleyre. She delayed Peyris army."

"Don't you think that all this is a farce?" Joffroy asked, pointing at the camp.

"War is never a farce, but Bucur as candidate King is the worst one I've seen in my life, and I am not a young man. I don't know how the Circle could go so low. This thing related to Codrin should stay between us, no one else know, not even my commanders. Go now, Sandro and Doren are waiting for you."

Chapter 32 - Codrin

It all started with a small line of clouds at the edge of the sky. It was little more than a smudge, white and thin, almost shy. The wind blew them back toward the ocean, and they vanished from sight. The clouds were stubborn, though. They came back some hours later, and their color soon changed to dark blue, then to black. It was almost as if they wanted to scare the wind, still trying to blow west. In a few minutes, the wind changed its mind, moved east and gained strength. The clouds rolled over the sky, and the soldiers began to look uneasily around. Strong gusts came from nowhere, and the men on the plain leaned into the wind to avoid being thrown down. Some just lay down in the grass. In the eerie light beneath the clouds, the walls of Poenari looked impregnable and sinister. In less than half an hour, the blue sky vanished, and it was almost like the night came at noon that day. The first drops were so huge that they left holes the size of a child's fist in the dust. The wind stopped. The flood came a few moments later. It was like someone had broken a dam in the sky, and the green plain morphed into a pool. It was not deep, just three feet, as Codrin blocked the bottom of channel dug by the Albans for the water to move away from the plain. In the middle, over the road from Orhei leading toward Poenari, the water was less than a foot deep. Only the eastern part, close to the small ridge where the road mounted toward the gate, was not yet submerged. Chased by the rising water, the soldiers gathered there, and the place soon became crowded. Angry eyes followed the water, which was still rising.

"Blast this rain," Pierre cursed. "Companies three, four and seven, move the carts with the food over here. We still need to eat." These companies were Mountes, men from the Pirenes Mountains in the south, and they were tall and strong.

"We can even climb on them, if the water rises further," Bucur added, trying to take some initiative.

"It will not rise further." Pierre used his hand as a roof for his eyes, trying to see something through the almost darkness. "The water stopped rising when it reached the discharge channel at the other end of the plain."

"Whoever built that was an idiot. Two-thirds of the plains are flooded."

"It works as it was expected to work," Pierre snapped. "The floor of the channel is not much higher than the plain, and that deceived us. I should have thought about it. My guess is that Codrin had partially covered the channel. As soon as the rain stops, we should prepare for battle."

"Do you really think that they will attack?" Bucur snorted.

"It's what I would do. We were herded here without our horses." Pierre glanced up. "Reno, move fifty people onto the ridge. You go with them. I don't want them to rain arrows on us."

Reno moved swiftly and took two companies with him. Some men cursed, a few fell on the wet stones, but in ten minutes the ridge was secured.

The rain stopped as fast as it came and, herded by the wind, the clouds broke, then shredded and flew overhead. It was day again.

In the middle of the plain, the soldiers clustered around the carts, ten men to a cart. The water was up to their knees. Two harnessed themselves at the shaft, the other eight were grouped two by two at the wheels. Some carts moved immediately, some did not. The men cursed and pushed harder. It took them almost an hour to finish.

“The dam will break soon.” Boldur pointed at the thing they had built more than a month before.

It was not really a dam at first, just four poles, thirty-foot long and thick as a man’s thigh, stuck six feet into the ground. There were two for each side of the ravine. When the rain stopped, the Mountes lowered thirty-foot long beams between the poles. Soon they formed a dam, stopping the furious water in its tracks. It was not a water-proof dam, but it didn’t need to be. Water was plentiful. A pool, five hundred feet long formed in the ravine.

“We need to release the other side before this crumbles.” Boldur strained the huge muscles of his back. “You two, come and help me. And you,” he pointed to three Mountes who were almost as large as him.

The ravine had two mouths, and the other one had been blocked by the Mountes at the end of Spring. It was similar to the first one with the exception that the poles keeping the beams in place were only stuck two feet into the ground. This dam was better built, with skins between the beams to stop the water from flowing through. The poles were kept in place by one large beam, halfway up, bearing two iron rings, the size of a man’s head, attached to it. One Mounte went down and passed a rope through them. He passed the ends of the rope up and climbed on the ridge. The four Mountes passed the rope behind their shoulders, two on each length.

“One, two, now,” Boldur said, and they moved to pull the rope and the beam. They worked in short bursts. “One, two, now.” Each time Boldur said ‘now’, the beam moved slightly up on the side with the iron rings. “One, two, now.” The head of the beam was now half out from its place in the wall of the crevasse. “One, two, now.” The head of the beam sprang up. “We are done.” The four men were breathing hard, and they let the rope fell from their shoulders. It went down into the crevasse with the falling beam.

At first, nothing seemed to move, and only the frowns on the men’s faces revealed that they were expecting something to happen. Then the top of the left-hand pole moved an inch. The men did not see it, but they heard the hard wood complaining with a muffled sound. The horizontal beams moved slightly too, and a thin stream of water flowed down. The pole was now moving slowly from its vertical position. Then it fell. The pressure of the water pushed the upper beams down. A waterfall formed and water surged down from the pool. With an astounding crack, the dam broke, and hell came down with the torrent.

The wave swept away half of the fifty Tolosa soldiers on the ridge overseeing the plain. The other half spread like chickens, running from the stream. Their screams reached the soldiers at the foot of the ridge just seconds before the water came down, sweeping away men and carts. All who were caught by the main stream were dragged into the middle of the plain. Some of them escaped. Almost none of those who wore armor stayed alive. In ten minutes, the pool from the ravine had exhausted its water, and the soldiers on the plain moved out toward the end of it, in the opposite direction from the castle. Most of them were walking on all fours, only their heads above the water. They looked like rats trying to flee a sinking ship. But they were not swimming, just crawling.

"Form companies!" Pierre thundered as soon as he emerged from the water. It took him all his will to stand up. Almost half of his men were still down, in the water. "Move! Move! We could be attacked any time."

"Sir," one soldier gasped.

Pierre drew his sword before the man could finish. He turned. Codrin's cavalry was coming from the forest like another deadly wave. *I am so tired*, Pierre thought. "Form companies. Turn!" he ordered, raising his sword. The men moved to form battle lines around him. Some of them had only daggers with which to defend themselves.

In front of his men, Pierre was the only one giving a real fight. "Do we have spearmen?" he asked.

"Only four," said one man whose voice the Spatar could not recognize.

"Give me the spears, one by one." He grabbed the first spear, balanced it briefly, then made it fly with all his force, and Pierre was a strong man. It pierced the chest of the first rider.

"Spear," he grunted, and the second spear put down another man. From four spears, only one missed its target, as the skilled rider deflected it with his sword. "Someone, give me a shield."

The first incoming rider rose in his stirrups, sword poised to strike, and Pierre swung his shield up to deflect the blow. The impact pushed him one step back, and his shield was gone in splinters. Rocked back, the rider felt the strap breaking and, unable to redress, he slid down. Before the rider could stand, one man moved forward and planted a heavy axe in his head.

By then, a second rider was attacking again, and his sword's tip caught Pierre on his shoulder. Pain moved down his arm. *I was lucky*, Pierre thought, as he did not feel a hard wound. He ducked low, as the rider's sword searched again for his head. Pierre's long sword almost cut the bent rider in two. For ten long minutes, Pierre fought, and his soldiers rallied behind him. He was so exhausted that he'd begun to feel lazy. His head was throbbing, and when he brought his sword down upon a rider's waist, it seemed to descend in slow motion. It was then when Laurent's column moved away, toward a band of disorganized soldiers.

The rest of Codrin's cavalry swept through the foot soldiers much like the flood before. It was a low-speed charge; the soil was wet and slippery, and that caused even more deaths. Some horses slipped and neighed in fear. Their riders fell. The other riders did not stop when they passed through the sieging army. They turned left, their horses in two feet of water, and exited the plain on the western side. Codrin rose in the saddle and glanced to his left where Pierre was gathering his soldiers again. He pondered for a few moments, then canceled the second wave of the attack and pushed his horse toward the forest.

The turmoil in Pierre's camp continued for a while, but he whipped them into shape with his harsh words, and sometimes hit soldiers with the flat of his sword. They were now better prepared to fight against another charge. Standing still, their hands gripping cold iron, they waited.

"You men at the back; break formation and take care of the dead," Pierre said after a while. "Then see what you can salvage from our food." Slowly, he stuck his sword into the ground and leaned on it. He'd taken blows, and beneath his mail ring, his body was darkening with bruises and contusions, and he was soaked in sweat, as if it were a sunny day.

"They did not attack again. What happened?" Bucur asked.

"The earth is slippery because of the rain, and even more so after the horses have trampled it. Codrin cares about his soldiers. I counted seventeen horses with no riders. That's how many soldiers he lost during the charge. We lost many times more." *How could they select such a dumb man for a Candidate King*? Pierre shook his head and ignored Bucur's next question.

In the evening, they finally counted the dead both from the flood and the attack: six hundred and thirty-two soldiers. When the camp was settled, Pierre went to the channel which was draining the water from the plain. Verenius and a few soldiers from Tolosa followed him. Walking through the shallow water, he arrived at the entry point in the channel. His hand slipped on the stones.

"Just what I thought," Pierre said. "There is almost no vegetation growth on the last three feet. The floor of the channel was raised recently. I should have checked it earlier."

"Only three feet," Verenius said. "It was raised enough to flood the plain, but not enough to attract our attention. It still looks like a deep channel."

"Something like that."

Mercifully, the storm blew over in the night, leaving only a steady drizzle in the grey overcast early morning.

The siege trailed for the next month and half; Pierre army did not try to assault the walls while Codrin vanished in the forests around Poenari. There were skirmishes from time to time but, over the years, the siege of Poenari became known as the Sleepy Siege.

"Blast this siege," Pierre growled. "I will not stay a day longer. Send an embassy to Codrin. I want to meet him before we leave."

"I forbid it," Bucur snapped. "We have to take Poenari."

"Be welcome to forbid whatever you want, but you will not command me." *We have food left for only ten days.*

"I am the Candidate King."

"Then take Poenari and win your crown," Pierre said and turned abruptly.

Behind him, Verenius gestured to Bucur to calm down, and followed the angry commander. *Bucur had the finesse of a blunt spade*, Verenius thought. *It's quite strange because he is an intelligent political player. War is getting the worst in him.* "Pierre," he said, his voice calm. "Would you agree for a talk? There must be some facts behind your decision, but I am not a military man."

"We can't take this fortress by force. That was clear from the beginning, and I did not hide it from you. We need more than ten thousand soldiers and the right attack equipment to mount a successful assault on those walls. Once we failed to burn the gate, there was no way to enter by force. My plan was to starve Poenari, and make it fall before winter comes. We lost most of our food and almost half of our soldiers. In a few days, we will start to eat our horses. Here, the second half of summer is rainy. In one month, we were able to deepen only half of the three-hundred-foot-long channel which collects the water from the plain. With each rain, we have to move on the hillocks because of the flood. You know that the floor of the channel was raised recently with three feet of stonework. Everything around us was prepared for siege, even the ravine's stream. Why were you not able to find this before we came here?"

"We tried, but all the spies we sent were captured."

"I can fight men; I can't fight water. We should have stuck to the initial plan and take Deva. I know Deva, and I've guaranteed you that we would have taken in a month."

"I may agree with you, but that will solve nothing."

"This happens when women with no military skills make decisions on how to fight a war. Was the decision because Codrin took Leyona?"

"Partially. It was more because Codrin became an alternative to the Candidate King, and more people started to look at him.

Devan sent troops to help Codrin. In Peyris we could not get all the soldiers in time. Some nuclei of resistance appeared here and there. They could spread."

"After this," Pierre gestured toward Poenari, "*they will* spread. Why did you allow Codrin to take Poenari?"

"Fate," Verenius shrugged. "Garland surprised us by giving him the fortress. We did not know much about it, and thought that taking back Leyona was more important." *Well, I knew about Poenari, but...*

"Perhaps Garland did not like the pressure Maud put on him." *Or perhaps Garland tried to help Codrin*. Pierre knew Sava, and a courier from Tolosa went to Leyona just after Codrin left the city. He learned that Codrin helped Garland to free his wife, even when she did not want to be freed from her lover. "Change your strategy, Verenius. You've bet on the wrong man for Frankis. Do you have more questions?" Pierre asked and Verenius shook his head. "Then inform that helpless Bucur. I will send couriers to reach Codrin."

Codrin stopped in the middle of the road, as did Pierre, both men studying each other under the brilliant blue sky, and they dismounted at the same time.

"Sir Pierre," Codrin bowed slightly.

"Greetings, Lion's Cub. Your fangs and claws were sharper than mine. There is not much to talk; we will leave tomorrow."

"It was about time," Codrin said, a touch of a smile on his lips.

Pierre frowned for a moment, then he smiled too. "Yes, yes, I remember; you said the same words when I freed you from that jail." He extended his hand and Codrin clasped it. "I am still accustomed with Tudor, but Codrin is not a bad name either. I bet that it will become even more famous than the Wraith of Tolosa. It was unfortunate that we had to meet on the battle camp, and... Fate take both the Circle and Bucur. Fight for Frankis; you deserve to be the king." He nodded and turned abruptly.

Pierre kept his word and, the next morning, all the soldiers of Tolosa left the camp. All others could do nothing but follow, and the siege of Poenari ended.

At the Burned Forest crossroads, the armies split, Tolosa going south, the others riding north. From a nearby hill, Codrin was watching the departing soldiers with his spyglass. Pierre was riding in front of his army with his captains. In the middle of a six-hundred-foot long, thirty-foot-tall ridge, a bush moved slightly, and a man threw a brief stare at the road. Three paces behind him stood Veres, in a state of intense agitation, wriggling his hands. They were just sixty feet from the army riding at leisure, its soldiers happy to return home. As the army came closer, the man in front retreated a few inches inside the bush.

"Now," Veres whispered.

A bolt flew and hit Pierre on the left side of his chest. With a deep growl, he clutched a hand on the shaft and fell from his horse.

"Run," Veres ordered, his voice filled with a morbid excitation, and he turned toward the horses waiting for them thirty paces away, guarded by a third man. "One traitor less," he shouted, and raised his thumb up once they were all mounted. *That bastard from Tolosa disobeyed our King, and I brought justice. After this, Bucur will return Midia to me*, he thought, his mind working in a feverish state. *I must solve the issue related to Saliné too. I am the head of the family now, and I will order her to accept Bucur even before the marriage. She must obey, or I will beat her how I beat Vio. No, I will beat her worse. She deserves it.*

"Company one, take the ridge from south. Company two, take the ridge from north," Joffroy shouted, dismounting at the same time. He ran toward his father and found him still alive, albeit almost unconscious.

"Quite a pity to die such death." Pierre found some strength to whisper.

"You are not dead yet." Joffroy eyed the bolt's shaft, which was moving up and down in the rhythm of Pierre's breath, and his face became grim.

From the top of his hill, Codrin pushed his horse down, and a column of thirty riders followed him. "Vlaicu, take twenty men, and ride toward that ridge," he pointed forward. "Pierre was shot. Fall behind the ridge and find than man or men who did this. I suspect that it's the Circle's game, and they will place everything in my hands." Zor had no equal and Codrin reached Tolosa army, two hundred paces before his men. "Make place!" he shouted when some soldiers from Tolosa tried to stop him. One of them came dangerous closer with his spear and Codrin had to unsheathe Flame and hit the spear away. "We are not here to fight. I came to see Pierre." A minute later, sneaking between the nervous riders and the ridge, he arrived at the place where Pierre was lying in the grass, and he dismounted swiftly.

"Who did this?" Joffroy asked with a tone implying that Codrin was involved, and his look was stern.

"I don't know, but it was none of my men. Why should I kill Pierre? Let me see him."

"Ah, the Lion's Cub," Pierre said in a weak voice. "Let him come, Joffroy; Codrin would not do such thing to me."

With expert eyes, Codrin checked the bolt: the point where it entered the body, the angle on which it pierced the flesh. His fingers measured the distance to the shoulder, the distance to the collarbone and the distance to the breastbone. "You had chance. Your heart was not even scratched, and you don't spill blood through the mouth, so the lungs are fine too. Did you hit your head while falling?"

"I suppose so," Pierre said, and Codrin moved to take his helmet down, then his fingers went through the thick hair.

"There is a lump here, in the back. That's why you feel weak. You must come in Poenari. There is no way to ride home with these wounds."

"This was quite a good strategy to finally enter in Poenari," Pierre said with a wry smile.

"Joffroy," Codrin looked at him, "tell your army to march toward Tolosa, after they finish the search around the ridge. I have twenty soldiers doing the same thing. They are led by Vlaicu. Tell this to your men; I don't want more issues. Take twenty men and come with me. Pierre should mount your horse in front of you. It's the fastest way. I can't take the bolt out here, and he will need a few weeks of rest."

Joffroy helped Pierre stand, and two more men came to raise him on the horse.

"Careful," Codrin warned in a low voice, "don't break the bolt's shaft."

With all that pain in his chest and shoulders, Pierre did not complain, but they rode slowly, and Vlaicu caught with them an hour later. "We could not find the rats," he spat, "but I bet my sword that they were from the Circle."

Chapter 33 - Codrin

Of the thirty-seven hundred soldiers who besieged Poenari, less than two thousand remained alive. The mood was sour, and there were not many words spoken between the northern commanders. Even worse, all of them avoided Bucur like the plague. Having only fifty soldiers left, Bucur tried to attach his troops to the two armies going north-east: the one from Peyris and Orban's army. At the first main junction, both turned north, leaving him alone. That was not by chance; the commanders had decided that it was better not to be seen with Bucur; Codrin's army was following him.

By the time he arrived in Severin, more than forty of his soldiers had deserted, and Bucur entered the city followed by only seven guards. The Sages of the Circle came with him too.

"We could not take Poenari," he growled, seating his tired body in a chair in Aron's office. "And the cowards ran away, leaving me alone. Rats!"

"How many soldiers have returned?" Aron asked, keeping his calm.

"Seven."

"So many deaths?"

"No, so many traitors. I had fifty when I left Poenari."

"Go and see Saliné."

"The last thing I want is to see that tramp. Oh, yes, she will keep her calm and hide her joy that her dog won the fight."

"Bucur," Aron said coldly. "We may not have enough soldiers to defend Severin. Saliné is the only thing keeping us from defeat."

"Fine, I will make her my woman, tonight."

"That should have happened a long time ago, but you in your pride insisted on seducing her, instead of just spreading her legs. Now be the chevalier with her and forget about your pride. She may be our only chance of escaping alive. See to her, and then we need to talk with Verenius."

Codrin took the plain in front of Severin in a methodical way. First, he cut off all the roads, with an invisible hand. His scouts were waiting, hidden in the forest, and grabbing anyone who tried to enter or leave Severin. The road looked peaceful. It helped him gather information and stop the flow of food going into Severin. After three days, Aron guessed what was happening, but he could do nothing apart from sending no more couriers for help.

In his camp hidden deep in the forest, Codrin read the two letters Aron had sent the day before. While numbers were not mentioned, the request to Maud for help was desperate. Although no more couriers had left Severin, he was still waiting for the Mountes to build the assault ladders, and mostly he was waiting for Ferd to tell him how many soldiers Aron still had inside the walls. Once he had the information, he occupied the plain, in one sudden move. The ten assault ladders were laid in front of the soldiers, a warning to Severin. At the same time, a patrol marching around Severin market was attacked by a mob of people. Their clubs and arrows were merciless, and when the people dispersed, it was difficult to recognize the five soldiers lying on the street. It took Aron a while to send another, much stronger, patrol to recover the bodies.

That evening, in his office, Aron met Verenius, the Primus Itinerant, again, and the other Sage, Octavian, who was Maud's right hand. "Negotiate a deal," Aron growled.

"I tried, but you stopped me," Verenius replied with a shrug.

"Do it now, before those cowards in the street assault the palace. I don't have enough soldiers to fight two wars."

You don't have enough soldiers to fight anything. "Free passage for you and Bucur, and whoever else wants to join you. Saliné will stay. Make sure Bucur does not harm her."

"I thought that you were worried for us, not for that bitch."

"Harm her and there is nothing left to worry for."

"Fine."

"Read this." Verenius placed a sheet of paper on the desk. "If you agree, I will send it to Codrin."

"The surrender of Severin," Aron growled. "Can't you find another word?"

"What's more important? The word or your lives?"

"Fine," Aron grumbled and threw the paper across the desk. "Tell me when it is done."

Codrin agreed as soon as he read the proposal, and he was surprised how well Verenius had represented his interests. The Primus Itinerant did not try to negotiate; he wanted the document signed fast. He had his own worries, which could not be shared with Codrin.

"Thank you, for the good work, Sage," Codrin said and signed the document, which was effectively a treaty between the new owner of Severin and Aron, who was free to leave with Bucur and their soldiers. Saliné was left in Codrin's custody. Through Verenius, the Circle was the guarantor of the treaty.

Verenius returned quickly to Severin, and tried to find Aron, when Octavian took him aside. "We need to talk," Octavian whispered, and both left the room. "The document you've negotiated is not acceptable to the Circle."

"Severin will fail in an hour without that document, and it's up to me to decide what is acceptable or not."

"Maud and the Conclave of the Circle have a different opinion." Octavian pulled a letter from his pocked and gave it to Verenius, who took his time to read it, then read it again.

I am trapped, Verenius thought. "Then we should renegotiate the document."

"The document was already signed, but we will interpret it in a creative way."

"Will you do the interpretation?"

"That's a Primus Itinerant's task." Octavian smiled in a gentle way, hiding his satisfaction. *Soon, I will take your place, Verenius. The Primus Itinerant position should have been mine. You are too weak.* At least, in this he was right. Octavian had been sick when Belugas was killed, and the healers did not think he would live. The Conclave named Verenius, who was next in line. He survived in the end and saw Verenius more as an imposter than a Primus. Octavian had both seniority and Maud on his side.

"I have two more letters." Octavian pushed them forward. "In one of them, Baldovin, the Duke of Tolosa agrees to marriage between his daughter, Marie, and Codrin, and he will become Duke at Baldovin's death. In the second one, the Circle makes Codrin Grand Seigneur of Severin. With Severin, half of Mehadia and the north-east of Leyona, he has enough lands. As you see, everything has been prepared in the finest detail. Now let me explain what we will do." Octavian spent almost half an hour revealing the details of the new plan.

"It may work," Verenius shrugged. "Except that you have forgotten one thing: Codrin's reaction." *And it will fall on me.*

"Grand Seigneur today, Duke of Tolosa tomorrow and King of Frankis the day after." Octavian set a crooked smiled on his lips. *Verenius is more stupid than I thought.* "What more could Codrin want?"

"We shall see. Let's talk with Aron and Bucur."

The sun was not yet risen in the east when Aron opened the metallic door of the tunnel. It screeched, and two men with torches moved forward. Aron followed, then Verenius, then Bucur and Saliné. One by one, all the soldiers who had decided it was better to follow Aron than stay and bear the grunt of Codrin and the people of Severin went inside the tunnel. No one took care to close the door, and it remained open. At the end of the tunnel, everything was repeated in the same sequence.

Outside, the light was not strong, but they saw a group of soldiers waiting for them, together with Octavian.

"There is a change in plans," Octavian said. "Codrin has agreed to take only Severin and let Lady Saliné go with you, Bucur. Laurent can confirm this; he is the Knight of Seged, and one of Codrin's trusted people."

"By the authority that was given to me by Seigneur Codrin, who will soon be Duke of Tolosa through his marriage with the young Duchess, I guarantee your passage."

"Was this necessary?" Verenius whispered.

"Yes," Octavian replied. "That little bitch must understand her place. She will marry Bucur. For the future of Frankis, Codrin must marry the young Duchess."

All this time, both kept their eyes on Saliné. She was standing still, her face calm, without visible reaction. Knowing her better, Verenius guessed what was in her mind.

Saliné did not see them. She was looking intently at Laurent. She knew that he was the Knight of Seged, but she also knew that he was lying. *Codrin would never agree to such an arrangement*, she thought yet, while she absolved him of treachery, deep in her mind, she thought him guilty of not being careful enough. Guilty of shattering their dreams. She had fought for and dreamed of a new life for almost a year, and what had happened in Severin was her last chance to escape. There was little hope from now one. She knew it.

"Tell Codrin, that we thank him for his generosity," Aron said, playing the role for Saliné. She was becoming important for him now; Octavian had made it clear that Bucur had to marry her the day they arrived at the place the Circle had given them to hide in. *They want her out of Codrin's way, and they will give him that bitch from Tolosa.* He also understood that Bucur's marriage to Saliné, and their children, would help them survive. Codrin would not harm Saliné's family. "We should go now."

"I need to talk with Saliné," Verenius said. "Come, my dear. There are things you need to know before your journey," he said, loud enough to be heard by everyone. "Don't oppose this," he whispered and, taking her by the arm, pulled her away. "I don't think that it will mean anything for you, but I apologize for what has happened." He stared at Saliné, who ignored him. "I did not have this end in mind, but..."

"Enough," Saliné said coldly, turning her head away from him. The wind whipped aside her cloak and plastered her riding pants to her legs. She did not care.

"You have to abide me a little longer. The Circle changed my plans. I..."

"You have no honor."

"No, I did not have, and neither had the Circle. Life brought you an unexpected twist today. The next one may be in your favor. Goodbye, Lady Saliné." He took her hand to kiss it, and despite her pain, she forced herself not to slap him. "Farewell," he patted her palm, still in his, and she felt something sneaking under her sleeve. She forced herself not to look down. His body shielded her from other people's sight, and she pushed the thing up, hiding it completely; it felt like rolled-up paper.

Laurent had brought enough horses, and all seventeen people leaving Severin mounted. Led by Aron, the group rode west. As planned, Saliné was flanked by Bucur and another soldier. The remaining soldiers made a larger cage around her; far to the left, the ten men Codrin had sent to watch the tunnel were lying dead in the grass. With the first light of the day, Laurent's twenty men strong patrol approached them as friends and killed them all. She could not see the dead. Sage Petronius and his two guards joined Aron at the front of the troop. Together with Octavian, he was the only one who knew the destination; even Verenius was not aware of it.

"Laurent," Octavian patted his shoulder. "Your efforts are seen very favorably way by the Master Sage. Go to Leyona. The position of Itinerant Sage is waiting for you there. You deserve it."

Laurent bowed to Octavian, then to Verenius, who ignored him.

"Now let's go inside and wait for the young man who wants to be our king," Octavian said, and walked toward the tunnel. *He will make children with our Duchess, and get the crown at some point in time, but the Circle will still rule Frankis. Once we have his children... Later... Now I have to convince Codrin to kill that weakling, Verenius. He reneged on his signature on the treaty after all.*

The gate was open, but there was no one in sight, not a single soldier. Vlaicu was a prudent man, and even with the signed treaty, he decided to stop his troop two hundred paces from the wall. He waited a few minutes more, then felt the need to decide.

"Charge!" he ordered and pushed his horse to a gallop. Fifty riders followed him. Speed was the easiest way to overcome a trap. They found no trap, and for a moment, Vlaicu felt ashamed. *Better ashamed than dead*, he mused. Once the first moments passed, feelings from the past came to him. It was his gate, his garrison, his city to protect.

Once the gate was secured, they took over the palace too, and found only a few scared servants. "No one will harm you," Vlaicu shouted, and sent a soldier back to the gate. Codrin's banner was raised, and the raven on it flew in the wind. A few minutes later, two hundred soldiers came through the gate.

Codrin dismounted in front of the main stairs, and climbed it in haste, jumping two or three steps at once. In the hall, he turned swiftly on the main corridor, and ran until he got to Saliné's suite. Swiftly, he pushed the door open and entered. He found Verenius.

"Saliné is not here," Verenius said. *Neither is Octavian.*

"Where is Saliné?" Codrin asked, as if unable to hear, his eyes piercing Verenius.

"Women are so volatile sometimes. We negotiated hard, and she chose at the last moment to leave with Bucur, but let's forget about Saliné; we have more pressing things to discuss."

"Where is Saliné?"

"With Bucur. What's so hard to understand? She likes him, and they will marry soon. This is for you," Verenius pushed a letter across the table. "The Duke of Tolosa is..."

"How did they get out of Severin?" Codrin's voice went dangerously low, close to a feral growl, and his hand rested on the hilt of Shadow, his long sword.

"Through the secret tunnel under the castle," Verenius said, his voice thinner than he would have liked, and he coughed, to hide his weakness.

"We signed a treaty."

"You are the Seigneur of Severin, and with all other lands, you will become Grand Seigneur. This is the letter recognizing your title," Verenius pushed another envelope across the desk. "Our rules constrain us to keep Bucur as Candidate King, but we already consider you the next in line. In eight years, we will nominate you. That was the real agreement. Everything else is just a trivial detail in the larger scheme." *This is the last time I play such a dirty game, and Fate take Maud and the Circle.*

"Your larger scheme, not mine. What happened to my men who were guarding the tunnel?"

"I have here a letter from the Duke of Tolosa. He grants you the hand of his daughter, and you will become Duke at his death. As you know, he is sick, and no one gives him more than a year to live."

"The same girl you promised to Bucur before."

Surprised, Verenius frowned and took some moments to think before answering. "Things change. The Circle approves your marriage."

"Approves, disapproves. That girl is Maud's granddaughter and under the Circle's control. The last thing I need is a spy in my house. Anyway, the Circle has deceived me again... There will be consequences."

"There was no deception. Saliné wanted to go with Bucur. What's so difficult to understand?"

"If she had wanted that, she would have talked to me. You just sneaked her out, even though we had an agreement. A written one. You betrayed your own signature, and you killed my men guarding the tunnel. There is a price to pay for that."

"Codrin," Verenius said in haste, the memory of Belugas's decayed hanged body resurfacing inside his mind. "I killed no one. Severin and this," he pointed to the letters, "are the most important things. They will help you rise. Frankis needs you. Frankis needs a king. You may bring order and put an end to this period of lawless. Let's not make a rash decision."

"I will try. Where is Saliné?"

"I don't know where they have gone. I swear. Sage Petronius knows..."

"Then you have no value to me."

"My value is in those letters. They will..."

"You disrespected your own signature. Why should I believe you?

"I am a soldier of the Circle, and I do what I have to do for my order. You would expect the same from your soldiers. You are right that I disrespected my signature, but I am right that in a few years Frankis will have a king again. You. My shame and your feelings count less than the task of bringing stability to a kingdom which was torn apart by civil war and lack of order. There is more at stake than a woman, however intelligent and beautiful she is. You need the Duchy of Tolosa."

"That would sound good in the mouth of a decent man."

"It sounds right. You may do whatever you want with me."

"There will be no stability with the Circle manipulating everything. You don't want a king; you want a puppet on the throne; you want to rule. That's why all the Candidate Kings were wrong. They were only pawns in a greater game. Maud wants to be the hidden Queen."

He may kill me, but I will not tell him about my letter to Saliné until he makes his decision. "Then do what it must be done and end the game. Frankis needs a real king. You." Verenius cocked his head and, silent, left the room. Unable yet to think straight, Codrin let him go, knowing that he could not leave the palace.

"Severin," Codrin whispered, walking alone with no aim, feeling no life in the empty rooms where Saliné, Jara, Vio and Mohor once lived. He stopped again in Saliné's room and, mechanically, went to the right side of the fireplace. His hand maneuvered twice a small ornament Saliné told him would open the secret door. One went north and the second one south. He felt nothing moving in the wall yet, when he pressed against it, the door appeared. Inside the hidden corridor, he found her second bow, and he took and pressed it to his chest, as if Saliné was inside the springy wood. He closed the door and went to the window, staring away, seeing nothing, the bow still pressed against him.

"This place will haunt me as much as Arenia. I lost my first family there, and the second one here. I must be cursed by Fate. I can't live here. I will write to Jara that Severin will stay in my custody until Mark can claim the Seigneury. Severin," he repeated and leaned against the window, "a bunch of cold rooms and walls. An empty thing, like my life."

Behind Codrin, a white silhouette appeared from nowhere, and Dochia, the Empress, stared at him, a smile playing on her white lips. She raised her translucent hand, and a sphere, resembling the texture of her skin, materialized in her palm. She blew gently, and the sphere flew slowly toward Codrin. It touched the back of his head and vanished.

He shivered and turned abruptly. The room was empty.

Appendix

Poenari

Codrin, son of the slain King of Arenia and the legitimate King. After his father's death, he finds sanctuary in the former kingdom of Frankis, sometimes using the name Tudor to conceal his real identity. Seigneur of Poenari in Frankis

Mara, the Secretary of Poenari

Vlaicu, Spatar of Poenari (commander of the army). Former Chief of the Guard of Severin before Severin fell to Aron.

Sava, Chief of the Guard of Poenari, former Chief of the Guard of Leyona

Ban, Chief of the Archers of Poenari and Sava's right hand. Former Chief of the Archers of Severin before Severin fell to Aron.

Bernart, custodian of Poenari before Codrin took the fortress

Vlad, born in Litvonia, he followed Codrin to the former Frankis Kingdom. Chief Scout of Poenari

Calin, former Secretary of Mehadia and Mara's father

Laurent, Knight of Faget, Garland's brother

Pintea, Vlad's brother

Julien, Sava's son and captain

Neira, Sava's wife

Nard, Aron's second son, taken prisoner by Codrin after the conquest of Faget

Siena, Bernart's granddaughter
Amelie, Bernart's granddaughter
Mihail, Mara's son

Severin

Jara (Stejara), Signora of Severin, former Grand Signora of Midia. She lost her castle to Grand Seigneur Orban after her first husband, Malin, was slain in battle. She lost Severin to Aron when Mohor was killed.

Mohor, former Seigneur of Severin and Jara's second husband

Cernat, former Grand Seigneur of Midia and Jara's father
Saliné, Jara's daughter
Vio, Jara's daughter
Veres (Snail), Jara's son
Mark, Jara and Mohor's son

Aron (Big Mouth), Seigneur of Severin after killing Mohor, former Spatar of Severin (commander of the army)

Bucur, Aron' son, and new Candidate King of Frankis
Karel, Spatar of Severin (commander of the army)
Martin, guard
Geo, guard
Gria, servant of Aron used to keep Saliné under control
Milene, servant in Jara's house
Ferd, mercenary from Valer's army
Senal, Secretary of Severin

Cleuny

Calin, former Secretary of Mehadia
Mara, Codrin's Secretary and Calin's daughter

Frankis Wanderers

Dochia, the Fourth Light of the Frankis Wanderers
Valera, the First Light
Livia, the Second Light at her death

Drusila, the Second Light after Livia's death, the First Light after Valera's death

Derena, the Second Light

Splendra, the Third Light, converted Serpentist and High Priestess of the Serpent in Frankis

Sybille, the Fifth Light

Olmia, the Eight Light

Chloe, the Ninth Light

Viler, Drusila's nephew, and Chief of the Men Guard of the Frankis Wanderers. He was killed by Codrin in a duel.

Arenian Wanderers

Ada, the Second Light of the Arenian Wanderers, and the strongest Light of all the Wanderers

Litvonian Wanderers

Ingrid, the First Light of the Litvonian Wanderers

Salvina, the Fourth Light, converted Serpentist

Mared, the Fifth Light, converted Serpentist

The Circle

Cantemir, former Master Sage

Maud, the new Master Sage

Aurelian, Sage and Primus Itinerant, killed in Severin

Belugas, Sage and Primus Itinerant, hanged by Codrin

Verenius, Sage and Primus Itinerant

Octavian, Itinerant Sage

Petronius, Itinerant Sage

Hadrian, Itinerant Sage

Paul, novice Sage

Arad

Orban (the Beast), Grand Seigneur of Arad

Cantemir, Secretary of Arad and Master Sage of the Circle

Panait, the first Mester of the Merchants Guild in Arad

Delia, Panait's wife

Doren, the Spatar of Arad (commander of the army)

Vasile, Jara's agent in Arad

Leyona

Garland, the new Grand Seigneur of Leyona

Leyonan, former Grand Seigneur of Leyona, slain in a battle against Codrin

Maud, Secretary of Leyona and the new Master Sage of the Circle

Sava, Chief of the Guard of Leyona

Bartal, second Secretary of Leyona

Lina, Garland's wife

Farcu, Chief of the Guard of Leyona's castle

Dobre, governor of Orhei in Leyona Seigneury

Peyris

Stefan, Duke of Peyris

Cleyre, Stefan's granddaughter and member of the Council of Peyris

Albert, Stefan's son

Nicolas, First Spatar of Peyris (commander of the army)

Reymont, Secretary of Peyris and Hidden Sage of the Circle

Gilles, second Secretary of Peyris

Tolosa

Baldovin, Duke of Tolosa

Leon, the old Duke of Tolosa

Laure, Baldovin's wife, and the real ruler of Tolosa. Maud's daughter.

Marie, Baldovin's daughter, promised to Bucur, and the Circle's real choice for the Candidate Queen

Pierre, the Spatar of Tolosa (commander of the army)

Celeste, Pierre's wife

Joffroy, Pierre's son and captain of Tolosa

Masson, Secretary of Tolosa, Hidden Sage of the Circle

Deva

Devan, Grand Seigneur of Deva

Filippo, Devan's son

Balan, the first Mester of the Merchants Guild in Deva and Sage of the Circle

Mona, Balan's wife

Dan, Chief of the Guard of Deva

Long Valley

Matei, Half-Knight and mercenary in Valer' army

Varia Matei's wife

Livia, daughter of Varia and Matei

Damian, elder son of Varia and Matei

Lisandru, son of Varia and Matei

Boar, Knight

Sara, Boar's wife

Little Boar, Boar's brother

Balint, Boar's second Chief of the Guard

Sharpe, Black Dervil, mercenary captain, slain by Codrin

Valeni

Agatha, Signora of Valeni, Jara's aunt and Hidden Sage of the Circle

Bran, Chief of the Guard of Valeni

Maxim, Bran's right hand

Mercenaries

Valer, Black Dervil of Tolosa, mercenary captain

Eagle, Black Dervil of Peyris, mercenary captain

Bear, Black Dervil in south if Frankis, mercenary captain

Sharpe, Black Dervil for north-west of Frankis, mercenary captain, slain by Codrin

Assassins

Scorta, Assassin Master

Dorian, Assassin Master

Serpentists (followers of the Serpent God)

Meriaduk, the High Priest of the Serpent

Arenia

Tudor, an Assassin renegade and Codrin's mentor

Ioana, Codrin's twin sister

Radu, Codrin's brother

Baraki, Chief of the Royal Guard of Arenia

Iulian, captain of the Royal Guard of Arenia

Gaspar, Knight, Baraki's nephew

Others

Konrad, Knight

Boldur, one of the Mountes' chieftains

Manuc, Duke of Loxburg

Iaru, the third Mester of the Merchants Guild in Dorna

Lenard, Seigneur of Dorna

Miscellaneous

Spatar, Chief of the Army

Vistier, administrator of a castle and coin master

Wraith, most successful Lead Protectors (only four in Frankis)

Black Dervil, mercenary captain (only four in Frankis after Codrin killed Sharpe)

galben (galbeni at plural), gold coin, ten grams weight

turn, alternative time unit of measure, equivalent of one hour

cozonac, Arenian cake

Months of the year:

Gerar, January

Florar, May
Stove, July

Wanderers ruling councils
Inner Council of the Three
High Council of the Seven

Printed in Great Britain
by Amazon

77716906R00205